Praise for ...

'A brilliantly dark tale'
Mail on Sunday

'Clever, pacy, compulsive'
Sunday Mirror

'A fresh, witty writing style'
Daily Mail

'Punchy and energetic . . . a rapid-fire ride'
Irish Independent

'A contender for the most arresting opening paragraph of the year'
Sunday Express

'Enthralling – Spain dissects her characters' secrets
with razor-sharp precision'
JP Delaney

'A clever novel . . . gradually exposing a chilling history
of dysfunctional families'
Sunday Times

'I can't praise *The Confession* enough. Brilliant writing,
great story . . . a really cracking read'
BA Paris

'A dizzying tale of lives falling apart that has you addicted from
the very first page. I found it impossible to put down'

THE CONFESSION

JO SPAIN

First published in Great Britain in 2018 by Quercus
This edition published in 2018 by

Quercus Editions Ltd
Carmelite House
50 Victoria Embankment
London EC4Y 0DZ

An Hachette UK company

A CIP catalogue record for this book is available
from the British Library

PB ISBN 978 1 78648 837 4
EBOOK ISBN 978 1 78648 838 1

10 9 8 7 6 5 4 3 2

Typeset by CC Book Production

Printed and bound in Great Britain by Clays Ltd, Elcograf S.p.A.

For a friend from Derry, who never got to write his own book.
Rest well, mo chara.

Prologue

Present day, 2012

It's the first spray of my husband's blood hitting the television screen that will haunt me in the weeks to come – a perfect diagonal splash, each droplet descending like a vivid red tear.

That, and the sound of his skull cracking as the blows from the golf club rain down.

There's something so utterly shocking about that noise. I'd never heard it before and yet, the moment I did, I knew instinctively what it was. The crunching sound of a fractured head is strangely and horrifically unmistakable.

A few minutes earlier, the two of us had been watching a crime thriller on that television, now criss-crossed with blood. We were sitting separately in our armchairs – expensive black leather recliners. A particularly scary scene was playing out on the wide LCD screen. The killer in the show was on to his third victim and as he hunted her in deserted, creepy woodland I placed my hands over my eyes, unable to watch the inevitable. Harry laughed at me for being so girly.

That was when the stranger walked into the centre of our living room.

We hadn't even heard him enter the house.

A golf club dangled loosely from his right hand, but he didn't seem threatening, if you ignored the unexpectedness of the situation. A pair of jeans, a T-shirt. It was like he'd just strolled in off the golf course that sat to the rear of our property.

Harry turned to me, completely bewildered. Then my husband stood up, his body faster than his brain, a mammal reacting to this peculiar invasion of our space. His mouth was just opening to form the first indignant question when the man swung the golf club at him.

Harry buckled, momentarily winded. He was stunned but his eyes met mine and I saw him make a quick calculation. My husband has always been great like that. Throw him into any awkward situation and he'll negotiate himself out of it in minutes. Charm the birds out of the trees, my mother always says. Although, this time, it didn't look like words were going to work.

Harry is a strong, athletic man. He works out several times a week and one of those sessions is with a boxing coach. He's had a lot of stress in the last few years and there's nothing like laying into a punchbag to let off steam.

So when he pivoted to deliver a right hook to the man standing so nonchalantly in front of us, I thought, *This is it*.

Except it wasn't.

The man hit Harry again while my husband's fist was mid-air.

And again and again, and he's still hitting him.

Harry didn't stand a chance.

My husband is on the floor now, his attacker visibly sweating and grunting from his exertions as he brings the golf club down repeatedly. His knuckles are white on the iron, his arm muscles tense. Every time the weapon lands it makes a stomach-churning thumping sound, and each blow draws fresh blood, cartilage, saliva, teeth. There's vomit spewing out of Harry's mouth and a damp patch has spread down the leg of his beige trousers.

I'm still in my chair, watching all this.

I don't speak.

I don't run for my phone.

I don't launch myself at the stranger.

What I really want to do as all this is happening is cover my eyes. I want to block out the sight of the horror, just as I did with the thriller on TV.

At last the beating stops. The man releases his grip on the golf club and surveys the damage.

Harry is unrecognizable. There's blood everywhere. This is what they mean when they use the expression 'beaten to a pulp'. This . . . mess. A barely human form. Here lies the man I've known nearly all my adult life. A man who has held my hand, kissed my lips, lain beside me, been inside me – I know every inch of his body and recognize not a bit of it right now.

Then the intruder bends down to Harry's ear and whispers something, quietly, softly, like a lover's sweet nothing.

What? What did he say?

The man stands up and studies me. He has dark eyes – black, in fact. Black hair too. Not dark brown – coal-like. Thick eyebrows. Full, red lips. Younger than me but not by much, maybe ten years or so. He is good-looking. Even covered in my husband's blood.

I know what he is.

3

A reckoning.

We aren't perfect, Harry and I. All of us have our secrets, don't we? The little petty lies. The bigger sins.

But what has Harry done to provoke this?

My eyes are drawn back to his body, and I whimper. I've imagined Harry dead many times but not this . . . I never thought it would be like this.

Then the man turns on his heel and walks out of the living room door. Just like that, he's gone.

I dimly register the front door opening and slamming shut.

I'm alone, bar the bloodied and battered form on the floor inches from my feet.

That's when I finally do something, when my body throws itself into action.

I wet myself.

Part One

Julie

When I first met Harry, he told me he worked in finance.

What does that even mean? I asked. To me, finance was a title sharp-suited men gave to ambiguous jobs in new-build office blocks in the capital. They weren't *real* jobs. I grew up in a little village in rural Ireland. I was used to men in overalls, with calloused hands and bent backs, weather-beaten faces and an all-round lesser sense of entitlement.

In the early nineties in Ireland, 'finance' took off in a big way. The eighties had been bleak for our little country – mass emigration and unemployment, high taxes, politicians up to their necks in brown envelopes and dodgy deals. But in the nineties there was a shift. None of us knew it, but the state was about to embark on its Celtic Tiger journey. Wealth was flooding into Ireland and, Jesus, you've never met a nationality that could get comfortable with money faster. You'd swear we'd always had it.

My background didn't prepare me for what was coming. Dad managed a small farm long before the European Union made it profitable, and Mam stayed at home, rearing child after child. She'd missed the memo in the seventies that said nobody gave a shite any more what the Pope thought about condoms and what went on in the marital bed. Luckily, for me. I was the youngest of our large family. I was adored and spoiled, for all that you could be spoiled with what little we had.

But I was never content. Leitrim had nothing to offer. Thankfully, as the last of the brood, there were no expectations on me to hang around the farm or live close by. My older siblings carried all those responsibilities. I was allowed to finish school, and I worked hard – hard enough to earn myself *the* golden ticket: a place at Trinity College Dublin to study the arts. My plan was to become a teacher. I'd read Maeve Binchy's *Circle of Friends*. New pals, the capital, three months off every summer and a great pension? Yes, please.

Leaving the county was the first indication I was a breed apart. My poor grandmother almost had a heart attack when she heard where I was headed. Fair enough, it was the nineties, but she was of her age – eighty-five – and she'd had a number of rules beaten into her over the decades. Firstly, single girls didn't move from Leitrim to Dublin on their own unless it was to deal with an unpleasant and unwanted surprise in their bellies. Secondly, they didn't go to college unless it was to learn hairdressing or secretarial skills. And thirdly, if they were going to flout every rural tradition going, they certainly didn't go to Trinity, which was bursting at the seams with sneaky, superior Protestants. She still thought the college had its ban on Catholics.

Turns out, she was right. Trinity would prove very dangerous for me. Not the place, but the people I would meet there.

I first saw Harry McNamara at the college ball in my third year, 1994.

My date had got, as we country people say, langered, and it wasn't even midnight. My pal Grace had also abandoned me, in order to suck the face off a PhD biology student. Left to my own devices, I walked around the various old stone courtyards, my face changing colour every time I passed one of the multicoloured ground lamps strategically placed to illuminate Trinity's Victorian-era walls. I hoped I'd bump into one of my friends to finish the night in company. I was never comfortable being alone.

I heard a low whistle, followed by the words:

'Well, now, if it isn't Jessica Rabbit.'

Harry called out to me through a circle of people, all gathered around him, the centre of their universe. He was leaning casually against the wall of the provost's garden, holding court. His bow tie hung open around his neck and a cigar stuck out of the side of his mouth. He was, without exception, the most handsome man I'd ever laid eyes on. He was so *un*-Irish-looking. Thick, wavy brown hair framed a tanned, sculpted face, and his tux was expensive – perfectly tailored, the way a man should wear a suit. And tight-fitting enough for me to see he had the toned and muscular body of an athlete.

But his smile – oh, his smile was the clincher.

The group parted like the sea for Moses as he moved towards me, all of them envious at the newcomer who'd unintentionally and so easily won his attention.

'Are you addressing me?' I said, eyebrows raised as I looked around, pretending to check he hadn't intended the comment for somebody else. 'Is that your thing? Yelling sexist remarks at random women?'

I was well able for him, used to the attention of the opposite sex. I'd been born with natural flaxen curls, sky-blue eyes and plump red lips. Attractive to most men, I guess. My curves, though, as Harry had so evidently noticed, were my selling point. I've always been petite (Polly Pocket, my older sisters affectionately termed me early on). But as soon as I hit my teens, I developed, big time. All the Ferguson girls were alike, blonde curls and pretty faces. But none of them got my chest. My sisters were disgusted.

The night I caught Harry's attention, I knew I looked sexy. I was wearing a tight emerald-green evening gown. It had started out as a cheap thing from Primark but had been transformed into something magical after Grace's mam got her hands on it and gussied it up on her sewing machine.

'Jesus,' Grace had said, green-eyed. 'Mammy, you wouldn't let me across the threshold in that get-up, and you practically stitch Julie into it.'

'I love you, petal, but Julie has a figure to work with,' Mrs Delaney had replied, giving poor Grace's two fried eggs the once-over.

'Everything I haven't got, I inherited from you, you horrible old woman,' Grace grumbled.

The dress would have been put to better use on my sex-mad friend. Unlike many of my peers in college, I wasn't there to find a man. I loved that our mam had always been home, but the thought of being a young, settled housewife sent me into a panic. And I certainly didn't want to end up with a bun in the oven before I had a ring on my finger.

I'd kidded myself into thinking I was Ms Independent.

I knew nothing about myself.

Harry had laughed when I snapped my retort back at him, then tutted playfully.

'Is it sexist to point out you're the best looking woman here? Honestly, I don't know who you came with tonight, but the man is a simpleton leaving you alone. Unless you figured that out yourself and it was you who abandoned him?'

I smiled, despite myself.

'He's . . . somewhere.'

'I see. So, while he's somewhere, I'm going to seize this opportunity to woo you, and I'll start by getting us some champagne. It's just not right, you gliding around, goddess-like, without a drink in your hand. And it can only be the best.'

'It's far from champagne I was reared,' I snorted. 'And did you just say "woo"?'

He blushed.

'I did, didn't I? It's your dress. It looks like it was made for you and your . . . eh, assets. I can't remember my own name, let alone what century we're in.'

'Wow. Tell me. Did you practise in a mirror before coming out tonight, or is this just you?'

'Seriously now – would you fake being this cheesy?' He lowered his head and smiled out at me from under his fringe, an adorable brown-eyed puppy. 'Please. Don't torture me any longer. That gang behind me are watching to see if I can pull this off and if you knock me back my reputation will be ruined, utterly. Can you even pretend you don't think I'm a total arse?'

'I would take pity on you, but you promised me fancy champagne and they're not serving it.'

'Well, now. I see light at the end of this tunnel you're making me crawl through. They have it all right. You just haven't been to the right bar.'

'U-huh. Just so you know, I can't be bought. Fizz or no.'

'Are you saying you're priceless?'

'Got it in one.'

I'm not a cliché. I didn't fall for Harry McNamara just because he was a smooth talker and happened to have a case of bubbles behind the bar reserved for the alumni of the college. And, even with him charming and me tipsy, there was no way I was jumping into bed with him. I was still a girl from a small country village – nowhere near cosmopolitan enough for one-night stands.

We talked and, as we did, I discovered that he was actually a former, not a current student, which explained his access to the alumni bar.

'Dear God, how old are you?' I asked. 'Is the college aware you're here, preying on young, vulnerable women? And what is your actual job – in finance, I mean?'

He was amused by that.

'I'm twenty-seven,' he said. 'I hope that's not too old for you. What are you – early twenties? Come on. I'm hardly a predator. And my job? I'm a banker. Of sorts.'

'Oh! Well, why don't you just say that? You work in a bank. Why does everybody have to use fancy terms these days like "finance" and "consultancy"? I'm going to be a teacher. Not a "provider of knowledge". What? What are you laughing at?'

'You,' he said, leaning in, until his long-lashed chestnut eyes were centimetres away from mine and I could feel his breath hot against my lips, mint and alcohol-flavoured. 'I could listen to that accent all night. It's melodic. Are you always so frank?'

'Oh. I thought you were laughing because I just want to be a teacher.'

He came close to my ear and whispered, 'Come on, now. You could never be *just* anything.'

I pulled back, blushing, alarmed at how much my body was responding to his. I was still a virgin but all I could think was *I want this man to fuck me senseless.* Turns out I was a latent harlot.

'Do you want to get out of here and we can get a drink somewhere more private?' he asked.

'No. My friends are here too. I need to find them. We have a policy – no woman left behind.'

'Ah, go on. Ditch 'em. The night is young. It's only . . . shit, it's not even light out yet. I'm not giving up on you.'

'Yes, well, I don't give up easy either,' I said. 'And I can see my pal Grace over there. It looks like she's come up for air. I have to go.'

Everything about Harry was an aphrodisiac. It wasn't just his looks – it was his confidence, the power he exuded, that assuredness. He was that little bit older and he was seducing me, but not in a sleazy way.

And there was something about him. Something . . . dangerous. Like he didn't play within normal rules.

I'd always been a good girl. Good girls are meant to go with good boys. But being the focus of Harry's attention was intoxicating.

In the end, there was more pulling me towards him than even I knew. I was an ambitious young woman but I was used to being loved. A large, tight-knit family will do that for you. I might have wanted to carve my own path in the world but I didn't want to do it alone.

And I think I sensed something similar in Harry. I'd learn, as time went on, that he wasn't as confident as he came across. He liked having people around him, lackeys and sycophants. But he'd never really had anybody who mattered. No family, I'd later find out, and no real friends. He let very few people get close.

The night of the Trinity Ball, I gave him my number.

Here's something I didn't know at the time.

Harry had come to the ball that night with a date. She wasn't with him when he saw me – maybe she'd gone to the loo or to touch up her make-up or something. Harry was gone by the time she got back.

You could say it was love at first sight and she was incidental to the story.

That would be the romantic interpretation.

Would it have mattered, anyway, if I'd known how easily he could pick up and drop women? Harry probably would have just spun it another way and I'd have most likely chosen to believe him. We were both good at that, but him especially.

Like when he told me that night that he was a banker – what he failed to mention, or at least correct me on, was that he didn't just work in a bank.

He owned one.

In his early twenties Harry had started his own bank; it dealt predominantly with funding up-and-coming property developers, headed by an up-and-coming financier. Here was a man well used to getting what he wanted.

I resisted him for months, which made the chase all the more exciting.

By that stage, I was head over heels for him and he with me.

You see us, don't you?

Young, innocent, hopeful, in love.

That was us at the beginning of our fairytale.

But here's the thing about fairytales.

Sometimes they're darker than you can ever imagine.

Alice

'Rummy.'

'What? What do you mean, "Rummy"? You can't have Rummy. We've only started.'

'Rummy.'

Doherty held out his hand so they could see the four jacks and three aces.

The officers around the table groaned and threw their cards down in disgust as the young Guard swept up his winnings.

'You're a jammy cunt, Doherty,' Station Sergeant Dean Gallagher grumbled, at the same time thinking he should start a lotto syndicate and get Doherty to place it every week. Only Alice was luckier, but she'd never waste her time on something as trivial as gambling.

Where was she, anyway?

The sergeant lifted his cup to take a sip of tea, spitting it back in when he realized it was lukewarm. He used his feet to shunt his chair back over to his desk, tossing the remains of the tea into an artificial pot plant. His quack kept telling him to walk around more. That was the best cure for sciatica, apparently. But his treatment of choice when his back seized up was ibuprofen, a heat patch, the occasional muscle relaxant and venting at anybody who dared to look at him sideways.

'Doherty,' he called over his shoulder, 'I'm giving you a chance to redeem yourself and be my favourite again. Make fresh tea and, while the kettle is boiling, nip out to the all-night garage and get some biscuits.'

Gallagher pulled a bundle of paperwork towards him, glanced at the top sheet and dropped his head into his hands. He was on a week of evening shifts and it was the early hours of Sunday morning. He figured he should get a commendation just for turning up, not be expected to clear up after the day shift as well. He envied his detectives who still did a job that could be considered proper policing, not this desk shite.

He was getting no sympathy at home from his fiancée of two years. She was planning the wedding of the century – by herself, apparently – which left her totally exhausted and absolutely not in the 'bloody humour for a bloody early night'.

'Are you at least in the humour for sex?' he'd quipped recently, and got slapped in the head with a bridal magazine the size of a block for his trouble.

Doherty was back, hovering over his boss.

'I don't see any Jammie Dodgers,' Gallagher said, his eyes fixed on the charge sheet on the top of the pile. He scratched at a spot beneath his beard – a bite or a hive, he wasn't sure which, but it was bloody itchy. It was probably a hive. He was very stressed.

Doherty didn't reply. He was wringing his hands.

The sergeant looked up at the lanky lad and noticed his regular, poker-straight face was filled with panic.

'Spit it out.'

They'd been busy earlier, a typical Saturday night, but it had eased off over the last few hours. He should have known.

'There's a man downstairs, covered in blood. He says he's killed somebody.'

'You're joking me.'

'No. Really. I am definitely not joking, Sarge.'

'I know you're not bloody joking – it's an expression. Jesus wept. Right. Where is he? Who is he saying he killed?'

'Nobody. I mean, no, he says he killed somebody, he's just not saying who. Somebody, anyway, by the looks of things. He's in the holding area.'

'It's like listening to Shakespearean prose.'

'What?'

'Forget it. The holding area. Is he covered in his victim's blood or is it his own blood? Nobody is to go near him without gloves, you hear?'

'He doesn't seem to be hurt himself. He's sitting on the ground, not saying anything. He hasn't said a word since they put him in there. It's . . . creepy. He's creepy.'

'Creepy? You sound like a five-year-old. I'll be down now. A mystery wrapped in a conundrum tied up in a riddle at 1 a.m. on a Sunday. Marvellous.'

Gallagher was about to attempt a painful standing position when Sylvia from reception came jogging up the stairs. Even while trying to process what he'd just heard from Doherty, the sergeant couldn't help but admire the way Sylvia's tits jiggled in her jumper as she trotted into the open-plan office.

Three weeks ago, he'd been tempted. They'd gone out for a work do and, rat-arsed, she'd told him how miserable she was. Thirty-five and not a sniff of a date, let alone a relationship.

'I've more pyjamas than going-out clothes,' she'd snotted on his shoulder. 'And really, Sarge' – she'd lowered her voice and breathed heavily into his ear – 'all I want is a good ride.'

It was a devastating reminder of why he'd stayed single into his early forties.

'What now?' he sighed as she made a beeline for his desk. Not fifteen minutes ago they'd been playing cards.

'We've just received a call. Harry McNamara. He's dead. Murdered.'

Sylvia nearly vomited the words out.

'His wife rang. Their house is in Dalkey. We're the closest fully manned station. She—'

'Hold up.' Gallagher felt the colour drain from his face. 'Harry McNamara? *The* Harry McNamara?'

'Yes! That's what I said. Harry McNamara. His wife rang 999. It took a while for Emergency Dispatch to calm her down, but she says a man just walked into their home and attacked him. *A total stranger*. There's an ambulance there now.'

'Whoah.' Gallagher held up his hands, as if he could stop the force of the oncoming train wreck. 'This can't land with us. McNamara is rich. He's famous. He's . . . this is huge. I knock off in a few hours.'

The sergeant sat back in his chair, an idea dawning on him so ludicrous that he almost couldn't articulate it.

'The man who's handed himself in downstairs. There's no chance . . .'

Gallagher, Doherty and Sylvia looked at each other, all thinking, *No, it couldn't be, could it?*

The sergeant clutched the arms of his chair, assessing how to respond to both situations or whether he should even consider them linked. He needed his best on this. The bigger the crime, the more intense the media focus, the greater the risk of a cock-up.

'I presume a First Response car is already on its way?' he said. 'And where's moody Alice?'

'My name is Alice Moody, you twat. I'm here.'

Gallagher's senior detective sergeant arrived at the top of the stairs, sweat patches already forming under her armpits from the three flights, her thin mousy-brown hair gleaming with the perspiration emanating from her scalp.

Every time that woman took the stairs she gave a convincing performance of somebody on the verge of a heart attack.

Gallagher shook his head as he watched Alice gasp for breath. She has a record-breaking solve ratio, he told himself, not for the first time. Her size shouldn't matter. And yet he couldn't get over the sheer height and girth of the woman. It was breathtaking. A walking sequoia.

'I'm just off the phone with First Response,' she said, propping herself against the banisters at the top of the stairwell. 'They were in the area and got to the house sharpish. The paramedics say Harry McNamara is alive. Barely.'

'Right, then,' Gallagher said, standing. 'He's not dead; we have breathing space. You come with me, Detective Sergeant Moody. Let's check out this fruit loop who's turned himself in before we do anything else.'

Alice groaned at the prospect of having to take the stairs, even if this time it was down, but it looked like Gallagher was going to make it easy for her. He limped over from his chair, each tentative step accompanied by a wince. Sylvia the receptionist was about to return to her post but, observing the slow progress of the walking wounded and the barely breathing, turned back towards the kitchen area at the rear of the office to make a coffee.

'So, is this McNamara's attacker, Sarge?' Alice asked. 'Or another headache? Could we be that unlucky?'

Gallagher shrugged.

'Of course we could. I've no other detectives available this week. Murphy is off sick and Tweedle Dum and Dumber are dealing with the gang hit. Of course something huge and horrendous could plant itself in our laps.'

Alice sighed, but he knew she didn't care about the absence of other detectives. She preferred working alone. It was easier than having to drag idiots along with her to every obvious conclusion.

Downstairs, he opened the door to the holding room.

It had been cleared of other suspects for its newly installed resident. He was sitting in the centre of the floor, arms wrapped around his denim-clad legs, rocking back and forth. His light T-shirt was splattered with blood. As were his hands, his arms, his face. He was youngish. Maybe early thirties? Black, almost tar-like hair, the same colour as his furrowed brows. An attractive-looking man, beneath everything.

His eyes were two big moons on a blank face as he stared up at them.

Alice opened her mouth to say something, but no words came out. Gallagher was only slightly less taken aback. It was like the man had arrived fresh from some sort of blood sacrifice.

'Eh – Station Sergeant Dean Gallagher and this is Detective Sergeant Alice Moody,' he said. 'We're told you've handed yourself

21

in, claiming that you've murdered somebody. Who do you think you might have killed?'

'I did kill him.'

Gallagher exchanged a glance with Alice. She took the reins.

'Would you be more comfortable sitting over on one of the benches, sir?'

The man said nothing, but kept rocking.

Psych assessment, Alice mouthed at Gallagher.

The sergeant shook his head, growing more irritated with each passing minute. He was too tired for this drama. Not to mention there was no way he was blowing his budget getting some suit into the station to tell them the fella on the floor was nuts. That much was obvious.

'Can you tell us your name, sir?' Alice said.

'JP.'

'JP. As in Jay Pee, or are they your initials?'

'JP, for the pope, John Paul. I was born in 1980. The teachers shortened it to JP when I came to Ireland because there were about five of us in every class and my surname was common. I grew up in London but my parents were Catholic.'

Lots of words and still the rocking. Back and forth. It was almost hypnotic.

'And what is your surname?'

'Carney.'

'Hmm. Common enough.'

The two officers stared at the man, who now had a name. It was progress of sorts, but they were still unnerved to hear calm, normal words from a man clearly in turmoil.

'So, JP,' Gallagher said, 'we just need you to tell us the name of the person you think you killed. We can hear all the details as soon as we have you in a proper interview room. There's a solicitor on duty – we can get her over here, unless you'd like to call one yourself?'

JP shook his head.

'You don't want a solicitor?'

'No. I don't know the name of the man I killed.'

'Excuse me?'

Gallagher and Alice looked at each other, then back to JP.

'How can you not know – did you run into him with a car?' Alice asked. Maybe he had concussion. That would explain the weirdness. They'd a doctor en route to check him out; they'd know soon enough. 'Or did you have a fight with somebody? How did you end up covered in blood?'

JP shrugged.

'I kept hitting him,' he said slowly, like he was in a daze. 'I just walked into their house. I don't know who he was. The back door was open and I walked in and they were in the sitting room, a man and a woman.'

Alice felt her blood run cold. This had to be the man who'd attacked Harry McNamara.

'Sorry,' she said, 'but you're saying you gained entry into some couple's house, a house unknown to you, and attacked the man inside? Where was this?'

JP shrugged.

'I don't know. Somewhere nice. I was walking and walking and I couldn't shake this feeling . . . I–I couldn't . . . I was just so full of anger. Then I was on this golf course and the lights were on in the house—'

'Don't say any more,' Alice said, holding up a finger. 'Sarge, can I speak to you for a minute?'

Gallagher nodded, and they stepped outside.

'The McNamara house backs on to a golf course,' she said, once they were out in the corridor.

'How do you know that?'

'How do you *not* know that? It was in all the newspapers during the trial. Big pad, floor-to-ceiling glass windows. No houses overlooking it, obviously. He shouldn't say any more until there's a solicitor present.'

'Agreed.' Gallagher nodded.

'He obviously thinks McNamara is dead,' Alice said. 'It'll be interesting to see how he reacts when he discovers he's alive.'

'I imagine he'll be relieved. I am. This will all wrap itself up nicely.'

'Seriously?' Alice cocked her head to one side. 'You believe it was just a random attack, then?'

'You don't?'

'Harry McNamara has just been cleared of multiple counts of financial fraud in the High Court. Most of his colleagues in HM Capital were convicted. He was up to his neck in all sorts as the head of that bank and has come out of the manure smelling of roses. People are probably queuing around the block to do him in. Do you really think the Teflon man could be so unlucky that, having come through all of that, some stranger just arbitrarily strolled into his living room and started beating the crap out of him? Your man in there must have recognized him for a start.'

Gallagher frowned.

'Recognition is not a given with bankers. He's not a reality-show star. He's mainly known from news clips outside a courthouse or the odd pic in *The Times*. Most people filter that out. I know him by name and reputation but even I'm not sure I'd recognize him in the street or relaxing in his own home in civvies. And just because he's been lucky in business doesn't mean he has a free pass to be lucky in life. Believe it or not, wealth can't buy you immortality.'

'You need a pysch assessment.'

'You're killing me, Moody. Right, let's get one of the oddballs in here with their crystal ball to confirm that JP is a few sandwiches short of a picnic.'

'That's a psychic, Sarge, and I think you need to bring in an expert to prove he's *not* nuts,' Alice said. 'I'm telling you now, if that man didn't know he was attacking one of most famous bankers in the country, I'll buy the whole shagging station a round of drinks next Friday.'

'Ha. Mine's a triple whiskey. Bad things happen to good people, Moody.'

'That's the thing, though, Sarge, isn't it? Harry McNamara is not a good person.'

'Maybe not. But if that poor sod in there is crackers, it doesn't matter if McNamara is the devil himself. Looks like Harry got unlucky, that's all I'm saying.'

JP

They say if bad shit happens to you when you're a kid, your memories are more vivid.

It's true.

Not all mine are bad. It's funny that it's this one in particular that fills my head while I sit here thinking about what just happened.

What I did.

I don't know what time of the year it was. I think it was hot – sunny, anyway. Mum was taking me to the seaside. That was a big deal. We lived in a tower block in East London and I'd only ever seen the sea on the box.

We got on a train at Victoria. It was crowded – office workers legging it to East Sussex for the weekend – but we got a seat, anyway, because she had me. I sat on her lap, almost five, all limbs and sharp angles.

'Where're we going?' I asked.

'Away,' she said.

I wondered why Dad wasn't coming. I knew enough not to ask. Sometimes Mum and Dad would fight and she would scream a lot

26

and hit him. Then she'd have to go away for a little while. I guess I thought that maybe this was one of those times and she was taking me with her.

I watched through the window as the city disappeared and was replaced with suburban housing estates, then fields. I slept at some point and then we changed trains and were there.

I was tickled pink with the golden sand of the East Sussex coast and ran around barefoot, whooping as I kicked the soft surface up into the air. I wanted to go in the water but she hadn't brought any togs for me. I wondered why anybody would go to the beach and not bring a swimsuit.

Mum seemed more nervous and worried than usual. I thought she went away on these trips to 'get well'. That's what I'd overheard Dad say to our neighbour this one time. I couldn't understand why she wasn't enjoying herself with me. We were on our holidays; it was the best day ever, in my head.

But she kept clutching her stomach and whispering things to herself about babies and everything being better this time.

As the hours wore by she seemed to relax a little, the corners of her mouth turning up as I raced at the waves with my trousers rolled up almost to my bum.

'Let's go get supper,' she called. 'You must be starving, John Paul.'

We walked along the pier and she bought us fish and chips – the tastiest I'd ever had.

'Wha' are those men doing?' I asked.

'We'll have a look, shall we?' she said, and brought me over to the fishermen who sat at the end of the pier.

'All right, lad?' The first man we arrived beside had perched his bum on a fold-out chair like I'd seen in the allotments beside the playground. He'd a bucket beside him, a flask of tea, and was smoking Benson and Hedges. He held his rod in one hand the line disappearing into the water beneath us.

'Wha' are you doing?' I said, nosiness overcoming shyness.

He smiled up at my mother.

'London?'

She stared at him, frightened. Her grip tightened on my hand. 'Why would you say that?' she asked.

He shrugged.

'Just the accent, missus. Sorry. No harm meant.'

'Oh. Of course. Yes.' Mum's hand relaxed a little. 'Sorry.'

'What's your name, lad?'

'JP. My mum is called Betty. Two Ts.'

She clicked her tongue in annoyance, her hand squeezing mine, hurting me. I didn't know what I'd done wrong.

He looked up at her and then back to me.

'You don't get out of the city much, eh, son?'

I shook my head.

'Well, see that fish you're munching on? I probably caught that for you.'

'How?' I said. I wasn't so stupid that I didn't know a fish was a living thing, but I was that innocent you could have told me they lived in trees.

'The fish are in the sea,' he laughed. 'I'm fishing with this line. Look in the bucket there.'

I peeked into his metal bucket and saw three or four small dead slippery things staring back at me; blank black eyes.

'You got them out of the sea?' I asked. 'You've loads.'

28

His mouth twitched. His rod wobbled a little and he gripped it with both hands.

'Well, they're not out of the shop. That's only a dozzle.'

'A wha'?'

'A small few. I'll need to catch a few more before I go home, but it looks like I'm about to get another one. Do you want to help me?'

'Can I? Can I?' I was jumping up and down with excitement.

Mum hesitated before relenting.

'Go on, then.'

The old man let me sit on his lap and wrap my hands around the rod while he reeled and released, reeled and released, slowly drawing in his catch.

When the fish appeared into view, it was wriggling and leaping about on the line.

'It's alive!' I said, astonished.

'Of course it's alive. I'd have to fling him back in if he was dead. He'd be no use to anybody.'

'But the ones in the bucket are dead.'

'You miss nothing. They are indeed. Let's put that to rights.'

He set me down off his lap and grabbed the body of the fish. It was then I could see how it was stuck on the end of his line. A nasty silver hook had pierced its mouth; a speckle of blood gleamed on its surface. Before I could say anything, the man unhooked the fish and whacked its head on the edge of the bucket then flung it in.

I let out a cry.

'It's all right, lad,' the man said. 'He's dead now. He didn't feel nothing. Bloomin' 'ell, the colour of you. I'm not sure you have a fisherman there after all, missus.'

Mum kissed the top of my head.

'He's just young, isn't that it, John Paul? He doesn't like to see God's creatures harmed.'

The man started to thread a squirming worm on to the end of his hook and I turned my head in distaste.

I didn't know how anybody could hurt another living thing. I wouldn't hurt a fly. I wasn't a typical little boy. I didn't delight in pulling the wings off dragonflies or scaring girls with spiders. Not even five, but I'd already seen too much by way of violence.

The next morning the nurse from the clinic and two policemen came to our B&B. They told Mum we had to go home and that she'd need to be minded for the next few months, for the baby's sake. I didn't know what the nurse was talking about. I wasn't a baby.

It was years before I realized what had happened that day. Before I knew what Mum was.

Why, all these years later, am I sitting in this cell thinking about that day?

Maybe because I'm wondering if there's a lot more of my fucking crazy mum in me than I'd ever realized.

Julie

He looks like a mummy.

I'm sitting beside Harry, my hand resting on the stiff blue hospital-issue blanket.

I'm afraid to touch my husband. His head and face are covered in bandages. The parts of him still visible are swollen purple and red, his nose bent at a strange angle, stitches sewn in his lips and cheeks. They only managed to save his left eye.

When he opens his mouth he'll be missing his front teeth. His hair has been shaved and, if it ever grows back, it won't grow over the two long scars that now run along the side and base of his skull.

Even at forty-five, Harry was still very handsome. All the years of worry and nerves after the banking crash – all those sleepless nights – none of it left the marks they would have on an ordinary man. The papers said he was Teflon – nothing stuck. When he was found not guilty, it seemed they'd called it right. Eighteen counts of financial fraud. It took the office of corporate law enforcement years to compile the charges, all those grey-suited little civil service clerks wading through piles and piles of data on my husband and his business. The trial was postponed multiple times and when it finally went into session it dragged on for months. I only ever attended court twice – for the opening arguments and the verdict.

I suspected how things would go that first day. The jury looked terrified at all the complex financial jargon. They were completely out of their depth. And of the six women on the bench, I could see five of them looking at Harry sympathetically as he sat hunched over in the dock, hands clasped together, sad and shocked at how everything had unfolded. The sixth woman was just bored to tears.

It killed Harry, but his defence team had decided to paint him as an innocent bystander to the goings-on at his own bank, of which he had been only chair by the time the bubble burst. They were throwing all the dirt at the then CEO who'd replaced Harry.

'As if I'd have let that fucking stooge make any decisions on his own,' he said to me that first night as we lay in bed together, staring at the ceiling.

'Oh, Harry, that's your bloody ego talking,' I replied irritably. 'What do you want to do, go into court tomorrow and make some grand statement about how it was all you, how nobody in HM Capital moved an inch without the great McNamara say-so? And then what? You'll be sent to prison for ten years. We'll lose everything. I'll lose you.'

He squeezed my hand under the bedclothes and turned to look at my profile in the half-light.

'Julie, you'll never lose everything. You know what to do if anything ever happens to me. You know where the money is and how to secure it so it can't be found. Don't you?'

Of course I did. He didn't even need to ask.

There's a soft rap on the glass and I look up to see an extremely large woman staring in at me through the blinds. She's not a nurse – she's wearing an ill-fitting black suit jacket and a light blue blouse, the buttons of it ready to pop. She doesn't look like press and it's unlikely they'd get this far into the hospital anyway. She can't be police, can she?

I make myself stand up, gently pat Harry's hand and go out to the corridor to see what she wants. Every time I leave his room I'm seized with terror that it will be the last time I see him alive. I might look normal as I emerge into the corridor but inside I feel like I'm trudging through emotional quicksand. Every fibre of me is screaming *STAY WITH HIM*! I'm convinced he'll die if I'm not beside him – as if my hoping and praying is the only thing keeping him alive.

I need a second chance with him. That's what this whole episode has taught me. I need another chance. I need to say sorry.

'Mrs McNamara, I'm Detective Sergeant Alice Moody. My apologies for disturbing you at your husband's bedside. I need to talk to you for a couple of minutes, if that's okay? Bring you up to date?'

I nod, surprised to discover I'd been wrong about her. Maybe it doesn't matter what size you are in the police force these days.

She's not an ugly woman, I realize, despite her pear shape. Her hair is awful, sure. Greasy and thin, an insipid brown scraped back in a severe, unforgiving ponytail. But her face is very pleasant. Warm eyes and a generous smile, deep dimples in her cheeks. She's wearing a nice scent, something almondy and feminine.

What's wrong with me?

I'm standing here assessing this woman's looks while my husband lies feet away with a fractured skull and barely breathing. I've never been that shallow. It's the shock. It's stripped me of my ability to function properly. Thoughts skid around my head like marbles on a plate.

'There's a family room,' she says, guiding me by the elbow. I look like I need to be guided places. I caught sight of myself in a mirror in the bathroom earlier and thought I was looking at somebody else. It's as if I went asleep and woke up ten years later – my face shadowed and lined and freeze-framed, like it's going into the drop of a rollercoaster.

We enter a room of cream – cream walls, cream curtains, cream sofas. I look around at the soft furnishings and shudder. I've had a vision. This is where I'll be sitting when they tell me Harry won't pull through. They'll bring me here, to this comforting room of cream nothingness, and break the news.

She's handing me something, and I reach out and take it, without knowing what it is.

'Your phone,' she says, seeing she has to explain. 'Forensics let me take it from the house. It's been ringing non-stop. Relatives, I imagine. You'll want to speak to them. I'm sorry, but it's already been leaked to the media. The emergency personnel are usually good about these things, waiting for family to be informed, and so on. But in these circumstances, with Harry being who he is . . . Anyway, sorry.'

I look at the screen. Forty-five missed calls have been logged, and countless texts. Even as I'm holding it it rings, and I jump. It's my mother.

'I . . . I can't,' I say, and drop it on the couch beside me. 'I'll ring them later. Don't you need it for evidence?'

'We've already examined it.'

She scrutinizes me, studies my reaction to the phone. She's wondering why I'm letting our family and friends stew in panic.

She doesn't understand.

I can tell them that Harry is in the ICU.

I can tell them a man came into our home and attacked him.

But I can't answer the questions that will follow.

What did you do? Did you phone the Guards? Did you scream? Did the man hit you?

Because then I'll have to tell them how I did nothing during the onslaught.

How I sat there and watched as Harry was beaten to within an inch of his life.

How, when the man left, my first act wasn't to call the police. It was to hurriedly change out of my pee-stained trousers and put them in the wash. I was embarrassed to be discovered in them.

I didn't even check Harry's pulse. I assumed he was dead.

Who wants to have that conversation?

'You should ring them soon,' the detective says. 'The news is saying he's alive, anyway, so they know that at least. Does he have any immediate family you'd like us to talk to? I know you've no children, but siblings? Parents?'

I bristle, even though her voice is gentle.

'No. He's an only child. His parents are dead.'

'Sorry, but doesn't he have a stepmother? I recall reading something. Is she dead too?'

'I doubt it. She's a modern-day miracle.'

'She's what?'

'The woman's a hypochondriac. She pops prescription drugs all

35

day long. She'll probably go until she's one hundred, outliving all her peers. He can't stand her. He wouldn't want her here. She has another family somewhere, anyway. Wouldn't want to know.'

'Ah. I see. Families. Complicated, huh? Well, if you think of anybody . . .'

'Thank you.'

She hesitates. I guess she's wondering if she should keep questioning me or if I should be lying down somewhere, sedated. I know I'm coming across as very odd. I want to tell her that I feel like I'm a few seconds behind myself, but she'd never understand what I mean.

'Mrs McNamara, can you talk me through what happened last night?' she says, her mind made up. 'I imagine this is very painful for you, but we need to know the sequence of events and you're the only witness we can talk to properly.'

I nod. The only witness. There were three of us in the room, but the man who did it won't be volunteering information.

The words spill out of me, just as they did when the woman at the end of the 999 line asked me to explain what had happened. I add a ridiculous amount of unnecessary detail. It seems important to give an exact picture.

I tell DS Alice Moody about the show we were watching. The Scandi thriller that everybody is talking about. We were relaxed. We'd had a late dinner – linguini in a tomato and garlic sauce with clams – and stayed up to let it digest. We didn't want to go out. We're still adjusting to our new lives, being liberated from the demands of solicitors and barristers and the High Court.

I suppose we were quietly celebrating, but I don't tell DS Moody that. We're not meant to be celebrating.

Then the man walked in. I describe to her, calmly, what he did, and what I didn't do. I leave out the part about wetting myself.

'You were in shock,' she says.

'Don't you think there's something wrong with me?' I whisper. 'I did *nothing*.'

She pauses, uncrosses then recrosses her legs, shifts her massive weight on to the other bum cheek. 'Mrs McNamara – Julie – let me tell you a story. When I was eleven, I was attacked by an Alsatian dog. I was running to the newsagents' and he saw me from a neighbour's garden and jumped the gate. I froze – I mean, completely froze – and he ran at me and bit my leg. Just one bite, then he was gone. I yelled my head off as soon as he was out of sight.

'Afterwards, in the hospital, my mother kept asking me why I hadn't screamed and fled when I saw the dog coming. The doctor who was dressing my wound looked up and said, "Mrs Moody, your daughter's reaction saved her life. If she'd run, that dog would have taken her down by the throat." Now, Julie, let's ignore the fact that even at eleven I was already ten-ton fucking Tessie and wouldn't have got more than a couple of feet. Do you get the gist of what I'm saying?'

'You think if I'd tried to escape, or to protect Harry, that man would have killed me?'

'Maybe. There's no wrong or right reaction when something like this happens. The human body does what it does.'

I look down at my trainers, thrown on hastily with a tracksuit before the ambulance arrived.

'My husband was dying and I did nothing to help him. He knew I was doing nothing.'

DS Moody eyes me curiously.

'And you had never met this man in your life? You didn't recognize him?' she asks. 'Did your husband appear to know him?'

'No.' I shake my head. 'Not at all.'

'Well, Mrs McNamara, the good news is we already have a suspect in custody whom we believe is the man who attacked Harry. We're running DNA tests to confirm that the blood about his person is your husband's. He handed himself in, claiming he murdered a man. He doesn't know yet that Harry is still alive.'

'What?' This information leaves me reeling. 'Say that again? He handed himself in?'

'Yes. His name is JP Carney. He claims he doesn't know the identity of the man he attacked, but his statement of what happens fits with your description. Is the name familiar at all?'

I shake my head, still in shock.

'He's mid-thirties. Jet-black hair and eyes—'

'I—I don't know. Yes. That could be him.'

DS Moody is nodding.

'Well, we'll know soon enough, anyhow. As I said, Mrs McNamara, he claims that he had no reason to attack your husband, that he just walked into your house and—'

'That bloody back door,' I say.

'What?'

'Harry. I spend my life telling him to lock the back door. He goes out to smoke, and when he comes in he always leaves it unlocked. Just when we're up, obviously. We lock everything at night. We even have an internal alarm. But during the day he leaves it open. I'm always taking him to task on it. I told him somebody would just walk into the house one day.'

DS Moody is peering at me with an intensity that is just

soul-stripping. She's being perfectly nice to me, but I can sense something at the back of it.

Suspicion.

'I see. So the attacker didn't have to break in to enter. And you're absolutely sure it wasn't you who left the back door open? It was definitely your husband?'

'I never leave it open. I'm the one who goes around the house at night, making sure everything is locked and switched off.'

'I see. Actually, we did notice, Julie, that in general external security is pretty lax. No electric gates, walls that are easy to climb. Harry is . . . well known. And you're a very wealthy couple. Were precautionary measures not considered at some point?'

I sigh.

'Not really. Harry could be very stupid about that sort of thing. We have a top-class alarm system, as I said, but my husband has this notion that . . . I'm sorry, I don't quite know how to explain it. He thinks we're untouchable. We live at the top of a quiet hill, we're surrounded by wealthy people on all sides. We're not idiots. I keep my jewellery in a safe and we never keep large sums of money about the place, but—'

'But?' she says.

'He takes chances.'

'Chances?'

'Yes. Harry isn't risk-averse. Does that make sense?'

She gives me a peculiar look that implies it makes absolutely no sense. She doesn't know Harry though. She doesn't get how arrogant he can be, even now, after everything that's happened.

'Right. Anyway, as I was saying – it's important, you see, to establish whether Mr Carney did just randomly attack your husband or is lying and has a motive. We've established he must have picked up the golf club from your husband's bag in the hall and that he didn't arrive armed. But anybody can source a weapon in your average home. Premeditation is a serious matter, do you understand? It will make a huge difference when it comes to prosecuting and sentencing – if what he did was planned. If he knew Harry and targeted him.'

'We don't know him,' I say adamantly.

'So you say. Can you think of a reason why he might have wanted to harm your husband? Why anybody would?'

I look at DS Moody, wondering if the question is as innocent as it seems.

I can think of one hundred and one reasons somebody might have for harming Harry. Unless she's been living under a rock for the last few years, surely she must be able to as well.

I shake my head. At the question, not in response to it.

'Was there anything else?' she asks. 'Anything the man did that struck you as odd? I mean, aside from the whole thing.'

'There was something,' I say, thinking of the unexpected move at the end of the attack.

'Yes?'

'He whispered something in my husband's ear.'

'What?' She leans forward eagerly.

'I don't know. He bent down and whispered something.'

She considers this.

'I see. Very interesting.'

You know, I think the shock is beginning to pass. In its place something else is growing, an all too familiar feeling.

DS Moody is so intense. It's like she knows everything.

40

A yearning takes hold.
Thirst.
I want a drink.
No.
I need a drink.

JP

A solicitor has just been in to see me. She's all right – somebody who's been appointed to a case that should be a lost cause and yet, when she talks about my defence, she's like a Duracell bunny. She says none of this is my fault, and I'm inclined to agree with her.

I didn't want to do what I did.

I had to.

She thinks people will pity me, because I've had a shit life. I understand her methods but I hate the thought of everybody knowing my business. More than that, I really can't stand them putting me in a box and feeling sympathy for me. A working-class sod who never stood a chance. That's just bollocks. And very middle class.

This wasn't written for me. Yeah, I didn't have the best start. Mum had her problems, and Dad wasn't around much. He was a bricklayer but could have worked on an oil rig, for all I knew, he was away so much. Mum used to tell me when he'd been in the flat, like he was this magical figure who could pass through unnoticed. He would leave early in the morning so he'd be the first in the queue for the van collecting the labourers. Then he'd work late into the night and have a few jars after. I'd be in bed by the time he got home.

I saw more of him the year my sister Charlie was born. She came along a few months after Mum took me to the seaside. The nurse was in our flat a lot and I heard her tell Dad that he had to keep an eye on Betty after the 'incident' with her first baby. Dad had his head in his hands and muttered something about having to earn a living. I sat on the floor, colouring in, pretending to watch the telly, but they were ignoring me anyway.

'Mr Andrews – Seamie – your wife's condition was exacerbated during and after her last pregnancy. We all know what happened with the . . .' She looked over at me, but I kept my head bowed and scribbled furiously with the crayon. 'With the little lad. I understand times are tough, but you don't want her to do something silly again. Doesn't Betty have any family who could lend a hand?'

Dad shook his head.

'The Carneys are fucking useless,' he said. 'Always have been. They could have warned me about her . . . issues, but they were happy to just wave her off at the church and leave me to deal with it. I didn't figure it out until it was too late. I just thought I was a lucky bastard, having a gorgeous blonde like that chasing me.'

When the nurse left, he smacked his hand angrily on the table and shouted at me to turn the telly down. Then he said sorry and came over and ruffled my hair. It was as close as he got to showing affection. Dad never did hugs.

He got himself a beer from the fridge and cursed because there was nothing in for my tea. Mum had forgotten to do the big shop again.

I was five when Charlie was born. She was named for Charlene in *Neighbours* — you know, the Kylie Minogue character. It was 1986, the show had just started, and Mum was obsessed with it. Monday to Friday, she'd tune in at 1.30 p.m. for a half-hour of yellow Aussie sun. Really, when I think of it now, all Mum gave Charlie was her name. She wasn't around for much else. Straight after she had her, Mum went on one of her special trips. This time, though, it lasted months.

Looking back, I can only imagine how hard it was on Seamie. He wasn't the most expressive of men; he just got on with things. But he was old-fashioned. It was his job to work and provide for his family. Not to take care of a newborn and a small child.

His brickie work fell by the wayside, and I remember those first few weeks after Charlie was born being filled with visits to a big building full of cubicles and lines of people sitting on red plastic chairs. Dad said it was a benefits office and I could see him tense every time we left the flat to go there, even though I'd no idea what was wrong with the place, other than it being boring as hell.

I didn't notice much else. I was too in love with the new arrival. I'd wanted a puppy, but she was better than any pet. Charlie was a good baby — if she'd cried and griped all the time, I'm sure I'd have had no interest. But she slept mostly, and it was like an extra special treat when she opened her eyes and grabbed your finger.

As hard as those days must have been for Seamie, to be honest, I remember them as being really happy. It was the eighties, nobody really had anything, so I didn't know what I was missing out on, if anything. I did worry about Mum but, in secret, shameful moments, I thought everything was a bit better without her. There were no tears, there was no shouting, and Dad kept things together.

The solicitor has zoned right into Mum's head problems. She

says her mental health probably had far more of an effect on me than I'm aware of. That whatever Mum had might be hereditary.

That that's what might get me off.

It's nothing I haven't considered myself.

Alice

By the time Alice returned to the station, JP Carney was kitted out in an over-sized shapeless grey tracksuit and cheap white trainers, no laces.

He'd showered since she had last seen him, all traces of Harry McNamara washed from his skin and hair. They'd taken DNA samples; they knew now for definite that this was the man who'd attacked McNamara.

Alice perched on the bench in the holding cell, trying to appear friendly, relaxed. She was chancing her arm coming in here like this, but she had to see how Carney reacted to McNamara's name. She had to figure out if he'd known him. It made more sense than the alternative: Carney being a violent psychopath who might have targeted anybody.

Whatever the truth of it was, what she didn't believe, for a second, was that Carney hadn't planned to hurt somebody. Nobody normal just 'snapped'.

'Mr Carney, I know you've spoken with your legal aid solicitor. I just want to have a little informal chat, if that's okay. Last night, a man named Harry McNamara was assaulted in his home in Dalkey. I spoke to his wife, Julie, a short time ago. Harry is the man you beat up.'

Carney looked at her, eyes uncertain.

'Harry McNamara?' he asked, as if it was news to him.

'Yes. You may have heard of him. He was just cleared on charges of multiple counts of financial fraud by the highest court in the land. He's been in the news quite a bit. He's very recognizable. Didn't you realize who he was when you attacked him last night?'

JP shrugged.

'I don't watch the news,' he said. 'I'd no idea who he was. I figured he was rich, all right. His house was . . . it looked like they'd money. The couple who owned it.'

'Yeah. They've a few bob. So you're positive you didn't know who he was? You never met him on a previous occasion? He didn't owe you money, or you owe him money? You'd never fought with him over anything?'

JP shook his head at Alice's questions.

'I've never even heard his name before.'

'Come on, JP,' Alice said. 'He's one of the most famous bankers in Ireland. One of the most famous men. Are you really claiming you'd no idea?'

'I don't pay attention to those things. I don't know shit about politicians or bankers or anything like that. I left school when I was fifteen. I don't follow what's going on in the news.'

'So you didn't know him. And when you woke up yesterday you really had no intention of hurting anybody? You didn't think about finding somebody and just smashing their head in?'

'No. Of course not. I know what I did but I didn't . . . I don't

47

know what came over me. One minute I was outside, the next I was in their house and just hitting this man. It was like something had taken over. Like I was possessed.'

'Okay, okay. Don't get upset. This is just a little chat. I just wanted to let you know the name of the man you attacked. There'll be quite a lot of attention on this. He's very well known. And he's still alive.'

JP's eyes widened.

'He's alive?'

'Yes.'

Alice watched as the emotions scattered across Carney's face. Confusion, in the main. Followed by what looked like relief. Looked like.

'Thank God,' he said, and started to cry.

Alice nodded.

'Hm,' she said. 'I'm just wondering something, JP. If you didn't know who Harry McNamara was, what did you whisper to him when you'd finished attacking him?'

'What?'

'What did you whisper?'

JP looked at her blankly.

'I didn't whisper anything.'

Julie

Love is blind.

I *was* warned. God, I was warned.

Even before Harry proposed.

I ignored what everybody close was telling me. I ignored my own gut.

I didn't want to hear it. I was already too far gone.

The first piece of unwanted advice came at the Christmas party of my final year in college. A gang of us were squashed around a tiny table in the Buttery Bar, drinking cheap wine and the occasional shot of what the barman claimed was tequila but tasted like lighter fuel.

I was sitting in between my sister Helen and my best friend Grace. Helen was the oldest in our family, ten years my senior, but we were the closest. She'd come to Dublin to shop and was staying in our bedsit with us. I kept apologizing for the size of our place and having to go out that night with college friends, but Helen had dismissed all my concerns with a wave of her hand.

'Pet. I left a two-year-old at home. I'd sleep in the back of a car and be happy to squeeze the dregs from a barman's sock. That's how thrilled I am to be liberated for the weekend. Hang on a minute.'

She paused.

'What the hell are you wearing in your ears, Julie Ferguson?'

I'd tucked my hair back so I could tip a shot glass into my mouth without using my hands. In doing so, I'd put my earrings on display.

'They're just costume, aren't they?' Grace said, squinting at the large diamonds.

'They are not costume!' Helen exclaimed. 'Christ, you're a lost cause to womankind. They're real diamonds. You can spot that from twenty miles away. 'Course, I've exceptional taste.'

'And still you married Barry the civil servant,' I snorted, and got a flick to the side of the head in return.

They *were* real diamonds. An early Christmas present from Harry. It was 1995, and we'd been going steady for over a year. HM Capital had grown and Harry was doing very well for himself.

'I tell you, you've landed on your feet, girl,' Grace said. 'He's either smitten with you, or he thinks you're a high-class hooker. Here, let me out. If I don't pee, my bladder is going to burst.'

'Get some drinks on the way back, will you?' I asked, not wanting to join the five-person-deep throng at the bar. Grace was shagging one of the barmen; she was our go-to woman for supplies. 'A vodka for me this time. The wine is burning the lining of my stomach.'

'Do you think she's capable of carrying drink back to the table?' Helen asked, as we watched Grace's tinsel-wrapped head weave unsteadily through the crowd.

'As soon as she emerges, one of us can grab the tray,' I said.

'It's serious, so.' Helen couldn't let the topic of the earrings go. 'They cost more than few bob.' She moved my hair back to look at them again.

I blushed and waved her hands away, pulling my curls over my ears.

'You know we're serious,' I said.

'He's older than you.'

'By a few years, Helen. The blokes my age are . . .' I indicated the far side of the table, where one of the lads from the course was standing on the couch, flexing his muscles like he was Popeye, the front of his shirt splattered with Guinness.

'Yeah, but he's *older* older, Julie. He wants to settle down. You can see it in him. He's got the job and the money and now he wants a wife. He'll be proposing to you next, and you've seen nothing of the world. You're only just about to get your degree. You've so much potential, pet. I don't want to see it wasted.'

'Says the woman who lives three miles up the road from Mam and Dad!'

'I'm the settling sort. You know what I mean about Harry. Don't play dumb, Julie.'

I did know. Harry had no family of his own. His parents were both dead, though he had a living stepmother, with whom he had no contact. His mother had died a couple of years after Harry was born, back when they were still diagnosing cancer in Ireland post mortem. He never outright criticized his father, but I got the impression he'd been a cold fish. He was good with Harry when he was very small, reading to him each night before bed, bringing him to rugby matches, that sort of thing. But when Harry entered his teens their relationship changed. I guess his father didn't know quite how to cope with having a moody, lanky strap of a lad hanging about the place. He sent him away to boarding school, a bit of a rarity in Ireland.

His father married again but then suffered a stroke that killed him. He'd left his wife and Harry well off (he'd been a banker too, though in the far more traditional, conservative sense) and the two had gone their separate ways. They'd never got on, according to Harry, who had filled the gap of his real mother with all the romance and myth that only premature death can allow. It didn't help that his stepmother spent her life diagnosing herself with various maladies, when Harry had watched his mother die from a real illness.

He'd been popular in boarding school. Harry was smart, a keen sportsman, quick-witted and handsome. He'd fitted in perfectly and it was there that he started to build up the vast network of contacts he'd need to start his own business. But that feeling of abandonment by his father, following on from his mother's death, marked him in ways beyond my comprehension.

Harry was looking for family.

'Well, what if he does ask me to marry him?' I snapped at Helen. 'Do you think I could do better? I love him.'

'I know you do. I'm just saying that when you came up to college you had more ambition than marrying the first man you met. And he's possessive. Anybody can see that. You must be able to. I just worry, though, that he might have double standards for himself.'

'He's not the first man I met,' I said. 'And in any case, aren't you getting ahead of yourself a little? He bought me some bloody jewellery. It's not a ring. And he's not that possessive. He loves me, he doesn't own me. I'm out alone tonight, aren't I?'

'I don't want to fight with you,' she said, sliding out of the seat to help Grace at the bar. 'I'm just telling you to be careful. Be young. Live your life. Harry will please himself. You should too. That's all I'm saying.'

A week later, Harry popped the question.

I was due to go back to Leitrim for Christmas Eve. It was the first time I wasn't looking forward to the trip. I was leaving Harry alone, and while he spoke convincingly about the friends' houses he'd be visiting and all the festivities he'd be a part of, I knew he wished I was staying.

But I couldn't avoid going home for Christmas. Mam would never have forgiven me. The unspoken condition attached to me moving to Dublin had been that I would return for every special occasion – no exceptions. Nor did I have the option of inviting him down. Mam was Catholic to her core. She only made up the spare bed if you were married.

Harry had booked a table in a little Italian restaurant off Dame Lane, and we took our seats just as soft flakes of snow started to fall on the shoppers who dashed about under the street lights outside, laden with Christmas packages and last-minute purchases.

It was our final night together before I left. He seemed anxious, and I put it down to him wanting it to be special.

When we got to dessert, Harry produced a little box wrapped in gold paper and tied with a red bow.

'Happy Christmas, baby,' he said, smiling as he placed it in my hands. He fidgeted nervously in his seat, not at all his usual calm self.

'Harry,' I tutted, taking it from him. 'You already gave me a present. This is too much.'

I was thrilled, but also a little irritated. I'd bought him something small and thoughtful – a rare copy of *The Count of Monte Cristo*, a book he'd loved since childhood. It had cost me a week's wages. It was important to me that he didn't think I was with him because he spoiled me. He had enough people around him sniffing after his money, and I was my own woman, after all.

I opened the box, perhaps expecting to see a watch or a bracelet to match the earrings.

Inside was an engagement ring set with a large diamond solitaire.

'Oh my God!' I gasped, realizing immediately. Harry was kneeling beside the table, smiling from ear to ear. The restaurant was more or less empty bar us and the waiting staff, but my heart still beat like I was on a stage under a spotlight. My mouth felt dry and I couldn't summon any words.

'You shouldn't have bought this,' I managed to get out eventually.

'You don't want me to propose?' Harry looked panic-stricken. I noticed then that a waiter was hovering in the wings with a bottle of champagne in an ice bucket. He'd thought of everything, and it was as romantic as anything I could have dreamt up. My dad had proposed to Mam with the words: 'I think it makes sense that we wed, Mary, what with the two of us stepping out a year now and me needing help with the farm.'

Harry's eyes were so full of hope and desperation, I think, even if I'd wanted to, I couldn't have said no.

'Of course I do, Harry,' I said. 'But this ring? You must have spent a fortune. It's too much.'

Harry laughed, trying to sound relaxed, but there was still more than a hint of nerves in his voice.

'You're worth every penny. Are we going to keep casually chatting about this ring or are you going to answer the question? Will you marry me, Julie?'

I smiled.

He leaned close and whispered, 'I'm not as young as you, sweetheart. That old rugby injury in my knee is fucking killing me and I don't think Giovanni there can keep the cork in that bottle much longer.'

'Do I really want to marry some old fogey who can't pop the question without whining about joint pain?' I whispered back.

'A *rich* old fogey. You left that part out.'

I laughed and put the ring on my finger. 'It fits.'

'Of course it fits. It's meant for you.'

'It really is,' I said, admiring it.

'Is that a yes, then? Can I get that in writing?'

'You and your bloody contracts!' I smiled. 'It's a yes. Holy crap. It's a yes. I'll marry you.'

Harry whooped and planted a big kiss on my lips.

'I love you, Julie Ferguson,' he said, as the kitchen staff emerged and began to clap and the hovering waiter poured us a toast.

'I love you too,' I said, and I meant it.

And yet a little part of me, a very small part, wondered about the timing of his proposal, a day before I was due home, hours before he was going to be left to celebrate Christmas on his own.

Just a little part, but it was there nonetheless.

And there was Helen's warning, her prophetic words ringing in my ears, making the champagne taste a little more bitter than it should. Was it too soon to be getting engaged? I was madly in love, but still young.

Still, I resolved to let nothing ruin the moment.

Even then, I think I'd already accepted that Harry could be manipulative.

I was so crazy about him, I just didn't care.

Alice

'There's something's not right about this whole thing,' Alice said.

'There's something absolutely not bloody right,' Gallagher grumbled. 'I haven't been home in thirty-six hours.'

'Aside from your human rights being infringed, Sarge.'

Alice took the seat across from her boss and drummed her fingers on the desk. Carney had just been transferred from the holding cell to a nearby detention centre. She'd watched him go, wondering how many days – or would it be only hours? – he'd spend in an actual prison. Everything was moving at lightning speed in this investigation, including the scheduling of a series of psychological assessments to determine responsibility. Harry McNamara was too famous. All eyes were on the justice system, and its wheels were spinning faster than a Formula One car.

'I wonder what, if any, Julie McNamara's involvement is in all this.'

'You mean the blonde with the big tits who appeared with him as the Good Wife on his first day in court?'

'I thought you said people filtered out the news clips of infamous bankers?'

'Yeah, they'd be looking beyond his face to her tits, Moody. What do you not like about her?'

'I don't know. I can't put my finger on it yet. She was in shock when I spoke to her, obviously, but there was something off. She was cold. She hadn't told her relatives what had happened and wouldn't answer the phone to her own mother.'

'You gave her phone back to her?'

'Of course. I want to see who she rings. The phone company are monitoring it for us. Anyway, at the start I could barely get a coherent sentence out of her, but you should have heard the detail she gave me when I asked for her version of events. She stopped short of telling me how much garlic she'd used cooking the dinner. And she was well able to tell me that her husband had left the back door open for Carney to walk in. She was insistent it was him, not her. It's not like we can check, is it?'

'Well, there's logic to how Carney got in, and she's trying to find something that makes sense in all this madness. What's wrong with that? Alice, I hope you weren't treating the victim's wife like a suspect. At her husband's bedside, of all places.'

'Of course I wasn't. I'm offended you'd even think that. I am full of compassion when I want to be. But . . . what if it was her who left the door open? She did absolutely nothing, you know, to stop Carney. Would you just sit there if somebody walked into your house and started beating the crap out of your Angela?'

Gallagher shrugged.

'Stop it, Sarge.'

'I'm messing. So what if it was her who left the door open?

Maybe she feels guilty about it. About that, and about not jumping in. But from what I remember, she's tiny, right? Aside from boobs. What sort of defence would she have been able to put up?'

'She might have left the door open on purpose and she might be feeling guilty for a reason,' Alice said.

Gallagher leaned back in his chair.

'Where are you going with this?'

It was her turn to shrug.

'Why did she take so long to raise the alarm?' she said. 'At least twenty minutes passed between Carney leaving and her ringing. And do you know what's even stranger? First Response told me the washing machine was on when they arrived. As in, the initial stage of the wash cycle.'

'People do funny things when they're in shock, Moody. You know that. I had a wife go up to wash and blow-dry her hair before coming in the car to identify her husband's remains. I just can't see what your point is about Julie McNamara, other than her reacting strangely to something that wasn't exactly normal in any case. What did she say about the washing machine?'

'She claims she doesn't remember turning it on. Forensics took everything out and looked through the clothes but nothing was stained with blood, which it would have been if she'd helped her husband at all. And another thing. She didn't tell me about that alleged whisper until right at the end. She'd all this detail but forgot that and only remembered to mention it when I told her how important premeditation is. Let's say Carney was hired to do McNamara in. You know as well as I do that it's more than likely somebody close to him who ordered the hit.'

'True,' Gallagher said. 'But what possible reason could Julie have for wanting to have her husband murdered, Alice? They're the golden couple, aren't they? She's stood by him through everything. If you're going down that avenue, you'll need to find a chink in their relationship that they've kept very well hidden.'

'Yeah. Well, I'm going to concentrate on Carney for now anyway. Try to figure out what makes him tick. Where he comes from, what his background is.'

'Do that. I think you're mad considering the wife. Because anyway, if she hired Carney to do it, why tell us in such detail what he did? It's enough to turn any jury's stomach.'

'No, Sarge. The more interesting question is, why has he handed himself in?'

Article from *Ireland Today*

5 October 2012

An Garda Síochána have confirmed that they are holding a suspect in custody following last weekend's brutal attack on Mr Harry McNamara, former head and founder of HM Capital.

The well-known financier was assaulted in his home on Saturday night. Mr McNamara's wife, Julie, witnessed the attack.

The family home in Dalkey, a €5.4 million detached residence, designed by renowned architect Michael Stewart Bannon, was sealed off following the attack, but Mrs McNamara has since been allowed to return. Images of the house were used during the McNamara trial to highlight the former banker's wealthy lifestyle, with the building's layout described in detail across several media outlets. Police have refused to say whether this provided Mr McNamara's attacker insight that enabled him to gain unlawful entry.

Mr McNamara was recently cleared of all charges relating

to fraud at HM Capital during his period there as chairperson. The Trinity graduate and son of the late Lorcan McNamara founded the bank in 1990, filling the role of CEO until early 2006, by which time HM Capital had become one of the largest funders of property development in Ireland and Eastern Europe. In 2003, the bank recorded share growth in excess of 100 per cent per annum.

HM Capital required a state bailout of €20 billion following the financial crash in 2007.

Mr McNamara remains in intensive care at Our Lady of Hope Hospital in Dún Laoghaire.

An Garda Síochána have declined to comment on a possible motive for the attack, but a solicitor representing the accused has issued a statement to say her client will present shortly in front of a judge to ascertain if he is fit for trial. Leading criminologist Dr Mary Batten has confirmed for *Ireland Today* that this implies that Mr Carney's defence, if the case does go to trial, will lodge a plea of not guilty by reason of diminished responsibility.

Julie

So that's his game.

The hand I'm holding the phone in shakes as I scan the article.

He's trying to get away with what he did by claiming he's mad.

'It's disgraceful, that's what it is,' my father says, looking up from the knot of wires he's attempting to untangle. He's decided to mow the lawn. I've explained to him we have gardeners who come in to do that for us. They're the only staff we've ever had over the years. At first I told Harry I was uncomfortable having a cleaner or live-in help, because there were only two of us and I wasn't raised that way. But later the reason changed. I didn't want anybody else about the house, any strangers judging me.

Dad finds the plug amid the tangle and sticks it in the wall, removing an air freshener to do so. He looks at the air freshener like it's something that fell off the bottom of a spaceship, before casting it aside. He needs to have a purpose, my dad. It will take him hours to do the acre behind us, but I think that's why he chose the task. He'd probably do the golf course too, if he could get on to it. Eighty years of age and he still lives by the old adage – the devil makes work for idle hands.

The sitting room has been scrubbed, the rug removed and the floorboards sanded and revarnished. My family did it all before I returned, in a matter of days. I still can't go in there.

My mother is making sandwiches.

'Outrageous,' she agrees, halting the butter train momentarily to snatch the phone away. 'Nobody should have to read what's happening in their own lives in the bloody newspapers. The police should have been out to you first thing to tell you what your man is at. And as for you, missy' – she picks up the butterknife and waves it like a warning at Helen – 'stop showing her rubbish on that phone. If you want to help, find me some tinfoil. This batch can go in the fridge with the others.'

'She's well used to reading about her life in the newspapers,' Helen replies, playing musical plates. She gives me a sympathetic smile.

God, how often have I seen Helen over the last few years? I've been so lax with my family and friends. I just let everybody drift.

It doesn't matter to her. Blood is blood. Throughout the trial she rang and checked in with me regularly. Some of my siblings didn't bother. Nobody would have said anything bad about Harry to my face, but their silence when we needed support spoke volumes.

Not Helen though. Even *with* how she felt about Harry.

She picks at the crumbs discarded by our mother, all the time watching me to make sure I'm coping okay. I love her to bits but, in this very moment, I just want to scream.

You're wrong. I was wrong. Harry doesn't deserve to die. I want him to live.

64

'Little pickers have the biggest knickers,' I say instead, sweeping up the crumbs with my hand.

She sticks her tongue out at me, trying to cheer me up, but I look away. I wish they'd all stop being so nice. I'm not worth it.

The mound of sandwiches on my kitchen island is growing again. Ham, cheese, chicken, tuna, salmon. This invasion of my home is like a continuation of the attack the other night. They're all wrapped up together, a chain of events there's no escape from — the assault, the police, the arrival of concerned loved ones refusing to leave me alone, a constant stream of well-wishers in person and on social media. Yes, an event hasn't truly happened until you've posted about it on Facebook — even my husband's coma. What's the emoticon for *Isn't this awful, but they sort of had it coming, didn't they?*

I just want everybody to leave me alone so I can think.

'Mam,' I say, exasperated. 'Why are you making so many fucking sandwiches?'

She flinches.

'Language, Julie. I know you're upset, but there's no need for language. People will call in. We have to offer them a cup of tea and a bite to eat. Your colleagues from the school have all been ringing, asking when they can drop by. Nobody expects you to do anything. They just want to be here for you. Why don't you go upstairs and have a rest?'

My mother has an entirely innocent interpretation of people's concerns; of course she does. She can only view them through the filter of her own good heart. All my co-workers — even my friends — gave up on me a long time ago. I tried to renew the friendships when I went back to work but it was never the same. Too much time had passed. Too much had happened in my life.

My dad has got the mower going and I can see him through the French doors, already scratching his head as he tries to work out the logistics of our sprawling garden. The grass doesn't even need to be cut.

'Oh, Mam, as if she'll sleep,' Helen says. She takes my hand and gives it a squeeze. '*I* couldn't sleep last night and I had a Xanax before I went to bed. I might try one with a bottle of bloody wine tonight. Oh!'

She freezes. We all do.

I want wine. I want to take a bottle of wine and crawl into my downy-soft bed, drink it dry, then open another one. I'd sleep if I'd a bottle of wine to snuggle up with. I'm parched, the inside of my mouth craving just a drop, the syrup to make all things better.

That's the thing with alcoholism, isn't it? You're never really recovered. It's always just there, on the sideline. Waiting.

'Helen,' my mother says, her voice falsely cheerful, 'I'm out of bread. Why don't you make yourself useful instead of sitting there and . . . and talking fucking nonsense.'

I nearly fall off the stool. Helen's eyes widen.

'That's put me in my place,' she says, and swings her legs off the breakfast-bar stool. 'Three Hail Marys for you, Mammy.' She mouths 'sorry' in my direction before grabbing the car keys from the counter. I shake my head dismissively. She meant nothing by it. They're all on tenterhooks, terrified that this trauma will knock me off the wagon.

'I know you're upset, Mam, but there's no need for language,' I say when Helen has left.

'Don't start. This is not the time to be talking about drink and

66

drugs. Sure, why don't we all break out the happy tablets and have a . . . what do they call them? A rave. Indeed, we'll have an oul' rave.'

I snort. She rounds the counter and cups my tear-swollen face in her hands.

'You need to sleep, my beautiful girl. I can see your brain working overtime behind those tired eyes. We're here, and we'll take care of you. All you have to do is mind yourself so when Harry wakes up you'll be there for him. He's going to need you. Don't fall back on alcohol. It won't help. You've been strong for so many years. Harry needs you to stay strong.'

I nod. I don't tell her that I'm equally afraid of Harry dying and of him waking up. Afraid of what he might say to me when he does.

You just watched.

I go to my bedroom, the largest room upstairs. The floor-to-ceiling windows here give us a view of a glistening Dublin Bay stretching into the distance. Once the door is closed, I get the footstool by the rocking chair in the window and carry it into the walk-in wardrobe.

There, I reach up to the back of one of the top shelves and retrieve the hidden laptop. The Guards had no search warrant for the house when they arrived in response to my call for help. We were the victims for once.

But for all I know they did an illegal search. I've a very suspicious mind when it comes to the law, these last few years.

Harry and I spoke about what the police would do next if the attempt to prosecute him for fraud was unsuccessful.

'They'll come after our assets, Julie,' he'd said. 'The Criminal Assets Bureau. It will move beyond financial irregularities and fraud at the bank to a criminal investigation into me, and that will give them the power to search and seize.'

'What do you want me to do?' I asked.

'Well, I can't move anything while the trial is going on. They're watching everything. Afterwards, when they're looking for a new file to be opened, we're going to move everything into your name. The house is already switched and I'm making weekly payments from my bank account into yours, but I need to talk to you about something else now. The other accounts. The ones they don't know about.'

After all those years of being married to a financier, suddenly I was getting a crash course in where to hide money and how to grow it.

And finding out that my husband had been keeping yet more secrets from me.

He never learned. After everything that had happened between us, he still thought it was a good idea to hide stuff.

The fucking idiot.

The accounts are one of the many reasons I can't have a drink. I need to set the process in motion, the one that should have started as soon as the trial was over. I suppose we were both so taken aback by the verdict that we got a bit carried away, thinking everything was going to be all right. Who knew there was something else coming?

Before I input the complex password that will launch me on the cyber trail to access the private banking, I go back on to the webpage Helen showed me, and the article about Harry's attack.

I read it again, and that same feeling of anger and confusion tears at me.

Diminished responsibility.

68

It's bullshit. No matter what he says – JP Carney – I know it's all lies.

He knew what he was doing.

That detective one, Moody, isn't worth her socks if she isn't wondering if I'm somehow involved in the attack on Harry. If she isn't yet, by the time she's done a full background check on us and discovers our many problems, she will be.

She'll try to connect me to that animal Carney, no doubt.

She'll just be doing her job. But they won't find anything linking me to the attack on my husband.

I shut down the article and go back to the system that will take me into the offshore accounts.

Whether Harry wakes up or not, it's time to start moving that money.

And then I'm going to figure out exactly what JP Carney is up to.

I need to know why he has wrecked everything.

JP

If things had been different, we would never have come to Ireland.

If we had never come to Ireland, none of this would have happened.

If, if, if.

It was both their faults. Mum and Dad.

Mum was in a psychiatric institution for months after she had Charlie. When she came back, she was never the same.

Dad must have thought that when she came home everything would return to normal. He'd go back to his routine of working hard during the day and having a few drinks with his mates at night. She'd be able to cope with us. Normal service would resume.

It wasn't like that though. At the end of the first week, Dad came home one night to find Mum cutting up all his trousers at the kitchen table. I was sitting on the sofa with Charlie in my lap. Even as a baby, you could see Charlie was going to end up looking like her namesake, a tiny Kylie with blonde curls and the face of an angel. The complete opposite of me. I was the spit of Seamie – a black-haired, dark-featured, sullen-looking thing.

Mum snipped away and muttered under her breath. A cigarette hung out of the side of her mouth, its ash falling on to the discarded material.

'What are you doing?' Dad's mouth fell open when he arrived at the door to the flat and saw what she was at.

'*I know*, Seamie,' she said matter-of-factly. 'I know what you've been getting up to with that hussy downstairs. Do you think I don't see these things? All that time I was away, you had her – a *tart* – in my bed and minding my children. *My* children.'

'Rose?' Dad choked. 'The woman who helped me hold this family together while you were in the fucking funny farm? The bleedin' nerve of you, Betty.'

He spotted me and Charlie.

'Why in the name of Jaysus are the kids still up? It's nearly midnight.'

'They wanted to see their father when he came home from the pub. If you didn't stay out so late drinking, they wouldn't be still up. If you earned proper money, maybe we could live somewhere nicer and I would get better. If you . . .'

She was still going when Dad packed us off to our room. I heard the fight continue through the paper-thin walls and then Mum started crying and Dad's voice went quieter and I knew he was trying to make her happy.

That night, it worked.

'Betty, why can't you believe I want everything to be okay, my lovely girl?' I heard Dad say in between the hushing and the soothing sounds. 'Don't you remember how we used to go dancing when it was just the two of us, and we'd stay out all night? I've only ever had eyes for you, girl. You know that.'

Mum sobbed quietly and then started to talk, and soon they were laughing and things were okay again.

But even I knew Mum was getting worse, not better.

The next time she left, she went for good.

She couldn't have timed it worse. Dad, unbeknownst to her, had taken a job that morning up in Northampton. When she locked the door behind her that night, she must have assumed he'd be home late, as always. But he didn't come back until the following evening.

'Where's Mummy gone?' Charlie asked me the next morning. She'd wet her bed, something that happened a lot now she was three and no longer in nappies. Mum had taken her out of them, saying she was big enough to be toilet trained, but she'd forgotten to do the training part.

'Dunno,' I said, trying to be the little grown-up so she wouldn't be scared. I changed her out of her pee-soaked nightie and made us bowls of Rice Krispies. I was eight; old enough to know something was up, especially when I couldn't open the flat door.

We ate our breakfast in front of the telly and I tried to keep Charlie entertained for the day and not get too panicky myself. I thought she was all right. She was used to me taking care of her anyway. But that afternoon she started to cry.

'What's wrong, Charlie?' I asked.

'I'm afraid.'

'Why are you afraid?'

'Has Mummy left 'cos of me?'

'Why would Mum leave 'cos of you?' I said.

She wiped the snot that had rolled down on to her lips with the back of her hand, her chubby cheeks puffy and red.

'She gets angry when I do a pee-pee in my bed. I try not to, JP. It just comes out of me.'

I shook my head.

'No, you silly boo. Mum loves you. How could anybody be annoyed at you? She's just gone to get something.'

'Will she and Daddy fight when she comes home? I don't like it when they shout.'

'I know,' I said. 'Me neither. But if they fight you can come sleep in my bed, okay?'

'Promise?'

'Promise.'

I held her hand and we watched more TV, snacking on whatever I could find in the presses.

When Dad got home that night and found the door locked from the outside he knew Betty was gone, but he still checked every room in the small flat. He couldn't believe she'd left us. He couldn't believe she'd left him again, and this time it wasn't even because she'd checked into hospital. She'd just gone.

He brought us down to Rose the next morning and asked her to watch us for a few days while he went off looking for Betty.

'I can't keep doing this, Seamie,' she hissed. 'I've three of me own. Look, I'll take 'em for a couple of days but, love, you might want to think about sorting something full-time. Betty could be gone a while. It's not good for 'em to be always shifted from pillar to post, and they've already seen too much for kids their age. You're just lucky that she never tried anything funny with Charlie, after what happened to John Paul.'

'I know, Rose. I know. Jesus, I need a drink.'

73

'Seamie, be careful now,' Rose said. 'Have a drink, but just remember – you're all these mites have.'

Dad cursed again and muttered that he didn't need a lecture. He stomped off down the balcony and Rose watched him with a worried look in her eye. I held Charlie's hand tight. She was all I had, really.

That night Rose put us to bed head to toe in the flat's tiny box room. She'd heard nothing from Dad since that morning. She sat on the floor beside us and watched Charlie doze off, then talked to me like I was older than I was.

'Do you know what's happened, John Paul? You know your mummy has gone? The silly cow. If she'd just told me, I'd have taken you down 'ere . . .' Rose swiped at the tears that had sprung up in her eyes. 'The thought of you, up there on your own all night!' She stroked Charlie's curls, her soft baby cheek, and swallowed.

'Is Dad going to find Mum?' I asked.

She shrugged.

'I don't know, son. That's the God's honest truth. Do you want 'im to find her?'

I didn't know what to say to that.

'Sorry,' she said, misunderstanding. 'Of course you do. That's a stupid question. I hope he does. I hope it works out for you all. You've had it tough, 'aven't you, pet?'

It was my turn to shrug. I didn't think I'd had it tougher than anybody else.

'What did you mean, what you said to Dad about him being lucky Mum did nothing funny with Charlie after what she'd done to me?' I asked.

Rose's jaw dropped. She'd said that right in front of me but assumed it had gone over my head. It wasn't the first time I'd heard something like that though, and I'd picked up on it.

'Ah, nothing, John Paul. Don't mind me. I'm talking out of school. Anyway, I'm sure Seamie will find Betty and everything will be grand. But until he does, you'll make sure to 'elp 'im now, won't you? You be a good big brother for Charlie.'

'Yeah,' I said. 'I always am.'

'Good. Your dad has had it tough, John Paul. Don't forget it. First having to emigrate and then your mum's . . . condition.'

I knew very little about Dad's background. He rarely talked to us about anything, let alone his life before we came along. I knew he was Irish and that meant he was different from Mum and us in some way. His accent, mainly. In the European soccer championship that year he'd told us we were cheering for the green team, not the white team. But everybody in school was cheering for England and, when he wasn't around, I was too.

'You know your poor dad didn't want to leave Ireland, love. He had to, for work. And then, when he came, some people weren't very friendly.'

'You're friendly,' I said.

'Yeah, but I'm one of your own, sweet'eart. The poor's the same, no matter where you're from. And my mum was Irish, so I really am one of your own. Anyway, your dad came in the early seventies, long before you were born, and it weren't a great time to be gettin' off the boat. Your dad couldn't get a proper job and ended up doing backbreaking work for a pittance. No guarantee of even getting a day's labour. You know he grew up on a farm?'

'No.'

'Yeah. He did. He was used to seeing the land, outdoors and greenery. And he ended up in a shithole tower block here in East London. Then, when Betty got pregnant on you, she was very ill. That 'appened again with Charlie, and your dad couldn't even try to work then; he had to go down the dole office every week to get abuse from some slag looking down her nose at 'im like her own crap didn't smell. Most other men would have cracked by now. Seamie's done his best. He's done his best.'

For all she was praising Seamie, I could see that same worried look on Rose's face that had been there when she watched Seamie storm off that morning. She sensed something bad was coming.

Dad looked for Mum for weeks. There was no sign of her. It was like the time after Charlie was born again – just the three of us in the flat and having to go to the benefits office all the time for meetings. He started to drink a bit more. He was a lot angrier too.

A few weeks later he phoned his mother, a grandma in West Cork we didn't know we had. Twenty-four hours later, all three of us were in Holyhead waiting for the boat to Ireland.

I sat in the ferry terminal bar hugging my sister while Dad downed Guinness.

'It's the only way,' he said, half to me, half to the empty glass. 'We can't wait for her to come back and even if she does, what fucking use is she? I should have realized years ago.'

'Are we leaving England?' I asked.

'We'd hardly be getting on a bloody boat for any other reason, John Paul,' he said. 'Don't worry about it. Ireland is better anyway. I should never have stayed.'

'But what about school?'

'They do have schools in Ireland. You know the greatest poets and writers in the world come from there? Never let anybody tell you Ireland is not a great little country, lad.'

Dad drank more Guinness, and the hours passed. We were hungry. I was afraid to ask for money. Dad had slipped further in his chair and was muttering to himself. I didn't think he was that happy to be going back to Ireland at all.

I couldn't wait any longer. I asked him for a pound for the chocolate machine.

'I'm not made of money,' he snapped.

'But we're starving,' I said. 'You forgot to get us something.'

Dad looked confused, then realized I was right. His face flushed red as embarrassment turned to anger. He was too drunk to think logically.

'I do my best, you ungrateful little shit. Don't take that tone with me.'

He made to swipe at me but Charlie leapt up.

'Don't you touch my bruvver!' she yelled, this tiny tot, stamping her feet and making as much noise as only a three-year-old can make. The barman looked up from his paper to see what all the excitement was about. Dad was mortified.

'All right, all right,' he said. 'Don't be getting upset. Sorry. I'm sorry. Here, go buy some crisps.'

He gave me the pound and eyed her like she was some kind of devil-child.

The pressure was getting to Seamie.

The funny thing is, Seamie was a good person to begin with.

No matter what people think, I've seen it first-hand. Sometimes, in the right circumstances, even the best of us can just snap.

Alice

'I love seeing you, Moody. You bring the sunshine with you. I knew you'd be over when I heard what happened. Not sure how I can help, though.'

'Don't be a wanker.' Alice blushed despite herself. Jimmy Doyle in Fraud was a world-class flirt. The myth went he'd been inside the knickers of half the women in the station. He hadn't been in Alice's, but she wouldn't say no. Not that she'd ever get a chance. His MO was the charm offensive, but in her case she knew he was just being charitable.

'You must be punching the air with delight, seeing old Harry get what he deserves.'

Doyle shook his head.

'Nah. You want him banged up for what's he's done wrong. But that taking the law into your own hands shite is not on. Anyway, I sort of liked him a little.'

'You liked Harry McNamara? Even though you helped build a case that had him up on eighteen counts of fraud?'

Doyle laughed, rubbed his chiselled jaw.

Channing Tatum. That's who he looked like. Gorgeous.

Alice gave herself a mental slap and an order to cop on.

'Yeah. I did. He was self-made, Harry. Fair enough, he wasn't born into poverty and the father sent him to a good school, but that was all he gave him really. He was an aloof git by the sounds of things. Harry was left on his own in a world where network is everything. He made it work. Those men he ended up surrounded by – they'd have looked down on him and envied him in equal measure. Shrewd enough to get close to the money but still thinking of him as a little upstart with nobody behind him.'

'And when you say money – what are we talking? How wealthy was McNamara when all this was going on?'

'Oh, he's still wealthy, Alice, my little flower. We couldn't even begin to track down all the money. But at the height of it, I'd say he was Ireland's first billionaire. Mainly on paper, but that didn't matter until stocks went belly-up.'

'You're shitting me.'

'Scout's honour. Why do you ask?'

'I'm trying to figure out if he knew JP Carney. Or if Carney knew him. Carney is piss-poor by Harry's standards. How the hell would two men like that ever interact?'

'Hmm. It's a puzzle all right. But only if you're thinking of money as being whiter than white. Harry's money wasn't clean. By any stretch.'

'How do you mean? Are you just referring to the illegal trades at the bank?'

Doyle raised an eyebrow.

'Ah, Alice. Let me take you for a drink and explain it.'

'Here is fine, *flower*.'

He laughed.

'Okay. Well, look, nobody as young as Harry could make that much money, that fast, without being naughty from the start. And we know he got rich early because he was spending money hand over fist as far back as the mid-nineties. The tales about his wedding would make your eyes water.

'But if you really won't take me up on my offer, then let me steer you to somebody even better than me on this stuff. There's a woman you should talk to. She's a busy gal but I'm sure I can sweet-talk her into seeing you. She'll give you everything you need about Harry's world. See if you can find a chink of light there that leads you to your Carney suspect. Can I have a kiss now?'

'Only if it's you planting one on my arse.'

'Such a tease, Alice. Such a tease. You're breaking my heart, you know that?'

She smiled, so hard it was painful. If only.

Julie

People think they know us. The papers, the magazines – they love revealing our 'secrets'. The details of our lives.

But nobody knows *us*. They just know *things*.

It's still not very pleasant, but it's the cost of being in the public eye. With Harry's name a symbol for wealth during the Celtic Tiger years, and then a warning for excess during the crash, we were never going to avoid it.

Money defined us.

On my hen do back in 1996, in a luxurious spa hotel, my friends and sisters took turns pointing out the sort of wealth I was marrying into and what they'd do with it in my place.

'How rich is he do you think, Julie?' Grace asked. 'I mean, are we talking millions or billions?'

'Billions?' my sister Lynn snorted. 'Do billionaires even exist? Wouldn't he be flying around in a shagging hovercraft rather than driving a BMW, if he'd that sort of Monopoly money in the bank?'

'He owns a bank,' Helen murmured from underneath a face mask. 'He can print money.'

'You're wrong,' I said, taking a sip from an exotically named pink-hued cocktail. 'Harry can't print money. Only the Central Bank can do that. HM Capital makes its profits from interest on loans and returns on its investments.'

'Hark at her,' Lynn laughed. 'J. D. Rockefeller's missus. Please tell us some more about banking – it's riveting.'

'You're just jealous.' I pouted.

In truth, I'd no idea how much Harry was worth when it came to his personal wealth. But I was starting to suspect he had more money than I could imagine.

He planned most of our wedding, taking it in hand like it was another business project. It never would have occurred to me to marry outside Ireland. Maybe in a county beyond Dublin – but abroad? Nobody did that in the nineties. And he insisted on keeping the final venue a surprise.

I thought it was romantic.

Looking back, I see it was just another way of Harry controlling things.

We flew to France, the wedding party and the guests, all together, on a chartered private plane.

'Harry, my family haven't closed their mouths since they got on,' I said, snuggling up to him in the front row.

He was reading the *Financial Times*, his features fixed in concentration.

'Good,' he said. 'They might even invite me for Christmas dinner this year, seeing as I'm spoiling them.' It still rankled with him. He couldn't understand the word 'no'.

A young air hostess arrived beside us and I accepted the glass of wine she offered me.

'Would you care for something yourself, Mr McNamara?' she cooed, her make-up exact, hair delightfully coiffed.

The studious gaze fell from Harry's face as soon as he saw her, replaced with a look normally reserved for me. It turned my stomach to ice. I'd seen him do that a couple of times, and I didn't like it.

'I think you can tell me now where exactly in France we're going,' I said, drawing his attention with a little squeeze to his upper arm.

He turned to me immediately. I caught the flash of disappointment on the girl's face. For a moment, with his eyes on her, she had been elevated. She trotted off, ignored.

'We're going, my little princess, to a fairytale island,' he said, and planted a big kiss on my lips.

'Your little princess might need an actual marriage certificate from an actual registrar. Do they have civil servants on this fairytale island?'

Harry smiled cheekily. 'I'm not saying another word unless you make me a member of the mile-high club.'

'Bloody hell, Harry. A bit risky, don't you think? With everybody we know onboard? What if my dad wants to use the loo?'

'It's the risk that turns me on.' He winked.

We flew into Rennes and drove in a private coach through Normandy, staying that first night in a luxurious hotel en route. The following morning, after a breakfast of croissants and Bellinis, we continued by coach. My family, the rural Leitrim dwellers, were settling into this lifestyle like they'd been born to the manor. I heard my mother say she was going to buy peach juice to make her own Bellinis at home. Like we had champagne lying about in the drinks cabinet under the picture of the Virgin Mary in the back room. Like you could buy peach juice anywhere in Leitrim.

'Are we actually getting married on an island?' I asked, determined to get the information out of him.

Harry nodded.

'Yup. The coach will bring us right up to the gates.'

'The gates?' I repeated. 'Just so you know, I can't walk anywhere. These are car-to-bar heels, my love. And if it's an island, are we not going on a boat?'

He laughed. 'No boat and don't worry, it's not far to the hotel once the coach leaves us off. I'll give you a jockey-back. There are no private vehicles allowed inside the walls. There are hotels – but only a handful of families actually live there. It's like a fortress built around an abbey.'

'An abbey? Do they have many weddings?'

'I'm starting to think I should have hired a tour guide.'

'I'm sure you could just click your fingers and get hold of one,' I snorted. 'Seriously, Harry. Tell me everything.'

'Oh, I could never tell you everything.' He gave me a cheeky grin. 'But it is time to reveal where we're going.'

He got out into the aisle of the coach and clapped his hands.

'Everybody, the bride-to-be would like me to play tour guide for the remainder of our trip.'

There was a cheer from the semi-tipsy bus occupants.

'Now,' Harry continued. 'On your left, you'll see a great big bloody sign telling you we're en route to the island of Mont-Saint-Michel.'

More cheers.

'We will, of course, be approaching the island via a causeway – I

84

won't be asking Julie to swim because as we all know, she is, in fact, a shite swimmer.'

'Nearly drowned in the bath once,' Helen piped up.

'Two inches of water,' my mam added.

'And these days Julie likes to drown in champers,' Harry intervened, and held my hand up to show them my glass.

'Piss off,' I said, to laughs.

'So,' he continued, 'this place was once a proper island. But most of the land around it has been reclaimed. The legend goes that in the eighth century, the archangel Michael appeared to a bishop named Aubert in his sleep and commanded him to build an oratory there in his honour. Up the abbey went, on a massive rock in the sea, battered by currents and waves. Then, after years of being a religious centre, it was used as a prison during the French Revolution.'

'We're getting married in a prison?' I said. 'Très romantic!'

'Don't worry.' Harry smiled. 'There are no crooks there now.'

'We're bringing a bus full of bankers,' my dad called from the back. This got the loudest clap. Dad stood up and bowed.

'I'll take that as a compliment,' Harry said. 'Now, we're about to round the bend on to the causeway. One last piece of information. You reprobates have to behave yourselves. Mont-Saint-Michel is a tourist island, and they don't generally allow marriages in the abbey. I had to promise them our first child for the use of the Magdalene chapel. No skinny-dipping, Mr and Mrs Ferguson. Ah – there it is.'

We all turned and looked out the left side of the coach.

Rising out of the sea, high into the mist, was a huge rock, climbing up, up, various turrets stretching to the clouds, the final point of the abbey lost in the vapours.

'Oh my God!' I gasped. 'It's . . . I've never seen anything like it. It's like something from *Indiana Jones*!'

'Fuck me,' Helen said, leaning over the top of my chair from the seat behind.

Even she was impressed. Harry knew how to pull it out of the bag.

On the morning of the wedding he had a bouquet of blue freesias delivered to my suite, along with a long, slender box containing an exquisite sapphire and diamond tennis bracelet.

Not as beautiful as the blue of your eyes, the note said, *but there isn't a jewel in the world that is*.

I sat on the end of the bed and started to cry. That's where my mother found me.

'What in God's name has you upset?' she said, dabbing gently at my eyes with a handkerchief, not wanting to make them puffier than they already were.

'It's too good to be true,' I said. 'This – all of this. Harry is perfect. I've just been going along with all this like it's normal, but I'm from bloody Leitrim, Mam. I haven't even got a proper job yet. How did I end up here? How did I end up with him?'

She knelt in front of me and took her hands in mine.

'You daft girl,' she said, 'getting yourself in a tizzy. There's nothing wrong with where you come from, and of course he's not perfect. For a start, he works fourteen-hour days. You haven't minded up to now because you're young and you have your independence and he makes a fuss of you every time you're together. Wait and see how you feel when you're at home with a house full of screaming tots and you don't see Mr Perfect from one end of the week to the next. Jewels won't cut it then. And what is it he does, exactly?'

'What do you mean?' I bristled. 'You know what he does. He works in finance.'

How easily it had slipped into my everyday parlance.

'He's a banker,' she said, her grey eyes holding mine. She'd been blonde once, like me, but now her hair matched her eyes. She still had the fine bone structure, was still a good-looking woman.

'He's not just a banker, Mam. He's the CEO of Ireland's leading capital company.'

'Still a banker,' she said. 'In all my days, I've never known a glorified accountant to have money like he has. It strikes me he's more like a loan shark to other wealthy people.'

'Oh, Mam. Times have changed. The money that's swirling around nowadays – finance is the way of the future. Everybody's doing the same thing. Taking risks, earning big money.'

She sniffed, unconvinced.

'He has an eye for the ladies too. You said that yourself.'

'Mam! It's my wedding day! I said he looked at other women sometimes; he doesn't do anything more than that. That's normal, isn't it?'

'I know it's your wedding day, dote, but I'm speaking frankly. If not this morning, then when? You said he was perfect, as though that scares the life out of you, and I'm telling you he's not. He's a man. God never figured out the recipe for a perfect specimen. The world has been washed in women's tears because of it. But Harry clearly loves you, he has means – Divine Mother, we all see he has means – and he makes you happy. And you've decided that's enough. You're right to. It's more than what most women settle for.

'Just don't think you don't deserve this because, if you ask me, he's the one getting the bargain. He has nobody, Julie, and you have a whole family that adore you and are taking him into the fold. Now, wipe away those tears and let's get you into this dress. Your sisters are already merry on bubbles. We're going to have to carry them the three thousand bloody steps to the chapel if we don't get a wriggle on. Honestly, only a man would pick a church you had to climb the side of a shagging mountain to get to.'

It was a testament to the woman that my mam could still be so measured in her opinion of Harry at that wedding. Everybody else was blown away. He spent a fortune spoiling me, spoiling everybody. Buying his way into their good books.

I met several of Harry's business colleagues for the first time in Mont-Saint-Michel. Most of them were older than me – most of them were older than Harry – but they were important in his life and I wanted them to take me seriously.

I knew some of them by name even before I'd met my husband. Richard Hendricks part-owned a new Irish airline that was challenging the existing market monopoly. It was Richard who Harry had rented the private plane from to fly us to France. Tadhg de Burca was a famous Irish horse owner who'd won the English Grand National several years previous and ran a world-renowned stud farm. The rest were lesser known, but in some cases even wealthier, businessmen.

Some of them managed to keep their riches in the crash that came later. Some, not all.

But that day, in the courtyard of our hotel, surrounded by sweet-scented roses and fairy lights wound amid the jasmine vines, not one of us had a care in the world.

'They call these little things "Napoleons",' Harry told me, holding a fork of the millefeuille dessert to my mouth. We were sharing a rare private moment, everybody else from the top table up dancing. I took the bite, making the act as provocative as I knew he wanted it to be, licking the custard with my tongue and clamping my lips shut on the end of the fork.

'They used to call your beloved Napoleon in college,' Richard Hendricks said. He'd appeared suddenly and crouched down between us, interrupting the intimacy. 'Even then he had an uncanny ability to strategize for the future.'

He handed me an envelope, his little finger stroking mine. I didn't think Harry had noticed, but he had nothing to worry about anyway. Richard was twenty years older than me, balding, his face lined with telltale broken capillaries, his overpriced suit almost bursting at the seams as it tried to contain him. He made my skin crawl. There was something very creepy about the man.

'Your wedding gift.'

I took it gracefully.

'Does that make me your Josephine?' I said, looking back to Harry.

'Sweetheart – I think you're my Waterloo.' He kissed me full on the lips, deliberately, inches away from his friend's face.

Later that night, up in our honeymoon suite, I opened Richard's card, withdrawing the large wad of money. My eyes widened.

'Jesus, Harry. Look at all this cash.'

Harry laughed, but there was an edge to it. He'd lit a cigar, and exhaled a cloud of bitter-smelling smoke.

'Go on, then,' he said. 'Count it. Let me see your teller skills. I might give you a job in the bank yet.'

I raised an eyebrow and waved away the cigar smoke.

It took me three minutes to count out the notes.

I looked up at Harry, my jaw nearly on the floor. He had an expression of mild amusement on his face. At the sum, or at my reaction, I don't know.

'Harry. What the hell? Who are these people?'

'You know who they are,' he said. 'You know how wealthy they are too.'

'Yes, I know, but – seriously? Is he using us for money laundering or something?'

'That's Richard. He thinks he can buy anything. Still thinks he can buy me. He hasn't a clue. I can outspend him in a heartbeat.'

'But this . . . Christ, we could buy a house with what's in these cards. Outright.'

'We already have a house,' he said. 'But you can get another if you like. You could buy one here, in Normandy.'

'Sure. I'll buy a house. I'll nip down to an estate agents in the morning and see what they've got.'

He laughed.

'Did you enjoy today, wifey?'

He'd switched a gear. Talking about Richard made him uneasy. I didn't know why. I didn't know what Richard had on him. What he knew about my husband that I didn't.

'It was all right,' I said, answering his question. 'As weddings go. To be honest, I think I would have preferred a quickie visit to the registry office in Leitrim and a bag of chips for afters.'

'A bottle of cider and a romp in a field?'

'That too.' I smiled.

Harry grabbed me around the waist.

'I'd do anything for you. I love you to bits, Julie Ferguson McNamara.'

He did. No matter what happened afterwards, he really did love me.

I know what's on your mind. You're wondering – did Harry get a second wind on our wedding night? Did we throw all of Richard's cash on to the bed like confetti and go on top of it like rabbits?

Absolutely. Who wouldn't? Money was like a Viagra drip for Harry.

We were the Celtic Tiger generation, and while my background might have been simple, even I couldn't escape the allure of real money.

Maybe that was why I turned a blind eye to how Harry earned it.

Alice

Alice leaned close to the one-way glass of the interview room, the tip of her nose almost pressing against it, watching the interaction taking place inside.

The psychologist was just about to conclude his third interview with Carney and Alice, irrationally, found his gentle manner irritating. Carney's solicitor sat beside him, her face set in an expression that said she was very pleased with how it was going.

The door to the interview room opened and Sylvia from Reception popped her head around it.

'Do you want me to bring the psychologist in here when he's done and have Carney taken back to the detention centre? The unit officers who brought him over are waiting down in Reception and getting on my nerves.'

'Bring the doc and the solicitor in here,' Gallagher answered. 'Let Alice obsess over Carney in the fish bowl a bit longer. And get us some tea, will you? Good girl.'

'Excuse me?' Sylvia arched a thinly plucked eyebrow. 'Have you mistaken me for Catering? And by the way, if you call me a good girl again, I'll have you up in front of a tribunal. Arsehole.'

'I love it when she talks dirty,' Gallagher said loudly over the slamming door.

'What are you on about?' Alice barked.

'Sylvia wants a go on me.'

Alice snorted.

'No, she doesn't.'

'She does.'

'She really doesn't. You'd be no use to her.'

'Do you think I can't perform because of my sciatica, DS Moody? Because I'm telling you, I don't mind letting a woman do the hard yards on top.'

'That's fierce gentlemanly of you. I'm sure your Angela would be proud. But it's less about your back and more to do with the fact that Sylvia is gay.'

'She is not. She was practically begging me for it in O'Donnell's at the last work do.'

'Really? She must have got a whiff of your vagina.'

Alice smiled smugly. Gallagher was a good copper but, like many in the force, a misogynistic little git.

The door opened again and in came the psychologist, a bland, balding man with a weak chin and a self-important air. Carney's solicitor, a tiny little woman from the legal aid centre, followed him. She had a quiet squeak of a voice and avoided direct eye contact. Alice, who'd dealt with her before, knew they were deliberate affectations to hide the woman's truly ruthless nature. Still, she admired her and had groaned when she'd seen who'd been assigned. It took something to be an achiever in a predominantly male workplace. Alice of all people knew that.

'I'll be doing up a report for the Director of Public Prosecutions,' the psychologist said before anybody else could get a word in.

'We know that,' Gallagher interrupted. 'We just want to get an indication of your thinking. DS Moody is in charge of this investigation.'

'Hmm. Well, from the monitoring sessions and the interviews, I have garnered enough information for a preliminary evaluation.' The pyschologist massaged a carefully cultivated evening shadow and furrowed his eyebrows in academic concentration. 'I must stress, it's all early-days conjecture. I've never had to work this fast before. It's unprecedented. But I appreciate everybody is under pressure in this instance to be seen to be acting. That's certainly the impression my boss gave me.'

'And?' Alice said impatiently. 'We're all dying to hear your take on this.'

'Look, all I can give you is a synopsis.'

'That will do.'

'Right. So, Mr Carney has been through a number of traumatic events recently. His father died last year in tragic circumstances. He fell into a canal on the way home from his local. His father had an ongoing drink problem and his relationship with JP was fractured. JP's mother left while he was still a child and that, alongside the loss of his father, left a mark. JP has very few memories of her but it seems she had some form of mental illness. He doesn't know if she's alive or dead, but I imagine you can track her down easily enough.

'As a teenager and younger man, JP fell in with a bad crowd and experimented with soft drugs. But he says he steered clear of alcohol – up until recently, anyway. The night before his attack on Mr McNamara, he consumed a large quantity of booze and cocaine.'

'There were traces of alcohol and drugs in his bloodstream,' Gallagher said. 'Not enough to have prevented his actions, obviously.'

'Yes, though you would have to imagine that, unused to hard drugs in particular, it would have had quite an effect on his thought process. Anyway, after a difficult start he seems to have straightened himself out. That fell apart in the last year, following the death of his father and then the loss of his job last month. The company he worked for shut down as a result of economic pressures. JP has spiralled downwards in the weeks since.

'You know already that on the night he attacked Mr McNamara, he was under the influence. He's insisting he doesn't remember how he got over to the south side of the city. Most of that twenty-four hours seems to be a blur for him. However, he is absolutely clear on one thing. He recalls exactly what he did to Mr McNamara. Notwithstanding his admission that he has no recollection of how he got there, he knows what happened inside the McNamara home. He's not claiming he blacked out. JP says he felt something snap when he entered the house and had no control over his subsequent actions.'

Alice held up her hand.

'Okay, this is all great stuff, Doctor, but none of it is new. Here's what we actually need to know. In your professional opinion, is he attempting to con us? Did he leave his home that day determined to kill somebody? Did he enter the McNamara home intending to kill Harry McNamara?'

Carney's solicitor started to protest but stopped when she saw the psychologist shake his head.

'Look, as I said, this is just an initial review but having watched JP closely for the last week, read the notes from his daily interview sessions with my colleagues in the detention centre and listened to his account of events three times, no, I do not believe that was his intention. He has suffered intense anguish and upheaval in his life. It is not beyond the realms of possibility that his recent unemployment triggered a delayed response to that trauma and he experienced a clinical episode of some sort on the night of 1 October – a unique psychotic response. But of course I can't make a definitive statement. JP will have to be moved to the Central Mental Hospital in the meantime for further assessment.'

'But why?' Gallagher asked. 'Why did he snap? What was it about Harry McNamara?'

The psychologist sighed. 'The McNamaras are wealthy, their home reflects that, and their security and stability might have been a tipping point for Mr Carney. JP is very convincing in his assertion that he had no clue as to the identity of the man he assaulted. If that's the case, then he was attacking what the man represented. And he's not denying that. So in answer to your first question, Detective Sergeant Moody, no. In my opinion, he's not trying to con you. He didn't act with criminal intention.'

'He walked into the man's sitting room with a fucking golf club,' Alice growled. 'What was his plan – to ask the owner of the house for a tour of the course? How can we be sure he's not a psychopath?'

'He committed a crime, we're all agreed on that. It's whether he acted *compos mentis* that's the question. And no, you don't have to be a psychopath to have a psychotic episode. Like I say, it's absolutely possible that Harry McNamara, in the moment of the attack, symbolized everything Mr Carney is not, everything that is wrong or absent in his own life – happy home, happy wife, happy man – and it flicked some sort of switch in him. That is credible and also not without precedent. I reviewed some international cases before coming here this afternoon. A teamster in America lost his job in railway construction during the financial crash. He walked into an estate agents and shot the owner, a man completely unknown to him. Why an estate agent? Because his home was about to be repossessed by the bank.'

'Well, that's a flawed example if ever I heard one,' Gallagher said. 'The teamster clearly knew he was killing an estate agent – he targeted him. He'll have been done for first-degree murder, regardless of whether he knew the man personally or not. Carney there is saying he'd no idea who he was battering, or why he did it, which is important from our perspective. It precludes motive. And let me warn you, just in case you're thinking of becoming some sort of celebrity quack in this case and doing interviews spouting that kind of shite, it's not going to happen.'

'I'm sensing a lot of hostility from you,' the solicitor said, just as the psychiatrist began to protest. 'Towards my client and towards the court-appointed medical professional.'

'Not as much hostility as your client showed Harry McNamara when he was smashing his skull in,' Gallagher snapped, bending down so his face was level with hers.

She frowned, trying to look apologetic and sympathetic at the same time.

'I understand your irritation,' she said, 'but let's take a moment to reflect. I'm having to convince that young man to let me mount a defence. He *wants* to take full responsibility for something he's clearly not responsible for. He did not want to talk to us about his childhood and he's insistent we don't use it, though we can all see he's a very damaged individual. That's no ordinary hard-done-by whiner we've got. He handed himself in, for heaven's sake. He's a young man who's as much a victim in this as anybody else.'

'He's the victim?' Alice said, her voice thick with sarcasm.

'Detective Sergeant Moody,' the solicitor squeaked, 'can't we all be happy that my client will cooperate all the way with your good selves in clarifying his role in this tragic affair? We all want to see this cleared up, don't we? A little bit of compassion might go a long way here.'

'I'm reserving that for Harry McNamara – something I never thought I'd hear myself say.'

'I understand why you're sceptical. I really do. But, of course, after this assessment is written up, we will be asking a judge if JP is fit for trial and, if it's determined that he is, we will be looking at a plea of diminished responsibility and a verdict of not guilty. And of course if Mr McNamara pulls through, we will all be relieved.'

'If Mr McNamara pulls through, he'll be a fucking vegetable,' Alice retorted, shaking her head. 'By the way, you know Julie McNamara says JP whispered something to her husband as he lay almost bleeding to death? Sounds a bit calculated, doesn't it? And yet JP says he doesn't remember saying anything. Which would be a very deliberate lie if Julie is right.'

'He told you that when you paid him a little visit in his holding cell, isn't that correct? When I wasn't there?'

'It was just an informal chat.'

The solicitor frowned as Alice danced on the head of a pin.

'Mrs McNamara must be mistaken. It was a very shocking episode; I imagine her recollection of it is quite shaky.'

'It's actually incredibly vivid,' Alice retorted. '*I* imagine she sees it replayed in her head every time she closes her eyes. Probably will for the rest of her life.'

She plonked herself in a chair when the two had left, giving the closed door a one-fingered salute.

'There you go,' she sighed. 'Temporary insanity, a few years in the funny farm. Even if we get attempted manslaughter, what sort of a sentence does that carry versus attempted murder? Five years, a little bit of rehabilitation, then what? He'll be back out on the streets, the rest of us hoping he doesn't have another fucking moment. Unique psychotic episode, my arse.'

Gallagher tugged at his beard.

'I don't know, Alice. There's nobody who thinks more than me that it's voodoo science, the whole head-doctor profession. But maybe I'm getting soft in my old age. There seem to be a few simple facts we can't ignore. McNamara has led a charmed life; JP, anything but. He got sozzled and lost the plot and Harry in his big fancy house was on the receiving end. I know it's not nice to imagine Carney not getting the full hammer of the law but, you know – he hasn't exactly had it easy up to now and he won't have it easy if he ends up in the funny farm.'

'Very liberal-minded of you, Sarge,' Alice replied. 'You know you're just being contrary, don't you? If that solicitor had started on about human rights and the plight of the working classes, you'd have been preaching about bringing back the death penalty. Hellfire and eternal damnation for shoplifters.'

Gallagher shook his head. 'Give me some credit, Moody. And look at it this way – if we do get this into court, there's no guarantee that a jury wouldn't stand up and start applauding

99

Carney. McNamara is a banker, after all. Who hasn't wanted to kill one?'

'I don't buy it,' she said, ignoring him. She stood up and went back to the one-way glass to stare in at Carney. He was still sitting, gazing at a spot on the wall across from him, oblivious.

'Is that your line for the Director of Public Prosecutions? You don't buy it? Have you any actual proof JP Carney wanted to kill McNamara? Like a shred of evidence that he knew the man?'

'You know I don't. So far, we haven't found a single determinable line connecting JP Carney to Harry McNamara. They moved in completely different orbits. McNamara was a leading banker and Carney has had nothing but really shit to average-shit jobs. Yeah, sure, he'd every reason to resent and hate Harry McNamara for being a rich prick while he had nothing, but he'd had to have known him at least to want to kill him. It's only been a week though. I need more time.'

'What're your next steps?'

'I'm going to talk to somebody who knows about men like Harry. Some finance whizz-kid who might help me see the link between Harry and JP. She can't fit me in until next week. So let JP have his little stay in hospital while I get to the bottom of it. And you know I will.'

'Do you need more back-up? One of the other detectives? You can't do this all on your own.'

'I'm fine. I've plenty of support. Doherty is tracking down Carney's family. The mother, anyway. There doesn't seem to be anybody else, unless he's estranged from somebody and not telling us. All his early records are in London, and the Met are tighter than a wasp's arse when it comes to giving us the time of day.'

'Yes, well, don't let anything slip because you don't like asking for help, Moody. I know you.'

'Have I ever let you down, Sarge?'

Gallagher didn't reply. Not yet, she hadn't. But there was a first time for everything.

JP

Cork was certainly cleaner than East London. Greener. It seemed bigger, because it was more open, which probably sounds ridiculous, given where we were coming from.

Clean, green and spacious. What more could you ask for?

I yearned for the tower blocks.

Dad's old home was a stone cottage and his parents had resisted the temptation to install mod cons like radiators. We were used to underfloor heating in our flat, every season of the year. In Cork, Charlie and me shared a bed, and the two of us had feet like ice blocks every night as we desperately tried to warm up under the scratchy blankets.

Our grandmother was an odd woman. She'd had Seamie, her only son, late, and was now in her mid-seventies. Her face was weather-beaten and slack, not aided by the fact she'd no teeth and refused to wear false ones. The combination of gumminess and her thick Cork accent meant we kids couldn't understand a word she was saying, which she in turn interpreted to mean we were thick. The only thing we did pick up on was that she seemed to call us *poxy* an awful lot. I told Dad one night and he broke his heart laughing.

'She's saying *paistí*, you daft bugger,' he said. 'It's the Gaelic for "children". Christ, I got you home to the old country just in time.'

Seamie fought with his mother a lot. He told me one night, when drink had loosened his tongue, that she wanted him to ask for work on the big farm nearby but he had point-blank refused.

'My father – your grandad – used to own the land over beyond,' he said. 'Then that McCarthy shower came in and starting buying up acres and industrializing the farming process. They bought my oul' fella out and said he could stay on working for them, but of course they fired him within the year. He was too old and too expensive. I should have inherited that land. He didn't even get a good price for it.'

Seamie was bitter about his lost inheritance, the very event that had forced him to emigrate to London in the first place. Being home again reminded him of that.

He decided to move us to Dublin.

What a bad decision that turned out to be.

Seamie figured the capital could offer a better selection of jobs, if he could organize some sort of childminding there.

The problem was in the meantime he had to go back on the dole.

Our dad wasn't built for handouts or pity. It dented his pride in ways I only understood when I got older and realized it was a trait we shared.

He started to drink more, and our surroundings didn't help. We hadn't been well off in London – we'd been right at the bottom of the ladder – but it had been a different sort of poverty. A less lonely sort. It was the eighties and nobody had anything. But Ireland in the nineties was a different kettle of fish.

Seamie managed to get us a council house in an estate in the Dublin suburbs. It was bigger than our small flat back in London, and the whole place was certainly newer. The Irish were starting to build, big time. Alongside the fancy new estates and apartment blocks, concentrated pockets of social housing with Formica kitchens, brown windows and thin walls were being thrown up.

But while you could hear your neighbours flushing the toilet and having sex, there was none of the family feel to the areas, not like there'd been in the tower blocks. The new council estates were planned like somebody had flung darts blindfold at a map of Dublin. A few here, a few there, mainly on the rougher northside of the city, a token couple on the softer southside. A young lass could end up in a house in our estate, alone with a gang of kiddies, and have to take two buses across town to see her mum.

Nonetheless, little gangs of newly resident kids sprang up about the place, and I was in none of them. I stood out because I still had a cockney twang that, apparently, made me sound like a fucking muppet off *EastEnders*. Charlie was so young she picked up the Dublin accent straight away. Between that and the difference in how we looked, you'd never guess we were related.

It wasn't all bad. There were days when Dad would bring us out to the fishing village of Howth, not far from the estate we lived in. There, Charlie and me would run along the pier, before we all hiked up to Howth Head. We'd get chips on the way home, and if it was a Friday night, we'd watch *Cheers* and *Only Fools and Horses* on the telly. They were happy times, moments when Seamie really made the effort. Glimpses into what life could have been like.

As the years passed, Dad's reasons to be at home all the time dwindled. I was old enough to let Charlie in after school and make a basic meal. Seamie could have got a job, but by that stage the rot had set in. Alcohol, combined with bitterness, had started to addle his brain.

I saw it – but I didn't see it. I was only a kid, and I'd responded to being picked on by other kids by toughening up and becoming a bit of a shit myself. I mitched off school and smoked joints in the park. I shoplifted and scammed and generally did what I could get away with.

Nobody spoke to me about my mum leaving. Nobody explained to me the effect it must have had.

And nobody checked up to see how Dad was doing on his own. We were between the cracks.

I found Charlie crying in her room one night. She was usually such a happy-go-lucky kid, even in our circumstances. Seeing her upset like that gave me a fright.

'What's the matter with you, silly boo?' I said, sitting on the end of her bed.

'It's nothing.'

'It must be something.'

'It's stupid. There's a tour tomorrow to the zoo, and everybody is going except me.'

'Why aren't you going?'

'Because Dad didn't sign the permission slip and he says he has no money.'

My jaw clenched tight. She never asked for anything.

'I'll sort it,' I said.

I went downstairs to the sitting room, where Seamie was asleep on the couch. I called his name, but he was out of it. Carefully, I reached into his pocket, and I just about had his wallet out when he woke and grabbed me by the wrist.

'Whash you after?' he slurred.

'Just the remote,' I said.

He blinked and closed his eyes again. I opened the wallet, took out a tenner and put it behind him on the couch so he would think it had fallen out. I'd fake his signature and Charlie could have her little trip. It was as I was taking my hand away that I brushed his jeans and realized they were wet.

Dad had pissed himself.

I felt like crying.

It decided things for me. I would leave school. I was only fifteen, just the legal age to do it. My teachers all reported that I had brains, or at least was smart enough to pretend I was stupid, just to try their collective patience. But the Irish education system was expensive – uniforms, books, lunches – and money was tight. Seamie got the full gamut of social benefits on offer, but more and more of it was going on booze. I might have been a little wanker in training, but I loved my sister and never stopped feeling like I was somehow responsible for her. If I worked, the two of us would have our own cash.

I got a few hours as a lounge boy in the evening and stacked shelves during the day.

I was at that for a whole month before Seamie realized I'd quit school. A letter had arrived from the headmaster to say I hadn't returned after the junior certificate exam and it would have been the norm for him to have sat down with my parents and discussed my options. He was a nice bloke. It must have been like having a small stone removed from his shoe, me leaving, and yet he had the decency to say in the note that I was a bright kid who was wasting an opportunity.

I came in from work that evening to find Dad sitting at the kitchen table with Charlie, a glass of whiskey in his hand and an empty glass in front of my seat.

'Sit down,' he barked, his voice telling me he'd had a couple already.

He poured the whiskey into the second glass and pushed it towards me.

'What's that for?' I asked.

'You're a man now, aren't you? Making decisions for yourself. Leaving school without telling me and getting yourself a job. Charlie here tells me you've been working for weeks. Not that I'd have known. You haven't been handing anything up. That's the proper thing to do, John Paul. To contribute to the running of the household.'

I pushed the whiskey back towards him.

'I figured we could divide the expenses,' I said sourly. 'You take care of buying the alcohol and I'll take care of the other bits. Food and that.'

Seamie banged his hand on the table.

'You've never gone hungry on my watch,' he shouted.

That wasn't entirely true, but I let it go. When he was in this humour there was no winning an argument with him.

'It's late,' I said. 'Charlie should be asleep. I need to go to bed. I'm up early in the morning.'

I started to walk back out of the kitchen, but he grabbed my arm.

'You should have told me, lad,' he said, and he looked sad. For a moment he was his old self, not the man who'd been beaten down by life.

'You're too young to be out working when you don't need to be. You should be getting yourself schooling so you can get a decent job. I don't want you to end up like me, and that's where you're going.'

Teenagers are cruel. The man meant well. It wasn't all his fault I'd left school, though his neglect and drinking had contributed to it.

But all I could see was a drunk, slurring his words and having a go. I was the one doing my best. I could have been out with my mates all the time, meeting girls, getting stoned. Instead, I was working and helping my family.

I shook his hand off my arm.

'I'll never end up like you,' I said. 'You're a pisshead. No wonder Mum left. You can't even get a job. I'm out working so she' – I pointed at Charlie – 'doesn't need to ask you for money for school stuff, and you think I should be in school too? Why? So I can be home early every day to listen to you feeling sorry for yourself while you sit on your throne in the sitting room drinking and watching telly? You're a fucking failure.'

Whatever else I was going to throw at him never made it out.

Seamie pushed himself up from the table and punched me so hard in the face I went flying. He was still a strong man. His fist, when it hit, broke my nose and knocked out two teeth.

Charlie screamed as the blood spurted everywhere. I lay on the floor, dazed, but not so out of it that I couldn't see Seamie staring at his own hand, looking in absolute shock at what he'd done.

'John Paul,' he choked, and tried to pull me up. I batted him away.

'Get the fuck off,' I choked through a mouthful of blood.

He staggered backwards and then, in shock, walked right out of the house.

Charlie dialled 999 before I could tell her not to and then sat on the floor beside me, trying to stem the bleeding with her housecoat.

'I saw this on *Casualty*,' she said, in an attempt to make me smile so she'd know I was okay. Her face was white and she was shaking. In all her short years, she'd never witnessed anything so violent. 'If you can't breathe, tell me, and I'll stick a pen in your throat to let the air in.'

'Please don't stab me with a fucking pen,' I said, then started to cry, which set her off. I was so grateful she'd stayed with me. I felt sorry for myself but deep down I knew I'd provoked Dad. I'd set this train in motion and I did not feel good about it.

The cops came with the ambulance. I told them I'd been in a fight. I was terrified that if I told them what happened, Charlie would be put into care. Seamie was a shit dad, but everybody knew the system was a cesspit for kids.

The cops asked a few questions but they weren't all that interested. I'd left school, I was known to hang around with bad lads, and they discovered Seamie was on his own with us. It was assumed I was just a mess.

We came from a certain area, a certain class.

Seamie tried to stay off the drink for a couple of weeks afterwards. The sight of the bruises on my face was a constant reminder of how he'd lost it, in every sense.

But as they faded, so did his willpower.

It was 1996. Apparently, Ireland was doing well. There was money in the country, lots of it. People were well off and happy.

That's what they said on the telly, anyway. It wasn't like that in our house.

The Celtic Tiger wasn't lifting all boats, and I was starting to resent both it and all those smug wankers who seemed to be doing so well for themselves.

Julie

Money does funny things to people. To the people who have it, and the people around them.

I tried to keep things normal. I enjoyed the treats that came with wealth, but I didn't particularly want to be a kept wife. Not then. Not at the start.

I got my first job shortly after we were married, in a secondary school not far from where we lived in South Dublin, just on the Wicklow border. It was a relatively new school and took on a gang of us recently qualified teachers all at the same time. My pal from college, Grace, got a job first, teaching history and German. She was only in the door and saw that they were advertising for an English teacher. I was interviewed the following week and started a month later.

Those first few years teaching were the probably the happiest I'd ever been. Harry worked long hours, but the staff at St Mochta's were a lovely bunch and we got on just as well outside of work hours. We ended up in the pub every Friday night and, depending on how late our last class was, sometimes during the week too. It's amazing those kids ever learned anything, the hangovers we'd have going in some mornings.

There were four of us in particular who hung around together. Grace and me; Anna, a redhead from Donegal, who taught Gaeilge in a dialect that none of us, including the kids, could understand; and Toby, the PE instructor, who was holding a candle for me but was gentleman enough not to be too obvious about it, me being a married woman and all.

Anna used to drive me mad at times. She was always making little digs about the staff I probably had, the holidays me and Harry must have taken – jibes that were repeated often enough to have lost any humour they might have once held and by then had an edge of meanness to them. She seemed offended by our wealth, even though I didn't think I rubbed anybody's nose in it. I actually spent most of my time trying to downplay it, to compensate for having what others didn't.

We were out one Friday night, as per usual, when my mobile went. Harry had finished up early for once and was at home.

'Where are you?' he asked.

'Where do you think?' I shouted over the noise of the packed bar.

'She's working very hard,' Grace yelled. 'We're correcting essays. Tell him we're marking, Julie. A double G&T for every twenty foolscap pages.'

Harry laughed.

'Who's there?' he said.

'The staff room minus the Trunchbull.' We'd nicknamed our very lovely headmistress after the awful one in Roald Dahl's *Matilda*, thinking we were hilariously ironic. The woman threw parties for us on our birthdays, and her idea of student discipline was having a stern conversation with them and suggesting some quiet meditation.

Telling Harry everybody was there was a tiny white lie on my part. The evening had started off with more, but of course it was us four hard-core drinkers who'd hung on behind while others drifted off. Harry suspected Toby had a thing for me. It was just easier not to make a big deal of it.

Toby, especially after several vodka and Red Bulls, wasn't so diplomatic.

'Tell him we're hitting Coppers after this and not to stay up!' he called out loudly, a hint of the devil in his eye.

'Is that the bachelor PE teacher?' Harry said into the phone. He managed to make 'PE teacher' sound like an acronym for sad, desperate bastard who can't get a real job.

'Yup,' I said. 'Pissed as a fart and doubling his own body weight with vodka.'

'Why don't I pick you up?' Harry said, his voice still casual. 'I booked us a table in that French restaurant you like in the village. I thought we could treat ourselves this weekend, given I've been working so hard lately and neglecting you.'

'That sounds divine. I'll see you soon.'

I put down the phone. I didn't really want to leave, but it was so rare for Harry to finish early and he hated sitting home alone. Inviting him to join us wasn't an option. We'd done it a couple of times and while he'd been perfectly polite, his very well-observed opinions afterwards on my friends' lack of maturity had stung.

Anna had just arrived at the table with four sambucas and over-heard the tail end of the conversation.

'You're not abandoning us just because Richie Rich has snapped his fingers, are you?' she said.

Out of the corner of my eye I could see Grace draw her finger across her neck in an attempt to tell Anna to kill the conversation.

'I know you take issue with my husband earning slightly more than your average impoverished state worker, Comrade Anna,' I said, 'but you can piss right off. He's taking me out to Le Bar à Huîtres and, I have to say, the prospect of a bottle of Bolly and Tabasco-drenched oysters beats Coppers any day of the week.'

Anna pursed her lips.

'So we're only of use to you when your hubby is not around to splash the cash, is that it?'

'Give it a rest,' I said. 'I'm out with you lot all the time. How often does Harry get home early?'

'It's not how often it happens,' Anna said. 'It's the fact that, the moment it does, you ditch us. It's very telling, Julie. But I suppose some things matter more than friends. Money talks.'

I looked to Grace, expecting some support, but she was nose deep into her sambuca and not making eye contact. Toby was resting back in his chair, his arms crossed, not looking best pleased either.

I shrugged.

'Sorry, lads, but I think I contribute plenty to our little socials. I am married, ye are aware of that. Last time I checked, it wasn't to any of you. And I'd still be married, Anna, even if Harry was ringing and asking me to come home for a pizza and a few beers. When the rest of you grow up, you'll understand.'

I started to collect my things. I knew Harry wouldn't arrive for at least a half hour, but I was angry and not willing to sit there and let Anna snipe at me for the next thirty minutes.

'That's right, little wifey. Off you run. Your husband has said "Jump".'

'You know what,' I said, prepared for a fight by that stage, 'bitter and single is not a good combination, Anna. You'd want to watch that.'

Toby and Grace sat forward, realizing we were on the tipping point of a full-blown argument that we'd both regret in the morning.

'Don't worry, Anna,' Grace said. 'We'll go dancing and leave poor Julie to listen to Harry the Boring and the Tale of his Great Big Bank.' She winked at me so I'd know she was only slagging Harry to calm things, and not to have a real pop.

It worked. Anna backed down.

I stood up to go and she followed me out to the door.

'I'm sorry,' she said, grabbing my hand.

I shook my head.

'Forget it. What happens in the pub stays in the pub.' I smiled. It would all be forgiven by Monday.

'Just . . . just be careful,' she said. 'Look, it might be the drink talking, but I want to say this to you anyway. You're a nice girl, Julie. You're smart and you're fun and you're gorgeous. I'm not saying you shouldn't have a Friday night with your husband. I'm saying that, most of the time, I think of you as being a single woman, because you're always out with us. He obviously doesn't give a fuck what you're doing when he's busy, but the minute he's free, he expects you to be. It's always the same with people who have it all – they think the world revolves around them. It would do no harm to remind him he doesn't call the shots. And whatever you do, don't drop your friends just because he wants you to himself. He doesn't own you.'

I bit my lip. It was the sort of stuff Helen said to me regularly, but I didn't want to hear it.

I knew it was true, which was why I couldn't defend Harry – or myself, for that matter. And I was loyal. I wouldn't be speaking about my marriage to Anna or anybody else.

'I'll see you Monday,' I said, and pushed open the pub door. As the cold wind hit my face, I saw the look on hers. It wasn't the usual resentful look. It was pitying, and I didn't like it one little bit.

Alice

'Have you noticed the change in him?'

Alice swiped at the crumbs that surrounded her mouth and took a slug from the bottle of Coke to wash down the mouthful of toasted ham-and-cheese sandwich she'd sourced from the hospital's visitors' canteen.

Gallagher squinted back through the window.

'What change? Do you mean the stubble? I think he's trying to copy my beard.'

'Not the stubble. Jesus! That look in his eyes. He looks calmer, don't you think? There's none of that eerie, distressed shit that was there at the start. He's happy. He's got what he wanted.'

They'd just finished a session with JP Carney, newly resident at the central mental hospital. He was sitting now where they'd left him, among his fellow inmates, in a large television lounge of soft furnishings and tables stacked with board games and books.

This was the low-to-medium security ward of the hospital. Carney had cooperated at every step: allowing the assessments, complying with the psychiatrists who examined him, willingly being admitted to the hospital; insisting he wanted his victim and his family to have their day in court so he, Carney, could plead guilty to the attack on Harry McNamara. He was happy to talk to the police. He wanted to see justice done.

Alice still didn't believe a word of it.

'I didn't see anything different about him,' Gallagher said. 'And I'm starting to think you're the one who belongs in here. Look at him – in there with a bunch of fucking nutters. Do you really think this is where he wants to be?'

Alice sighed. Gallagher had insisted on accompanying her to the interview. He'd been inserting himself more than usual in this investigation. She wasn't sure what help he brought.

'This place is better than prison, Sarge,' she answered. 'God knows what lies ahead for McNamara.'

Alice had gone to the hospital earlier, where Julie McNamara had sat with her husband every day for almost two weeks. She was aging fast in the artificial lighting, holding Harry's hand as he lay there, unresponsive to all treatment. You had to give it to her – she was a wife in a million. All that public shaming of Harry the banker, all the humiliation she'd been put through because of it, and still Julie wanted her husband to live.

'I don't believe Carney,' Alice had said, passing Julie a surplus-to-requirements package of grapes. She always brought something when she went to the hospital. She'd been reared with manners like that.

Julie took the punnet of fruit without a murmur.

'Believe him about what?' she asked.

'The whole "I just snapped" story. Have you thought about what

118

I asked – making a full list of your husband's enemies? Somebody who might have had the wherewithal to work with Carney?'

Julie sighed.

'It's all I think about. I don't have much else to do when I'm here for hours every day. It's not like I can't get Harry to shut up. But I don't even know half the people Harry did business with. Believe me, I want to know what's going on in Carney's head too. It scares the life out of me.'

Alice kept stressing that she wouldn't use anything Julie told her about Harry's business dealings against him later on. For the moment, his wife said she accepted that. But she'd come up with nothing of use, and Alice knew Julie was holding back. You weren't married to a man – you didn't live with somebody for all that time – without knowing the skeletons in their cupboards.

Alice tutted in frustration. Julie, whether she meant to or not, was helping Carney get away with this.

At the rushed preliminary court hearing that Monday morning, the judge had declared JP unfit for immediate trial on the basis of both the medical assessments and the lack of a convincing book of evidence from the Director of Public Prosecutions showing that Carney had a motive. He'd directed a temporary stay in the hospital for ongoing monitoring, which also gave the police more time to build a case.

Alice looked in at Carney, who was sitting where they'd left him, alone on a beige sofa, pretending to read a book. He hadn't turned a page in all the minutes she'd been watching. She had the distinct impression that he was watching her right back.

He had everybody convinced. The doctors, with their prestigious qualifications. The judge, who saw mad and evil bastards every day of the week. Even some of her colleagues, who, once it was determined that McNamara wasn't going to croak and they weren't looking, in fact, at a murder, dismissed Carney as a loony and McNamara as unfortunate (though most were secretly glad he'd got the hiding he deserved) and moved on to other, more pressing cases.

'I'm still convinced it's something to do with cash,' she said, to Gallagher and to herself. 'Follow the money, isn't that what they say?'

'I thought Julie McNamara was cooperating with you on that stuff,' Gallagher retorted. 'Harry's enemies in the finance world, and so on.'

'Oh, Sarge.' Alice sighed. 'Do you know anything about women at all? Julie's priority is protecting herself and her husband. She'll tell me what she's happy for me to know. I'll never get their secrets out of her.'

'It's not always money,' Gallagher said.

'What makes you say that?'

'Nothing. It's just, sometimes emotions go deeper. Love, for instance. Lovers scorned. That sort of thing.'

'Have you done a full one-hundred-and-eighty? What, Julie and JP were shagging and she got him to whack Harry?'

Gallagher shrugged.

'I'm not saying that happened at all, and I definitely think JP is a few shillings short. If Julie and JP were a secret couple, maybe she didn't realize he was nuts. Or she did and used it to her advantage, but now it's backfired. I'm only speculating, anyway. It's you – you've infected me with your paranoia.'

Alice looked at the sergeant, impressed.

'Well, good. Sometimes, they are out to get you. You're right too. I'll have a look at Harry's personal life as well. See what he's been getting up to there. Thanks, Sarge. And here I was thinking you were as useful as a chocolate teapot.'

JP

That woman copper doesn't like me.

I can see her beady little eyes sizing me up through the window outside the patients' lounge. Her colleague, the sergeant, is bored, and dying to move on from all this. She'll keep going. She's a bloodhound, that one. She wants to sniff me out. And she's smart. She has this whole sloth-like thing going on, but you can see her brain is working overtime, reading between the lines of everything I say, making connections where there are none.

No matter how much I say I'm sorry for what I've done, that I want to be punished, she doesn't believe it. She thinks I have a cushy number here, sharing a ward with the cast of *One Flew Over the Cuckoo's Nest*.

She won't be happy until I'm in a proper prison.

She's convinced I'm faking and that I deliberately went after McNamara. She suspects I knew what I was doing, but she can't prove it. She's looking for a motive and scratching her head because she can't find one.

And she won't, because I'm telling the truth.

No, really.

I'm telling the truth.

That's all I have to keep saying.

I've been too clever.

And if they're looking for people to come forward and tell them JP Carney's secrets, they'll be waiting a while.

It looks like Julie is being clever too. I wonder how long she'll last?

There's nothing linking me to Harry McNamara. As long as I stick to my story – I was overtaken by this blind rage, I didn't know what I was doing, I just wanted to hurt somebody – everything will be okay.

The cops think I'm a loner and that I've nobody. I'm so close to getting what I want. Harry McNamara can't possibly come through what I did to him. Even if he wakes up, he'll be nothing like the man he was before. I hope I get to speak to Julie before then. I'll be able to have an honest conversation again. That should be fun.

Part Two

JP

What made me this way?

I don't know. Can you ever really know why you are the way you are?

I guess in more ways than I was comfortable with, Seamie and me were very alike. We were both the quiet type, happy to keep our heads down and work away, prone to self-pity and anger when the status quo was upset. Especially when we were forced to deal with other people's messes impacting on us. For him, that meant Betty. For me, it meant him.

In another life I might have followed his path, step for step.

But I'd my sister to think of.

Seamie was of a generation that believed the job of a father was to get your offspring to eighteen alive. He wasn't a bad father before he took to the drink, but he wasn't a model one either. I never really looked for parenting from him. Despite her problems, Betty was the adult I'd known the most during my early years. But Charlie, abandoned by our mum so young, wanted a proper daddy. One who'd give her jockey backs and take her to fun places, one who told her stories and gave her hugs at bedtime. In the absence of anything resembling that, she turned to her big brother, and there was something in me, something good, that made me the person she wanted me to be.

She held our small family unit together, but she couldn't keep it going for ever.

Not long after I turned seventeen, I had the run-in to beat all run-ins with Seamie.

He was drinking every day by that stage. I'd come in late from work, having stopped at a mate's house for a joint en route. I was relaxed and instead of heading straight for my room, I sat with him in the sitting room.

Big mistake.

Seamie generally drank alone, quietly, quickly, until he passed out. But then it got so he liked to have an audience.

That night, he started off with his usual routine – talking about his life and how tough it had been. I was barely listening, keeping half an eye on the *Match of the Day* results flashing up on the telly screen.

I realized he was talking about Betty and lowered the sound.

For years I'd been angry at Seamie about our mum. I reckoned if we'd stayed in London she might have come back to us. Sometimes I'd direct my bitterness at her but as I'd got older, I'd begun to accept she had an illness that she hadn't chosen. Betty had an excuse for being a terrible parent; Seamie had inflicted the drink on himself.

Yeah, probably unfairly, I loved her more in her absence.

That night, he was going on and on about what a dreadful wife she'd been, what a shit mother she was to us, and something in me just snapped.

'Funny thing is,' I said, and he stopped, shocked to hear me speak, probably having forgotten I was even there, 'she never landed me in hospital, Seamie. She never used her fists on me, like you have. She walked out because she was a sick woman, but how hard did you try to find her? Charlie was only three and you moved us over here, where Betty couldn't even make contact. And then you set about drinking yourself stupid while we dragged ourselves up. And you reckon you can sit in judgement of my mum? Give me a break.'

Seamie's mouth fell open and his eyes swivelled in his head as he tried to fix his gaze on me. I'd never spoken to him like that. I barely spoke to him at all.

'How dare you!' he roared. 'How dare you speak to me in that tone when I have sacrificed everything for you! Who was here? Who stayed? I could have put you into care. I could have just left you starving and alone. I gave up everything. I couldn't even work because I had to mind you – a grown man sitting at home with two children. It's . . . it's not right!'

'Yeah?' I snapped, jumping up off the couch. I knew the argument was going to escalate, and I was prepared for him this time. If he took a swing at me, I was going to land a punch on my dad that would put him back in that bloody armchair for good. 'Maybe at the start, Seamie. But what about for the last few years? Once Charlie started school there was no need for you to hang around here. You sit in this house, drink and sleep. You're not here for us. We live around you. At least Mum cared.'

Seamie looked like he was about to stand, and I tensed my fists.

But he stayed sitting. He'd sized up the situation and could see that I'd grown. I wasn't going to be pushed about easily.

There was that, and also the fact that over the years drink had made him meaner.

He could hurt more with words than slaps.

'Your mum. Your mum took care of you, did she, John Paul? Ha! Did I ever tell you what she did to you when you were a baby?'

I'd heard words like that before. The nurse who'd visited our flat when Mum was pregnant. She'd said something about me as a baby and what Mum had done. Rose, our neighbour, too. I had wondered at the time what they were on about but had long since forgotten to ask.

Seamie squinted at me as I towered over him.

'When you were only five weeks old, your mum put you in your pram and wheeled you up to the big bypass behind ours. She walked to the middle of the bridge, stopped, took her bag out of the bottom of the pram and turned around. She left you there, John Paul. Alone. A five-week-old baby, with cars and lorries racing by. You were on that bridge for hours. It wasn't used much by folks, and the motorists driving past just thought somebody had dumped a pram.

'Six hours later, a car broke down. The fella had just got out to look under his bonnet and he said he heard this godawful screaming. He ran over to the pram. You were almost blue from the cold and the crying. It was November and she hadn't even left a blanket on you. But do you know what the worst thing was, John Paul?'

I could feel myself physically shrinking. I couldn't tell him to stop. I wanted to hear the end of the story, but I couldn't bear it.

'I was working away that night, so I wasn't there for it. The cops did a door-to-door in the tower blocks, asking if anybody had seen a man or woman crossing the bridge behind the flats earlier that day with a pram. They knocked on our door and Betty spoke to them. You'd think she'd have broken down, wouldn't you? Confessed, said it was her baby. No. She told them nothing. The cops said she even offered to make them tea and kept on about what a terrible thing it was, to leave a poor baby like that.'

I opened and closed my mouth like a fish. Even though, in the back of my head, a voice was screaming *She was ill!* I still felt sick. What sort of mother could do that to her child?

'I got back the next day,' Seamie continued. 'She wouldn't tell me where you were. I couldn't wait to see you, my little son. I went down to Rose to see if she'd left you there, and it was then Rose put two and two together. You were in foster care for a month, John Paul. They wouldn't let me take you home even after Betty was admitted to the hospital. That was your lovely mum who cared so much for you.'

I fell back on to the sofa and put my head in my hands. Then I started to cry.

Seamie said nothing. He'd won.

But, as always, his satisfaction was fleeting. Seamie's tongue was wickeder than his heart. His attacks were always followed by guilt.

'Sorry,' he said. 'But you had to know.'

I shook my head. I didn't need to know that my mother had abandoned me twice. He'd only told me to hurt me.

I stood up to leave.

'John Paul,' he said feebly.

'Fuck you,' I answered. 'Fuck you, Seamie.'

The damage was done.

Julie

No, I never thought Harry was a saint.

But we were married a few years before I started to see the real man.

Harry had become ridiculously, filthily rich, and we had all the trappings of that in our home and belongings. At the same time, I was still teaching in St Mochta's and hanging out with my fairly normal pals, dressing and acting like I was just one of them.

I was straddling two worlds, thinking I was comfortable there.

It got to the point, though, where Harry had so much money it made me nervous. Unlike him, I was afraid that if I got used to living with it, I wouldn't be able to live without it.

And I knew that meant I wouldn't be able to live without him.

In 1999, he took me to Capri for our holidays. Harry had business associates there he wanted to catch up with and the offer of a friend's house to stay in, so off we went.

The friend's home was a villa built on to the side of one of the island's cliffs, our view every morning the shimmering blue and green of the Tyrrhenian Sea.

'You don't mind that I didn't book us a hotel?' Harry said.

'Yes, I'm disgusted. You expect me to live in this dump for the next two weeks?' I flapped my arm at the Italian marble kitchen, stocked to the brim with fresh food and fine wines, like I was at ease with my surroundings and not overwhelmed.

Harry smiled.

'I know. I'm a cheapskate. I'll bring you somewhere more exotic next time, but given I have to do a little business on the mainland, Johnny's offer of the house seemed like perfect timing. I'll try to make it up to you. Multiple orgasms tonight, I swear.'

'You want me to fake more than once? Ah, Harry. I'll be exhausted. What are you . . . put me down!'

Harry threw me over his shoulder.

'How very dare you, Mrs McNamara! I always make good on my promises. Jesus, the weight of you for such a tiny thing.'

I squealed as he carried me up to the bedroom.

Harry had organized the trip so we had most of the first week alone together. In the mornings we explored the island, sailing out to the Grotta Azzurra or climbing the rocky hills. In the afternoons we swam lazily in the gentle waves. Rested and relaxed, we'd stroll to the secluded restaurants frequented only by locals and eat food so delicate it was like sitting at the table of the gods. We left the island twice, once to visit Sorrento, the second time to drive along the Amalfi Coast, in a rented red Ferrari with the top down.

Towards the end of the week, Harry had scheduled meetings and I was left to my own devices for a day or two.

It wasn't a hardship, sunbathing on the terrace, reading, sipping ice-cold white wine.

On the Friday I decided a second day lounging about would be too decadent. I would walk into the town instead, perhaps browse in some of the stores I'd yet to visit.

Morning was my favourite time of day on the island – those few hours before the boats of tourists arrived, hordes of them in their bright summer get-ups, swarming the island's small streets and restaurants like multicoloured ants.

As I strolled down to the centre, I was filled with a feeling of wellbeing. The sun's rays were warm on my face, the sweet smell of Italian honeysuckle filled the air and the salt from the sea tickled my nose. I was wearing a light cotton dress and thin-strapped sandals, the soft breeze that rippled overland dancing lightly on my exposed skin.

This, I thought, *is bliss*. And I could have this every day if I wanted it.

Even as the thought entered my head, I shook it free. I had no idea what on earth I would do with myself if I didn't teach, if I was at home all day long while Harry was at the bank. And I would have been embarrassed to be one of those wives who turned up at the many galas and events organized by HM Capital with nothing to talk about but the latest fashions and boring Irish celebrity gossip. That wasn't me.

I knew Harry hoped that I would get pregnant, and he was convinced I'd give up work if that happened, but I wasn't sure. It was a bridge I'd yet to cross. In any case, two years into marriage and there wasn't a blip on the pregnancy front. There was no explanation. We certainly hadn't slowed down in bed. If anything, I'd have described Harry's appetite for lovemaking as insatiable. I'd wake up some nights to find him kissing my breasts and nudging his knee between my legs. I think the knowledge that he could get me pregnant at any time (I'd flung out the pill on our honeymoon) was a huge turn-on.

But still, there was nothing. I'd gone from thinking I didn't really mind whether or not I had kids to being vaguely concerned that I mightn't have a choice. Every month I wondered if my premenstrual belly was a little too swollen, my breasts more tender than usual – anything that would indicate the seed had been sown. Every month, when that telltale trickle of red splashed into the toilet bowl, I felt a strange pang of disappointment, more at my own inability to conceive than at anything else. I wasn't quite at the stage of panic. After a year of unprotected sex I'd insisted we get checked, and after two visits to the leading fertility expert in Ireland we knew we were both fine medically.

So it was just a matter of waiting and not stressing about it, because, as everybody told us, stress would only prevent it from happening. And anyway, I really enjoyed our life as it was. I was the youngest of a very large family and used to being minded, not having to do the minding. Harry probably wanted a baby more than me, but even he didn't seem in a panic to tie us to night feeds and dirty nappies, for all the rewards we were promised that would bring.

It would happen eventually. And that morning in Capri, I was too relaxed to worry about it.

The first store window to catch my eye on the cobbled street that led into the town contained just one dress – an elegant red strapless affair for an evening event. It was striking, and I knew Harry would love it. When he bought me lingerie, red was his colour of choice. I bent down to squint at the infinitesimally sized price card at its foot.

'Jesus Christ!'

I stood and looked up at the name of the shop, wondering what kind of store would think it normal to advertise a dress in its window that, converted from lira, cost about €10,000.

Gucci.

I looked beyond it to the inside of the store and saw two women beside the till chattering in Italian, gesticulating and throwing back their heads as they laughed. It was impossible to guess who was the customer and who was the sales assistant. Both looked like they'd fallen out of the pages of a *Hello!* magazine spread, their dark hair gleaming like gossamer, French-polished nails, clothes styled like they could glide from the shop to a catwalk – effortlessly chic.

I looked down at my own attire and suddenly felt like the scruffiest woman on the island.

I knew I was being ridiculous. We were staying in one of the plushest villas on Capri. My husband was – or at least seemed to be – of immeasurable wealth. I had chosen to wear a dress I'd bought in Topshop and sandals from Mango. I painted my own nails and sometimes, because it was so bloody curly and nobody would know the difference, I let Helen or Grace cut my hair. But I could have worn the sort of clothes those women were wearing if I wanted to. I could have visited stylists and salons to my heart's content. It was just that, on a regular day, teaching in a secondary school didn't really require labels or manicured hands.

Feeling a little despondent, and silly with it, I carried on down the street, averting my gaze from the windows that followed as well as from the other island inhabitants, the ones that belonged there. The sun had been obscured by a rare cloud, and it was the first time I'd felt out of sorts on the holiday.

It didn't last. As I emerged on to one of the famous squares, the clouds drifted on and yellow light started to creep over the cobble-stones. The restaurants had set tables outside for their mid-morning patrons and I decided to treat myself. Eleven a.m. was practically lunchtime.

I took one of the quieter tables and perused the menu while I waited to be served. The look the waiter gave me when he arrived improved my mood that bit more. He was no more than twenty, and he really didn't give a toss about my cotton dress not being up to scratch. All he saw was blonde curls, smooth, tanned skin and a generous display of cleavage.

'*Un caffè espresso e un bicchiere di vino bianco piccolo, si prega di,*' I ordered.

If he thought it was too early in the morning for a glass of wine, he gave nothing away.

'*Qualsiasi cosa per una bella donna,*' he said. *Anything for a beautiful lady.* He leaned over me to take the menu in a manner that indicated he hoped he might fall into my breasts.

When it arrived, I knocked back the espresso, taking an imme-diate sip of the Pinot Bianco to rid my mouth of the bitter taste.

I hadn't brought anything to read, so I texted Grace and Helen to tell them where I was. Grace didn't reply, which meant she was, typically, out of phone credit. Helen texted back with a 'You lucky wagon, don't bother coming home without an Italian stallion for me, per favore, and buy some nice clothes!!!'

I smiled and put the phone down. I wished Helen was with me. We would have sat there all day drinking wine and laughing about that Gucci dress.

I people-watched for the next hour or so. The square began to

138

fill with the day-trippers, who in turn stared at those of us already settled at tables, like we were tropical fish in an aquarium.

I'd finished my second small glass of wine and was deliberating whether to move on somewhere else for lunch or return to the villa. Nicely oiled, I was even considering taking Helen's advice and making another clothes-buying attempt, if I could find a store that sold anything less costly than a spare kidney.

That's when I saw them. Harry had just entered the square with a group of men and women, all Italian or of some other Mediterranean origin.

My waiter appeared at the same time, and it was his enquiry as to whether I'd like a complimentary glass of limoncello from the cellar that made up my mind. I accepted and sat back in the chair, watching as, across the square, staff rushed to seat my husband and his colleagues, as though a flock of VIPs had just arrived. Which was what they were, I guess.

I was being voyeuristic, but what harm?

I asked little about Harry's work but any time I did, he told me anything I wanted to know. In truth, it both confused and bored me. Building on the success of HM Capital in Ireland, Harry had branched out, financing big building projects in other property markets – London, Madrid, Dubai. It sounded fascinating on the surface but, in reality, it involved hours of meetings about strategy and profit analysis, engagement with the Central Bank about capital reserves and risk liability, dinners with shareholders – monotonous, dull, laborious. I turned out for the fun nights, the charity dinners and the annual party for the shareholders, but as for the rest of it, well, I just tuned out.

In my head, when Harry left the house I imagined him in an office with a group of men in sharp suits – spectacles, laptops, briefcases, copies of the *FT* and the *Irish Times*, and folders of files. I knew they had money and houses like the one we were staying in now, but that was all outside work – beyond the stifling, boring boardrooms.

Yet here was my husband, surrounded by Italian men and women who could have starred as extras in a James Bond movie.

I was intrigued.

Harry fitted right in. He was wearing a white Armani shirt, tailored grey trousers and Versace sunglasses, perched perfectly on his lightly tanned face. He was always at me to spend money on clothes, but I'd never really appreciated how different we must have looked together, not until I saw him in that company.

The woman on his left removed her large sunglasses and looked over her shoulder, revealing dark, cat-shaped eyes, to go with an Egyptian nose and bee-stung red lips. Her hair was long and glossy, like the women in the shop – not a strand out of place – and fell down to her waist along a toned bare back. She gathered it around to the front of her body as she turned back to the table, revealing the clasp at the neck that held the backless dress in place – and my husband's hand between her shoulder blades.

It was like being electrocuted.

I'd seen Harry flirt with women many, many times. He'd flash them his pearly whites and turn on the charm to the point of them blushing ridiculously. He was shameless, doing it openly in front of me. But it was harmless. In fact, me being a witness confirmed that.

I always thought that if the worst I had to worry about was my husband chatting up other women, I really didn't have a lot to worry about at all. It was just something I had to accept about Harry's personality.

But that day I watched from across the square as his hand slid down the woman's back, coming to rest at the top of her buttocks, where he caressed the light brown skin in gentle circles with his thumb.

It was too intimate.

And there was more. There was something telling in the bored looks on the women's faces as the men made their orders and resumed their business talk. Their expressions told me that they weren't there for financial matters and clearly weren't wives or girlfriends of the other men.

They looked like prostitutes. High-class hookers. Whatever you'd call them.

Harry hadn't come home the night before, telling me when he'd left that morning that he would probably stay over on the mainland and come back to the island with the clients to view land they were purchasing.

I had this awful sinking feeling.

Harry could be reckless. I might have liked a bit of danger (I'd married him, after all), but I was more old-fashioned. Especially when it came to sex. We had a passionate love life, but there were some things I wouldn't do. I wouldn't screw outdoors. I didn't mind games and role-play, but only up to a point. And he'd asked me to do coke with him before sex once and I had said no.

I didn't think we needed anything to make it more exciting. What if I'd been wrong? Perhaps, the night before, he had cut lines of white powder along her stomach. Hookers and cocaine, they sort of went together, didn't they?

Had he been with more than one of the women?

I gawped over at the group as the waiting staff appeared with thick crystal glasses of mojito and silver trays of fresh shellfish, all other customers coming second to that table.

What was going on?

His company didn't look like bankers, or at least no bankers I'd ever seen. Were they Italian developers? If you'd asked me to guess and I didn't know the context, I'd have laughed and said that they looked like mafiosi.

And who were the women? Were they part of the deal – throw in some escorts and I'll sort you out with a loan?

The words of my mother on the morning of my wedding came back to haunt me.

He's not perfect.

What is it he does, exactly?

He has an eye for the ladies.

The waiter appeared, producing the limoncello with a flourish and then studying my ashen face with concern.

'*Va tutto bene?*' he asked. *Is everything okay?*

I forced a tight smile and accepted the glass. I placed a note larger than was needed for my bill and waved him away with his inflated tip.

No, everything wasn't okay. It was far from okay.

I left the table and melted into the throng of tourists, completely unnoticed by my husband as I blended in with the cheaply dressed, invisible plebs.

Why didn't I cross the square and confront him? Catch him red-handed and call him out?

It crossed my mind. Striding over and smacking him full on the face. Screams, tears, recriminations.

It's hard to explain what was going through my mind.

For a start, I was embarrassed. I felt shabby in comparison to the people he was sitting with. I didn't want to go over when he was in their company.

And then – as I moved away from the square – other thoughts filled my head.

Yes, I had a suspicion – but it was easy to tell myself it was just that. That I was being paranoid. I made myself see it from his point of view. Him, sitting down to lunch in a public place with work colleagues – yes, his hand on some woman's back, but he's a tactile person, he's a flirt, I know that. And he has to be Harry the charmer, fun Harry, to make his business work.

Even though, in my gut, I felt something, I talked myself out of accepting it as quickly as I had talked myself into thinking it. The mind and the heart do funny things for self-preservation.

It wasn't like I'd caught him in bed with another woman.

Surely, knowing I was on the island, he wouldn't have taken the risk of intentionally touching another woman so intimately?

I was imagining things.

That's what I told myself as I fled back to the villa, and all through the glasses of wine that followed that night.

And I reminded myself of everything I had to lose.

I'd had six years of Harry smothering me with love and affection, sorting out any problems I encountered, sheltering me from the rest. Six years of laughter and adventures and firsts. Whatever my sisters or my pals in work thought, he was my best friend as well as my husband.

I didn't want that to end.

The next morning he brought me breakfast in bed, tea and

143

pastries and two Nurofen (he'd spotted the wine glass and bottles beside the bedside table).

'Sore head?' he asked, his face a mask of sympathy.

'Hmm.' I knocked back the painkillers. 'How was business? You must have been lonely without me over on the mainland. I missed you.'

'I missed you too. It was okay. Richard was over. I told you I'm lining him up for a board appointment, didn't I?'

'No?'

'Yeah. He's perfect for it. By the way, I've a bit of a confession to make.'

I felt my muscles clench.

'What?'

'I got a bit carried away too. This is for you.'

He left the room and came back with a black box. When I opened it, it was filled with satin-like tissue paper and the red Gucci dress from the store. It had caught his eye too.

I pretended to be amazed at my gift, chiding him for spending so much money while he told me I was worth every penny.

It made me sick to look at it.

Blood red. The colour of guilt.

And I'd told him I couldn't be bought.

JP

Life was better after I got away from Seamie.

There was no coming back from the massive fight we'd had that night. I stayed in a mate's house at first, and a few weeks later I got my own place, a basement flat that I'd found in Drumcondra, just outside the city centre.

At first, Charlie was just 'staying over'. She'd go back to Seamie's house after school, and her stuff was still there. She'd leave little notes to tell him she was calling over to mine, in case he was worried where she was. He never was. He'd given up.

After a while Charlie moved in with me, and we left him to his bottle. A man who'd been married and had two children and a job now alone with nothing and nobody. It was sad, but it didn't change how I saw him. My sister cried for him more than I ever did.

I got work in a garage, where I learned on the job how to be a mechanic and on the side how to fence cars and deal cannabis. I was rolling in it and could afford our rent and other bits with ease. I smoked a bit of blow, snorted the odd line, just to relax a bit. It was all around me. Getting drugs in Dublin in 1998 was piss-easy. And that was before the really big boom happened and you'd yuppies snorting cocaine in nightclub toilets. Yuppies like Harry McNamara.

But I never let a sip of drink pass my lips. I didn't want anything to do with Seamie. Not even his name.

I only saw my dad once after that. Surprising, considering how small Dublin is. But then, I didn't hang out in pubs much. Ironically, the canal he died in was just yards away from our first bedsit in Drumcondra, and not far from where he himself lived then. Even more ironic was that he died from drowning in water and not whiskey, which anybody would have assumed was where he was heading by the time we'd moved out.

I didn't go to his funeral.

Even Charlie stopped bothering with him, in the end. She started to have a life of her own life and realized that it didn't have to include dealing with a grown man passed out on the sofa every night.

I was lucky that she chose me. I was angry at the world and could have slipped. But taking care of her gave me a focus. It was my job to make sure she kept on the straight and narrow – that just because she didn't have parents didn't mean she could do what she liked.

And I had plenty to worry about. Charlie was a stunner, no doubt about it. Even at twelve, you could see young fellas stopping in their tracks to stare at her. She didn't have a clue, and she certainly wasn't aware of how much danger it posed.

I was working late one night, a delivery of three BMWs that needed paint jobs and plates changed so they'd be ready for export the next day. I had to leave Charlie alone that night, but she was always fine.

The shift over, I headed home, too knackered even to stop for chips.

I was taking the wrought-iron stairs from the street down to the bedsit when, through the window, I heard Charlie giggle.

Then I heard another voice. Male. Who the hell did she have there at that hour?

In the seconds it took to descend the last three steps, I'd come to the conclusion that Charlie was a two-faced little wench who had a boyfriend over every night that I was out. If she was going to be abusing my trust, she could go right back to Seamie's.

I threw the door open to find one of my suppliers sitting on our recently acquired two-seater settee. His legs were spread wide as he relaxed on the couch, a bottle of beer in one hand, joint in the other. Charlie was standing by the kitchenette, her arms wrapped around herself, a false smile forced on her face. She was shivering in her pyjamas, pink princess ones she'd bought in Primark. Seeing her in the flesh, I realized the laughter I'd heard had been the nervous sort.

'What are you doing here?' I asked the dealer, whose name was Rick.

'I came by to drop off some gear and have a few beers with you, man. Then I met your lovely little sister. You've been keeping her quiet, haven't you, John Paul? I was just telling her she could be a model. I bet you've all the fellas after you, Charlene, eh?'

Her name sounded filthy on his lips. He looked her up and down and smiled, a dirty, disgusting gesture, all for my benefit.

'Outside,' I growled, still holding the front door open.

He laughed and stood up, giving Charlie a mock-bow before heading out the door.

'See you soon, love,' he said, winking at her. It was all I could do not to smash his teeth in.

Out on the pavement, I took the baggies off him and handed over the cash. I'd been expecting him at the garage and, when he hadn't turned up, I assumed he'd find me the next day. But not at my home.

'Don't come here again,' I said. 'We're not friends. I don't want your beer. And I don't want to see your face in my flat or near my sister.'

'Chill the cacks, man. Who do you think you are? Grant Mitchell? She's a bit young, even for me. Just saying, though, if you ever run up any debts, I might know a few lads who'd pay you a few bob for a go on that. The young wans are all the same. She'll be giving it out for free any day now, probably is already. You may as well make something off it, considering you're more or less fucking rearing her, from what I hear. She owes you.'

I grabbed him by the throat, pushing him up against the railings. I'd never felt such rage.

'Are you some kind of paedophile?'

His eyes bulged as he strained against my grip. He clawed at my arms until I dropped him, coughing and spluttering. The desire to kill him filled me like a white heat, frightening me almost as much as him.

I guess there were some parts of Seamie that it wasn't easy for me to shake off.

Starting on Rick was reckless. He worked for one of the city's leading dealers. I was only on the periphery of that world, and I wanted to stay there. What I didn't know was that this kingpin had a thing about kiddy-fiddlers, having been through an infamous

Christian Brothers' school and with tales of woe to prove it. My use of the word 'paedophile' had sent Rick into a state of panic and instead of having a pop at me, as soon as I released my grip he just swore and legged it.

Downstairs in the bedsit, Charlie was already in bed, her back to me when I came in.

'Charlie,' I said, touching her shoulder.

'I'm asleep.' She shrugged her arm away.

'You sound it.'

She said nothing.

'I'm sorry,' I said. 'He shouldn't have come here. It won't happen again.'

'Why do you know people like that, JP? Does the garage not pay you enough? Is it because you have to mind me? Should I go back to Dad's?'

She wouldn't look at me. She didn't want me to see that she was crying.

'Charlie, this is your home now. You know that. As long as I'm your brother, you'll always have somewhere to stay.'

She turned and sat up. 'JP, please, I don't want you to get into trouble. Maybe I should leave school and get a job?'

'Are you kidding me? Charlie, seriously. You've nothing to worry about. That fella is just a plonker. I said I'd do him a favour, just this once. I won't do it again, I promise. Do you believe me?'

She stared at me for a few seconds before breaking eye contact. She saw what the situation was but was neither old nor confident enough to challenge an outright lie.

'Yes,' she said.

I took it, feeling ashamed.

'He's a creepy git, isn't he?' I said. 'Did he say anything to you . . . anything bad?'

She shrugged, embarrassed. Clearly he had, and it made my skin crawl.

From the very start, Charlie attracted the wrong sort of man.

Julie

It's funny to think that, back when I should have been concerned about what Harry was getting up to at the bank, all I was worried about was whether he was being unfaithful. Like him having an affair was the worst thing that could happen.

After Capri, I buried deep the seed of doubt that had been sown. I had the conversation I should have had with Harry so many times in my head, it was like it had actually happened.

'*Did you cheat on me in Capri, Harry?*'

'*What the hell would make you think that?*'

'*I saw you. That day in the square. You had your hand on that woman's back.*'

'*I had my hand on a woman's back? Have you lost your mind? You saw me? Why didn't you come over?*'

'*It was more than that. It was how your hand was on her back.*'

'*Julie, you sound like a madwoman.*'

'*And you bought me that Gucci dress. You felt guilty.*'

'*I bought you that dress because I thought you'd love it. What is this?*

When have you ever felt that I don't love you, that you mean so little to me that I would cheat?'

In all versions of it, the Harry in my head talked me out of my suspicions. He was as convincing as my husband would have been in real life – I didn't need to play the conversation out loud at all.

And then, as time moved on, I became distracted.

Ireland had entered the new millennium in a whirl of positivity about the future, and it was hard to feel anything but good about life.

The excitement in the country was contagious.

Everybody was enthralled with the hope offered by the noughties. People had jobs and were on good money. Suddenly there were 'oo cars on the road, Mercs and BMWs and Jags. Restaurants were opening of a quality and price we veterans of spending usually only saw abroad. Satellite dishes sprang up on the walls of council houses and companies targeting decking in the middle classes' back gardens were making a killing.

This was the 'trickle-down' prosperity promised by Harry and his ilk – wealth ending up in the hands of even those on the lowest rung of the ladder. Those poor people, of course, had no clue how tenuous their footing on that ladder was, how easily they could be knocked off it completely when economic catastrophe hit, while the rest of us merely feared slipping down a little.

I didn't see the unevenness as much as I should have. I lived in a bubble. Okay, I worked in the school, but it was a nice school and the kids there came from moneyed backgrounds anyway. It might have made me a better, less selfish person if I had realized how the other half lived. Less self-absorbed.

How easy it is to get used to money. Even if I conned myself that little things, like not having a live-in chef, somehow meant I was still an ordinary country girl in touch with her roots.

My first big mistake was moving to teaching part-time. It hadn't been my idea. Harry had pushed and pushed for me to work fewer hours, taking the odd morning and afternoon off himself so we could spend more time together.

I started the 1999–2000 school year on a fifteen-hour week.

To begin with, Harry and I had a ball. We'd go for long, boozy lunches and catch a film in the afternoon, or take walks on Killiney Hill and go shopping. But then, at the end of 2000, he started working more. The school had hired somebody into my job share so I had no option but to stay on part-time hours. He told me to keep having fun. I'd endless resources at my disposal.

I got bored. I had a lot of time on my hands. Everybody else was in work.

I started to drink a bit more. A glass a night. Two glasses a night. A half a bottle. A full one, because it was the weekend.

It wasn't just boredom. I drank, too, because I knew the real reason Harry wanted me working part-time.

My husband was convinced that with more time on my hands and me relaxed, I'd get pregnant. Ha! If only life was that easy. The time off had absolutely the opposite effect. I was becoming quietly desperate and, to be honest, slightly obsessed by my inability to conceive. Getting pregnant had become my ultimate goal, even more than actually having a child. Every single one of my siblings had a baby by then. Every single one. What the hell was wrong with me? And I wouldn't even consider adoption or artifical methods. I wanted to prove I could do it.

Towards the end of 2000, you could pick me out in the local

Tescos by my shopping basket – wine and pregnancy kits. What a combination.

It just wouldn't happen. We tried everything, from old wives' tales to the scientific. Ovulation cycles. Legs in the air after sex. Worrying. Not worrying.

And there was still absolutely no medical reason for it.

At the same time, Harry was growing more distant and, unfairly, I started to worry that it was because of me, that he was angry because I wasn't pregnant. Like it was my fault.

The doubts and suspicion crept in, especially during his long absences from home.

What was he doing? Who was he with?

It was his idea that we have a New Year's Eve party in our house that year.

I didn't drink much that night, to begin with. Over the Christmas I'd gotten more than a little carried away and was carrying that sluggish hung-over feeling. So, in my only slightly tipsy state, I saw her come in, the woman with the long dark hair in a tight red dress.

I'd begun to suspect that Harry fancied a certain type of woman. I'd catch him eyeing these girls, who could have all been sisters, his eyes lingering on them even as they moved away. You'd be forgiven for thinking that type was me – blonde, petite, curvy. In a perverse way, I think I would have understood that. Some men do that – fantasize about other women who look like their wives but don't answer back, don't know their flaws and weaknesses, don't come with the same baggage.

But Harry seemed to have a thing for skinny brunettes. They weren't paler imitations of me. They weren't anything like me.

The way the woman in the red dress looked at me that night

– nervous, defensive, pitying, scornful, resentful – it tore a hole in me. I'd never met her, but she knew me.

I wouldn't have even considered her that pretty. Her teeth were too big for her mouth. She had no tits to speak of. What could she offer that I didn't?

Again, I silenced the doubts. I'd never had a single piece of concrete evidence that Harry was going with other women. No whispered phone calls or hang-ups on the line when I answered. No smell of perfume on him when he came home. Importantly, no lack of sex or desire in our own bed, which would have made me guess he'd found it elsewhere. And yet, the suspicion lingered. A little lump in my throat that I couldn't swallow.

If he had slept with that woman, I told myself that New Year's Eve, there was no way he'd invite her to our home.

I took a deep breath, held my head up high, stuck out my chest and greeted the brunette and her date with all the sense of entitlement I had.

'Welcome! I don't think we've met. I'm Julie McNamara, Harry's wife. Do you work for my husband?' I addressed the man who accompanied her, as if she was insignificant in the conversation, not smart enough to work for HM Capital.

'I work for Harry,' she said, extending her hand with its sculpted, talon-tipped nails. 'I'm Lily, a project manager at the bank. Hasn't he mentioned me?' She smiled icily.

'No. Never.' I smiled back. I took her hand limply, then dropped it as though worried I might catch something.

Around 11 p.m. I noticed that Harry wasn't mingling in any of the rooms downstairs. I'd been watching him up until then, but had got distracted seeing to a guest who had to leave early. My husband looked really handsome that night. He'd discarded his tie and left his sharp white Jasper Conran shirt open at the neck. There was a hint of evening shadow about his jaw and he smelled of musky cologne. *He belongs to me*, I thought as he moved through the room, everybody watching him.

But Harry seemed on edge, annoyed even. He circled Lily, almost as if he were trying to avoid making eye contact with her. And it struck me – he hadn't invited her. She'd turned up unannounced.

Who would do that?

Only somebody making a point.

As the evening wore on, Harry made a fuss over me, fetching me glasses of champagne and telling me to relax, that it was my night too.

When I realized I'd taken my eye off the ball and the two of them had gone missing, the first places I checked were the bedrooms.

That was how bad it felt to be inside my head.

They weren't there.

I went out to the back garden and negotiated my way through the smokers under the marquee we'd erected. People delayed me, wanting to chat about trivial things like the winter floral displays I'd imported for the occasion – white roses in baskets rimmed with frosting – and how nice the fairy lights twinkling in the trees were, and the logs crackling and blasting out heat from the chimeneas.

Harry and Lily weren't there either.

As I walked back through the kitchen I noticed the man she'd come with, a glass of orange juice in his hand.

'Oh, hello, I was wondering if you knew where your date went?' I smiled. My voice slurred a little – I'd had countless glasses of Moët by that stage. My brain was working though, and already a theory was forming. If he wasn't drinking, it was probably because he'd driven, which meant his was one of the many cars that currently lined the hill up to our house.

'She went out to get something from the car,' he said, barely able to contain the simmering resentment in his voice.

He knew.

I thanked him, weakly, and moved towards the hall in a daze.

This couldn't be happening. I'd have to see it to believe it.

I draped a shawl around my shoulders and was out the door before I could talk myself into staying inside.

The air, cold and unadulterated, hit me hard, showing me just how intoxicated I was. How drunk my husband had wanted me to get, so I wouldn't notice him sneaking off.

Stumbling down the drive, I paused and turned to look back at our home. It was like peering into a doll's house, a perfect little world lit up with soft lighting and candles behind sheets of pristine glass, everybody inside enjoying themselves.

That was my house. That was my life. And it was about to be destroyed.

I closed my eyes.

I imagined tottering down the hill in my heels, not caring if Harry heard me. I imagined finding them. Othello's *beast with two backs*. He'd be fucking Lily hard, with all the anger and lust he would have been feeling all night, the red dress bunched up around her waist. Punishing her for showing up and getting him all hot and bothered in front of his wife.

The bottom fell out of my world as the images played out in my head. It was physical, the pain I felt at the thought of him screwing another woman.

I couldn't do it.

I knew I was being a coward, but I couldn't bear physical witness to my husband cheating. I'd wait until he came back and confront him, once I'd got everybody out of the house. Once I'd summoned up the courage.

I went back inside, and waited.

Just before midnight she arrived in the kitchen, her cheeks flushed, grinning at everybody with those fucking buck teeth.

Harry came in a few minutes afterwards. He was with Richard.

'Sorry, darling,' he said, and grabbed me around the waist. He smelled of cigarette smoke. I'd been at him to quit and he'd taken to covertly smoking outside so I wouldn't catch him. 'Richard decided tonight was as good a time as any for a bit of shop-talk. I only got him to stop by telling him it was nearly midnight.'

'Oh, yes, blame me,' Richard said, laughing. 'It was my idea to go out in the freezing cold. Nothing to do with cigarettes at all, at all. You've some view from the top of this hill, though, Julie. I'm fierce jealous. Harry, what will I get to warm us up? Whiskey?'

I opened and closed my mouth, unable to process what had just happened. I was so sure Harry had been outside with Lily. Where had she been, if he'd been with Richard?

I looked back over at her. She was talking to another man now, one I hadn't noticed before. He was leaning in close to her ear, and she laughed and put her hand on his arm in a familiar way. I had got it completely wrong. She had been with him.

I felt a weight lift. I was so relieved Harry was here with me now and that nothing had happened. I kissed him hard on the mouth and he responded, surprised at first and then happily.

'Here, you two, the clock hasn't struck yet. You need to top up your guests. Are you giving those kisses out to everybody, Julie, or what?' Richard smiled lasciviously as he handed Harry a whiskey.

'Yes, top-ups!' I gasped, ignoring Richard's other, sleazy comment. 'Harry, help me.'

He knocked back the whiskey and we both grabbed champagne bottles and started moving through the crowd.

I was so busy filling glasses I barely looked up to see who was holding what, but just as the countdown began, I found myself standing in front of Lily.

At the same time, Harry called my name.

He grabbed my hand and started to pull me towards him, but not before I saw it.

Her smile. A vicious, sickening smile that lit up her face and said everything.

I entered the year 2001 thinking about that smile and what it meant, even as my husband kissed me.

Alice

'Thanks so much for seeing me. I know you're a busy woman. Right, I'll start, shall I? I want you to speak to me like I'm a retarded six-year-old who hasn't figured out how to count to three yet. That's how simple I need you to make this.'

The finance expert raised her eyebrows. She studied the policewoman sitting across from her who'd so casually made the very non-PC statement and was now tackling the foot-long sub she'd strolled into the office with, chilli sauce oozing from either end.

'My son has a mental disability and can't count to three,' she said, passing a Kleenex over the desk.

Alice's jaw fell slack. She tried to swallow her current mouthful and apologize at the same time.

'M'sorry, m'fucking idiot. What's wrong with him?'

Doyle had said Sam Carter knew about Harry's world and could be of huge assistance. He hadn't mentioned anything about her family, and now Alice had put her foot in it.

'He doesn't have a disability,' Sam said, arching her eyebrow. 'And if he had, asking what's *wrong* with him would have been another entirely fucking inappropriate remark. Jesus. Don't they have courses on this stuff for Guards these days? What is it you want to know, exactly? You can't just say "Tell me everything about dodgy banking" and expect us to complete the conversation in this calendar year. You need to narrow it down. What's this for, anyway – are you thinking of changing career, gamekeeper turned poacher?'

Alice flushed. This woman was smart as a whip. She immediately liked Sam Carter, even if she'd just been on the receiving end of a smack. And Alice normally reserved judgement in first meetings. This woman was worth something.

'Okay,' she said. 'I'll give it to you straight. You know I want to talk to you about Harry McNamara. I want to know what he was up to all those years, what all those fraud charges related to. I'm like most people, Sam. I know he was doing something naughty but the actual details of it are over my head. It's in the details, though – that's where I need to start looking if I'm to understand the man and those he moved with.'

The financial expert pursed her lips.

'The High Court has just decided Harry McNamara has nothing illegal on his conscience,' she said.

Her tone was acid. She clearly hated the bankers who got away with it.

Alice had a hunch that there was more. The detective scrutinized the financial expert's face, the flawless skin, the two giveaway red spots in her cheeks.

'Did you know Harry personally?' she asked, the penny dropping.

'In a manner.'

'Ah. Right. So you really do know all the juicy gossip.'

'Yes.'

'Well, can you make me understand what he was doing without frying my tiny little brain?'

Sam tilted her head to the side.

'I can try,' she said. 'But you'll need to pay attention. Unlike the poxy, moronic jurors at his trial. But I'll tell you something for nothing. If you're looking for dirt on Harry McNamara, don't just concentrate on the money.

'If you want the real nasty stuff, look at how he treats women.'

JP

I wasn't blessed with the best of the genetics in our little family. I might have left school early for other reasons, but I don't think I was any great loss to the world of education. I was always street smart, but I didn't have the attention span for books – one of those lads better at learning through doing. Give me electrical parts or a tool set, and I can build or fix anything. But I can't read a novel or follow an instruction manual to save my life. I guess, had I gone to school in more recent years, they'd have diagnosed dyslexia or attention deficit disorder and maybe they could have helped me.

Charlie was the cleverer of the two of us, by a long stretch.

'You could be a barrister, a surgeon, anything you want,' the headmistress wrote in her report card in Charlie's final exam year. 'You have brains to burn, Charlene.'

Charlie had the world at her feet. She could get a student grant with ease and could choose any course she wanted to do in college – the first person in our family to go. I was that proud of her, I thought I'd burst.

What did Charlie put on her college application form?

Fucking nursing.

She didn't even want to be a doctor. Nursing.

I spoke to her about it, and it went like this.

'Charlie, you'll be on a government wage, twenty-five thousand fucking euros a year if you're lucky, and wiping other people's arses! Don't you want more?'

'More than this palace?' she laughed, throwing her hands out at the room. We'd come up the property ladder and had a two-bedroom apartment in Clontarf at that stage, facing the north side of Dublin Bay.

I sighed.

'I'm not saying there's anything wrong with nursing.'

'It certainly sounds like you are.'

'I'm not, really. I'm only saying, you're so brainy. Why not a proper medical degree? Jesus, you could be a shagging brain surgeon.'

But she didn't have the confidence for it.

'I like taking care of people,' she said, to explain her choice. 'It's a job I'll be good at. You should be happy for me, JP.'

'Right. I am. I just thought you'd want more.'

She flushed red, embarrassed. I immediately felt ashamed. Who was I to push her when I did nothing for myself?

'Well, I can always train up once I start,' she said, staring at the floor. 'I'm still going to college, JP.'

'I know. Sorry, Charlie. I just want the world for you. At least promise me you'll marry a bloody doctor.'

'Ha! Whatever makes you happy. Please don't be disappointed. I'm looking forward to this, and I'm happy. You know I'm very grateful for everything you've done for me, don't you?'

I did. She told me all the time, even though I didn't need or want her to.

'You're all I have,' she'd say. And then give me a lecture about lifestyle choices.

'You need to quit that job in the garage and quit dealing, JP. You're risking going to jail for the sake of a few extra quid a week that we don't even need any more. And I don't like it when you smoke blow. It doesn't make you relaxed. It makes you . . . stupid.'

'Oh, well, I'm *awfully* sorry to be such a disappointment to you with my big, thick head.'

'Oh, shut up. You're the smartest person I know, which is why you smoking blow is all the more ridiculous.'

As sensible as she was, I was still convinced somebody would fuck it all up for her – get her pregnant and lead her down a bad path.

The problem was, Charlie was a people pleaser. Whatever my problems with our parents, my sister had been more or less completely overlooked. Seamie and Betty had little time for her and she spent her life trying to make others like her, not realizing she didn't have to try. Like all attractive people, everybody came to her, whether or not she was trying to impress them. Especially blokes.

I tried to keep tabs on her – a habit formed when she'd first come to live with me so young. But it was the one area of her life where, bizarrely, she didn't think she owed me anything.

'Who are you out with this weekend?' I'd say.

'Well, as you ask,' she'd answer, 'we're going to hit a club on Friday and then, apparently, we're going to an orgy. I mean, I'm a bit nervous, JP, but my mates tell me the heroin will calm me right down. You should be happy, now I'm planning to take some recreational drugs.'

'That's not funny, Charlie.'

'It really is. Seriously, JP, nothing is going to happen to me. You're going to worry yourself into an early grave, old woman.'

I did worry. It was inbuilt in me. I skirted around happiness, examining it from every angle, looking for the cracks. Being happy made me unhappy. I wondered when it would end. If I worried, I thought I could keep trouble at bay. And it made it very hard to enjoy life, no matter what my sister wanted. We weren't the same.

Charlie organized a party in our apartment one New Year's Eve – gave me no warning, of course. I heard the music out in the hallway and landed in the door to a disco in the living room.

I was gobsmacked. I grabbed her as she emerged from the loo.

'What the fuck, Charlie?' I said, loud enough to be heard over the music, but not for the twenty-odd people there to notice.

'Oh, shit. Ah, look, JP – what were your plans tonight? To be in bed by eleven? Come on, let your hair down. I've ordered pizza. Do you have any money, by the way?'

One of her girlfriends had propped herself up against the wall outside the bathroom. She clutched a West Coast Cooler. Pink, the same colour as her hair.

'Charlie Andrews, your brother is a ride. If I shagged him, we could be like sisters.'

'Fucking hell,' Charlie groaned, as I blushed to the roots of my hair. All her friends were girls in their early twenties, but I saw them as kids.

The girl kept smiling at me as Charlie escaped back into the open-plan area.

'At least have a drink with me?'

'I don't drink,' I said.

She broke her heart laughing.

'What the actual fuck? The two of you are throwing a party and neither of you drink?'

'It's not my party, that's for sure,' I said, but I'd lost her attention.

I was going to kill Charlie when this lot left. The doorbell rang, and I went to pay for the pizzas. I was stung for €100 and never saw a cent of it back.

We got everybody out the door sometime before two (apparently telling people to shove off home at five past midnight on New Year's Eve is not the done thing) and started the clean-up.

'Sorry, JP,' Charlie said, waving a dishcloth at me. 'If I'd told you I was throwing a party, you'd have told me not to or just stayed out. You're like the anti-fun police.'

I took the cloth and started drying the cups and glasses.

'I'm not anti-fun, Charlie. I just don't feel the need to be the life and soul of the party, like you. I'm happy for things to be quiet.'

'No.' She shook her head. 'That's not it.'

'What are you on about?'

'Yeah, we're different. I do get that. I like having people around me and you . . . well, you're a misanthrope. You're so wound up all the time. I know you took on a lot when I moved in, but you can stop worrying now. I'm grown up.'

'I have no idea what "misanthrope" means, but it sounds like an insult, and also, have you ever thought that you might be the one with the problem? Would it kill you to not have so many friends, to not need company all the time?'

'I don't need it, JP. I want it. I enjoy it. You had fun tonight, didn't you?'

'Absolutely. I loved coming in the door to find my gaff colonized by raging sex maniacs—'

'My friends.'

'Yeah, them. Then leaving myself broke for the weekend so you could all stuff your faces with Domino's—'

'That's a yes, then? You had a ball. And if you come out with me next week, I won't have to bring the party here. Let's start the year as we mean to go on.'

'I'm getting a restraining order for next week,' I said.

'Mm-hm. And I thought we could go travelling a bit this summer, when I finish my exams. See a bit of the world before I settle into studying.'

'I've no interest in foam parties in Ibiza.'

'Well, you'd better get interested, you boring sod. I'm making this happen.'

'That sounds more like a threat than a promise.'

I laughed, despite myself. She was infecting me. Nursing me to happiness, you could say.

Julie

When I was a little girl, I used to dream about meeting the love of my life. I grew up with parents who adored each other – in an understated way, sure – but I always had that comfortable, secure feeling that my mam and dad were in love. That that was what a 'couple' looked like – always there for each other; easy, unquestioning loyalty and affection.

I didn't understand the complexities of marriage. I certainly didn't envision the compromises.

My biggest fear when I first began to suspect that Harry was unfaithful was that it would end up in us separating. That's why I lived in denial for so long. I thought that once I'd actually caught him, he would say he didn't love me any more and leave.

So I said nothing and Harry never left. Life went on.

Ignorance is bliss. Does that make me sound stupid? Naïve? Deserving of everything I got?

Perhaps. In reality, it probably made me like a lot of other women.

Two of my siblings were already divorced, I reminded myself.

One had gone through an extremely acrimonious split and ended up with nothing, not even access to his kids. He was back living with our parents, at the age of forty.

I didn't want that. I had a very nice life. I could be content with my lot.

One of Harry's biggest problems, though, was restlessness. For him, 'content' equalled bored. I found that out with a bang.

It was a warm Friday evening in September 2004, and I'd just opened a bottle of Bollinger, my little heart skipping when the cork popped and the fizz swelled up in the glass. It never grew old, and it was the one luxury I'd never had to talk myself into.

I was managing my drinking better. I kept it to the house, mainly, and just at the weekend (that stretched from Thursday to Sunday). I squeezed all my teaching hours into Monday, Tuesday and Wednesday. Sometimes I met up with my workmates for nights out but, more and more, I drank at home. I'd gotten lazy.

I was sitting out in the garden that evening, the Indian-summer sun's rays still warm, surrounded by the scent of late-summer blooms. That morning, I'd started reading the ridiculously entertaining *Da Vinci Code* and was absolutely gripped. I was thinking about planning a trip to Paris so I could enjoy that city again in the light of all the book's revelations.

My phone rang and I picked it up to see Helen's number flashing.

'Well, hello stranger,' I answered.

'Hello stranger yourself,' she retorted. 'I've tried to ring you twice this week already.'

I took the phone away from my ear and looked at it like there was a gremlin inside, hiding my calls.

'Really? I didn't see any missed calls.'

'I rang the landline, you div'. I've free house-to-house calls. Ringing your bloody mobile costs a bomb.'

'Oh, God. Sorry. Here, let me ring you back.'

'Don't be stupid. I've got you now. Listen, I just want to ask, are you coming down for Mam's birthday on the sixteenth? It's just, she's determined not to have a party so I thought I'd book a dinner in that hotel she likes beside the river.'

I hesitated. If I said yes, I'd have to ask Harry to come down for the weekend, and he had this weird thing about making the effort for my family. He liked it when they came up to us, when he could be all flash and show off our home, bring them to restaurants which they never felt entirely comfortable in but where he was best friends with the maître d'. I knew it annoyed my lot, but I could see it from his perspective too. It was intimidating to be an extra in our noisy, large family. Especially so when you had no experience of that in your own background.

'Julie,' Helen said into the silence. 'You could come down on your own if Harry is busy. Mam shouldn't suffer.'

She could read me like a book.

'Don't be silly,' I said. 'Of course he's busy – he always is. But I'll just get him to cancel whatever he has on. This is more important.'

'Okay. Well, let me know if you want me to book you a room at the hotel or if you're staying at mine. You're always welcome, you know. And don't put yourself out for the kids with presents. They don't appreciate fancy gifts, pet. A big bag of sweets from the supermarket will do them rightly.'

I laughed and said 'Fine' before saying goodbye.

I heard Harry inside; he was home from work and fixing himself something in the kitchen. I didn't look up from my book until he sat down on the rattan chair beside me and I heard a clink of ice in a glass.

Harry had a large tumbler of whiskey in his hand and a look of utter desperation in his eyes. I found the whiskey the more unusual of the two. He'd eased off on the drink in recent years, in direct contrast to my intake.

He'd been on edge all week, since returning from a business trip to Estonia. I hadn't been able to work it out. Usually, Harry came back from these trips full of the joys. But this time he'd come with bags under his eyes and his face drawn, looking twice as old as his thirty-seven years and as though he had the weight of the world on his shoulders.

I didn't want to ask what was wrong. The day had been perfect. I was happy. Why ruin it?

For better, for worse.

I sighed and put my novel down.

'What is it?' I said. 'Is it trouble with that deal you were after? I knew when you extended the trip something was wrong.'

He shook his head.

'The deal is fine,' he said. 'It should be, anyway. It's costing a bit more, but it's a good investment.'

I took a sip and eyed him over the glass.

'Then what is it, Harry? You've being going around all week like somebody has died.'

He stared into the glass of whiskey, his silence sending little ripples of alarm through me. He raised the glass and took a gulp, then placed it on the mosaic-tiled table.

My husband leaned over and placed his hands on my bare, tanned legs. Horrible possibilities started to run through my head.

Was he sick? He looked fine, despite the haunted look in his eyes.

Oh my God. Was he about to tell me he was leaving me?

Or worse, had he fallen in love with somebody and got her pregnant?

My breathing quickened. It was that. That was the absolute worse thing that could happen.

'You know I love you, Julie,' he said.

'Harry, you're scaring me.'

'I love you with all my heart. I would never, ever do something intentional to hurt you.'

'Harry, I don't want to hear it. Please. Don't say it.'

I placed my hands on top of his, trembling. He took them in his own and squeezed them tight.

'I'm in trouble, Julie. I have to tell you. This is serious.'

'Why? Harry, what's happened? Just pull off the plaster, will you?'

He took a deep breath.

'There was a girl, in Tallinn.'

My hands were clammy. I pulled them away from his and wrapped my arms around myself. I'd started to shake. I was so tempted to put my hands over my ears. This was it. The moment I'd been dreading.

'She accused me of something.'

'What?' That confused me.

'Julie, she accused me of rape.'

He couldn't look at me.

My mouth fell open.

'W-what?' I stammered.

'Julie, you know me,' he continued. 'I would never, ever harm a woman. Never. We were having a party to celebrate the deal. It was a bit . . . wild. There were drugs taken. I fell asleep, and when I woke up she was in the bed beside me, screaming. This bloke and his friend ran in and started to shove me around. They said I'd assaulted the bloke's sister. They were security for the Tallinn investors. They'd brought her to the party.'

His face was so desperate and angry.

'I was set up,' he said. 'I didn't touch her.'

I could feel that familiar feeling of relief – absolutely fucking ridiculous in the context – but this time . . . this time, it was tinged with something else. Shame.

I was an intelligent woman. This had to stop.

'You were set up?' I said, my voice incredulous.

'Yes.'

I grabbed his hands again. Then I jumped off the cliff, before I could talk myself out of it.

'Harry. Tell me the truth. I mean it. Did you sleep with that woman?'

'What? No, Julie. Of course not. I was off my face on cocaine. You know I can get a bit . . . mad sometimes. Of course I didn't sleep with her. I wouldn't have been able to if I'd wanted to. I was out of it.'

'So, what, Harry? How come you're here and not over there in a cell? What did you do?'

'I . . . Richard sorted it. He paid off the girl and the gang. I'd done nothing wrong. They just wanted money. It was easier to just make it all go away.'

I flinched. Richard Hendricks. Always just on the edge when bad things happened.

'Well, if you did nothing wrong and it's all sorted, then why is it still bothering you? Are you afraid of more blackmail?'

I didn't even recognize my own voice. It was as though somebody else was speaking, somebody detached from the conversation.

He looked down.

'Sort of. I . . . I'm afraid if anybody finds out then it will lend legitimacy to another claim, one that was made previously.'

I could barely hear what he was saying. My head felt like it was rushing through a tunnel of sound; there was a huge roaring in my eardrums as blood rushed into them.

'Julie? Are you okay?'

I'd started to hyperventilate. I opened my mouth and sucked in huge gasps of air. None of it reached my lungs.

Harry told me to breathe, then rushed indoors and arrived back with a brown paper bag he'd found in the kitchen. It was a long baguette bag, not like the square paper bags you see when they breathe into them in the movies. The absurdity of it would have made me laugh if I'd had any oxygen to spare. I felt the hot air enter my body as I puffed in and out. The dizziness lifted. He knelt beside me and kept talking as I took great, shuddering breaths, tears streaming from my eyes.

'Julie? Oh, baby, I'm sorry. Are you okay?'

'Who?'

'What?'

'Who, Harry? What other claim?'

He stopped rubbing my back. He'd been massaging away at it like I had trapped gas. Like a back rub would make it all better.

I let go of the bag, letting it float to rest on the ground.

He looked down at it, not able to meet my eyes.

'A woman in the bank – she claimed I tried to rape her. At a work party. Her name was Nina Carter. She followed me up to my hotel room and started kissing me as soon as I opened the door. We were both drunk, but I–'

I'd started to cry. I shook my head, again and again. I couldn't bear any more.

'I pushed her away,' he said resolutely. 'I'm a wealthy man. This stuff happens. Julie – what are you doing?'

I'd stood up quickly, sending him rocking backwards.

'You need to leave,' I choked, every bit of me quivering with anger and sadness.

'What?'

'You need to leave. Get out, Harry. Get out of the house.'

He took a step towards me but I held my hand out ready to push him away.

'J-Julie.' He spluttered out my name, his face shocked. 'It's not true. None of it is true.'

I turned and ran into the house and up the stairs. I locked myself in our room and stayed there while he banged on the door. I heard him slump down on the landing, heard him crying, and still I lay on the bed and refused to move. If I'd looked at him or let him talk to me, he would have won me round, and I was too angry.

What he'd told me had horrified me to my core. Even if I believed everything he said, this man, this version of him – I couldn't believe that was my husband. I was a *teacher*, for crying out loud. He knew everything there was to know about my job, my life, and I knew nothing about him.

Who the fuck had I married?

JP

I beat Harry McNamara into a coma.

Into a coma.

Sometimes I just say it to myself so I can believe it.

And it all started with a chance meeting. Way back in 2004.

Things were going well for me. I'd given up the dealing. It was too risky, anyway, and life was taking a different turn. I had to leave the garage where I worked to get away from the circle I was in. I'd built up enough dough so that I wouldn't have to panic about rent and bills for a couple of years.

I got a job with an office supplies company, repairing broken office equipment. It was a bit like working as a mechanic, to be honest. I just had to get my head around photocopiers and printers and the like, which I did easily. They were a lot more predictable than engines.

'You're quick, John Paul,' my boss told me one day. 'And reliable. Keep going like this, you could be made a supervisor. We could send you for some training, even. Get you familiar with computers. There's better money in IT.'

I was excited by that. The offices where I was sent to replace parts and remove broken cartridges hummed with money. I'd begun to realize that there might be a way of earning a really good living without scratching it out through crime or the minimum wage. I hadn't finished school but, as Charlie always pointed out, I wasn't as thick as I let on. And in Celtic Tiger Ireland, you didn't need a degree to make something of yourself. You just needed some get up and go. That's what we were told, anyway.

Not long after I'd started with the company I was sent on a job to a large suite of offices in the city centre. I was there to replace all the copiers on the sixth floor, the boss man's floor. The man himself came in, wearing a suit that looked like Armani had flown over to personally sew it on to him. He strutted like he didn't just own the buisness and the building: that man walked like he owned everybody in there too.

He had a head of hair ridiculously shiny for a bloke, his nails were manicured, and on his wrist was a watch that even I recognized the value of. A Bulgari, probably half a million's worth, less if you were fencing it. He pretended not to notice everybody's eyes on him but you could see he lapped it up. He oozed wealth and the confidence that came with it.

Back in 2004, none of us ordinary joes knew what all these rich plonkers were up to. Nobody knew they were the dodgiest rank of criminal. I looked at this man and thought, *bloody hell*, if I could make even a twentieth of what he's bringing in, I'd probably be well off.

There was a living to be had in IT, certainly. But it looked like banking was where it was really at. Maybe I could get a job as a teller and try to work my way up a bit. I was pretty good with numbers – in all my days dealing I'd never needed to keep a book of who owed what and when, storing it all in my head instead. Not that I could put that on my CV.

But, yeah. Banking. Maybe I could give it a go.

That's what ran through my mind leaving HM Capital that day, the first time I saw Harry McNamara.

Alice

'Moody. Where the hell have you been all morning?'

Gallagher's sciatica was playing up badly, hot pain shooting down the back of his left thigh.

'Sarge?' Alice looked around to see where the voice was coming from, before spotting the two feet on the floor sticking out from behind Gallagher's desk. It was like the house had just landed on the wicked witch's sister, right down to the stripy ankle socks.

She walked around the table until she was standing beside his head.

'Moody, you have ugly shoes. What are they, Clarks?'

'They're €100 Birkenstocks and they're the comfiest shoes on the planet, I'll have you know. Just what, exactly, are you doing?'

'Looking to see if the ceiling needs a lick of paint. What do you think I'm doing? My back is at me again. Here, help me up. Don't pull me – I'll use you as a crane.'

Huffing, puffing, cursing, and with far too much bodily contact for either of them to be comfortable, Alice and Gallagher finally made it to the two chairs at his desk.

'The people of Ireland can sleep safe knowing you two are in charge,' Doherty called across the office, to a chorus of breathless swear words.

'Don't do that again,' Alice gasped, her hands planted on her knees. 'I'm a woman, Gallagher – I'm not designed to haul fully grown men off the floor. And here, have you thought about going on a diet? Might take the strain off your back. That, or go for retirement on health grounds. You're not exactly in great shape for a Guard.'

'Fuck right off. Jesus, I think I need a morphine shot. Do you reckon we've anything in the evidence room?'

'Nothing they wouldn't miss.'

'Nurofen it is, so. Now, tell me where you were.'

'Ah, now. See, while you were having forty winks on the floor, I was doing some research.'

'Into what?'

'Into the earth being round. What do you think? Harry McNamara. I finally understand what he was getting up to all those years in HM Capital.'

'Dodgy stuff.'

'Yes, but now I know what they actually mean when they say "dodgy stuff".'

'Alice, just a little reminder, because it sounds like you might have forgotten. Harry is the one in a coma. You're not building a case so the fraud squad can retry him. I hope this is all heading in the direction of you finding a link to Jekyll and Hyde?'

'Of course it is. I told you, if Carney didn't have a direct grudge, then he was hired to kill him. And my theory is that it might be linked to what Harry was getting up to over the years.'

'Ah, yes. You were theorizing at one point about the wife. I've been thinking about that. Wouldn't that be more likely to be a life insurance jobbie? Maybe he was screwing around and she's a woman scorned. Have you looked into their accounts, by the way?'

'Patience,' Alice said, holding up her hand. 'I haven't looked at their accounts yet: I'm struggling to get a warrant for that, him being the victim and all. But I did speak to Jimmy Doyle, and he was well aware of the contents of the couple's accounts during the trial. The McNamaras are still very well off – and probably even more well off than we know. Our lads suspect hidden bank accounts they haven't been able to find. She works, has a healthy bank balance of her own, and the house is in her name. He doesn't have a life insurance policy, so she has no real financial motive to do him in.'

'Weren't his accounts frozen during the investigation?'

'No. He had a great salary when he was at HM Capital and they couldn't find unusual lodgements large enough, or without back-up paperwork, into either of their accounts to warrant freezing them – that's why they suspect hidden bank accounts.'

Gallagher shifted slightly in his seat and winced, reaching for the pile of drugs on the desk and a bottle of Coke.

'I'm not a numpty, Alice. I know what McNamara was up to. He was loaning millions to developers all drawn up on the back of brown envelopes, with the payback dependent on property prices climbing ever upwards. That's the crux of it, isn't it? That and something to do with moving money around the books when the auditors came looking.'

'Not bad.' Alice nodded. 'But that is, oh, the mere surface of what Harry was up to. You were right to tell me to look at the personal. You told me to look for problems in their marriage. Well, let me enlighten you.'

Julie

It could have been so different, after I kicked Harry out.

My life could have gone in a whole other direction.

Then none of it would have happened.

That night would never have happened.

I phoned in sick the week after I threw Harry out, and the following Friday Toby turned up.

'Jesus Christ, Julie. I knew you had money. But this place? You must come home from work and bleach yourself to get rid of the germs.'

We were standing at the door. I had yet to invite him in, so gobsmacked was I to see him at my home. Nobody from school, except Grace, who I'd known years, ever came out here. I'd never liked to mix the two areas of my life, mainly because of Harry.

'Eh, is there a workman's entrance you'd like me to use?' Toby said, grinning but slightly nervous. 'Do I need to check in with the staff downstairs?'

'Oh. I'm sorry. Come in. I'm not with it – excuse me.'

I stood aside to let him pass and watched as he admired aloud the black-and-white diamond tiles on the floor, the spiral staircase to the balcony that overlooked the reception hall, the Baccarat chandelier.

'Is Harry here?' he asked, moving into the question seamlessly, as though it would naturally follow his exclamations about the wrought-iron stair railings.

'No,' I said. Then, 'Toby, why are you here?'

'I was worried about you,' he said. 'You missed your days. You haven't been sick since you started at St Mochta's. Is everything okay?'

I'd been on my own all week. I hadn't left the house. I had ignored calls from Helen, and then from my mam. I'd texted that I was too busy to talk, but I knew I couldn't speak to them because I wouldn't be able to lie and pretend I was fine. I still hadn't got back to confirm about Mam's birthday and I knew Helen would be fuming with me.

Is everything okay? It was one little question, and Toby had inserted so much feeling into it. The fact that he'd come here, when I only worked part-time in the school and barely went out any more – the fact that he'd known I wasn't all right because he was still in love with me, after all this time and no reciprocation . . .

I started to cry.

Toby practically skidded across the floor to put his arms around me.

I buried my head in his chest. It was unfamiliar. His body was harder than Harry's, who was fit but didn't teach teenagers how to play sport all week. Toby smelled of Lynx deodorant and aftershave from the chemist's. The sandy-coloured bristles on his chin tickled my forehead.

It felt strange, and yet it was an embrace I could get comfortable with if I let myself. Like a first cigarette must taste.

'You did the right thing,' he said, murmuring into my hair. 'Throwing him out. You were right.'

I nodded and pulled away. We moved into the kitchen and I poured myself a large glass of wine and him a smaller one, after he protested he was driving.

'What happened?' he said.

'I don't want to talk about it.'

'You don't need to give me the gory details. What did he do to you? Did he hurt you?'

Toby took my face and turned it this way and that, looking for signs I was a battered wife, which I think would have secretly pleased him. He could have come to my rescue big-style.

I gently removed his hand.

'No, Toby. Not like that.'

'He cheated on you.'

My eyes fell to the table.

Had he? Had my husband cheated on me? Was that worse than what he'd actually told me, what he'd been accused of? Raping somebody?

'That wanker. I knew it. I knew he didn't deserve you.'

I shook my head.

'It's not . . . he didn't cheat on me,' I said.

'Don't defend him, Julie. I know you're upset. I know it's your marriage. But you have to be strong. I'm here for you. All your friends are.'

'My friends?' I sobbed. 'I've been a shit friend. Why would you be here for me?'

He shook his head.

'Don't be silly. We don't have to see you every day to be your friends. I think about you all the time.' Toby flushed. He'd said more than he meant to.

I looked at him. Properly.

It might have been the drink (it wasn't my first that day), but it occurred to me that Toby was a very handsome man. He was the antithesis of Harry – shorter, stockier, fairer. But he had real character in his features, lines that said humour around his eyes and mouth, and a crooked smile that was endearing.

I'd felt so lonely all week and I was pathetically grateful for his company.

He stared back at me and I could see the yearning on his face, all that unspoken love he'd nursed for years. And I thought of all the times I'd sat in that kitchen on my own, wondering where Harry was and who he was with.

I could have been with Toby. With him properly, or having an affair with him, and I knew, I just knew, I would have been the only woman in the world for him.

He leaned towards me, his mouth close to mine.

I could have kissed him. I could have let him take me upstairs and make love to me. I would have been justified.

But there was an elastic band in my body that connected me to Harry and it snapped me back.

Toby was lovely, but he wasn't my husband. If I slept with him I would cry all the way through, wanting it to be Harry's body I touched, Harry's mouth on mine, Harry inside me. Then I would die from the guilt of it. I'd meant my wedding vows. I'd given myself wholly and completely to my husband. I couldn't be with anybody else. Not while I was still married.

I turned my head.

Toby pulled away like he'd been smacked.

'Sorry,' I said. 'I can't.'

'But he's not here.' Toby's voice was angry.

I put my hand to the side of my head.

'He's here,' I said.

I expected Toby to understand, but he didn't. He couldn't. He'd come so close and I'd yanked it from him at the last moment.

'For fuck's sake, Julie. When are you going to cop on? Anna was right. You are a sap for that man.'

He stood up fast, knocking back the chair.

'Toby!' I said, shocked.

'Fuck it. I'm sorry; I'm going to say this. You know I've fancied you for years, Julie. I've waited for you to see the light and leave that prick. He's not right for you. He's nothing like you. You're one of us. I've waited for you to grow up and stop acting like a lovesick teenager who can't see the fucking nose on her face, who can see beyond the money and the pizzazz. But you never will. He says, "Jump", you say, "How high?" You always will, no matter what he does. You're infatuated with him. I've been an idiot.'

My jaw dropped.

'What the hell? Who do you think you are, Toby, coming here and presuming to know everything about my life, about me? We're work colleagues. This is the first time you've even been in my home. You said you wanted to be my friend, but now you're saying you're only here because you thought you might get your leg over? Do you think I'm that easy? That any time my marriage faces a problem

I'll fall into bed with somebody else? Is that the kind of woman you could be happy with?'

'No,' he said, shaking his head. 'I don't think that about you. That would make you like a bloody normal person. Whatever you have going on with Harry, it's not normal.'

I recoiled. Then I realized something.

'Hang on. You came here because I rang in sick. You asked if Harry was here. I said no and you said I was right to throw him out. How did you know I'd thrown him out?'

Toby lowered his eyes, shamefaced.

'Toby? How did you know?'

'I saw him, all right. In town. He was propping up a bar, pissed. He started shite-ing out of him about how he'd messed everything up, how much he missed you. He asked me to . . .'

I covered my mouth with my hand. The bastard. The absolute bastard. Harry couldn't stand Toby, and he'd still appealed to him, he was that desperate.

'Get out,' I said.

'I—'

'Don't say anything, Toby. Just get out. Don't come here again. And by the way, you're right. You are a fucking idiot. I've never fancied you. I never will. It's nothing to do with Harry. You're just not my type.'

I wanted to hurt him. Partly because he deserved it, partly because I felt sick at the thought of what I'd almost done. What I'd considered doing. Letting Toby, an emissary sent in desperation by Harry, screw me because I wanted to feel better.

Toby stared at me, his fury making his face ugly.

'I shouldn't have come here. I'm sorry for that. I'm sorry for not being straight with you. I thought you had feelings for me, Julie. That's the God's honest. I thought you had some weird notion about marriage being sacred and that's why you wouldn't leave him. But now I see it. You're just addicted to him. Well, good luck with that. I'm sure he'll be back within the week. I won't say "Be happy" – I know you won't be. And it's not just bitterness talking. You're the only one who can't see it. Or maybe you can but you just don't want to admit it. He'll ruin you, Julie.'

With that, he left.

I stayed at the kitchen table and picked up the wine.

I tried to remain angry at Toby, but I couldn't. He'd put it all out there, and I'd thrown it back at him. He was jealous and hurt and rejected. So he'd been mean.

He hadn't meant what he'd said.

That's what I told myself as I picked up the glass he hadn't touched and emptied it into my own.

Alice

'It all started off fairly innocently,' Alice said, taking a swig from Gallagher's bottle of Coke. The sergeant had taken pain relief for his back and was looking a bit perkier. Alice wondered just how many pills he was popping every day and if he was in a technically fit state to be in charge of the station.

'He has a good entrepreneurial head on him, does Harry – can spot an opportunity a mile off. He could see in the early nineties that land was being rezoned left, right and centre in Ireland. The demand for houses and commercial property was growing and developers wanted to build.

'The thing was, nobody was lending big sums back then. So Harry took risks. Started throwing money at the non-established development firms and getting it back with good interest when their builds were flipped. All very legal, all very profitable, even if the construction projects were built on the back of corrupt planning decisions. You with me?'

'I'm with you,' Gallagher replied.

'In your dreams. Anyhow, in the latter part of the decade, other banks started to move in on the act. It didn't matter. Harry had a loyal customer base. He'd his pick of investors in HM Capital and his borrowers had good credit ratings. He was already expanding his horizons, looking at property markets abroad. Italy, Spain, Portugal – countries like Ireland, with pockets of greedy little politicians happy to zone land for development. The builders just needed the backing. Harry was personally agreeing to loans all over Europe. And guess how he usually sealed the deal?'

'How?'

'With a golden handshake for him and a line of coke off a hooker's arse.'

'You're shitting me!' Gallagher's eyes widened. 'He's a cokehead?'

'A functioning one, it seems. Enough for the thrill, not an addict. He liked dipping in and out of the high life. And he wasn't just lending money either. He made investments on behalf of the bank without his board's say-so. Even went in with the mafia in Naples.'

'No way.'

'Seriously. HM Capital invested €10 million in the hotels built by the Arnolfi family, including a controversial one on Capri that had no planning permission. He made €15 million back, a 50 per cent return. Only 25 per cent of it went to the bank, a percentage of which went to him anyway, through his CEO shareholdings and bonuses.'

'Where did the rest of it go?'

'To him.'

'And that wasn't legal?'

Alice sighed.

'No, Sarge. Investing your bank's profits in mafia business and siphoning off the profits of your deals is not legal. There were lots of episodes like that, which were all corrupt as the next and probably would have come to light anyway, even if everything hadn't gone belly-up.'

'But nobody gave a crap back then because everybody was making money?'

'Precisely. Bear in mind, people weren't just investing in HM Capital because there was a good return to be made. They – especially his friends who put in *millions* – were investing in Harry. Harry could spot a good deal. He was the man. He was CEO of a bank guaranteed by the Central Bank and the financial regulator, and he was running it like this was his bumbag of cash in a Las Vegas casino. But the dice rolled well for him, so that was all okay – up to a point.'

'What point was that? Hang on. *Doherty!* Turn that match down or, so help me God, I will rip off your head and shit down your neck! Sorry, Moody. I can't face a headache on top of everything else today. Isn't he meant to be working on stuff for you?'

Alice waited for Gallagher to settle back down in his chair.

'He is. Right. Well, Harry was clever, but he got cocky and took way too many chances. Buoyed by his European successes, he went east. Russia.'

'Now, even I know you never do business with the Russians.'

'From what? The movies? Dear God, sometimes you're like a bad parody of yourself.'

'Leave off.'

'Stop interrupting me! Anyway, in 2000 he invested with some fella called Kuznetsov. This chap had been in the ascendancy in Russian oligarch circles before Putin came to power. There was talk of him buying an English premiership team. Nobody knew then how long Putin was going to be in power, but this lad wasn't in his camp. He was waiting for Putin to be put out. 'Course, the big man stayed in charge.'

'So what happened to Harry's investment?'

'Flushed down the Volga. By December 2000, Kuznetsov was gone. As in, gone. He'd done a runner – God knows where – leaving all his investments to be taken over by the state and his creditors up shit creek. Harry had put in €25 million from HM Capital.'

'Wow. There's a hole on your balance sheet.'

'Indeed. Easily plugged in the years that followed, though. It just required some creative accounting for the auditors' sake. If that had been it, fair enough, but Harry made a few more reckless decisions. Like somebody losing at poker who keeps throwing down the chips.'

'I suppose with your own personal bank able to cover the losses, it's not too worrying. Speaking of chips, let's send Doherty out for food. My appetite is coming back. You?'

'I'm starving.'

They sent Doherty off with a list and relaxed back into their chairs.

'So, Harry is making stupid decisions during the noughties, but enough good ones to counter the bad. He's also not so thick that he can't see little blips in the market in the mid-noughties. That's why he steps out as CEO of HM Capital in 2006 and into the role of chair, which removes him from the firing line when the shit hits the fan. The High Court jury bought that one hook, line and sinker.'

'How, exactly,' Gallagher interrupted, 'when he was clearly up to all this shit in the preceding years? Why wasn't he done for all the illegal loans and investments?'

'Oh, all of that is just background crap that our guys know about. It wasn't part of the prosecution's case. There's no proof of what Harry was up to – unless you can find where he put all the money he was making and establish the paper trail. And our guys weren't going after him personally. They were going after him as an executive of HM Capital. The prosecution focused on the incidents they did have paper for – the loans and accounting discrepancies in the 2006–2009 period during and after the crash. The CEO then wasn't as clever as Harry at hiding stuff. To be fair to him, the place was in meltdown anyway. By that stage Harry wasn't an executive director, although, according to Sam Carter, he pulled the CEO's strings like Jim Henson.'

'Who?'

'Jim Henson? *The Muppets*? Christ on a bike. Anyway, to recap – and this is what you have a handle on already – the bank was loaning out money hand over fist from 2006 to 2009. Most of it was trying to shore up earlier bad decisions, but it was being loaned out on the basis of personal guarantees from developers. If the project didn't work, the developer would have to repay the loan out of their personal funds. Except the developer's own funds were actually a loan sitting in their account from another bank and disappeared as soon as HM Capital came calling – and so on. That was repeated across all the financial institutions. HM's risk assessment was all shit and they were lending into a vacuum. They started selling on books of subprime loans—'

'Wait. What's subprime? I've heard that word so many times, but I've no idea what it means.'

'Me neither, until about two hours ago. Subprime refers to loans that were made to builders and private individuals when there was a risk that they'd never be repaid. Not *optimum prime* loans, basically.'

'Oh, right,' Gallagher said. 'Why don't they just call them bad loans?'

'No idea. Because they want us to be confused, I guess. Anyway, the banks were selling packets of those loans to each other, and every time anybody came to look at the books they'd cook them, make those subprime liabilities look like assets, and so on – because a loan is an asset, do you get me?'

Gallagher nodded in a way that said he was completely in the dark but couldn't cope with another explanation.

'And that's what our guys tried to get Harry on,' Alice concluded. 'HM was the worst of the banks when it came to all that shit. But our prosecution strategy didn't work.'

'This, my dear, has been a fascinating insight into the life and times of Harry McNamara, the banker,' Gallagher said, holding out his hand for the brown paper bag from Romayo's proffered by Doherty. The office was already filling up with the smell of cheeseburgers and chips drenched in salt and vinegar. 'I'm kind of cheering for him – I've always liked a man who'll go all out in a gamble. So, you're thinking with all that in his past, Harry has a list of enemies as long as my dick. Yes, I can see why somebody would put a hit on him.'

'And not just ordinary enemies, Sarge. He ran with dangerous lads, our Harry. Lads who'd knife you as soon as look at you. He got in over his head. Luckily, he always had the money to buy himself out.'

'So if Carney was in one of these gangs – and we haven't been

196

able to make any link whatsoever, but let's go with it – or if he was hired to kill Harry by somebody, isn't there still a flaw in your theory, Moody? Why wouldn't Carney just take whatever he was paid to do the job and fuck off? Why do it in front of the wife and hand himself in? And, by the way, I presume you're still running the background check on Carney and haven't skipped straight to all this sexy banking shite?'

'I told you, Doherty is helping me with that. There isn't a whole lot to find out. The guy's a loner. I figure if I track down Harry's enemies I can trace a link to Carney that way. The only way I can see Carney doing this is for money. As for handing himself in, well, McNamara is infamous, Sarge. Whatever happened, it was going to be a high-profile investigation. I don't know for sure, but I can only imagine that Carney has made a strategic decision to go this way and there must be a huge pot of money waiting for him if he pulls it off, rather than wait for us to catch him and get done for life. That, or he's making some sort of point.'

'That is such a leap I'm thinking of entering you in the Olympic long-jump team. You're so determined to prove Carney is sane that you're going *in*sane. Can you really not accept the possibility that McNamara was just an unfortunate sap that karma came hunting? So, he was hated because of dodgy business deals. There were hundreds of bankers doing the same. Why him?'

'Sarge, I haven't even started,' Alice said, holding up a chip and waggling it at him. 'The personal stuff, remember? Harry's problems started with money, but money brought other things. Power. Drugs. Women. It's a very real possibility Harry pissed off somebody big time by hurting somebody close to them. Wait until I tell you the real scoop on Harry, the accusations that are so far under the radar not even our fraud squad colleagues know about them. This financial expert I met – well, she had family who worked with Harry. A girl called Nina. Sam gave me some real gems.'

Julie

Toby was wrong. Harry wasn't back within the week. I let him stew for a whole month. It was like a test of my own willpower, but I knew I had to make a point.

In that month, I managed to alienate my whole family. I missed my mother's birthday, sending down an expensive gift that couldn't compensate for my absence. I texted Helen, too cowardly to phone. My sister, who hated confrontation, responded in the most hurtful way she could – by not texting back.

I was consumed with guilt but too full of self-pity and heartbreak to do anything about it.

I phoned Harry on a Monday morning, knowing he would be busy in work, and told him to come out to the house. He was there forty minutes later.

When he came in I was sitting at the breakfast table, glass of wine in hand. It wasn't even 11 a.m., but I needed it.

He took one look and said, 'I don't suppose there's another of those going?'

I shrugged, and he fetched himself a glass.

He sat down, took a large gulp, then reached for my hand.

I wouldn't let him take it.

'Julie. I've missed you so much. Baby, I am so sorry for what I put you through. But you have to believe me. I didn't rape those women. I was stupid, and I got myself into two ridiculous situations. But rape? Women are going to say that because I'm loaded and they want money out of me. I'm not that sort of man, Julie. You know that, surely?'

'I don't believe you raped anybody,' I said.

His face flooded with relief.

'Thank God,' he said, as he tried to take my hand again.

I lifted the wine glass instead.

When I'd taken a sip, I had the courage to continue.

'But I do think you slept with them. How many, Harry? How long have you been cheating on me?'

He reacted like he'd been slapped.

'You slept with that Lily woman from the bank, didn't you? Was she the first, or were there more?'

'What are you talking about? I don't cheat on you, Julie. Why would you say that?'

'Don't lie to me!' I slapped my hand down on the table, making him jump.

'I . . . I—' Harry stuttered to a halt.

We looked each other in the eye.

He couldn't do it. He couldn't confess.

Did I even want him to? Really?

'I'm not a cheater,' he said, and stared down at the table.

He couldn't meet my gaze.

'How can I believe you?' I snapped. 'All that madness in Estonia is one thing, but you never told me about that Nina Carter girl. Why not, if you'd nothing to hide? I'm your wife!'

'Maybe because I knew you'd react like this. Jesus, Julie. You haven't a clue how stressful my job is. I have to be your big, strong husband all the time. You expect me to take care of you, but who's taking care of me?'

'Are you shitting me, Harry? I never said I expected you to take care of me. Any time I try to take care of myself, you're in there with "You don't need to work, Julie. Let me take care of everything, Julie."'

'I'm not talking about money, and stop being so fucking selfish!' he shouted. 'I'm talking about you drinking. I'm talking about us not getting pregnant. Other women take folic acid when they're trying to have a baby, Julie, not a glass of fucking Pinot Noir. Have you ever thought the two might be connected? Did you notice that I cut back on the booze? To give us a chance, because I want a family. And if you really wanted to get pregnant, there are ways. You've never even mentioned IVF. Do you actually want to have a baby, or do you just want know that you can?'

I winced. It was my most private thought and he'd just spat it in my face.

'And another thing. You never acknowledge how hard I work. You just take everything I give you for granted, turning up your nose at what you don't want and grabbing what you do, like it's fucking normal to be a millionaire and you can pick and choose your pleasures with good conscience. You drive into your job in a BMW, pretending you're just one of the gang and nothing like your boring square of a husband.'

'All those years you spent flirting with that toad Toby and getting pissed every other night. I've never thrown any of that at you, and the minute I confess my worst moments to you, you throw me out of the house! You're not perfect, and neither am I. But it's not fair for you to think the worst of me because I make a mistake. I'm only human. I needed you to support me for once. I've done nothing wrong. And you turned on me.'

I couldn't speak. I was so appalled, I wanted to disappear inside myself, to unhear everything he'd just said.

I knew what he was doing. The passive-aggressive nature of it, turning the situation around so, somehow, I was to blame.

I recognized it. It was the behaviour of an addict – somebody absolutely genius at deflecting attention from their own behaviour. I just wasn't aware what his addiction was at that stage.

Despite this, I let what he said affect me. Especially as he'd touched on a raw nerve when he mentioned Toby.

I needed an out. I didn't want my marriage to break up. I'd realized that the moment another man came on to me. If I could share some of the blame for Harry keeping things from me, then I could rationalize my decision to stay with him. I could shut the lid on Pandora's box and sit on it.

I let him move back in, but for weeks afterwards things remained awkward. He came home early from work Monday to Friday – early for him, anyway, just in time to make dinner. We stayed in, picked at dinner, watched television and moved around each other like we were the wrong ends of two magnets.

I couldn't live with the pained silences.

Harry was pulling on his trainers for a walk one Saturday morning when I made the first move.

'Can I come with you?' I asked, standing at the door to the guest room.

He looked up, his face arranged in the permanent worried expression he wore those days.

'Yes. Of course,' he said.

We walked in the direction of Killiney Hill and climbed for a while, both concentrating on keeping our breathing steady as we negotiated the steep incline and slippery grass, me taking his proffered hand when I lost my footing.

'Julie,' he said, when he pulled me up to face him on level ground. It was the first time we'd touched in weeks.

'No, Harry,' I said. 'I'll speak.'

'Okay.'

We walked again for a few minutes in silence, until we emerged on to the section of the hill that looked out over the sea. It was cold. Our breath formed clouds of steam, the two of us warm from the exertion. There was nobody around, most people having more sense than to be out on a chilly November morning shrouded in a light mist that threatened to turn to rain.

'When we met, Harry, I hadn't even had a serious boyfriend,' I said.

'I know.'

'I was only twenty-four when we got married.'

He nodded, his face set against the wind.

'But I'm not a bloody innocent.'

He looked down at the ground beside his feet, scuffing at it with the toes of his trainers.

'You're rich, Harry. Filthy rich, and I don't really understand how. You manage a bank – you're not a bloody tycoon. You tell me your job is stressful, and I don't know why. Who are these people you deal with? Are they kosher?

'And I know I drink too much. I'm bored out of my wits. I should have stayed working full-time. You pressed me to go casual, but I'm not blaming you. I should have said no. I should have put my foot down.'

'I know that's my fault,' he said, gracious now I'd claimed some of the responsibility for the fissure in our marriage. 'I thought we could spend more time together and then I just started working more. I'm sorry.'

'Thank you for saying that.' I sighed. 'But "sorry" is just a word. Here's what we're going to do. I told you when we met that I don't give up easily. I am not going to let us fall apart. I'm not going to be a divorcee in my thirties. I love you, Harry. I've loved you from the moment I saw you.'

'And me, too,' he said. 'I know things have been strained between us for a while, and I don't know how or why. Something happened. I don't know what, but you started to look at me differently.'

He was talking about Capri and he didn't even realize it. That's what had happened.

'I want us to go back to where we were, Julie. What do I have to do?'

I looked out at the water, watching the distant ripples of white against the grey sea and the ferry sailing out from Dún Laoghaire harbour.

'I just want you to be honest, Harry. That's all. I'm not going to look away any more. I want you to always be truthful with me and I want you to show some cop-on and start seeing me as your partner, not just your wife. If you don't want me teaching full-time, if you want me more involved in your life and your work, then I have to be involved. Where does the money come from? They say you're one of the wealthiest men in Ireland. What sort of salary are you paying yourself? Is all this going to last? And Harry, more important than any of that – you need to tell me if you've ever been unfaithful. Did you sleep with Nina Carter?'

I turned to look at him, and I could see him calculating – how much and how little I had to know to make this work, which card he was willing to play.

'No,' he said. 'I . . . I kissed her back. I was drunk, Julie. I swear, it was just a stupid kiss. Nothing else.'

I closed my eyes, barely able to swallow the disappointment. With each little push, he gave up a bit more.

'She ran off and straight into a colleague in the hall, bawling. She told him she thought if she had sex with me, it would help her career in the bank, but that she'd changed her mind and I'd raped her. He talked some sense into her. He told her he'd seen her flirting with me, how everybody had seen her follow me upstairs – how much danger her job could be in. She threatened me because I rejected her, Julie.'

'Which colleague?'

'What?'

'Who did she run into?

'Oh. Richard.'

'It's always Richard, isn't it, Harry? He's always there to smooth things over.'

His face hardened.

'He's my right-hand man, Julie. You know that. He's always there because he's always bloody there. It's not a set-up.'

I pursed my lips, unhappy.

'I want to be honest with you,' he said, and turned me around to face him. 'We're grown-ups. I know it must hurt to hear that I kissed another woman, even drunkenly, but please, believe me, that was it. If you told me you kissed another bloke, I'd want to punch his lights out but I wouldn't consider it cheating.'

'Right,' I said. 'I kissed Toby.'

'What?' His eyes grew dark, and he tightened his grip on my arm.

I laughed without feeling and shook my head.

'See how that felt, Harry? Of course I didn't kiss him. Are you still claiming I should be okay about this?'

'I'm not. I have to make it up to you. But you have to believe you're the only woman I've ever wanted. You're my family. You're all that matters. And I'll prove it. I'm going to tell you things that will make you understand just how much I trust you, baby. I will show you how much you mean to me.'

And then he told me everything about the bank. Afterwards, he pulled me into his chest and I felt the comforting familiarity of his body beneath his fleece top. I inhaled his smell, mixed with the outdoors.

I thought I was a good person. I saw the world in black and white when it came to morality. But the world Harry moved in was differing shades.

As far as Harry's business was concerned, that day he was completely and utterly honest with me.

In telling me, he made me cross the line with him. He made

real what I'd always suspected, what I'd been happy to be blissfully ignorant about.

In later years, when the ceiling came crashing in, the executives at my husband's bank and others would claim ignorance and stupidity to defend the actions that led to the financial crisis. But after billions were pumped into the banks by the State, with all that debt heaped on the taxpayers' shoulders, the public bayed for blood. That's when the Office of Corporate Law Enforcement decided to get involved and examine whether all the decisions made in the years leading up to the crash were as innocent as they seemed. Had the bankers been swept along by an acceptable and, at the time, legal tide of risky market ventures and overstretching? Or had they been criminally negligent in their businesses?

What Harry told me that day and in the years that followed meant I knew how calculated it had all been, the choices and the gambles that brought Harry's bank to ruin and eventually put the whole economy in peril.

Much of it was over my head. Subprime and falsifying capital reserves were things few people had heard about back then, but the gist wasn't lost on me.

Harry was playing a dangerous game, not just with our own finances but with those of many of our friends – his investors and bank shareholders – as well as his customers.

That's what I should have been worrying about.

Not whether he was cheating on me.

Harry trusted me with all that information.

I wonder, when he was on the floor being beaten while I looked on, did he regret placing his faith in me?

That Christmas, I drove to Helen's house on my own. I knocked on her door with two Dunnes Stores bags full of selection boxes and packets of jellies.

She opened the door, raised an eyebrow and put her hand on her hip.

'Think you can buy your way back into my good graces with a few sweets, do you?' she said.

'I've a voucher for a luxury spa weekend and a bottle of champers in the boot, but I thought I'd try these first,' I said. Then I started to cry.

'You daft mare,' she said, and pulled me into the house, wrapping her arms around me. She had tears in her own eyes. 'You know I can't stay angry at you. I was going to call up to Dublin at the weekend. Mam was coming too.'

'I'm sorry,' I sobbed. 'It was awful. Harry and I split up and I thought we were finished.' I felt her arms tense around me. 'We're okay now, but it's been so hard.'

She held me away from her and looked at me properly.

'Julie Ferguson. I swear, don't you ever do that again. I know you love that man and he's your husband, but we are your family. Do you understand? You tell us everything. What did he do? Was he with somebody else? Do I need to punch his lights out?'

I shook my head and gave her a watery smile.

'It was nothing,' I said. 'Just a silly thing. It's fixed now.'

Helen sucked in her cheeks and pursed her lips. She didn't believe me. But she wouldn't push it.

'Okay,' she said. 'That will do for me, pet. But Mam's in the kitchen, so we're going to have to come up with a story about a near-death experience in the next two minutes. All right?'

I nodded.

I was forgiven. I didn't even deserve it.

Tell them everything?

I couldn't even begin to tell them the half of it.

Part Three

Julie

Harry wasn't a perfect husband, and he sure wasn't a perfect businessman either.

During the boom years, he got lazy. Like everybody else, Harry assumed that everything could only get better. But as 2005 wound to a close, and after a series of problematic foreign investments, Harry was forced to take a step back and reassess. He began to look at the market in a way he hadn't since the early nineties, before he'd become complacent about success.

On the surface, everything looked great. HM Capital was making more money than ever and the annual dividend paid to its shareholders dwarfed those of all other banks. Property prices in Ireland would continue to rise for another two years and developers were still selling faster than they could build – overpriced, shoddy shoebox apartments and housing estates in the middle of nowhere. The Irish market was carrying all Harry's other business. Everything should have continued apace.

There were murmurs. The problem was, nobody was listening to them.

At home, some very prudent economists were saying Ireland was in an unprecedented property bubble and banks were over-leveraged. The government, greedy and bloated on property-related taxes, and the Central Bank and the financial regulator, bought and owned on the golf course by the banks' chief executives, had let things escalate out of control. It couldn't last.

Similar warnings were being whispered in the other countries where Harry had invested – Portugal, Italy, Spain, and further east, where the situation was particularly dire. There were more luxury apartments being built in former Soviet Bloc states than there were oligarchs to buy them. Harry and his pals had wrung the market dry.

While my husband was studying all this, I was studying full-time for my English Masters. I'd quit teaching. It no longer held the same appeal for me – neither the work, nor the people. I didn't take it up again until 2010, when we needed to look like we were just an ordinary couple.

Toby came to my leaving party. We'd avoided each other for months after the argument in my home. But he made the effort once he knew I was finishing up, and so did I. It was better to part on good terms.

'I guess we're all growing up,' Grace said. 'I can't handle mid-week drinking any more. Otherwise I'd miss you way more, Julie.'

We both laughed. It was a long time since we'd all been out together, but Grace was being kind, talking as though nothing had changed.

'You have a child,' Toby said. 'You're not supposed to be drinking in the middle of the week anyway. Leave that to the single people and the alcos.'

Grace had become a single mother, confiding in me one night that she couldn't even remember sleeping with the baby's dad, or his name for that matter.

'You don't need anybody,' I said. 'I can help.' And a little bit of me meant it, even if it never happened. It was too much, to be around somebody who'd got pregnant accidentally when I had all the jigsaw pieces and couldn't put the bloody thing together.

'I knew that husband of yours would make you quit altogether one day,' Anna said, voicing what everybody else at my table thought but no longer cared to say, not those days.

'Oh, Anna,' I said, too tired and too close to never seeing her again to have a fight. 'I'll miss your inability to keep an opinion in your head. Come here and give me a hug.'

She did, and it was the last time I saw her. Grace told me a couple of years later that she'd moved to New Zealand.

There had been another reason for me packing in teaching.

I started finally considering IVF. Time was against me and my hope of conceiving naturally. I was in my thirties and starting to worry. IVF would take a toll on my body that I didn't want to have to endure while trying to act normally in work at the same time.

I was optimistic it would work. The clinic doctor told us we were both healthy and it was just a fact that sometimes couples couldn't conceive on their own. With a little help, we might get there. We were sent off to think about it for a couple of weeks, and I'd more or less decided to go for it. Harry didn't need to think; he was raring to go.

Life, in general, was good.

But there was one cloud I couldn't shake.

I rarely thought about the rape allegations, so convinced was I that Harry was telling the truth. But sometimes, late at night, when I was alone, I wondered. When it was very dark and the world was very quiet . . . that's when the doubts crept in.

Harry had never forced me, but then he'd never had to. I never resisted. What would have happened if I had? At times, it felt like my husband needed sex like other people needed oxygen. Especially when he was stressed.

That's when I would worry the most that he was cheating on me – when we'd make love for hours and he would still seem unsatisfied and the next day he'd have to go to a 'work conference', or something else that had sprung up unexpectedly.

These thoughts crept into my mind every so often, but they weren't enough to upset the applecart.

I decided to tell Harry that I wanted to press ahead with IVF after the bank's annual 'board and partners' away dinner. The event was held at the beginning of each year and brought together all the senior executives and the board members, along with their wives (a couple of husbands, but mainly wives) for an overnight jolly. The dinner was to thank long-suffering spouses and act as a team-building exercise all in one. When the evening drew to a close, I would surprise Harry with the news and we could continue the celebrations.

I thought I'd experienced money. When Harry booked our wedding in France. When he brought me to Capri. The gifts he would shower me with.

But those away dinners! They made Louis XIV's extravagance look like a riverside picnic.

That year, the bank had booked a whole floor of a five-star hotel overlooking Lough Derg. The building was a converted former castle and, out of curiosity, I looked up the price of rooms and dinner before we went. Harry's bank would pay an average of €1,000 for each room per night (our room – the suite – cost €3,000). The dinner – the castle ten-course tasting menu – cost €245 per person, before alcohol.

Twelve board members, twelve spouses, six senior executives, six spouses. It was coming in at just under €30,000 for one night, and that was before they started ordering the oldest and best bottles of wine and whiskey from the castle cellar.

The spending lunacy of the Celtic Tiger had well and truly peaked, and it never failed to catch my breath.

We flew down to the event in a private-hire helicopter. I felt the whole thing was completely over the top and told him so.

'You've all lost the run of yourselves,' I said, shaking my head, even as the pilot was fixing my earpiece. 'You're like the kids on the island in *Pinocchio*. It can only end badly, Harry.'

He laughed.

'If you see me sprout a tail tonight, just give me a kick up the ass. Next year, we'll climb Croagh Patrick barefoot. A pilgrimage to atone. I promise.'

I tutted, then grabbed his hand as the helicopter started to rise into the air.

I was really looking forward to the night. I'd been on a self-imposed drinking fast for a couple of weeks. I did that regularly those days, to convince myself I didn't have an alcohol problem. It didn't matter if I drank like a fish most of the time if I could just stop whenever I wanted. And now the latest period of abstinence was about to be broken with the finest champagne. I was going to party and enjoy myself like only a woman about to give up drink for nine months can.

Harry had something else on his mind, though. What I didn't realize, and he didn't tell me until it was too late, was that he had decided at that stage to step down as CEO of HM Capital. He was going to stay at the bank, but he knew trouble was brewing and didn't want to be in the driving seat when it did. He planned to take a traditionally more hands-off role – that of chair of the board – but mould it to fit the role he actually wanted to play, which was to more or less still in charge, just not in the firing line. He needed to appoint somebody as CEO who would look like a good fit but be malleable and not smell the manure he was being dropped in.

The annual dinner that year had a new purpose, and I was ignorant to it, caught up in my own plans.

I stayed in the suite that afternoon while Harry went off for a pre-dinner round of golf. The beauty salon had been booked out for the ladies, but I skipped the pampering and ordered a bottle of Krug to the room. I never could bear making small talk with those women – most of them vacuous gossips who had carefully fostered superior snobbishness on the back of their husbands' earnings. Harry was king in their world and yet I was still my own person, determined to further my education and improve myself.

It was spring, and a light white frost covered the castle grounds, giving them a magical quality. I was in a fabulous hotel room, about to slip into a to-die-for dress (Harry had bought me a midnight-blue Valentino lace number for the occasion), and a bottle of the most expensive champagne he could find was open on my dressing table.

The bracelet Harry had given me as a wedding present sat alongside a recently gifted pair of diamond-and-sapphire earrings.

I sprayed my wrists with Chanel No. 5, took a sip of the Krug and smiled at myself in the mirror.

I had everything. No, my husband wasn't perfect. But was there ever such a thing, as my mam once pointed out? Helen's husband, Barry, was the most boring man alive. My friends used to go on about stuffy bankers, but they hadn't a clue. I always thought Harry was *exciting*. I could never say I was bored with him.

When Harry came in to get showered before dinner, I was waiting for him on the bed, naked bar the jewellery.

'I like it,' he said, eyebrows arched. 'I'd pay more for that than a designer gown any day. Wait until the rest of the board see you.'

'Shut up and come over here,' I purred.

By the time we went downstairs, I was the cat who'd got the cream.

Harry, though, had only been able to relax for the short time we'd made love. Among his colleagues, he became a ball of tension again.

The evening began to sour.

I felt so close to him when we took the grand staircase down to the banquet room but, by the time we sat for dinner, he was already flirting with the woman sitting beside him, caressing her arm and whispering in her ear.

It's just flirting.

For some reason, that night, telling myself that had no effect. I wanted him to be with me. To focus on *me*.

Maybe it was because we'd just had sex. My skin still smelled of him and his of me.

Maybe it was because it was so public.

Our relationship was on display, and all those bitchy wives were judging me, laughing at me.

But, most likely, it was because I was excited about telling him my decision about the IVF.

I had been positioned further down the table. The dinner was always organized so couples didn't sit together. We had to mingle. I made polite small talk with my neighbours. I sipped water. Every time I raised my wine glass to my lips, my throat felt like it was going to close up. The evening was ruined for me. All the while, I was watching Harry. I was waiting to get him on his own so I could tear strips off him. I watched the husband of the woman Harry was chatting up. He was pretending not to see what was happening under his nose. Everybody talked and laughed and acted like civilized adults, like nothing was happening at the top of the table, while Harry kept her entertained and she laughed like a fucking hyena.

The waiting staff cleared away plates of venison haunch and brought out trays of dark chocolate with amarena cherries. Harry excused himself. He didn't make eye contact with me once.

She left the room minutes later.

I had to get out of there. I left the table, a lump in my throat, just about holding the tears in. I headed for the castle gardens. I needed to breathe.

I walked among the low walls and neatly trimmed hedgerows, the cold, crisp air in my lungs. The sloping terrace led down to the lake and I drifted in that direction, sitting on a felled log by the water's edge, not caring what the bark did to my expensive gown.

I watched the waves lapping the shore, my chin cupped in my hands, and sighed.

An idea nudged itself into my head.

Was it worth it? Feeling this paranoid all the time? Suspecting Harry? He could have just gone out for a smoke and yet I immediately assumed the worst. Why? Why did I do that every time?

Because, in my gut, I knew.

I always knew. Somehow, deep down.

What kind of woman was I, to let him do that and stay with him?

I couldn't confront him, but neither could I keep pretending. That only left me one option.

Marriage in Ireland had long since stopped meaning marriage for life.

I would still be well off. I would finish my Masters. Then I could move back to Leitrim, be closer to my parents. I could get a house near Helen and see more of her children. I'd start teaching again.

I didn't have to do this any more. Maybe I could even get pregnant more easily with somebody else.

I would tell him it was over. Tonight. I'd pack a bag and go back to the house before him. Get my things and go home to my parents for a while until I sorted out an apartment in Dublin. Let him deny everything. I wouldn't listen. I was done. It would break my heart, but I had my pride to think of. Or what was left of it.

Would Harry even try to stop me?

I was so involved in these thoughts I didn't hear him approach.

'It's dull as fuck in there, isn't it?' Richard Hendricks sat down beside me, the log creaking under his massive weight.

He handed me a glass of champagne. I took it out of habit, but I didn't want it. I didn't want to cloud these thoughts that had arrived with absolute clarity.

'Your tipple of choice, my lady,' he said, smiling broadly.

When Harry had appointed Richard to the board of HM Capital a few years previously, I hadn't been able to understand why. Richard seemed to know everything about airlines and nothing about banks – but later I realized that my husband didn't want bankers on his board. He wanted soldiers, loyal to the cause of Harry McNamara. Richard became one of his chief lieutenants. A tiny part of me wondered if he had something on my husband. Why give him such an elevated position? Then, as I learned more about Harry, I knew I was right. Richard had seen everything. Estonia, Nina Carter, the dodgy business side. That's why Harry kept him close.

Richard had always been perfectly nice to me – maybe a little too nice. But I never let on that I was uncomfortable around him. I even felt sorry for him. His wife seemed obnoxious, and poor Richard was still as fat and ugly as the first day I'd met him, maybe more so. He was just an aging, probably unhappy, middle-aged man who admired an attractive young woman. Who could hold it against him?

'I noticed you'd left,' he said, as I continued to stare out at the lake, hoping my silence would speak loudly and he'd leave me be. 'You don't seem to be enjoying yourself tonight as much as usual.'

'Hmm.' I placed the champagne glass on the frozen ground. 'Has Harry come back yet?' My voice was bitter.

'You know Harry,' Richard said, his lip curled in a way that made my stomach turn. It was part of the job criteria, wasn't it? *Help me keep the missus in the dark. Don't let her know what I'm getting up to.* 'I'm sure he'll be back shortly. He's just off talking business. He never stops. Don't take it to heart.'

'Bastard,' I said. It just slipped out. I never, ever spoke about Harry to his friends. I barely spoke about our problems to my friends.

Richard placed a sweaty palm on my bare shoulder.

'He doesn't deserve you.'

I shifted on the log, feeling uncomfortable. I didn't want to have this conversation. If I started to talk about how I felt I wouldn't be able to stop, and a confidante of my husband's couldn't be my confessor too.

'You're shivering,' he said, and placed an arm around my shoulder. 'What were you thinking, coming out here without a coat, you silly thing?'

It was such a strange feeling, having another man's arm on me. I was so unused to it that I didn't immediately react. I didn't see it for what it was. And clearly he took that, and my utterance about my husband, to mean acceptance on my part.

At first, I thought he was just trying to kiss me. That he was about to declare his undying love or something, and offer to rescue me from Harry. Toby, mark 2.

But before I could fully process what was happening, Richard had pushed me back against the dead wood and was on top of me, his hand rammed up the inside of my dress, thumb prodding through the cotton triangle of my knickers. His breath smelled of garlic and whiskey; his fingers when they poked inside me were cold and unfamiliar.

He was so heavy, and I was so appalled and shocked, I couldn't react. I knew I had to; I could feel his erection pressing into my thigh and knew if I didn't scream or fight, he was going to rape me beside that lake and say my silence was consent.

'You're a filthy little bitch, aren't you?' he muttered into my ear, then licked my neck. I lay there, paralysed, violated, bile in my throat. 'You must be, married to that dirty dog.'

I gave a cry of terror and disgust, which manifested itself in one word.

'No!'

He grunted and tore my knickers down, even as my body began to resist, sending itself into survival mode while it waited for my brain to kick in.

It all happened so fast. He had my underwear around my thighs and was pulling at his belt.

I'd die if this man put himself inside me. I'd just die.

And then, weightlessness. Oxygen. Cold air. Harry.

He'd pulled Richard off and punched him, swinging hard as Richard, who had at least seven stone on Harry, fell to the ground and covered his head defensively.

I stood quickly and yanked my pants up, sheer panic throwing me into action while my heart beat like a racehorse's. I reacted to almost being raped like somebody who's tripped on the street and jumps up with a broken ankle, their only thought, *Did anybody see? Should I be embarrassed?*

What had Harry seen? Did he think I'd wanted Richard, that I'd met him for sex? I couldn't bear the idea that he would think I'd do that to him, with that fat old bastard of all people.

That was what was running through my head when my husband stood up and turned away from Richard, who lay bleeding and groaning on the ground. Harry had stopped himself from going any further, just a few punches, leaving Richard down but not out.

Harry spat and wiped his forehead with the back of his hand

I should have asked myself how he had found it so easy to stop, how it was that he didn't have to be pulled off Richard.

But I didn't think anything like that then because when Harry wrapped his arms around me and said 'Are you okay?' I felt like collapsing with relief.

'I'm okay,' I sobbed. 'The things he said, Harry. He said—'

'Shush. You're okay. It's okay.'

He stood back and looked me straight in the eye. His white shirt was splattered with blood and dirt, his face furious and determined.

'Do you want to ring the Guards?'

I blinked. Then I looked at Richard on the ground. *That's what we should do*, I thought. *Ring the Guards*. But what would I say? What bruises would I show them, when I'd just lain there and not fought and struggled, like you'd imagine any woman would? I'd said 'No' . . . At least I thought I had. I must have. Harry must have heard something to tell him I was resisting Richard's attack, even if it didn't look like I was.

Into the turmoil, Harry planted the seed.

'If you want to, Julie, we'll ring them. But if you're unsure, then we can sort this out ourselves. It's just . . .' He came close to my ear. 'He knows things. Richard knows things about me. There are better ways to punish him.'

'N-no,' I shivered, the adrenaline dissipating, leaving me shaking violently in its wake. 'I don't want the Guards. Just . . . sort it. Please, Harry, I just want to go back to the room. I need to have a shower. I n-need to wash him off me.'

He pulled me close.

'Go. Leave this to me. I'll be up to you shortly.'

I don't know what I thought Harry was going to do to Richard that night. I didn't care. I hoped he'd kill him.

And later, when he came back and took me in his arms, I cried with relief that he'd been there. He whispered into my ear and stroked my hair, promising me that he'd always protect me. All those thoughts I'd had earlier in the night about leaving dispersed like dust particles in the air.

When it really mattered, Harry had been there for me. He'd saved me. And in doing so, he'd saved himself.

Alice

'Are you still enjoying your little holiday here, JP? I'd say it's a laugh a minute, wha', between your one who thinks she's Princess Di reincarnated and that lad . . . what did he do when we came in, Sarge? Oh, yeah, he stuck his finger up his arse then asked you to smell it.' Alice smiled, and shook her head like it was the funniest thing she'd encountered in an age. 'Every time we come here it's crazier than the last. It could actually drive you nuts, being a guest, I'd say.'

JP stared at the table.

'They have problems,' he said quietly.

'We all have our problems, huh? You've had more than your fair share, we know that.'

JP had no reply this time, choosing instead to gaze at the white Formica table surface.

Alice studied the top of his head, the thick dark hair and furrowed forehead. He was so earnest looking for a man of thirty-two. Like he had the weight of the world on his shoulders. Every time she sat with him, she had the same thought. If you didn't know what he'd done, you would feel a natural sympathy for him – somebody who had been through so much as a child and had continued to get the rough end of the stick into adulthood.

And yet he had a self-containment and assuredness that said he was incredibly mature. He'd refused to have his solicitor present for any of these meetings – even though the woman had done wonders for him – stressing that he only wanted to tell the truth. It was either stupidity or arrogance.

But it was working. Alice had heard the whispers from the press and even some of her fellow Guards, ill-informed nuggets of stupidity that would soon be traded as facts . . . *if he keeps refusing legal aid, he must have nothing to hide*. Idiots.

'I was reading the report from your doctor again last night,' she said. 'You pretty much raised yourself, didn't you? That must have been tough. Especially with no other family. Seamie and Betty were terrible parents. Seamie in particular, by the sounds of it. You know he got arrested a few years before he died for beating a man half to death in a bar brawl? Like father, like son, huh? Did he ever hit you, JP? I suppose he did. Drunks can be nasty like that.'

Carney shrugged. He started to pick at the torn skin around his nails.

Beside Alice, Gallagher sighed. Moody's circular route to trying to provoke Carney was excruciating.

'Seamie was messed up,' JP said. 'I lost contact when I moved out. He hit me, yeah. But I got away.'

Gallagher felt his DS tense.

Alice leaned back in her chair, casting the sergeant a quick glance. She'd noticed something when Carney spoke. A tiny flex in his jaw, a little tic in the eye.

It was the first time Alice had any kind of inkling that there was anything at work beneath the preternatural calm Carney projected.

The family route seemed to provoke a reaction in their suspect that they weren't getting when they asked him about Harry McNamara.

'We found Betty,' she said, three little words that went off in the room like a bomb. 'It's interesting that you have her maiden name and not Seamie's surname. Though I guess he wasn't much of a father.'

JP looked up at her and Gallagher, eyes flashing from one to the other in shock.

He was like a child, Alice thought. An angry, bitter little boy, trapped in a man's body.

'W-where?' he stuttered.

'Sussex. She's still alive. She has a new family. Betty Carney, mother to Sarah and Clare. Two women, mid-twenties. I saw a picture. Gorgeous. Blondes. So unlike you. Maybe she never wanted a boy. Maybe she'd always wanted girls.'

The colour, what little there was, drained from Carney's face. He closed his eyes and hunched his shoulders, as though he couldn't sustain the blow of the words. Alice felt sympathy then. She felt it and dismissed it. She was projecting, thinking of her own circumstances as a child, the tall, tubby, plain-looking, quiet nerd in among a gaggle of handsome, sporty, loud brothers . . . how her mother used to look at her peculiarly, like the stork had gone off sat nav and dropped her in their house by accident. Alice had started comfort eating when she was six, already feeling too ugly for that family.

'Did you ever try to find Betty?' Alice said, giving herself a little shake.

'No.'

'Why?'

'It's not how it should be,' he said, voice low. 'A child shouldn't have to go looking for the mother who abandoned him. It was her coming to find us or nothing.'

'Us?'

'Seamie and me.'

'Hm. Yeah. I can see that. It looks like she just went on and had a great life, while you were left stuck with your dad.'

JP flinched.

'She had her reasons.'

How could he still love her? Alice wondered. She didn't love her own mother, and the woman had never been that bad. She'd never abandoned her.

'But still – to leave you?' she said. 'Her child? Sure, she probably had her reasons when she left. My colleagues say she was in and out of psychiatric institutions. Bipolar, apparently. But she got better. And instead of coming to get you, she went on to live the life of fucking Riley up the road with her new brood. She didn't even offer to come over to see you when our colleagues contacted her. Didn't want to know anything, or even speak to us.'

JP said nothing.

'That's very wrong, if you ask me,' Alice said. 'Isn't it, Sarge?'

Gallagher nodded.

'Disgraceful. I feel sorry for you, pal, if that's what you got landed with for folks. It would make anybody angry at the world.'

'Yeah,' Alice said. 'Especially when you see others who have it all, never having to cope with even a little bit of the shit you had growing up, and they don't even appreciate it. There you are – no childhood, forced to take care of yourself as the adults fall apart around you, even leaving school early. You were probably sliding down a bad road. And then – somehow – all credit to you JP, you straighten yourself out. After all the challenges put in front of you as a kid. Then, in the space of a year, your dad – your only family – dies, and you lose your job. You went through the mill and ended up on the shit heap again because the country has been ruined by bankers. It's the pits, isn't it, Sarge?'

'Absolutely,' Gallagher said. 'I mean, when you're watching the likes of that wanker McNamara on the telly, getting exonerated after what he got up to in his bank, and JP here is just trying to make an honest day's living. Talk about a tale of two worlds. I can see why that would make you angry. I took another pay cut last year, and between you and me, son, I'd like to fucking kill Harry McNamara for what he and his cronies did. So I'm with you, JP.'

'Me too.' Alice nodded. 'But is that really the only reason you did it, JP? Because McNamara is a rich, selfish fuck who has it all and gets away with everything when you never get anything for free?'

'I didn't know who he was,' JP said, the mantra so familiar. 'I keep telling you. It didn't matter to me who I was hitting. I barely knew it was a man. I just wanted to smash something.'

'Yeah, yeah.' Alice cast her eyes around the room, looking for inspiration. 'You see, the thing is, JP, I don't believe you. I don't believe you just wandered into that house and attacked the first person you saw. Why didn't you hit his wife? If you just wanted to lash out at somebody, how come you had the presence of mind to only attack him and not her? She was just sitting on the chair like a useless fucking lump, watching while you battered her husband, and that didn't irritate you? It irritates me and I wasn't even there.

I'd have smacked her just to get a reaction. But you didn't touch her.'

Carney flinched as Alice barked the words, his hands trembling on the table. Tears welled in his eyes and his jaw quivered. It was the performance of the century, Alice conceded. As it stood, they were better off not putting him in front of a jury. He'd have them convinced in minutes.

'And why that house? You had to walk through Dalkey village to get to the golf course. It was a Saturday night. There were people out drinking. You could have picked a fight with anyone. You could have gone into a pub and started a riot.'

She leaned across the table until her face was inches away from Carney's.

'I just don't believe you, JP. You're a liar.'

Carney backed further into his chair, his head hanging as she spat the words.

'I don't know,' he muttered. 'I don't know why I went to their house, but if you think I belong in prison instead of here, I'll say whatever you want me to.'

Alice clicked her tongue, sorely tempted to write out his confession for him. His words were right, but the tone was wrong. It was like he was playing at having emotions. It was utterly terrifying. She couldn't imagine this man weeping for anybody.

She leaned forward, bringing her face as close as possible to his without actually touching him.

'You did whisper in Harry's ear, JP, didn't you? Tell me, now – go on. What did you say?'

Carney met her eyes.

'I didn't,' he said. 'I told you already.'

Alice started to shake her head but then stopped when she realized he was still speaking.

'But if I had, I just would have said sorry.'

Gallagher's phone beeped and he pulled it out to read the message.

Alice didn't have time to formulate a new line of attack. The sergeant elbowed her and showed her the screen.

She glanced down at the text, her eyes widening as she read it.

Holy shit.

Now it had all blown up.

Julie

She's not difficult to find – the girl. I say 'girl', but eight years have passed since I first heard her name. She's a woman now.

It's more difficult to get out of the house without my self-appointed bodyguard, my dad.

'Really,' I say. 'I just want to pop into town and be normal for a while. Nobody will know who I am, Dad. I'll be back by tea and we can go to the hospital.'

He relents, his face still creased with worry. I'm starting to relax into his and my mother's company again. It's like being back at home. When I ran out of Leitrim in my rush to get to the big city, I don't think I knew just what I was leaving behind. My parents are both well into the winter of their lives. It's taken this for me to realize I want to see more of them; precious time is running out.

I've done my research. Luckily the girl is not married or, if she is, she's retained her maiden name. It would have been impossible to find her if she'd changed her surname. Nina Carter, the one who accused Harry of rape, works in the city centre, a senior accountant for a fashionable architecture firm. Thank God for Google.

When I arrive at the glossy set of offices on the quays, I feel myself wavering. I've been looking at this woman's profile picture all morning – it's like I know her – but can I actually approach her and have this conversation? And how? I'm stumped on that part too. If I just call in at Reception and ask to speak to her, will I even get past the first hurdle?

I sit on a bench near the Famine memorial sculpture while I decide what to do. I can't be thinking straight. In my quest to remain anonymous, I've dressed down in a pair of jeans and a black wool hoodie, large sunglasses to shield my eyes from the winter sun, my curls tucked in a bun. The building in front of me is upmarket and the people streaming in and out this lunchtime are stylishly cool. I'll stand out like a sore thumb if I go in.

While I'm rethinking my strategy, out she comes – Nina Carter, concentrating on her BlackBerry. She's carrying a cooler bag and only looks up to see if there's traffic coming, before crossing the road and walking to a bench a few up from mine.

It's definitely her. She's wearing a black trouser suit with a pale sweater underneath, a pink silk scarf knotted at her neck. The colour goes well with her olive skin and long brown hair. The frames on her glasses are so thin, they're barely there, but they still make her look smart.

A skinny brunette. Who'd have thought it?

The thing that really catches my eye about Nina Carter, though, is how young she looks. How young did she look when she claimed my husband raped her?

I can't believe it's her. Before I can talk myself out of it, I stand up and approach her. If I leave it any longer, somebody might join her and then the opportunity will be lost.

'Sorry to disturb your lunch,' I say. 'Can I sit here?'

She looks up from the tinfoil-wrapped sandwich in the cooler bag, her instant reaction a welcoming one. Her eyes flash discreetly to the empty benches to either side, but she doesn't suggest I sit on one of them. She just smiles and nods and moves up a little. I get the distinct impression she'd offer me one of her sandwiches if I said I was hungry.

It comes off her in waves. She's a nice person. Kind. She doesn't look like the sort of person who goes around falsely accusing men of disgusting acts. But I know better.

I sit there for a few minutes, trying to find the right words. If she'd seemed hostile or unfriendly, I might have found it easier. Now I feel off-balance. She'll be finished her lunch and back in her office if I leave it much longer. No doubt she rarely takes more than a few minutes. A home-made sandwich and some fresh air, before going back to her desk to earn a fortune.

'You're Nina, right?' I say.

She freezes in the act of chewing and her eyes widen. Her hands fall back towards her lap.

'Yes,' she says. She's still trying to be friendly but can't help the notes of suspicion and fear in her voice. 'Why do you want to know?'

'I'm Julie McNamara,' I say. It seems my incognito disguise is working exceptionally well, because she studies me intently when I tell her my name, her expression incredulous.

She finally realizes I'm telling the truth. Her jaw drops. For a moment, I think she's going to tell me she's sorry for my troubles. That she might say sorry for accusing Harry.

'What do you want?' she snaps.

'I . . . do you know what happened to Harry?' I'm taken aback by her sudden ferocity.

She wrinkles her nose.

'Yes. Couldn't have happened to a nicer man.'

Nina brushes imaginary crumbs from her lap, embarrassed at her own outburst. She's angry but well brought up and knows you shouldn't speak ill of the nearly dead.

I take a deep breath.

'You had a falling-out with my husband.'

She stares at me.

'"A falling-out"? Do you know what he did?'

'I know what you accused him of.'

Nina snorts. She zips up the cooler bag and rises to stand in front of me.

'And you believed him?'

'Of course I believed him. He's my husband.'

'Your husband lied to you. He raped me.'

Red heat fills my face and my eyes fall to her shoes, black high heels, office wear. She hasn't flinched. Her voice is calm but determined.

'He. Raped. Me.' She emphasizes each word, in case I didn't get it the first time.

'You say.' I look up at her. There is something so fierce in her face, something so resolute, I feel the ground start to give beneath me.

She blinks, slowly.

'Ah. Of course. The woman is always lying, isn't she? I mean, that's what we do. We just go around claiming men raped us.'

Tears prickle in my eyes. She's touched a nerve without realizing it. The memory of Richard pinning me against the fallen tree trunk fills my head.

'I . . . I'm sorry,' she says, when I don't speak. 'I can see you're in distress. But I don't want to talk to you. I can't see what good it will do. You believe your husband, and you're dealing with a lot at the moment. But I know what he did to me.' She wants to storm off but I can tell she's torn because she also wants to know why I've turned up. I seize on her hesitation.

'Please, I just want to talk to you for a couple of minutes,' I say. 'I'm desperate. Tell me what he did. I need to know.'

She doesn't move, but then she makes up her mind and sits down again.

'You don't want to know the gory details,' she says. 'Why would you? You're married to the man.' She paused. 'Or is it because he's dying? Do you want to know whether he's worth mourning or not? I can tell you, he's not.'

I bristle, but I don't react. I need to hear what she has to say.

'You claim he raped you,' I say. 'How did it happen? Did he grab you in work late one night? Force you?'

She swallows.

'It wasn't like that,' she said.

'No? He'd didn't drag you into a dark office? He didn't hit you? Leave you covered in bruises? Did you scream? Did you rush to the hospital and ring the police? I was nearly raped once. The man just attacked me, out of nowhere. I'd never so much as flirted with him. I froze. I didn't fight. But I remember it still hurt like hell, being pinned down and unable to breathe. I had little bruises up and down the length of my back from where he'd crushed me with his weight, scratches from his nails inside my thighs. You can talk to me; I know what it's like to be a victim.'

She gasps for breath and her eyes fill with tears.

'I . . . it wasn't like that . . . it was still rape. I went up to his hotel room.'

'Did you tell a man called JP Carney that Harry raped you?' I cut her off.

That's what I'm really here for.

I know Harry slept with Nina Carter. At some point, she decided in her head that was rape. She must have wanted revenge when nobody believed her little fantasy.

Is that why Carney attacked Harry? Does he know Nina?

I've surprised her.

'Who?' she says.

'JP Carney. He's the man who attacked my husband.'

Her head whips back.

She's a smart woman.

'That's why you found me? You think I've harboured a grudge against Harry all these years and found somebody to give him a hiding as punishment?'

I look out at the River Liffey and the large white gulls swooping along it.

'You stupid, stupid woman,' she says. 'Let me guess. Your husband told you I was some silly girl who threw herself at him and then cried rape when he turned me down – was that what he said? Those were the lines Richard Hendricks more or less used when he told me how they'd spin it. Did Harry tell you he paid me twenty thousand euro to keep his little secret? Did he tell you that?'

Twenty thousand euro? No. I had no idea.

I get up to leave. Suddenly I don't want to hear what she has to say. I want to run — far away from her. Far away from what I'm starting to suspect is the truth.

She pulls me back down and grabs my face, forcing me to look at her, sharp nails digging into my skin.

'Yes, I went up to your husband's room and kissed him, as you so obviously know. You want to know what happened next? He kissed me back and pulled me into the room. I took my clothes off, willingly. I knelt in front of him while he unzipped his flies, willingly. I got into his bed, willingly. And then I started crying, because that wasn't *me*. It was alcohol and the words of all my so-called friends in my ears. *Fuck Harry and you'll go far, Nina. He loves a brunette. You'll get a big promotion.* I started to cry and then I begged him to stop. He didn't. He should have stopped when I told him to — that was my right. He kept going until he was satisfied. And when he was finished, do you know what he did? While I was scrambling around the floor, ashamed and looking for my clothes, his semen leaking out of me, *he laughed*. He laughed and said: "Surely I'm not that bad? Nobody else has complained."'

Her voice is furiously indignant, but there are tears streaming down her face.

'I was twenty-one and stupid, but I didn't deserve that. I didn't deserve that arsehole Richard making me feel like a prostitute afterwards. I didn't deserve my doctor looking at me like I was some kind of slut when I asked for the morning-after pill. It took me years of counselling to get over it. Now, you tell me something. What kind of a woman stays with a man like that?'

I flinch. I shake my head and keep shaking it.

I can't believe her version. I won't believe it.

I know there was sex.

In 2007, Harry finally admitted that he'd been unfaithful. It was after something so horrendous happened that everything else paled by comparison.

He had to tell me the truth after *that* night.

I wanted no names. I wanted no details. I didn't ask him whether he'd cheated on me in Capri. I didn't ask whether he'd slept with that woman Lily who came to our New Year's Eve party. I didn't ask him about Nina Carter, or the girl in Tallinn, or the woman he left the dinner with the night Richard tried to rape me.

I didn't need to hear all the names, because I knew. All along I knew.

All I asked him was how many times and he said, 'Too many to count.'

I knew when I came here today that I would be sitting down with a woman who my husband had had sex with. Not been raped by. Sex. Consensual. Initiated by her.

It's not like what happened to me.

It's not, I tell myself, like a mantra.

And yet Richard's involvement in it makes me sick to my stomach.

My breaths are coming quick and short. I can feel my head filling with panic.

Coldly, and with far more calm than I feel, I speak. It's like I'm reading from a script, one I don't believe in.

'Harry never hurt me physically in our entire marriage. Never. You say you went up to his hotel room and offered him sex, that you . . . you got into his bed naked. Well, excuse me if I don't feel sorry for you for changing your mind. You knew he was married. I don't give a shit how young you were. You knew he had a wife.

You probably *met* me at bank events. And yet, for the sake of a promotion, you were happy to get on your back. You want me to feel for you, but you weren't exactly thinking about me then, were you? You tell me – what sort of a woman does that make you?'

Her eyes brim with fresh tears. She's angry now, and her grip tightens on my face even as I try to pull away.

'How dare you! It's not my job to make you feel better because your husband is dying. You can think what you like of me but you clearly know I wasn't the first or the last woman he screwed. How can you live with yourself, married to a man who uses women like they're pieces of meat? I'm glad he's in a coma. I'm glad you're upset about it because it means you're getting what you deserve too. You're a silly, dozy cow who deserves everything she gets. But no – I don't know any fucking JP Carney and I never told anybody bar my closest family what happened to me.'

She pushes me away and stands up, her head high, shoulders pushed back.

'Did you keep the money?' I ask.

'What?'

'The twenty thousand euro?'

Her face is unmoving, but I can see her eyes twitching frantically.

'I'll take that as yes,' I say. I want to hurt her as badly as she's hurt me. 'It's just, I wouldn't have been able to. If the man who attacked me had tried to give me money, I'd have set fire to it.'

'There's something wrong with you,' she says. 'You know what? I can see that you and that man are made for each other. I hope you burn in hell with him.'

She marches off.

I place my head between my knees and empty my guts on to the ground in front of me, again and again. When there's nothing left, I wipe my mouth and start to cry.

I've been a fool. I came here to try to establish a connection between Nina and JP Carney. There is none. She hates Harry, but she's moved on.

But what have I discovered instead?

That my husband is a rapist.

My husband is a rapist.

No matter how I try to twist it, to rationalize it – what he did to that girl . . . it makes me die inside.

After all this time, after everything that's happened.

It's the straw that breaks the camel's back.

If Harry comes back from this, I can't continue my marriage.

He can deal with all of this on his own.

I'm glad he's in that hospital bed. I'm fucking glad. And to think I was worried about him waking up and having to explain to him why I did nothing to help when he was being beaten.

Well, I don't want a second chance. We're finished.

My phone rings and I reach into my pocket for it. It's the hospital. I nearly laugh. Can you mind-read when you're in a coma? Does Harry know what I think of him?

Then they tell me.

JP

A tale of two worlds. That's what the sergeant said. Harry McNamara and me, one of us born with a silver spoon, the other – well.

I can see the tabloids loving that headline.

It's not that black and white. Everything was fine until Harry McNamara fucked things up.

By 2007, I'd made a great life for myself. I'd moved up the ranks to become a supervisor in the office equipment company. I still dreamt of getting into banking, but, for the moment, I was good where I was.

Charlie was about to graduate, and the hospital where she'd done most of her work experience was taking her on. It was a public hospital and she'd be working for the state but, as she kept pointing out, it was secure and came with a pension. I snorted when the words came out of her mouth.

'You sound like a spinster civil servant already,' I said. 'They'll have you doing twenty-four-hour shifts and you'll be coming out with about fifty pence a week.'

'At least I'll be working,' she retorted. 'I've read what they're saying. Did you not see that piece in the paper by that top economist fella? He says it's all going to collapse, and then who'll be laughing? Me, with my nice safe public-sector job.'

Man, did she call that right. And she loved nursing, so pay wasn't really an issue for her. She loved the company of the other girls in the job and talking with the patients, young and old. Most of all, she loved being needed.

I was still a bit of a loner. I kept my head down and did my job well, but I didn't really mix with my co-workers. I didn't have close friends, just my sister. I was a bit worried Charlie was slipping away from me. Already, her hours studying and nursing meant she was missing most of the week. I was so used to her easy company, it was hard to be without it.

'Fancy meeting up later and catching a film?' I asked over breakfast one morning. It was June, the sun was shining and the weekend was upon us.

'Oh, JP.' She laughed, but there was an edge to it. She'd been off for a few days, not herself. I thought she'd fallen out with a friend, but it was more.

'What?'

'You want to spend Friday night at the pictures with your sister? For the love of God, will you not get a girlfriend? I mean, I adore you and everything, but we're never going to expand our little family if you stay a monk.'

'I'm not a bloody monk, you cheeky mare.'

She raised an eyebrow.

I wasn't either. Plenty of girls fancied me, and the fact I didn't bother turned out to be a secret weapon in attracting them. I'd had plenty of one-night stands and the odd second date. I didn't go further. The girls my age were starting to have expectations. I couldn't imagine a long-term relationship because then I'd have to conceive of marriage and, terrifyingly, children. With Seamie and Betty as role models, that wasn't a road I planned to go down.

She frowned at me, stirring her cereal with the spoon, none of it making it to her mouth. There was definitely something on her mind.

'What about that girl in Payroll? The new one who started last week. The brunette. Ask her out. You said she's gorgeous.'

I blushed. The new girl was a looker.

'I knew it. Just make a move, will you?'

'Not this again. I'm only twenty-seven, Charlie, would you ever let up? Why are you so determined to marry me off?'

'You're an old twenty-seven, JP. Are you going to ask that girl out or not?'

'Maybe I will, maybe I won't. What are you doing tonight that you're so eager to get rid of me?'

'That, big bro, is my business.'

'So you can organize my life but I'm not allowed to know about yours?'

'Pretty much. Look, JP, one of these days we're going to go our separate ways. We can't keep living together, or we'll end up like one of those odd old pairs sharing a cottage down the country. Everybody will think we're having an incestuous relationship. I might have to move into digs at the hospital too, and I don't want to feel like I can't leave here.'

I nearly choked on the toast I was chewing.

'What the fuck?'

'Seriously. Live your life. I'm living mine. Sometimes you just have to move on. You need to stop crowding me. We're not kids any more – I don't need you coddling me all the time.'

She stood up angrily, scraping her chair off the floor. Seeing the look of hurt and puzzlement on my face, she hesitated.

'Sorry, JP. Don't mind me. I'm . . . tired.'

I didn't know then what the little episode had been about. Of course, it was nothing to do with me at all. She'd had a fight with a boyfriend. If I hadn't been so thick, I'd have figured it out. Instead, I felt pretty hard done by. I'd never looked for thanks for taking Charlie on, but I knew I'd made sacrifices. It was my job. She was my baby sister. To have it thrown at me like that – it was unfair.

In work that day, I sought out the new girl, Sandra.

I knew – I just knew – that Sandra was different. It wasn't just her looks. The girl was intelligent and carried herself in a way that told you she was worth something. I knew she was more than a one-night stand and it scared the life out of me. Other people are frightened of things like heights and spiders. I was frightened of falling in love.

'Do you fancy coming to the cinema later?'

I practically spat it out. I was better when women were coming on to me, not the other way round.

Her face lit up with a huge smile and she nodded.

'I would love to. I thought you'd never ask, John Paul.'

She gave me butterflies.

It was stocktake day and I didn't finish until 8 p.m. Sandra went home and got changed and came back in to meet me. We went straight into the city centre to have dinner first in a Chinese restaurant on O'Connell Street. I enjoyed it, enjoyed being with her. She was undemanding, funny, easy to be around. And I couldn't take my eyes off her. She was really gorgeous. Tall, long brown hair, big blue eyes. Like a model, and confident with it. She came in to meet me wearing a pair of jeans and a white silk blouse. She knew she'd look good in a black sack; she didn't need to put it all out there.

When I ordered a Coke instead of joining her on the wine, she asked me why I wasn't drinking.

'I'm not a fan of the stuff,' I said, feeling the familiar embarrassment. To be Irish was to drink. Charlie spent her life telling other revellers she wasn't pregnant or on antibiotics. When I said no, people just backed off.

Sandra studied me for a moment, then asked the waiter to scrap her order and bring her a Coke too.

'I only drink because I'm nervous, to be honest,' she said. 'I'm not a fan. It's a bloody scourge. It's nice to meet a man who doesn't think booze is the answer to all life's problems.'

We nearly missed the film, we enjoyed ourselves so much over the meal.

'I've had my eye on you,' she said, and blushed at her own directness.

'Have you?' I said. I was startled – I hadn't noticed.

'Oh, yeah. The whole strong, silent cowboy thing you have going on. I love it. The lads in the office spend their lives just talking shite. And they want you to talk shite back. There's only so many times I can change football-team allegiance and pretend to give a fuck.'

'I've absolutely no interest in football.'

'Glad to hear it.'

'Unless West Ham are playing.'

'Bollocks. Is that not a bit unusual for an Irish bloke? West Ham? Not Liverpool or Man U?'

'I grew up in East London.'

'I thought I detected a twang! So that's why I'm attracted to you. I've always had a thing for a wide boy.'

I groaned, and laughed.

Too perfect. She was just too bloody perfect.

We caught a late movie and settled into the dark and the action thriller.

I'd turned down the sound on my phone but hadn't turned it off, so I felt it buzz in my pocket when the first message came through.

It was from Charlie. She'd typed 'Haven't heard from you all day, are you annoyed at me? Sorry for earlier' and a sad face.

I put it back in my pocket.

A few minutes later it rang. I took it out again and saw her number flashing. I silenced the buzzing and was about to put it back in my pocket when a new message came in:

'Any chance of a lift home?'

'Is everything okay?' Sandra whispered. 'Do you need to be somewhere?'

'My sister,' I said. 'Looking for a lift.'

'I don't mind if you want to go. Really.'

I hesitated.

I could have left. I should have left. Saved myself from falling properly for Sandra.

Normally, I would have. I was always at Charlie's beck and call.

'No,' I said, decisively. 'She's a big girl. She'll find her own way home.'

I didn't want to leave Sandra. It was the first time I'd made a choice for me, and it felt good.

I didn't push it. I dropped her home like an absolute gentleman. All I tried for at the top of her road was a chaste kiss on the cheek, but she turned her mouth to mine at the last minute and our lips met. She was a soft, gentle kisser. No urgency, just generous and warm. It made me want to make love to her, proper like, not just a quick shag. I had a future with that girl.

She didn't want me to walk her to her house. She still lived with her mum and dad and didn't want the folks dragging me in for the third degree. It was only a couple of hundred metres down a well-lit road anyway.

I was so close to asking Sandra to come home with me, but it felt like a step too far, too soon. I'd have to introduce her to Charlie, and that was practically a marriage proposal as far as my sister would have been concerned. Turned out, the wagon wasn't even home.

I suppose the fact I was a little bit annoyed at Charlie for snapping at me that morning helped, but I think I would have ended up with Sandra anyway. Everything about that night had fate written all over it.

Julie

In eighteen years of a relationship, you have a lot of ups and downs and collect a lot of memories. Prior to meeting Nina Carter, if you'd asked me to balance the accounts, I would have told you that I'd had plenty of good times with Harry, for all the bad.

We laughed. We laughed a lot. Harry could be hilarious. We bounced off each other in just the right way. And we fit. We both enjoyed life. We wanted to live it with each other at the heart of it all. They say love at first sight is a myth, but we knew differently. That night, so many years ago, when he called out to me at that ball – that was it. The beginning of a deep, passionate, addictive love.

It was that love that made the things Harry did hurt so badly.

But our marriage was a fraud. Now I know what my husband was capable of.

I'm in absolute turmoil as I step into the plain black dress, place the black pillbox hat on top of my hair and prepare for Harry's funeral.

I have to go, of course. Even though I want to stay at home and pull the duvet over my head, just wait the day out.

I think if I could concentrate on one emotion, if I could just feel angry, then I could manage the next few hours. But I can't get a handle on what I'm feeling. I'm so confused.

For all that I hate my husband, I'm in shock that he's dead.

I want to feel that raw, violent rage that would overcome me when I suspected he'd been with another woman. That fury that made me want to kill him.

Instead, there's just numbness. And sorrow.

I'm not sad that the Harry I know the truth of is dead. I'm grieving for the Harry I thought he was. I'm grieving for myself and my marriage.

How did it go so wrong?

Yes, a little bit of me has always known that the problems in our marriage weren't all one-sided.

I remember the first and only time I fell pregnant, at the end of 2006. God knows – really, only He knows – how I became pregnant in that year, at precisely the same time I had upped my alcohol intake by about 100 per cent. We had been trying for ten years with not so much as a hint of a baby and there I was, up the duff, without even the expensive assistance of IVF.

And then, much less inexplicably, I miscarried.

Harry found me on the floor of our kitchen after discovering the bloody mess in our bed and bathroom. I was choking on sobs, drowning my sorrows with vodka straight from the bottle.

Harry wanted children more than me. He could have screamed at me and smashed that bottle in my face. I would have welcomed it, anything to stop the pain I felt, knowing I'd caused the loss, even if I hadn't realized I was pregnant at the time. But he didn't react with righteous anger. Instead, he fell to his knees and hugged me tightly.

'I'm so sorry, baby,' he said, crying hard.

And when I continued to drink like a fish, right up until *that* night, he still didn't lay the blame for the loss of our baby at my door.

Yes, I could point to Harry and say he was the reason I drank, but that would be far too simplistic, and a terrible cop-out on my part.

I could have left Harry. I chose to stay, and I chose to drink.

But how could a man who'd been that sympathetic, that caring, on the day I miscarried be the same man who could rape a young woman?

I knew my husband so well I could hear him in my head explaining away what happened, the blurred lines.

I was having sex with her, Julie, and she started crying out of nowhere. I was pissed out of my head. I'd no idea what the problem was. Maybe she'd a boyfriend or something and regretted it. I tried to cheer her up afterwards. I had to pay her so she'd go away. I was protecting us.

But Harry could justify anything to get what he wanted. He always had.

I slip on a piece of jewellery that I haven't worn in years. The sapphire bracelet. For so long, it reminded me of that horrible night in Lough Derg and that prick Richard. I want to wear it and feel that anger and pain. And yet, looking at it now, I'm suddenly walloped in the head with the memory of our wedding day. A happier time.

I pull it off my wrist in a panic, gasping as it clinks on to the dressing table, discarded.

The funeral will be huge. I knew that when I held his hand as he lay dying, the second bleed in his head the final blow. I didn't want to touch him, but there was some part of me that clicked into appropriate-behaviour mode, if only for the doctors' benefit. Or maybe I wanted, in those last couple of moments, to remember the good times and how much I had loved him.

The life ebbed from his body as soon as I agreed they could turn off the machines that had kept him breathing. Part of me wanted to keep the life support going, to avoid the oncoming spectacle. I knew it would entail having to deal with hundreds of people who called themselves our friends but really never knew the first thing about us.

My mother comes into the room and finds me sitting at the dressing table, unable to stand up. She walks me over to the end of the bed and sits beside me, placing her bony arm around my shoulders.

'I am so proud of how you're handling all of this, pet,' she says, her cheek against mine. 'Today is going to be tough, but you'll get through it. We will be standing beside you the whole time. You don't need to speak to anybody. It's only close family and friends allowed back here afterwards.'

She can always read my mind.

'You know, Mam, Harry really was a bloody bastard,' I say, and she squeezes my hand. 'And yet these bloody happy memories keep going around and around my head, like a tape stuck on loop. Do you remember our wedding day? When he lifted me over the threshold and everybody cheered? I was so happy. How come I'm thinking about that and not about all the times I wanted to kill him, all the times he hurt me?'

'Oh, Julie, love. I know Harry was no angel and that you had your troubles, but what else would you be thinking about on a day like this? What's done is done. What good would it do, to think about the bad? That sort of thing makes you bitter. Marriage is hard, but death is final. You need to remember all the happy times and let yourself and Harry be at peace with one another.'

I know this is why Mam came up and not Helen. My sister, given an opening, wouldn't be able to resist telling me Harry was a complete bloody wanker, I'm right to think so, and I should feel angry. They must have decided among themselves downstairs to send up the diplomatic corps.

'I don't want to remember all the happy times,' I sob. I might have wanted to before the meeting with Nina Carter. I could have forgiven everything in death. I could have held on to the image of him in the courtyard of Trinity College – that young man, so handsome, so full of fun and ambition.

Instead, every time I think of my husband now, I'll be thinking about how I was waiting for him to wake up so I could tell him we were finished – that I knew what he'd done to Nina Carter. I'll be imagining that scene she described, him pumping away on top of her as she cried her eyes out.

I want to spit on his coffin, not walk behind it.

'That detective is downstairs,' Mam says after a few minutes. 'She wants you to know she'll be at the funeral, but doesn't want the Garda presence to be obvious. It's not the day for it. Will you have a word with her before we go?'

'Sure,' I say, not really caring. Just for now, JP Carney is not to the fore in my mind.

DS Moody coming up the stairs is like the arrival of the T-Rex in *Jurassic Park*. The surface of the glass of water my mother has left on the dressing table starts to ripple as she stomps along the landing and bangs on my door like the Stasi police have arrived to cart me off. And this is her in compassionate mode.

'Two sets of stairs,' she pants, coming in and plonking herself down on the bed beside me. I nearly take flight. She's such a welcome distraction with her unintentional hilarity, I feel like kissing her. She is real. She's what normal looks like, not the sick, twisted reality Harry and I had.

'No wonder you're such a skinny Minnie,' she says. 'I'm very sorry for your loss, Julie.'

It's a marvel how she can move between sentiments with such ease.

I shrug.

'He was already gone. I thought he was dead, that night. When they said he'd survived, I knew it was only a matter of time. Nobody can come through that and live to tell the tale.'

I shudder.

She sighs.

'I suppose you're right. This does change things, though.'

'What do you mean?'

'Well, we've moved from attempted manslaughter to either actual manslaughter or murder. It puts pressure on my bosses. Now's the time, Julie. If there's anything of relevance that you haven't told me about Harry, you should tell me now. He's dead. There's no point in trying to hide anything any more, if there ever was. Look, I'm not having a go.'

She never ceases to surprise me. Most coppers just wouldn't give a fuck at this stage, but she's still gnawing away, like a dog with a bone. She knows – she just knows – that Carney did this on purpose. And she knows I'm keeping something from her.

DS Moody doesn't let my silence put her off. She changes tack in the face of it.

'Julie, I realize today is a very sad day for you. But I think we both agree that we want to catch Carney out. I need you to do something for me at the funeral.'

'I'm just not sure it's important any more.' I sigh. 'Why does it matter if he did it on purpose or not? Harry is dead, either way. He's dead.'

'I know that, chicken,' she says, and her voice is softer than I've heard it before. She's full of sympathy I don't deserve.

'And I know that right now it's very hard to think of anything other than burying the man you loved. But in a few days, in a few weeks, your thoughts are going to turn back to JP Carney and you are going to feel angry again. He stole your husband from you. And you'll want him to pay. You'll want proper justice, not whatever charade he's set up for himself. Why did he do this? Why did he hand himself in? What's the point of it all?'

I swallow.

'Well, what do you want me to do?' I snap irritably. It's like the shoe is on the other foot. She needs to see Carney caught out more than I do. 'Today of all days.'

She nods slowly, ashamed.

'Sometimes my job is not pleasant, Julie, but I only want to help you and get justice for Harry. I just want you to look at the people who turn up for the funeral. See how they act around you. If Carney was hired by one of your husband's former colleagues, one of two things will happen. The person who ordered his death will stay away from the church and that absence will be notable. Or they'll attend, but they'll act off. You know these people better than we do. Look for anybody behaving strangely or out of character, or somebody turning up you wouldn't expect. Do you think you could do that for me?'

I nod half-heartedly.

I'd laugh if it wasn't so bloody tragic.

JP

I'm not sure, as the one who remains, if you ever get over the shock of death. No matter how it comes. Not the long-drawn-out-cancer goodbye. Not the sudden exit – here one minute, gone the next. Knowing you have to live with grief, that there is nothing you can do to change what has happened, is just unbelievable.

You will never see that person again.

The loss and emptiness is permanent. You have no control over it. You can shut your eyes and cover your ears and, when you open them, you will still be there and that person will still be gone.

You have to experience it to understand it. Nobody can tell you what it will feel like to lose somebody close. Nobody can do it justice.

Thump, thump, thump.

The Guards have a special knock. Some bloke told me that once, when I was dealing. They train them in knocking, he said. It doesn't matter what news they're bringing, they'll hammer down the door until they get an answer. Big thick culchie fucks, he'd added.

I jumped out of my bed that morning, thoughts of Sandra in my head and at the same time knowing it was the police at the door. I'd an awful feeling one of my old jobs had come back to haunt me. I pulled on tracksuit bottoms and a T-shirt, determined to get to the door before Charlie did. I hadn't quite woken up. I was on automatic.

There were two officers, male and female.

'Are you John Paul Andrews?' the woman asked.

'Yes. I mean, it's Carney now; I dropped the Andrews, but yeah . . . Sorry, what's this about?'

They took off their caps.

It was that one simple act.

I knew.

Even then, with the realization that this wasn't some overdue arrest, that they were the bearers of bad news, what was running through my head? *Seamie*. That's what I thought. The stupid drunk bastard had finally killed himself or been killed.

But it would be years before that knock came.

'You know Charlene Andrews, date of birth the fifth of May 1986?'

'Yeah, I'm her brother.' I said.

'May we come in?'

I stood aside for them at the door, mute.

They sat at the kitchen table and asked me to join them.

I refused, preferring to stand, thinking I could prevent the inevitable if I didn't follow protocol.

'Charlene had you listed as her next of kin on the back of her ID,' the woman Guard said.

Had.

I put my hands over my face. It felt like I was having an out-of-body experience.

'Look, we have bad news, I'm afraid. Charlene was involved in an accident last night. We believe she was hit by a car while walking on the Malahide Road just before 2 a.m. She was unresponsive at the scene. The paramedics took her to Beaumont Hospital, where she was pronounced dead at 4 a.m. this morning. We're so very sorry for your loss.'

No, no, no, no, no, no, no.

I fell back against the counter and sank to the floor.

She knelt beside me, placed her arm around my shoulders.

'Is there anybody we can call? Your parents? A friend?'

'There's nobody,' I choked. 'There was just us.'

She glanced at the other Guard, the two of them shaking their heads sadly.

'Where is she?' I asked. 'I need to see her.' Then, a thought. A glimmer. 'Are you sure it's her? What if somebody else had taken her bag? Maybe somebody stole her bag?'

Yeah. That was it.

I hauled myself up and raced to Charlie's bedroom down the hall, throwing open the door.

The room was as empty as it had been when I went to bed last night. I had slept after dropping Sandra home, while ambulance men leaned over Charlie's body and tried to bring her back to life. I'd barely given my sister a second thought, so caught up was I in events in my own life.

'We need a member of the family to formally identify her,' the Guard said, having followed me into the hall, her face full of concern. 'But she had photo ID on her person, so we are certain it's her.'

'This can't be happening,' I said.

The officers talked me into getting dressed and getting into their car, me protesting the whole time that they'd got it wrong.

They brought me to the morgue and into a small white room with a cross at one end and a table in the middle, a sheet covering the shape of a body. Outside, they'd shown me the bag they'd found a few metres away from where they said Charlie had landed after the car hit her. The couple who found her had thought she'd collapsed drunk on the road and almost hadn't stopped. It was only when they'd slowed down and saw what looked like blood on her sweater that they pulled over.

The coroner showed me the clothes that had been cut from her body. Blue jeans and a pale wool sweater, soft, splattered with dirt and encrusted blood. I held the bag to my nose, thinking I could inhale the smell of my little sister.

All of her personal effects, wrapped up in plastic and marked 'Charlene Andrews, deceased. 8th June, 2007'.

In the room, they lowered the sheet from her head.

She didn't look dead. She didn't even look like she'd been harmed. The damage had been to her internal organs, and while her body was covered in bruises and cuts from the bang and the fall, none of that was apparent on her beautiful face.

I didn't believe it, yet I nodded, on autopilot.

'It's her,' I told the waiting assistant.

'Would you like some time with her?' he asked.

I did, because I thought she'd just sit up if we were alone in the room and tell me she was faking it, that everything was okay. Because I didn't trust the medical people or the police and I was sure they'd got it wrong. Because I wouldn't believe she was dead until I'd checked for a pulse myself and knew her heart had stopped beating.

The assistant pulled a chair over to the side of the table for me, and I sat. When he'd left, I reached under the blanket for Charlie's hand, so cold and small in mine. I squeezed it, but felt nothing back, only its lifelessness.

My little sister was dead. Hours before, she'd been alive. Now she was dead.

It was unreal. I kept waiting to come to, to awake from a nightmare. Except part of me knew I never would. That this had happened. That Charlie was gone.

'Charlie, do you remember,' I said, 'when we were little and you used to make me paint your nails and then do mine?' I stroked her skin, looking at the chipped pink nail varnish on her fingertips. 'I said I wouldn't because it would make me look gay and you said, "If you love me you'll do it, JP."'

I sobbed then, unable to see through the tears. Me, the hard man.

'I'm your big brother, Charlie. You know I'd do anything for you. Please, come back.'

I wanted to climb on to the bed and wrap her in my arms, just like I used to when we were kids. I wanted to protect her from all the bad in the world.

For so long it had been just the two of us. I couldn't imagine being without her.

They had to help me from the room.

I went through the whole gamut after that.

Shock. Denial. Devastation.

Confusion. Why had Charlie walked home alone that night and not waited for a cab or a lift? Had she been running from somebody or something?

Anger. She had put her safety at risk, taking a road that didn't even have a properly marked footpath, the police said. The driver had probably sped off in shock. The cops assumed he or she would hand themselves in when the realization of what they'd done sank in.

Fury. I had abandoned her that night. The one time I wasn't there for her, the worst had happened.

And loneliness. I felt so terribly alone in the world. I had nobody left. No siblings. No parents. No extended family. No close friends.

I picked a small church on the Coast Road for Charlie's funeral, near the graveyard where we would bury her. I thought there'd just be a handful of us. I'd had time to think it through – the normal three-day funeral ritual didn't apply in those circumstances. The cops wanted a post mortem and Charlie was held in the morgue for a week before she was released.

In that time, word had spread through her college and wider circle.

The church was packed to capacity, and the line of people coming up to shake my hand at the end seemed to go on and on. I was impatient, monosyllabic. I just wanted to get out of there, get her buried and go home.

For the first time in my life I felt myself longing for drink — anything that could send me into oblivion.

But then I realized that the numbers at her funeral meant something so special, it was worth enduring.

Charlie was loved. She was so loved.

Some of her best friends I knew. But with them were their families — all of them had met Charlie and brought her into their hearts. The rest of her nursing class came, her lecturers and tutors. One man nearly broke down as he shook my hand.

'She was amazing,' he sobbed. 'I'm so sorry.'

A colleague had to take his arm and move him so I could continue with the endless handshakes.

People returned to their seats and waited for me to lead the funeral cortege from the church. I stood up, almost crippled by the weight of grief. Five boys, her friends from college, joined me in hoisting her coffin on to our shoulders and carrying her for the last time.

Charlie had lived for such a short time. She'd had a horrible start, but she'd loved her life and she had been happy. Despite Betty and Seamie.

Just before we exited the church, I saw him.

I almost didn't. My head was bowed as we walked down the aisle, but at the bottom I looked up at the mourners who'd come to say goodbye to Charlie and hadn't even been able to get a seat for the Mass.

He caught my eye because something about his suit made me think he hadn't been in the line at the top of the church. Charlie's friends were all of a type, mainly students, and, while dressed in their best today, none of them had the money for what he wore.

I looked at his face, lowered as her coffin passed, his hands clasped in prayer, watch visible just under the suit. A Bulgari.

His eyes were red and puffy. He'd been crying.

It was *him*. The man I'd seen in HM Capital. What was he doing at Charlie's funeral?

Julie

I walk up the centre aisle behind the coffin, flanked by my mam and Helen. Harry is being carried by my dad and my brothers. The only family he had and, really, they're only doing it for me.

All I can concentrate on right now is putting one foot in front of the other. Getting up to the top of the church and into my seat. This must be what PTSD feels like. Everything that's happened over the last few weeks, over a lifetime with Harry, it's all come to this. Is it really happening? Is he really gone?

I can't believe the suddenness of it. The finality. Even with all those days he lay in that hospital bed.

The offertory table in the middle of the church catches my eye. We've left out Harry's boxing gloves, an Ireland rugby shirt and his most-read novel, the well-thumbed copy of *The Count of Monte Cristo*.

The sight of his favourite things brings a lump to my throat and I hang my head.

I hate you, Harry, I say to myself. *I hate you for ruining everything. What memories have you left me with?*

It's a large funeral, as I thought it would be. I know there are a few people here who've come because they are well-mannered, kind-hearted people. They're here to say a respectful goodbye.

But the rest of them are here out of either nosiness or nastiness.

At the end of the Mass they form a line and come up, one by one, to shake the hand of Harry's widow. His stepmother, despite the invite, hasn't bothered to come. Just as well. I can imagine Harry sitting up in the coffin and telling her to fuck off out of the church, miserable, hypochondriac bitch. Then she'd tell everybody she had some mad illness, just to prove she was actually sicker than dead Harry.

I almost smile. There are so many things only we talked about, little jokes only he would understand. In the last few years we'd started to settle into a nice middle-aged relationship that I hadn't even appreciated. We knew each other, our ways and thoughts. There was a relief to it, after all the drama.

Is that why I never pushed for the full truth about the women he'd slept with? Was it because we'd had to deal with so much pain I couldn't bear any more? There must be some logical reason for me not getting to the bottom of what had happened with the Carter girl. I knew Harry always got what he wanted. Why was I so quick to assume his innocence – every time?

And there's that little voice again.

You loved him.

That was my crime, for so long.

I take each proffered hand, making sure to make eye contact with the person in front of me, while my head spins with what ifs.

Harry lived for weeks after Carney's assault. But he never came back. I can't even remember the last words we exchanged. Was it something to do with the remote control? Had I asked him to make me tea?

No. I remember.

We were watching the crime drama and Harry said, 'I think he did it,' pointing at some character on the screen. I shushed him.

I shushed him.

I close my eyes, until Mam nudges me softly and practically lifts my hand to greet the next in line.

There's nobody I wouldn't expect among these fellow mourners.

Those who Harry really sold out in the bank, acolytes of Richard's and other board members, haven't come. Alice is right. I would have noticed, even unconsciously, if any of them had turned up.

Some of the people who lost badly in Harry's investments are here. But I know these men and women. They're decent. I can see it in their faces – the confusion over whether they made the right choice to come along and then their resolve when they see me, the woman left to deal with the fallout. There's no bitterness there, not towards me, anyway.

Not one of them would have wished Harry in that box just a few feet away from us, even if they had cause to.

The line is reaching a conclusion.

That's when I see her and my blood starts to boil.

Those bloody teeth.

Lily. The woman who came to our house that New Year's night so many moons ago. The woman he no doubt screwed while I was entertaining our guests.

She's like a gift from God. Seeing her, I'm no longer a mess of emotion, hating my husband one minute, wishing he was still alive because I miss him so much the next.

I feel only one thing in Lily's presence. Fury at what Harry put me through.

She arrives in front of me. Lily hasn't aged as well as me. She's put on weight and her skinny frame can't hold it. Her mouth and eyes are puckered at the sides. Her hair is scraped into a messy ponytail, her make-up barely there. She looks exhausted.

Why has she come?

I sit up, feeling more alert than I have in a long time.

'I'm sorry for your loss,' she says. I take her hand like she's just any other person in the queue but hold it tight. Too tight.

She tries to free herself, but my grip is firm and I pull her down towards me.

'Why are you here?' I whisper when she's close enough for those around not to hear.

She turns her face to mine and I get a waft of Chanel No. 5. My favourite perfume.

'I was in love with Harry,' she says.

And I can see in her mean little eyes that it's the truth.

I drop her hand like I've been scalded.

It had just been sex, that's what Harry had said. He'd never mentioned love.

Even from beyond the grave, he can hurt me.

My mother, sensing something is up, leans across.

'Hello, I'm Harry's mother-in-law. Will you be coming on to the graveyard?'

Lily straightens.

'No, I'm sorry. I have my son with me. He's outside. I must get going.'

My gut twists. I suspect something so terrible I can barely breathe.

'How old is he?' I ask.

She looks at me, unwavering, and I see a little fire in her eyes.

I wait for it, bracing myself. *Don't say eleven!* I scream in my head. *Please, don't say eleven.*

'He's one,' she says, and the fire dies. 'My husband is with him. I'd better go. Sorry, again.'

She moves on, and I feel like a tyre that has just had a valve opened, the air hissing out of my lungs in relief.

The handshakes finish and the priest completes the blessing. The rest of the day is a blur.

Later I lie alone in bed, calm after Mam consented to me taking a Valium (I've never had a problem with prescription drugs; Mam just thinks, because I drank, I must have abused all substances). I think about Lily coming and then wonder how many other women there were in that church who'd slept with Harry.

Women were always his Achilles' heel.

JP Carney must have known one of them.

It must be her, the one from *that* night, the one I've been avoiding thinking about.

The answer to what Carney did must lie there.

JP

The Guards told me it was natural that I would try to find meaning in Charlie's death. To look for answers where there were none. They didn't understand. I knew there had to be more to it.

In the first instance, how the hell did Harry McNamara (I looked him up and found out his name the day she was buried) know of Charlie's existence, let alone know her well enough to turn up at her funeral? I'd serviced office equipment at his bank. We'd never exchanged a word.

My mind went into overdrive.

Charlie was private when it came to her love life. I figured she didn't bring boyfriends around for fear of me scaring them off, intentionally and unintentionally. I was prickly and protective, the worst type of big brother.

But now I wondered if she'd had one boyfriend in particular and if she'd been keeping him secret because she knew I'd disapprove. She worried so much what people thought, and Harry McNamara was a married man. The only reason he'd be interested in somebody like Charlie would be for sex. She was smart enough to know that's what people would think and what I, for one, would probably point out.

What else had I not known? If she'd been keeping that big a secret, then perhaps there were more.

The driver who'd killed her still hadn't come forward, and the police considered that strange. The Guard who'd broken the news told me a week after Charlie's funeral that they would be appealing to the public for information.

'Normally, in a situation where the crash was an accident, the driver hands himself in quite soon after,' she said. 'It takes them a few days to deal with their own shock but when they finally realize what they've done they come clean. Very few people can live with the guilt. It's unusual for it to go this long.'

'Unusual why?' I asked.

She shrugged, as if she had no answer.

'Hold on,' I said. 'Do you think Charlie could have been knocked down on purpose? Are you even sure that she was knocked down? What if somebody hurt her and then just . . . just dumped her body?'

The Guard shook her head adamantly.

'That's what the post mortem was for,' she explained. 'The injuries Charlie sustained were compatible with being hit by a fast-moving vehicle.'

'But . . . could somebody have hit her on purpose?'

She shook her head again, but there was slightly less vehemence in this one.

'The stretch of road where she was hit – it's badly lit. There are no paths. It's more likely somebody was driving home and came upon her without even realizing. Maybe she stepped out on to the road to thumb a lift.'

'So why did you say it's unusual nobody has come forward?'

'Don't you worry, John Paul. There wasn't anybody in Charlie's life who wanted to hurt her. We've looked. She was a well-liked girl. And you don't think anybody was out to get at you, who then might have targeted your sister. So it had to have been an accident. We'll find whoever did it. It's very rare for somebody to get away with a hit-and-run. It's hard to hide the evidence when it involves a great big bloody car.'

As terrible as it sounds, the notion that Charlie had been killed deliberately was almost easier to grasp than what they said was the truth – that she'd died as the result of an accident – an arbitrary, random tragedy that could have happened to anybody. There had to be more to it.

But if somebody had driven into her on purpose, they would have had to know that she was on that road at that time, and alone.

Charlie's phone had smashed when her bag landed on the road, but the SIM card was retrievable. I put it in my phone to find her friends' numbers. Those jotted down, I scrolled through the contacts list to see if she had a 'Harry' there, or somebody I didn't recognize. There were lots of blokes' names, but none that began with H. It didn't mean anything. She might have had data saved on the actual phone and not the SIM card.

I went into the messages box and read through the few she'd saved. It took me a while to get past the first name in the folder, my own. Instead of John Paul, she'd saved me as J Pee-Pee Head – a term of affection, believe it or not, from when we were kids. The messages she'd sent me the night she died were there, asking me was I still angry and then for a lift. The crushing feeling I'd had in my chest ever since tightened as I re-read them.

If only, if only, if only.

I hadn't been back to work since and knew I couldn't go in there again. I couldn't see Sandra again. She'd tried to talk to me at the funeral, but the second she uttered the words 'You couldn't have known', I had to walk away. The poor girl didn't deserve it, but I knew that if she stayed in my life, every time I looked at her I would be reminded. I'd chosen to be with Sandra rather than answer my sister's call. I was all Charlie had in the world and I'd ignored her.

I shut my eyes to block out the sight of her last messages and then opened them again. I wanted to feel guilty. It was better than feeling despairing and hopeless.

There were other messages – very few, considering how often she was on her phone. Their content was what you'd expect. Organizing lunch dates, discussing outfits for parties, complaining about night shifts at the hospital.

Ten messages in total on a phone with a storage capacity for many more.

Had she been deleting texts?

I went into the trash folder on a whim and found an exchange buried there.

It was to her friend, Hazel.

C – You're right, I should put my foot down and stop letting him call the shots.

H – I sort of meant you should put your foot down & tell him to feck off. You're worth more.

C – I know hon. I wouldn't bother if I didn't love him & I know he loves me.

H – Ah, sorry. No lectures from me babe. Look at the fecking trail of destruction behind me last month. 3x1-night stands and pretty sure I have an STD.

C – Dirty bitch!!!

H – I'm messing. Delete that in case somebody sees it.

That was it.

My sister had been in love. I hadn't even known.

I searched her photos folder, but it was even more fruitless. There were a couple of the two of us that I hadn't seen before. They were the only ones she was in, really. She wasn't a bit vain. No selfies, like you'd find on most girls' phones.

In fact, I had very few photos of her. When you spend more or less every day of your life with somebody, you don't really need to take pictures.

I used this as a reason to ring Hazel. I rang and asked her would she drop over any photos she had of Charlie, so I could get copies.

She came over that night. She'd gone around my sister's friends and collected a bulky envelope of photographs.

'Thanks for doing this,' I said, welcoming her in. It was pissing rain outside and she was dripping wet, her dark hair stuck to her face. 'Shit. You should have called. I didn't realize it was so bad out – I'd have come to you.'

She shook her head and pulled the envelope from her bag.

'Don't be silly. It's our job to rally round you, not the other way around. Thank God they're dry. I was worried. This bag is new; I didn't know if it would keep the rain out. I must have looked like a right nut-job pelting down the road from the bus, trying to protect my bag and not my head.'

'I'll make you tea,' I said. 'If you don't mind staying for a while?'

'God, of course I don't. I meant to say to you before, John Paul, any time you want me to pop round, or if you need anything at all – you just have to ask.'

I got her a towel and hung her wet coat on the back of the chair while she sat on the sofa.

'Shit, we've no milk.'

'Black is fine,' she said, blowing her nose noisily into a Kleenex. 'Or green, if you have it.'

I was about to say I didn't drink green tea when I remembered that Charlie had bought a packet recently. I'd taken the piss out of her, telling her it would be quinoa and birdseeds next.

'You do that Neanderthal act really well,' she'd retorted, dipping the tea bag in and out. 'When you die, I'm going to have JP "meat and two veg" Andrews inscribed on your tombstone.' She managed to swallow the tea without gagging, just to prove a point, even though I could see she wanted to spit it out.

'It's Carney now, Charlie,' I sighed. I'd legally changed it the year before but Charlie still refused to acknowledge I'd dropped Seamie's name in favour of our mother's. She didn't like us having separate surnames.

The box was still there. I wanted to keep them – the teabags. If I used them all up, I'd be getting rid of the stuff that she had brought into our home.

How bloody ridiculous was that? They were shagging tea bags. In any case, her room was exactly as she had left it and would remain that way. Full of her clothes and perfumes, the books she loved, the glow-in-the-dark stars she'd stuck to the ceiling when she was still a teenager, the Take That posters she'd never got round to taking down.

'I don't think I'll ever stop feeling guilty about that night,' Hazel said, and I froze at the counter. I kept my back turned to her and tried to keep my tone neutral.

'Oh,' I said. 'Why?'

'If I hadn't left her there,' she said, her voice thick with regret. 'But she told me to go. There was a bloke – he was nobody. Not important enough for . . . well, considering what happened. But I fancied him and it turned out he was a friend of the fella who owned the house, the one who was throwing the party. Charlie saw me making moon eyes at him and told me to go for it. I asked her how she'd get home and she—'

'She said she'd ring me,' I completed the sentence.

Hazel stared at the floor. Her hair was drying into frizzy ringlets. She took the cup, still not able to look up.

'It was an accident,' I said. That was for her benefit. I knew my guilt was warranted. Hazel was a young girl who'd gone off with a fella. She shouldn't have to carry the weight of it. After all, Charlie didn't even drink. She knew how to mind herself and, in any event, her brother was always looking out for her.

'Tell me about that night.'

Hazel sat back, her hands warming on the mug of tea, and began to talk.

'She was knackered,' Hazel said. 'Most of us had finished working in the hospital so we could cram for the finals, but Charlie let them give her a few more shifts. I told her she had to get better at saying no, but you know what she was like. Anyway, the night out had been planned a while and she'd said she'd be there, so she came. None of us would have minded if she'd cried off.'

'Who was at the party?' I asked.

But Hazel had been drinking and only had vague recollections. She threw out some names but then just shrugged.

'Everybody, really.'

'Did Charlie have a boyfriend?' I asked, cutting to the quick.

Hazel stopped mid-sup, her mouth still open. Slowly, she closed it and started yanking down one of the ringlets in her hair, a nervous habit.

'No,' she said, glancing in the direction of Charlie's room.

It was like she thought the ghost of my sister was in there, watching her and warning, *Don't you fucking dare tell my brother I was seeing somebody!*

'Come on,' I said. 'She must have been seeing somebody. I know it doesn't matter any more, but I'm just interested in her life. She didn't tell me much. I . . . I know she thought I was possessive sometimes, but it was just because I loved her to bits. She was all I had.'

'I know that,' Hazel said, her face earnest. 'John Paul, your sister worshipped the ground you walked on. She had boyfriends, but she never thought any of them were good enough to meet you.'

'But there was one in particular,' I said, persisting, and trying to ignore Hazel's sympathy. If I let it in, I'd start to cry and that wasn't what her visit was about. 'Lately. Wasn't there? She was in love.'

Hazel sat back and sighed, relenting.

'You're right. I suppose it doesn't matter any more. Yeah. She was seeing somebody. It was rocky, but she seemed to have fallen hard for him. I never thought it would work out.'

'Was he there, the night of the party?' I asked.

She frowned.

'No. I don't remember everyone who was there, but he wouldn't have been at a student party.'

'Why?'

'He just – he was too old to be at something like that. He would have stood out like a sore thumb.'

'Why would that matter?' I asked.

She stared into the green tea.

'He was married, John Paul. That's what I mean when I say it wouldn't have worked. She thought it would, for a while, but I think she'd changed her mind. She was certainly cool about him the last time we spoke about it all.'

'Oh. Right.' My heart was pounding in my chest. A married man and my sister fixated on him. Had she been causing him hassle? Had she gone from being some plaything to a problem he had to dispose of?

'What's his name?'

She shrugged.

'Hazel, I'm not going to march around to his house to beat him up, if that's what you're worried about. Charlie is gone. What would be the point? I just want to know what her life was like these last few months. If she was happy.'

'It was somebody she shouldn't have been seeing. It's better to just let it go.'

It didn't matter. I knew who it was. I'd get it out of Hazel, but I didn't need her to tell me that Charlie had somehow ended up with Harry McNamara. It was the only plausible explanation as to why he'd been at her funeral.

Whether he did or didn't have a role in her death, he was some-body I wanted to speak to.

My sister was nobody's dirty little secret.

Alice

'See, the thing is, unless something fundamentally changes at a later date, this thing hasn't a snowball's chance of going to trial. Harry McNamara's death is incidental in that regard.'

Alice tried not to look sucker punched as the Director of Public Prosecutions laid out the facts as he saw them. He was a pompous man, prim and prudish, his shirt buttoned tight to his neck. He didn't like her, Alice could tell. Her or all women, she wasn't sure. But she'd a notion that if she was about six stone lighter, had a peroxide job and wore blouses that revealed her bra colour, he'd be a little bit more indulgent, whatever conservative persona he tried to put across. It was always the quiet ones.

Beside her, Gallagher bounced his knee up and down, impatient for the briefing to finish. The Carney episode was done. He wanted the best detective in the station on other cases. Tight resources meant they'd given it all the time it was going to get.

'JP Carney has been officially diagnosed as temporarily insane during the commission of a crime. His previous record of clinical depression — which you were unaware of — has contributed to the veracity of that conclusion. You have failed to establish any definitive link between the perpetrator and the victim that could have raised concerns. The suspect handed himself in, confessed to the crime and participated in all subsequent examinations, interviews and treatment. It's an open-and-shut case for the judge. I know it's quick but with a case this high profile, it was always going to move swiftly.'

Seeing the look of abject misery on Alice's face, the director unfolded his arms and spread his hands on the meeting table, trying to be conciliatory.

'I'm sorry if this comes as a disappointment to you, DS Moody. All I can tell you is that my office is inundated with open prosecution files and honestly, one that is wrapping itself up like this is no great loss to us. Harry McNamara was the victim of a terrible crime but ultimately, it would seem Carney had no motive for his murder and there was no premeditation. It was just damn bad luck that it was McNamara's house Carney happened upon. If any evidence to the contrary comes to light, then we can re-examine things. But surely, with all of the work you have on, you're happy to see this finalized? There's no need to get so upset, young lady.'

Alice turned to Gallagher, then back to the DPP, her face incredulous. Her mouth began to form the word.

'F—'

'Thank you, DS Moody, and thank you, Director,' Gallagher interjected. 'It was good of you to tell us in person.'

The man nodded and slapped his folder shut.

'Fucking twat.' The words exploded out of Alice's mouth when he was gone. 'Sometimes I wonder what bloody century I'm in. So that's it. Carney's going to walk.'

'He's not walking anywhere. He's going to be in the Central Mental Hospital for the foreseeable.'

'It's as good as walking. Aren't you a little suspicious that the DPP's office aren't pursuing this any further because Harry ran rings around the fraud squad and got away with that one? Doesn't it seem like they're in a bit of a rush to close up? It's only been a month. I know this is a high-profile case but, seriously, to close the file on Carney already just to look like you've got it solved? That stinks.'

'Jesus, Alice. Take off the tinfoil hat. Can't you let it go?'

'No, I bloody well can't! You've been to that hospital with me, Sarge. It's not exactly hard labour. And if he keeps being the model patient, he'll be released well before anything he'd have got for a prison term.'

Gallagher sighed. Alice had such a high solve rate that this case was demoralizing her far more than it would anybody else. He really didn't want it to affect other investigations he planned to send her way.

'Alice, you've exhausted every avenue on this, haven't you? You said so yourself. There doesn't seem to be any sphere in which the two could have met — am I right? And Carney has nothing on his record. Nobody in his family worked with McNamara or anything like that?'

She shook her head, despondent.

'Carney is the ultimate outsider,' she said. 'Doherty can't find any family bar the half-sisters in England that he didn't even know about. With the father dead and the mother not speaking to our English counterparts, I don't even know if Carney has shagging grandparents. He lives alone and there's no girlfriend or a best friend. His neighbours say there used to be a young one on the scene but she's long gone and they don't know him at all. It's apartments – everybody keeps to themselves. We had one or two of his old mates ring in just so they could be involved, and all they wanted to do was tell us he was a loner and a weirdo. But again, it takes time. People might be nervous about getting in touch. Not wanting to get involved. Eventually, they'll talk. We might get somebody who knew Carney properly coming forward.'

'What about through his work?' Gallagher was trying to be helpful, but even he felt he was reaching, and he hadn't spent the hours on this that Alice had. 'He was in office supplies, wasn't he? Could he have met McNamara through that?'

Alice scoffed.

'Harry McNamara didn't deal with that end of things. The company Carney worked for serviced virtually every business in Dublin city centre and quite possibly dealt with HM Capital, but it folded in 2010. The owner opened a new, similar but smaller venture, and Carney went back to work with him until that closed too. There are no files from before the first bankruptcy. And even if Carney went to HM Capital, say he did just bump into McNamara there, that doesn't give him a reason to kill him. He'd have to have had an ongoing interaction with him.'

'His other jobs?'

'Most of the places Carney worked in are either defunct or won't talk to the cops. I don't know – he could have met McNamara in a pub one night or fixed his car for him . . . but how am I supposed to find out if he did? He's either an unlikely assassin or a really bloody good one.'

'You seem to have looked under every rock, Alice. The wife has nothing more?'

'Sweet FA. She claimed she was telling me everything, but since the funeral she's clammed up. Most of Harry's background I got from that financial expert, anyway – the aunt of that girl who claimed he'd raped her. Nina Carter. I sense . . . ah, I don't know if my intuition is even working right any more.'

'No, tell me,' Gallagher said. He was being uncharacteristically kind, Alice thought. Indulgent rather than his usual smart-arse, dismissive self. She didn't like it. She preferred it when he was ribbing her.

'I could swear the wife's holding something back. I don't know if it's even relevant, but Harry was a more of a bastard than she'd have us believe.'

'So, what? She's protecting his honour, now he's dead?'

'I dunno. She definitely wants to know what Carney is up to. I believe that. So maybe she's decided that whatever she's holding back has nothing to do with the case.'

'That depression stuff – how come we didn't know Carney had been treated for it?'

'He didn't tell us. His solicitor and the doctors at the hospital have access to his medical file. We weren't aware of it until they presented the DPP with their case files. In record time. How can I be expected to match that pace with our lack of resources? You know legal aid threw themselves into this one. Working-class victim versus corrupt banker.'

'When did Carney have the depression?'

'In 2010, apparently. Handy, right? Two years later he's getting away with murder on the basis of temporary insanity with a history of mental illness.'

Gallagher stood up. He placed his hand awkwardly on Alice's shoulder.

'It looks like that's it then, DS Moody. Time to let it go.'

'Do you know what bothers me the most, Sarge?'

'What?'

'It's him not being found guilty of anything. He's getting the best of both worlds – admitting to killing McNamara but not being found guilty of it in a court of law. I don't know why he went after him and then handed himself in, but I do know there's a reason for it.

'It drives me mad that we'll never know what his motive was.'

JP

The café where I arranged to meet Harry McNamara a few weeks after Charlie's death was an out-of-the-way neutral venue in a village just outside Dublin.

I arrived early, wanting to watch him when he came in, to study his face for traces of guilt.

My imagination could have given Stephen King's a run for its money. Hazel had said that Charlie never went anywhere with the bloke because he couldn't be seen out with her, so I knew he hadn't been at the party she'd gone to that night. But was he the jealous type? Had it angered him, her cooling it off and going out without him? Had he gone after her? Maybe she'd rung him when she couldn't get me. He'd collected her, but she'd got out of his car after an argument, only for him to drive after her and hit her. Perhaps, when she told him she was no longer interested, he tried to force himself on her, then had to kill her so she wouldn't tell anybody.

That's the kind of mad stuff that filled my brain. I couldn't sleep for thinking about it.

Hazel hadn't a notion what was in my head when she agreed to set up the meeting. She refused to tell me who Charlie's fella was but instead said she would ask him if he would agree to meet me. He'd agreed.

I brooded over a coffee I hadn't touched, watching the minutes pass on my phone screen, going over and over what I would say.

My first question would be how had he met her. I couldn't imagine any situation in which the likes of this man would have encountered my sister. It had to have been an accidental meeting, and that tortured me – the thought that wherever she'd been that day or night, if she'd been somewhere different she might never have encountered him.

The wanker was late.

There were only two other customers in the café – a woman at a corner table eating a scone and a man who'd just come in and was ordering tea at the till.

I was so focused on the door that I didn't notice the man from the counter approach.

'John Paul?' he said.

I stared at him. He seemed familiar. I scanned my memories until I had it.

'I met you at the funeral, didn't I?' I said. 'You were one of Charlie's tutors?'

He nodded and sat down in front of me. He looked as bereft as he had that day in the church. *God*, I thought, *he wants to talk to me about Charlie*. I had neither the time nor the inclination to comfort a complete stranger about my sister's death.

'Sorry, I'm actually waiting for somebody,' I said, thick as two short planks.

He looked around, confused.

'Yes. I think you're waiting for me.'

It took a moment.

'You?' I said.

He nodded.

'You were having an affair with Charlie?' I had to say it to believe it.

'Yes.'

I sat back, stunned.

What?

I'd been so sure.

The man sitting across from me was harmless looking. A student-type – fair-haired, glasses, a beard covering what I suspected was a weak chin. He wasn't ugly. He wasn't anything, really. Non-descript. And he was married. What had Charlie seen in him? He was either very smart or very funny, because he wasn't a hunk and by the look of his well-worn denims and cheap suede jacket, he wasn't wealthy.

'I'm ashamed that I haven't contacted you myself before this,' he said. 'I didn't know what to—'

'Who are you?' I cut him off.

'What?' He looked up. 'I'm Chris. Chris Gaffney. I was . . . Charlie and I were . . . Shit. I'm making a hames of this.'

'How old are you?' The man could have been any age, an eternal student, somebody who lived in libraries.

'I'm thirty-four.'

'And you're married?'

He looked down, shamefaced.

'Yes.'

'What were you doing with my sister, then? Isn't there some sort of rule about teachers and students?'

'I wasn't her teacher. I convened her tutorial groups, but I'm a student too. I'm studying for my PhD in nursing. And Charlie was twenty-two.'

'Still too young for you to be messing around with.'

He flinched, then placed his elbows on the table and sank his head into his hands.

'It wasn't like that,' he said. 'You don't know the full story.'

'Let me guess. You're in a loveless marriage that you can't leave. Charlie understood you, and you, in turn, cared for her deeply.' I paused. 'Please. I could write the script.'

He shook his head.

'No. You couldn't. I loved my wife. I never intended what happened with Charlie to happen. And when it did, I resisted it. But in the end, I knew I'd found the love of my life. Charlie was the best person I'd ever met. I'd have thought that no matter what her age. I split up with my wife weeks ago. Just before your sister was killed. I'd moved out and everything. It wasn't fair to Niamh. I couldn't keep pretending I wasn't in love with somebody else. Charlie wasn't answering my calls – she was pissed off with me because I'd left it so long, and she was right to be. But I'd done it. And I never even got the chance to tell her. God, she meant the world to me.'

He started to cry.

I was still in a daze, unable to get my head around him not being Harry.

One thing was certain. The man in front of me was absolutely devastated by Charlie's death. Nobody could fake emotion like that.

I started to feel uncomfortable. I'd had one meeting all planned out in my head, and here I was in another, not knowing the point of it. And this bloke looked like he wanted to talk for hours.

'You didn't see her, then, the night she died?' I asked lamely.

'No. I tried to ring her, but she kept cutting the call short and then her phone was off. I'd have gone to the party with her – I'd have picked her up. I'm going mad thinking of all the what ifs.'

I believed him.

Despite myself, I felt a surge of sympathy for the man, but not enough to commiserate with him. He was older than Charlie and he'd held a position of power as her tutor. Charlie was a people pleaser, but she was also a kind girl. I couldn't believe that she would have tried to tempt a married man away from his wife. That didn't ring true for her. This chump must have chased her.

What kind of man studied for a PhD in nursing anyway?

We sat there for a few minutes, saying nothing.

'You really left your wife?' I said, breaking the silence.

'Yes.'

'And are you going to go back to her now?'

He looked appalled.

'Heavens, no. It's not an either/or situation. I'd fallen in love with Charlie. I still love Niamh, but not in the same way. I couldn't go back, even if she'd have me. I don't want to. Charlie told me once the most important thing she'd ever learned was that you had to leave the past behind to move on. She thought life was too precious not to live it to the fullest. She loved the bones of you, you know. She really would have wanted you to be happy, JP.' He hesitated. 'I know it's going to be very hard, but you should try to move on.'

I bit my lip so hard I could taste blood.

The use of 'JP' had thrown me. Only Charlie called me that.

She would have to be really close to somebody to refer to me that way. It stung.

And I couldn't be happy. I couldn't *move on*. All I'd been thinking about the night she died was myself. Now the only thought that filled my head was finding out what had happened to her, who'd done this to Charlie. To both of us.

I'd solved one puzzle – the man she'd been seeing. It wasn't who I'd thought though, which meant I was back to square one. There had to be a reason Harry McNamara had turned up at her funeral. I wouldn't stop until I'd figured it out.

Julie

Richard's attack that night in early 2006 left me traumatized, but it had one silver lining. For a little while after, I was the sole focus of Harry's attention. Not even the bank could compete. He reacted like some kid had tried to take his favourite toy from him.

Every night, he'd rush home from work with a gift for me. He'd make dinner, tell me about his day, and then we'd go to bed and make love. He was gentle and tender. It was like how we'd been at the start, the only two people in the world.

I told him that later in the year, when I felt back to myself, I wanted to begin the IVF process. Our fresh start would include a baby. It was time to settle down and put somebody else first. Lay all our problems to rest. I wanted him to pull back in work and be there for us more.

'You have enough money, Harry,' I said. 'What's the point in working all the time when you're not even enjoying the rewards? I want this child to have two parents. And I don't want it growing up in some sort of fantasy world, where you can have everything at a click of the fingers. I want my baby to live normally.'

He laughed and put a hand on my stomach like there was already a baby there.

'We'll see how normal you want everything to be when your little prince or princess arrives and you realize you only want the absolute best for them.'

It was a while before I could ask Harry what he'd done about Richard.

We were cuddled together on the sofa one night, his arm draped lazily over my shoulders, my body relaxed into his.

'What do you mean?' he said, and I felt him stiffen. He was obviously still furious at Richard for what he'd done.

I twisted around so we were looking at each other.

'You haven't mentioned him at all. Did you fire him?'

Harry sat up straight, forcing me to rearrange myself beside him.

'It's okay,' I said. 'We can talk about this, Harry. I'm ready. I need to know what happened. I presume you fired him, but did you do anything else I should know about?'

Harry's jaw fell slack.

'Fire him? Julie, I told you that night. He knows too much. About the bank . . . about me. I had to be more strategic.'

I blinked and slowly my hand came to my mouth. Had my husband been working alongside that man day in, day out since he'd tried to rape me?

'I thought you understood,' he protested, as I began to edge away from him on the sofa, horrified. 'I beat the living daylights out of him. But Julie, I've put him into the CEO role. I have to step back anyway, and he's perfect for it. With everything that's coming . . . it fits. And it means we can spend more time together. Isn't that what you said you wanted?'

'I–I . . . What the fuck, Harry? I can't believe this. Jesus Christ. I'm going to vomit. Get away from me.' I pushed him away and ran from the room.

I could see no logic to Harry promoting Richard to the CEO role. Harry, at his utmost stupid, hadn't told me about his fears for the bank. All I saw was a betrayal of the highest order. And when he tried to explain, I thought he was just spinning it because he'd been caught. The bank was doing fine. It was soaring, in fact. He was claiming to be preparing for a doomsday scenario but it wasn't coming.

I couldn't bear to hear his lies, whatever he was telling himself to excuse what he'd done. I shut him out.

Still, he persisted, trying to fix things with weaselly words.

'Julie, please, listen to me,' he'd whine. 'The promo— Shit, it's not a promotion even. You must understand, it's a long-term plan. The bank is going to be investigated at some point and—'

'Stop saying that. I don't believe you, and I don't care! I don't care what you think will or won't happen to Richard. I don't care what's going on in your head. All that matters is that you used what happened to me in some sick, twisted way. You and Richard Hendricks – I know what you both are. You live in a world where money matters more than wives, isn't that right? I'll never forgive you, Harry. Never.'

So he stopped trying to tell me.

I was heartbroken. I'd thought I meant more to my husband than anybody else. To be proved wrong in such a horrible way . . . it did terrible things to my head. I turned to drink.

Months later, I drank myself to the miscarriage.

All those nights when we'd been happy, when we'd made love

– I'd conceived. A miracle, ten years in the making. And I hadn't even realized until it was too late.

Fifteen weeks of wine every day.

And after, my drinking escalated even more.

By 2007, if you'd tapped my veins you'd have found alcohol.

You know what I realized later? Nobody decides to be an alcoholic. And you can drink for a long, long time before you accept you are one.

The biggest problem for me in the years leading up to that 2006, 2007 period was that I had a mental image of what constituted a proper drinker. In our village in Leitrim there'd been an old man who used to wait for the pubs to open in the morning, drink in one of them until he was thrown out, and then sit down by the river with a naggin of whiskey, arguing with himself, singing and trying to get passers-by to give him money. He was a pitiful sight, with a fat whiskey nose and a yellow tinge to his skin.

That was my idea of an alcoholic. Anything short of that (short of cirrhosis) was just somebody enjoying themselves. Living in Ireland didn't help. Here, you can throw a stone and hit at least five alcoholics in seconds, because there's a level of drinking that's just deemed acceptable.

While I definitely drank more than average, I'd always had a job or was studying. I had no real health problems, unless you counted a barren, dried-up fucking womb.

I was functioning.

We're the really problematic drunks. We keep telling ourselves we're just like everybody else, even while our trips to the bottle bank run to two or three times a week.

And then, suddenly, drink owns you. You're no longer drinking a few times a week. You're drinking every day, all day. Because it's insidious, alcohol. It waits until you're weak and it takes over.

For a short time after I went back on the booze, Harry did try to reach out to me. I pushed him away. And he grew distant – staying out at night, doing God knows what. Which, in turn, made me drink more. I should have left him. Any self-respecting person would have. And I think, had I not immediately turned to drink and got locked into that cycle, I would have. But we were well and truly in mutually assured destruction mode at that stage.

We exchanged words about the house – the weather, the news. But we didn't *talk*.

Sometimes I would think back to those months in spring 2006 and how happy we'd been. I'd resolve to find my way back there, to rebuild my life. But I couldn't. I was drowning.

People always say that you have to hit rock bottom before you can start to climb out from the pit that is alcoholism. That's true. But it's not as comforting as it sounds.

For a start, where the hell exactly is rock bottom? There's no benchmark.

For me, you might have thought it would be the miscarriage.

Or maybe that Christmas, when I rang up half my family and spewed vitriol down the phone like a woman possessed (well, there were spirits involved), summoning up every historic perceived slight and offence. Mam later told me that Dad had threatened to disown me if I ever upset them like that again. My poor parents.

The list of mortifying fuck-ups in my life over that period is too long to recount, even if I could recall the detail, which I can't. What I do remember, crystal clear, is waking up on many a morning with a deep sense of shame and regret and stomach-churning humiliation, and addressing that despair with a fresh glass of wine.

I don't know how I didn't kill myself, especially as I was starting to feel that's what I wanted to do.

But I didn't learn what 'rock bottom' was until the summer of 2007.

JP

Once I'd established that McNamara hadn't been having a fling with Charlie, I could only think of one other reason for him to have been at her funeral.

He'd had something to do with her death.

I was obsessed. Single-minded. I needed something to focus on, and that was it.

I decided to go back to the start, to try to discover what he'd been doing the night she was knocked down. But that was going to be tough. Even if I could confront him, I couldn't exactly ask him to his face and expect an honest answer.

The one thing I knew for definite about McNamara was where he worked. I hadn't gone back to my job and was officially on sick leave. I could renege on my own resolution not to return, but there was no guarantee I could get to HM Capital that way. It had been a few years since my company had held the contract for the bank's equipment supply and maintenance. I could pretend to be a sales rep and look for a meeting, but I'd end up in a room with their facilities manager, not any of the top guys.

No, I couldn't go back to work. Anyway, I couldn't face seeing Sandra again.

It was thinking of her that gave me the idea.

I was a decent-looking bloke. How hard would it be to get to McNamara via some woman in his life – somebody he worked with, or a relative or friend?

In the end, after discovering that the man was short on family apart from those on his wife's side (there were plenty of profile pieces about him online), I decided to concentrate on his workplace.

It took a few days watching the bank's headquarters and the people coming in and out to find my mark and, ultimately, Harry himself made it easy. I'd spotted a youngish woman, roughly my age, coming out almost every evening with him. The way he spoke to her – the way she deferred to him – made it obvious he was her direct boss.

One evening, he came out alone. I didn't know if she was sick or on a day off, but I hung around anyway, hoping she'd come out eventually.

An hour later, she scurried out of the building.

She was a chubby, pale girl. You could see she was pretty but chose to keep it under wraps. Her long hair was pulled into a plain plait and the glasses she wore were thick-rimmed and old-fashioned.

She crossed the road and rested against the wall behind me, waiting for her bus. When it came, I got on after her, not even knowing where the bus went, and stood beside her in the packed aisle.

I'd now found somebody who worked with McNamara. My new problem was that I didn't know what to say to her. I wasn't good at speaking to strangers, especially women, at the best of times.

We all swayed in the aisle as the bus moved through the city-centre traffic. I kept sneaking glances at her and tried to summon up some sort of opening line.

As the bus moved into the suburbs, it began to empty. A seat became available near me. I seized my chance.

'Do you want to sit down?' I asked, smiling.

'Oh. Thank you,' she said, surprised. She didn't see herself as the sort of girl people offered seats to.

Then I was stumped again.

Minutes later, the man to her other side got up and off the bus and she moved closer to the window.

'Do you mind?' I asked, nodding at the empty seat.

She blushed and shook her head.

'Not at all.'

'Your homework for tonight?' I said, pointing at the folder in her lap.

She looked down and sighed.

'You've no idea. I worked late, and now this. It's just endless these days.'

And then I made up a story about how much pressure I was under in work too, and wasn't it July, wouldn't it be nice to just go on holiday somewhere? I amazed myself with how much small talk I could conjure. A reservoir of chat.

'I'm John,' I said, before jumping off the bus.

'Oh. I'm Olivia.' She smiled.

It took a few such trips to strike up a rapport, but I could see with each passing evening that she was more and more thrilled to see me at the bus stop, waiting.

A week later, I'd asked her on a date.

We went out three times that first week and, even though I got her tipsy on the first two nights and drunk on the third, she was reluctant to talk about McNamara, or the bank. Years later, when what he'd been getting up to at HM Capital was all being revealed on the news, that made more sense. As head of the bank, the man had demanded loyalty and got it, whether it was with the carrot or the stick. Olivia was secretary to the board chair, his role, but she sensed her days were numbered. Harry had little time for her, apparently.

To get her to talk, I had to up the ante.

I had to make her start to fall in love with me. Of course, I never planned to feel anything back. I really was a naïve bloody prat.

I hit my first blip when I brought her back to my apartment and had to make up a story about a relative on her bus route, given I lived on the other side of town to the trip I'd been making with her every evening.

'Were you stalking me on that bus, John?' she goaded, laughing all the while.

I blushed furiously.

'Maybe a little. Are you going to report me?'

'I should. Yet here I am, a smart woman, thinking it's so fecking romantic. I'm a lost cause!'

All I intended in sleeping with her was to get information from her when she was relaxed with me. But I'd underestimated the girl. When she let her hair out of that plait and took off the glasses, I could see how lovely she truly was. She giggled all through fore-play, eventually making me laugh with her, then took over. What Olivia couldn't do wasn't worth talking about.

The sex was mindblowing.

I lay there afterwards, my mouth hanging open, willing myself not to like the girl, trying to talk myself out of having any feelings for her.

She lay in the hook of my arm, running her fingers through the dark hairs that reached down to my belly button.

'I don't normally do this – go to bed with a man I've only been on a few dates with. There's just something about you, John. I'm drawn to my stalker. It must be Stockholm Syndrome.'

I swallowed the lump in my throat. I was an absolute waste of a human being. That's what I wanted to say to her. *I'm a horrible person*.

And I felt even worse when I realized she'd started to cry.

'What's the matter?' I said, trying to lift her face so I could see her eyes.

'It's nothing.'

'It can't be nothing. Tell me.'

'I guess . . . it's just that nobody notices me. Not like you did.'

Oh, God. I was going to hell.

'I don't believe nobody notices you,' I said. If I could do one thing for this girl, it would be to make her feel good about herself. 'Look at the job you do – you're high up in that bank, aren't you? You must be, to be given all that responsibility. And that fella you work for – the famous one, I mean, he must really rate you.'

'Ha. I don't think I'll last there.' She wiped her eyes. 'I was put in to replace his usual secretary. Harry normally has stunners in his office. We all know why. He barely gives me the time of day.'

'What do you mean, "we all know why"?'

I tried to keep my voice as kind as possible when really I was dying with curiosity.

'They say he screws them – his secretaries. Well, the ones he fancies. Not me. Oh, God, that sounds awful. I mean, I wouldn't, anyway. I'm not like that.'

'Fuck, that's mad,' I said, my heart racing. 'Doesn't he have a wife?'

'Yeah. Apparently she knows exactly what he's like. That's what I heard, anyway. It's messed up, isn't it? I could tell, when I met her, that she's not a happy woman. How can you be when you're living with that? She must want to kill him.' Olivia shook her head. 'Anyway. I don't want to be talking about work. Can we . . .?' She smiled shyly and wriggled down under the bedclothes.

After all the stress I'd been feeling, Olivia was like some sort of godsend. The problem was, that wasn't what she was there for. If I had met her a year ago, it could have been so different.

We went on like that for a couple of weeks, and I found myself looking forward to seeing her each time – more than I should have.

It was difficult to bring the conversation back to Harry.

I had to, though. After we'd had sex one night, I leaned up on my elbow. She was yapping about some adventure course they were going on in work and how much she was dreading it because she wasn't the sporty type.

'Your work sounds like a barrel of laughs,' I said. 'Here, what you said about McNamara the other night – I can't get it out of my head. I can't believe he's never made a pass at you. The man must be blind.'

Olivia laughed and the post-sex colouring on her face and neck deepened.

'Why, thank you.' Her confidence was starting to grow. 'To be fair, I think he goes for bimbos.'

'Is his wife one?' I asked, shaking my head like I was fascinated. She frowned.

'I don't know. She didn't seem to be when I met her. To be honest, before she got rat-arsed she seemed really nice. Smart. She was kind to me, even though nobody else at the table even noticed I was there. But then she lost the plot. He was chatting up everybody and anybody and she was practically inhaling the drink at that stage.'

'Oh, you've actually met her?' I said. 'When?'

I was starting to grow very interested in McNamara's wife. If he treated her that badly and she hated him that much, maybe we had something in common.

'It was at a charity event last June. The bank bought two tables and I got to go because Becky in Personnel was sick. She was going because her brother killed himself – it was a suicide prevention charity. Anyway, she gave me her seat.'

'When was it?'

'In June. I said.'

'I mean the date,' I smiled back. 'I think I know the charity. We sponsor a suicide charity in work. It'd be mad if I'd been at the same event.'

She looked at me curiously.

'I think I'd have noticed you there, John! You're a bit of a ride. Oh, gosh, let me think. It was the weekend I got my new flatmate. When was that? Ah, the 7th of June. Yes – her rent comes in on the eight of each month and she moved in the day before.'

I felt my whole world cave.

If he was at an event that night, with his wife and hundreds of witnesses, he obviously had nothing to do with Charlie's death and this whole episode with Olivia had been a waste of time. There had to be more to the story.

'Do you want tea?' she said, about to throw back the covers.

'I'll get it,' I said. 'But first, tell me: you were saying the wife got hammered that night and made a show of herself. What happened then?'

Olivia looked at me funny and sat up in the bed.

'You're really interested in this. You're not—'

She stopped, her expression horrified.

I looked at her quizzically.

'Not what?' I asked.

'You're not a journalist?'

I laughed out loud, before I realized she was serious. Then I matched her look of horror, my eyebrows shooting up.

The funny thing was, it hurt. Even though her suspicion wasn't completely unfounded, I couldn't believe she doubted me.

'Are you for real?'

'Just tell me, John. Please.'

I swallowed.

'Holy fuck, you mean it. Are you mad? I've brought you to my home. We've slept together. I know journos take their job seriously, but Jaysus, that's a bit above and beyond, isn't it? All so I can get a bit of gossip about some wealthy banker I've never even met?'

I threw my legs out of the bed and sat with my back to her.

'Shit, Olivia. I told you I work for a garage. I'm thick. I can barely speak let alone write.'

I felt her hand on my shoulder, heavy with guilt and apology.

'I'm sorry,' she said. 'It's just, we've all been warned to watch out for journalists. There's . . . there's something happening at work, something bad. But you're right; I don't know what I was thinking.'

I bowed my head and shrugged like it didn't matter, when it so clearly did.

'Oh, John,' she said, hugging me from behind. 'Look, let me make that tea and then I will regale you with all the meaty gossip about Harry. Feck him. He's going to fire me out of that job anyway. I don't know why I feel the need to be loyal.'

She told me what had happened that night at the charity event, the night Charlie died. How drunk Julie McNamara had got while her husband flirted with other women and how she'd screamed at him on the dance floor and he'd had to drag her out of the place some time after 1 a.m, while everybody was still partying.

The event had been in the Coast Hotel in Malahide.

Olivia said everybody was staying in the hotel that night and she assumed the McNamaras had gone upstairs. But they had to have left the hotel. It was the only answer. And there was only one road he could have taken back towards the south side of the city, where they lived. The road Charlie had been killed on.

I knew what had happened.

Julie

Normal couples go out. They have fun together. Especially couples who have no children, no ties. When my drinking was at its peak, Harry and I avoided going out together at all costs.

But in the summer of 2007 my husband asked me to go to an event that the bank was hosting in aid of a suicide prevention charity. It was ironic, really. I'd slipped into a dark depression after I'd miscarried, not helped by the alcohol. I spent a lot of time those days thinking about killing myself. I mean, really thinking about it. Not just toying with the idea or seeing it as some sort of cry for help.

Sometimes it felt like just one more thing – it didn't even have to be a big thing – could tip me over the edge and I'd down a vial of prescription tablets. Quietly, when I was alone in the house, when Harry was away and I knew he wouldn't be back in time. I'd researched which ones were the best to take. I'd heard horror stories of people overdosing on pills that took a while to kill, then changing their minds. But I didn't think I had it in me to slash open a vein or hang myself. It had to be something I could do while drunk and, let's face it, after years of living with Harry, I really was very good at swallowing shite.

'I'd like you to come to this thing at the weekend, and for the love of God, Julie, stay sober at it, can you?' Harry said. 'I need some moral support. There will be people there . . . they're going to be making decisions about the bank in the coming months. I need them to think that I don't have much to do with the business end any more and that I'm spending time at home. Can you just back me up? Please?'

'What people?' I said, curiosity getting the better of me.

'Just politicians and that. I need you beside me, Julie.'

There was always something between the lines with Harry. Always some devious strategy, some plan I wasn't aware of.

Harry did need the politicians at the benefit that night to think that he was a small player at the bank over that 2007 period. He needed them to think that because he knew that the crash was coming and the bank would be investigated.

He could make them think it in one of two ways. Either by having me on his arm telling everybody how much time he spent with me those days, or by bringing me to an event he knew I'd get hammered at, with all those people to bear witness and assume that he was practically a full-time carer for his alcoholic wife.

Sure, they would say, *how could he have known what was going on in HM Capital when he was dealing with her*?

Which performance do you think I put on that night?

Even though it was win-win for my husband, he must have decided at some point in the evening that the drunk option was preferable to me being on my best behaviour, sober but dour. He needed authenticity, and I'm not that good an actress. I tried to laugh and say things like, 'Oh, Harry, I can't get rid of him these days!' but it was so forced, even I found it painful.

I wasn't privy to his change of tack. And before you get all judgemental, please know two things. One, you've never met anybody better at mind games than Harry. When he started flirting outrageously with the other women on our table, right in front of me, looking over to make sure I was watching, I met his eye and coolly reached out for an empty wine glass. He knew what buttons to push. I filled the glass to the brim and drank from it like I had a starring role in *Ice Cold in Alex*.

And two, Richard Hendricks, though having the sense not to sit at our table, was at the event. At least Harry had the good grace to be embarrassed about that when we arrived. Apparently, Richard was meant to be away that weekend but had cancelled at the last minute and turned up. I could see him from where I was sitting — his fat, ugly back straining his jacket seams, his meaty paw resting on his wife's shoulder. I couldn't look at his fingers, those things he'd stuck inside my body, without wanting to vomit.

'I wouldn't have asked you to come if I'd known he was here,' Harry whispered urgently in my ear when I spotted him.

'Wouldn't you?' I said, my shoulders sagging. 'You seem to expect me to endure plenty when it comes to him. I'll try to make sure I don't wander out to the toilet on my own in case he thinks it's an invite to rape me. I just hope he's not looking for another promotion.'

I turned my back on Harry and his flirting and chatted to the other table guests. I drank glass after glass, mixing white wine with red, picking up other people's dregs when my glass wasn't filled quickly enough.

I was the first person on the dance floor as soon as the inter-minable after-dinner speeches concluded, dragging up some poor unfortunate who happened to be sitting nearest and sending him and me into a heap during the first song.

That wasn't bad enough. After helping me back to the table, with apologies to my unwilling partner and the tables nearest the dance floor, Harry upped his game. He turned to the woman on his left, his hand resting so high up her thigh he could have been her gynaecologist, and began to whisper sweet nothings in her ear.

'Is the baby crowning yet?' I said, leaning over Harry and belching alcohol fumes into the other woman's face. 'You look about nine months now. What do you think, Harry? How many inches is she dilated there?'

'For crying out loud, Julie.' He grimaced, and she flushed a new shade of mortified.

Normally, I'd collapse after more than two bottles of wine, but that night I managed to make it to the toilet, throw up with only a little bit landing on my dress and return to the table for a repeat.

Harry was dancing at that stage, twirling some girl half his age in the centre of the floor as she giggled and fluttered her false eye-lashes for him. She held the attention of most of the men there, her blonde hair almost down to her bum, shimmying in a backless dress that stopped just high enough to protect her modesty while accentuating all her curves.

I don't know what it was about *her* that upset me so much. Per-haps it was because I suspected that the women Harry cheated with were normally skinny brown-haired girls, so very different. Like that was okay. But there he was, dirty dancing with what could only be described as a prettier version of me.

I stumbled on to the dance floor and got in between the two of them, pulled Harry's arms around me and began probing his lips with my tongue. He responded for a second, the habit strong, then pulled back.

'Jesus, Julie. You taste of vomit. Sit down, will you?'

She was still close enough to have heard, and I bristled.

'Well, at least I don't taste of shit, which is what comes out of your mouth most of the time, my darling husband,' I said, loudly and for her benefit.

'Right, I think it's time to take you home,' he said, the voice of reason.

'So soon?' I cried. 'After bringing me here and forcing me to have all this fun? I know, how about instead of running out, why don't we do what I imagine you normally do at these things? Why don't you take me to a room upstairs and fuck me senseless like I'm one of the slappers at the bank, huh? Isn't that how you usually end a night like this?'

I'd roared all this, completely oblivious to the band finishing the song they'd been performing and the crowd's polite clapping. The sound dribbled to a halt as they all turned to stare at the mad drunk woman.

Game, set and match to Harry.

'Outside!' he hissed.

He grabbed me by the arm and dragged me out of the ballroom. Everybody who was anybody – all of those he'd wanted to witness the little scene – got the full benefit of my husband's purple face and his most put-upon expression.

By the time we reached the reception area, the light bulb had gone on over my head.

'Oh my God,' I slurred, as the air conditioning and the bright lights of the lobby hit me. 'You wanted that to happen.'

'Sure,' he said, looking over my head, not meeting my eyes. 'I wanted you to embarrass yourself and me. Please, will you just shut up and come on.'

I stayed where I was, propping myself against a marble pillar for support.

'You did. You absolute fucking bastard. You wanted them to see what you have to cope with, have them think you're home trying to save me from myself day and night. You . . .'

I sobbed, unable to believe how low my husband would stoop, a man who would throw his wife's reputation to the lions for his own benefit.

Harry paled and stared at the floor.

I had caught him out.

'I'm not staying in this hotel,' I said. 'Give me the keys.'

'What?' he said.

'Give me the keys. I'm going home.'

'Julie, you can barely stand. You can't drive. You'll kill yourself.'

'I don't care! Give me the keys.'

It was the 7th of June. A night I'd like to say I would never forget but, to be honest, I was drunk and forgetting was my survival mode.

JP

I don't know if it made me a worse or a better person that I considered staying with Olivia and keeping her in the dark about my original intentions.

She'd grown on me over the few short weeks, with her funny little chats and her self-deprecating ways, even though she was really intelligent and very pretty when she let herself be.

I knew I couldn't, though. And as awful as it would be to break it off, it was better than the alternative – to maintain a relationship that had started on a lie.

More importantly, I had to deal with the fallout from my sister's death. I just didn't have room for anything else.

'But why?' she asked, her whole face miserable when I told her, tears glistening in her eyes. 'I thought we were getting serious?'

'So did I,' I said, staring out at the sea. I couldn't even look at her, coward that I was. I'd met her at the Bull Wall pier, somewhere nice and public from where I could make a quick exit. 'I'm sorry, Olivia. It's not you. It just isn't a good time for me now. I'm getting over somebody else. That's where my head is at.'

'But if you're enjoying your time with me, what does it matter?' she asked. 'I can handle you being on the rebound if you're actually happy with me, John.'

'Don't say things like that. You're worth far more than to be somebody's rebound, Olivia.'

She reached her hand out tentatively, felt my arm.

'Please. Give us a go.'

I shook her off, burning with shame.

'No. I'm sorry. I really am. I can't do it.'

I walked away. She had the dignity, God love her, to let me go.

I was a complete and utter bastard. Had somebody treated Charlie the way I treated Olivia, I'd have battered him. I felt like crying at my own behaviour.

I checked her out in 2012, before everything kicked off, to see where she'd ended up. She had lost her job at the end of 2007, just like she'd predicted. Her Facebook page showed her in Australia, where she was shacked up with some fella. She made good for herself in the end.

I never stopped being grateful for her help. I was convinced, because of her information, that I had the reason McNamara had come to Charlie's funeral.

He hadn't been having an affair with my sister. He'd been driving his drunk wife home that night and had smashed his car into Charlie.

The Guards were running a *Crimecall* special that August, the ten-week anniversary of my sister's death, to refresh people's minds about the details of the case and to try to get more information.

I knew where I'd be when it was on. Standing outside Harry McNamara's house, waiting to confront him when the show was over.

He'd be watching. How could he not, when the programme was directed at him? And when he opened the door to a knock that evening, I'd be there. Her brother, ready either to drive him to the cop shop or to kill him.

But first I wanted to get all my ducks in a row.

If he'd driven into Charlie, his car had to have been damaged in some way. That would be the confirmation I needed. Her blood would have been on his bonnet. He'd have brought it in somewhere, a place where they would deal with him with discretion, a dodgy garage.

And I knew all of them in Dublin and pretty much throughout Ireland.

I was going to track down his car and make sure that when I spoke to Harry, I'd enough evidence to hang him by the balls.

Julie

When I woke up on the 8th of June 2007, the world felt the same.

I sat up in bed, bleary-eyed, groggy and with a blinding headache. I made it to the bathroom just in time to expel the last of the alcohol from my system. After I'd vomited, I went to get the painkillers.

I had very little memory of the previous twenty-four hours. I did have that lingering sick, queasy feeling in my stomach, which had nothing to do with the hangover and everything to do with the suspicion that something particularly humiliating had happened the night before.

I tied a dressing gown around my waist, cold despite the warmth of the morning.

Downstairs, I moved gingerly around the kitchen, wincing at the noise of the coffee machine and fixing myself an Alka-Seltzer while I waited for it to brew.

I paused at the fridge when I went to fetch the milk, almost reaching for the bottle of wine I knew was sitting just inside the door. That would be how I'd normally treat a hangover this bad — hair of the dog.

But I didn't take it out. Something made me stop — that niggling bubble of nerves in my stomach.

It was Saturday, but I couldn't hear Harry anywhere in the house. I presumed he'd stayed out. Then I remembered. I'd been out with him last night.

The charity event.

I'd started the night sober, so how . . .?

The memories drifted like wisps of cloud through my brain. Him flirting and goading me. Me drinking, vomiting, dancing.

What sort of a state had I been in when he brought me home?

I went back upstairs and looked through the spare bedrooms, then in his study: all empty.

Back downstairs, I made my way through the various rooms — the dining room, the living room; I even checked the bathrooms.

He could have gone for a walk, I supposed. Normally, if Harry was there on a Saturday morning, he'd sit and read the papers at the breakfast table.

I made my way around to the garage to see if he'd taken the car, thinking that maybe he'd driven to the village to get them.

But still I had a growing sense that he was about the house somewhere, avoiding me.

That could only mean one thing. I'd made a holy show of myself.

I opened the garage door quietly, and almost didn't notice him. Then I saw the top of his head, bobbing up and down, his back bent as he worked at something on the bonnet of one of the cars — the Mercedes.

He looked up when he saw me, his face pinched and pale.

'You're awake,' he said. He used the crook of his arm to swipe at the sweat on his forehead, and it was then I noticed the cloth in his hand.

'Are you washing the car?' I said, bemused. 'Would it not be better to do that outside?'

He stood up straight, hands hanging by his side.

'Am I . . . Outside? Are you serious? Don't you remember, Julie?'

His voice was grave and strained.

He'd looked just like this when he'd told me about the girl in Tallinn and Nina Carter all those years ago.

This was bad.

'Remember what?' I said, and as I did, my eyes drifted to the cloth in his hand. It was stained, covered in something dark brown, something that looked like blood.

I wanted to move around to the front of the car to find out what he was doing, but my feet wouldn't cooperate. I didn't want to see, even though I knew I had to.

'Last night . . .'

He hung his head and seemed so desolate that I couldn't help myself. I walked over to him and looked at the car.

The side of the bonnet was dented; the headlight was smashed. But it was the dark drops staining its surface that caught my eye. That was what he was washing off with the cloth.

'I'll have to bring it to a garage and get it fixed and sprayed,' he said. 'There could be – I don't know – DNA or something on it, and the police might have been able to get paintwork off her body. I was thinking about getting rid of it altogether, but I can't risk it falling into somebody else's hands and the Guards getting it that way. I have to go with my gut. There's nothing connecting us to the girl. I'll get it professionally cleaned and keep it off the road. Don't worry, Julie. I'll get it sorted. I'll take care of this. I promise.'

My hands flew to my mouth.

I groaned.

'Oh God, Harry. What have you done?'

He turned to me and put his hands on my shoulders, looking like he'd seen a ghost.

'What have *I* done? What have *you* done, Julie?'

JP

Tracking down the garage took me less than a day. I'd been out of the game a while, but I still had contacts and plenty of currency. I put the word out that I needed to speak to anybody who'd turned over a Mercedes or BMW since June of that year, and within hours I had a name and an address. I'd already paid a quiet visit to his house to check out the layout. McNamara had two cars in his garage, but the Merc very rarely came out. If I was to bet, I'd say he was hiding that car.

My old boss rang me with the details.

'Do you want to come back, John Paul?' he asked. 'I could always do with a grafter like you.'

'Yeah, let me think about it,' I said.

He rang the garage I was headed to and let his guy know I was en route. The mechanic who'd done the job was waiting for me outside, smoking nervously and shifting from one foot to the other. He squinted at me as I approached.

'John Paul?' he said.

'That's me. Tony?'

He nodded, flicked his butt on to the ground and started walking.

'Can't bring you inside, mate,' he said. 'Let's go down to Gills. I'm on me lunch break – we can go there.'

'Gills?'

'Me local.'

He came back from the bar with two pints of Guinness and a Mars bar for himself.

'You're missing one of your five-a-day,' I said, trying to ease the tension. He was ridiculously skinny. Starved-looking – that kind of working-class skeletal appearance that told you he'd rarely had a nutritious meal as a child and his metabolism was driven by nervous energy. I should have looked like that, I suppose, but I had culchie-farmer blood in my veins, the one decent thing Seamie had given me.

'Fuck it. Curry later. Me appetite is gone anyway. Ever since Jim rang. Put the shits up me, it did. I knew there was something off about that job on the Merc. I knew it would come back to haunt me.'

I picked up the pint and sipped from it, probably only my third or fourth pint in my life. It was going to be one of those conversations.

'Sorry, we didn't mean to put the willies up you,' I said. 'Anything you tell me will stay between you and me, mate. You have my word.'

He studied me from over the top of his pint, then settled it back on its mat.

'That's as may be,' he said. 'But just to be clear, I'm doing this because Jim is me second cousin and I want a job over at his outfit. I reckon if this shit comes out it will be my boss's name that's mud – not us sods who do the dirty work – but I'd still rather be out of it.'

'Understood. Does he take many of these jobs, your boss?'

Tony sighed and shook his head.

'Too fucking many. I don't mind dealing with a hot motor, but the ones involved in accidents? Nah. That doesn't sit right with me. And the boss – he's in with all sorts of gangsters. You worry, you know? You'll fix up a car that's been used in a job where some kingpin has got whacked, and next thing a gang will be setting fire to your place of employment. Health and fucking safety shot to pieces.'

I almost laughed. Health and safety. Tony was a character.

'The man who brought in the Merc,' I asked. 'How does he know your boss?'

'He doesn't know him – but he was riding some bird who does. She's like a model or something, but her brother is selling charlie all over fucking Dublin.'

'What did you say?' I froze.

'Charlie. The white stuff? Cocaine?' He shook his head, looking at me like I'd just landed. 'Anyway, he uses the garage, and she must have given this banker wanker a calling card because not just anybody can rock up at the door and say, "Howya, can you help me cover up a murder?"'

My stomach churned.

'What was his name?' I said. 'The client.'

'No clue. Just that he was a rich prick who works in a bank. The boss is the soul of discretion. He'd cut my fucking tongue out if he knew I was having this little parley with you. Want another one?'

I looked down at my drained pint glass. How had that happened? And, yeah, I wanted another one so badly I would have strangled Tony to lick the dregs of his.

I shook my head. I needed to keep my act together to see this through. It wasn't the afternoon to turn into my dad.

'Fair enough. Anyway, your man drove it in. Brown hair, sunglasses, hoodie and jeans, like he was trying to disguise himself. He's driving a bleeding Merc and his sunglasses are Gucci. Like, actual Gucci, not me ma bringing me a pair back from a market in Spain Gucci.'

I pulled up the image on my phone, the screenshot from a recent profile piece McNamara had done.

'Yeah, that's him,' he said. 'Who is he?'

'Doesn't matter,' I said, putting the phone back in my pocket. 'How banged up was the motor?'

Tony shifted uneasily in his seat.

'Look, this is the reason I want to get out of this garage, you understand?'

'I get it. I told you, you've nothing to worry about from me. I'll never mention your name to anybody. Jim must have told you we go way back.'

'Yeah. Yeah, he did. He likes you. Trusts you.' Tony gave me his best dead-eye stare, trying to impress on me how much he was trusting me in that moment too, and the respect it deserved.

I took a bundle of notes out of my wallet.

'I discussed this with Jim,' I said, and placed it beside the empty Mars bar wrapper on the table. 'It comes with a firm offer of a job from his shop. There's nothing dodgy over there. Well, bar the obvious. He'll take you as soon as.'

Tony lifted the cash and counted it with his eyes. Fifties, at least twenty of them.

'There was no need,' he said, putting it into his pocket.

I wondered how much he'd been paid to panel-beat the car that had killed my sister, to remove any trace of her blood from its paintwork. Probably just his day's pay, €70 or €80.

'He'd hit somebody,' Tony said. 'Left side, passenger side. The bonnet was dented. Not too badly – I've seen worse. But it was a Merc. His victim would have taken the biggest dent. I saw the news. Some young one was killed walking home from a party a week before. I'd say it was her.'

I closed my eyes as the room started to spin around me.

'I gave it a few taps, replaced the front headlight and resprayed it a nice midnight blue,' Tony continued. 'Here, are you all right, bud?'

I nodded, then stood up.

'Thanks, Tony,' I said. 'Just – just write down the reg for me, would you?'

He turned over the beer mat and pulled a pen out of the front pocket of his overalls.

'I don't normally remember the numbers on regs,' he said. 'I'm usually changing them anyway, and I'm not bleeding Carol Vorderman. But this one stayed in my head. I told you, I knew it would come back to haunt me.'

He held out the mat but when I tried to take it, he kept his fingers on the cardboard.

'Jim didn't tell me your last name,' he said.

'It doesn't matter,' I answered.

'No,' he said. 'No, it doesn't.' He extended his hand for me to shake and as I did, he pulled me in close.

'Find him and fucking kill him. That's what I'd do if it was someone belonging to me he did that to. He has it coming.'

And with that, the atmosphere between us changed from one of shared suspicion to one of mutual understanding and agreement.

That's why Tony hasn't come forward.

He understood.

Julie

I wasn't sure I could live with myself when my husband told me I'd caused a crash that took a girl's life. And yet, each day, I got up and did it. I lived.

There were times, following the accident, when I would wake from nightmares, sweating and shaking. I'd go into the kitchen to get something and just start crying. Or I'd find myself walking to clear my head and two hours later, I wouldn't have a clue where I was.

But Harry was there for me.

What had happened brought us together. We closed ranks.

And I didn't touch a drop of drink.

Alcohol would have made it easier. I think that's why I didn't resort to it. I needed to feel remorse for what I'd done. I couldn't hide from it with booze.

That. That was rock bottom.

Harry went to work so everything would look normal but just like the previous year, after Richard, he rushed home each evening to be with me. We went for long walks. He ran me baths. We talked – not about what had happened, just about something and nothing.

At no point did either of us even contemplate going to the police. I know how fucked up that makes us sound, but you'd have to have walked in our shoes to understand.

Harry had spent years hiding his illegal activity at the bank. Not talking to the police was our norm.

I couldn't bear to know the name of the girl whose life I'd taken – to see her face or know what she'd been like. So I abstained from the internet, from the news, from anything that would tell me those things.

But it was unavoidable. Ten weeks to the day later, I was standing in the kitchen, idly buttering toast I wouldn't eat, when the news bulletin came on the radio that Harry had left playing.

'RTÉ's monthly edition of Crimecall will tonight focus on the death of Charlene Andrews, killed in the early hours of the morning of the 8th June. Ms Andrews, aged twenty-two, died as the result of being hit by a car on the Malahide Road, while walking home alone from a party. The driver of the car failed to stop and drove his or her vehicle away from the scene. Crimecall will show a reconstruction of events that night in the hope it will jog the memory of members of the public who may have seen something. An Garda Síochána have urged viewers to tune in this evening and say additional helplines will be in operation for the next seventy-two hours.'

I dropped the knife on to the counter with a clatter and had to grab hold of the granite to keep myself upright.

I had to watch that show. It was being made in order to find me. I had to see the girl. Charlene Andrews, twenty-two.

That night, I sat glued in front of the television screen as an actress playing the Andrews girl was shown at a student house party

329

in Malahide somewhere. She was a young, pretty girl, the actress. Blonde curls, smiley face. I wondered how close a match she was to the real Charlene.

Harry was in the shower. I'm not sure he even knew *Crimecall* was on. He would have turned it off and thrown the remote control out the window if he had.

'You've stood by me through so much,' he'd said, the morning I'd found him in our garage and he told me what happened. 'I will fix this.'

The reconstruction showed Charlene leaving the party alone that evening after unsuccessfully trying to secure a cab. She told friends she'd walk and grab a taxi along the road, and nobody had the good sense, or was sober enough, to tell her that wasn't a good idea. She was stone-cold sober. She didn't drink, apparently.

Why had I insisted on the car keys?

Why couldn't I have just passed out, like a normal bloody drunk?

I watched, horrified, and with the strangest feeling of the surreal, as the actress walked down the dimly lit road without a footpath, dangerous ditches on either side, eerie trees towering overhead. I was frightened for her. It was like watching a film. She'd got a full two kilometres down the road when we, the viewers, heard the car approaching. The Charlene actress turned to see if it was a taxi, her features illuminated in the headlights, and next thing – bang.

The car sped off.

My heart was thumping so hard I thought it was going to explode.

The camera returned to the studio, where the presenter said that nobody had come forward to admit to seeing Charlene on the stretch of road that night, which was unusual.

'We believe there may have been witnesses, other drivers, who are scared to ring in for fear of involving themselves with us,' a Guard explained to the presenter and the TV audience. 'But I want to stress tonight to anybody out there in that position that they should contact us, and that they have nothing to fear.' He turned to the camera. 'We need to talk to you to find out if you saw any other vehicles that evening, especially coming from the direction of Malahide.'

'And we're also appealing to the driver of the car involved, aren't we?' the presenter prompted.

'Yes,' the Guard said. 'We are saying to this man or woman that it's not too late to hand yourself in. Charlene's family and friends are devastated, and knowing that this was an accident and that the person involved is taking responsibility will help them to cope at this difficult time.'

The camera swung back to the presenter, who read out the relevant numbers as they appeared on the bottom of the screen. Then a photograph filled the television – Charlene Andrews as she was, the real person.

She was beautiful. So very beautiful. Friendly eyes, a wonderful smile. The sort of endearing shyness in front of the camera that you just don't see any more. The presenter spoke over her photo, saying that she'd just finished her nursing degree.

She was dead. That wonderful light had been extinguished from the world, because of me. I couldn't carry that guilt. I couldn't. I had to turn myself in.

I closed my eyes and, suddenly, I saw her. I saw it happening. Her hair. Her face as she turned towards the car. The look of shock as it hit her.

I hadn't heard Harry come in, but he was standing behind me, staring at the image on the screen. His hands came to rest on my shoulders at the same time as I looked up and saw his reflection in the large sitting-room window.

'Oh, darling,' he said. 'Why are you watching this? Why are you doing it to yourself?'

I jumped away from him like I'd been scalded.

'Don't touch me,' I hissed.

His mouth fell open.

'Julie? What is it?'

I looked around in desperation, seeking out the only thing to hand. His crystal ashtray, a cigar resting in it.

I picked it up and flung it at him as hard as I could.

He dived out of the way. The expression on his face when he stood back up was one of horror.

'What the fuck is wrong with you?' he said. 'Have you lost your mind?'

'I remember!' I screamed.

'You remember what?' Harry's voice was choked.

'I remember that night.'

I bunched my hands into fists at my sides. I was going to kill him. I was actually going to fucking murder him.

'I wasn't driving, Harry,' I yelled. 'You were.'

JP

Their house was like something from a magazine, one of those glossy ones Charlie was always wasting her money on. She'd point at celebrity homes with huge kitchen islands and indoor swimming pools and say: 'JP, what do you reckon our chances are for a mortgage on that one?'

The McNamaras' place must have cost a few mill', at least. Palm trees dotted the top of the lawn, their leaves swishing against the house's white walls. It had huge floor-to-ceiling windows, and the lighting was generously enhanced by the crystal chandeliers that hung in the centre of each room. A gravel drive, landscaped gardens. Imagine a house better suited to Los Angeles than Dublin – that was their home.

I found the glass offputting. It must have been like living in a goldfish bowl. Though I suppose they'd nobody looking in on them, up on top of that hill in Dalkey, with sea views to the front and a big golf course behind them. And it certainly helped my cause the night I went there, the night they were showing the *Crimecall* episode.

I stood in the garden among the trees by the boundary wall. I'd been there a couple of times to scout the place out. They'd electric gates but no security, so it was easy to get in. The tree's branches gave me a little shelter from the downpour that had started earlier in the evening, but wet drops still found their way down the back of my jacket collar. My eyes kept flicking towards the garage at the far side of the house, imagining the car that had killed my sister behind its sliding door.

At 8.55 p.m. the wife walked into what I guessed was the sitting room, but they probably called it the television lounge. I was taken aback for a moment. She was petite, blonde curls tied up in a ponytail, pretty. From a distance, and with the rain making everything beyond the glass a little blurry, I could have been looking at Charlie. I'd brought a little pair of binoculars, not knowing if I'd be able to get a good vantage point to see them inside. I trained them on the sitting-room window to get a better look at the woman. She wasn't much like Charlie at all, bar in superficial appearance. She was attractive – but older. Her mouth had a sorrowful downturn, dark circles ringed her eyes. She had probably been a stunner once. Now she just looked unhappy.

She turned down the ceiling light and flicked on the television with the remote. Then she sat on the couch across from it, her eyes trained on the screen, the lights from it playing across her face.

On the picture framed behind her, I saw the images reflected. Guards. A studio, a presenter.

She was watching *Crimecall*.

I watched as she got more and more upset, clasping her breast, then her hand across her mouth.

Why was it affecting her like that? I suppose I'd assumed that she'd been out of it in the car that night when her husband had driven into Charlie, but what if she hadn't been? Did she know what had happened?

More importantly, where was her husband? Why wasn't he watching?

I didn't have to wait long for the answer to that. One of the double doors opened behind her and Harry McNamara came in to stand behind his wife. He wore a polo shirt, and his brown hair was slicked wet. Straight from the shower, by the look of it. He placed his hands on her shoulders – for a moment I thought he was going to strangle her, and my own breathing stopped. I was that jumpy.

She whipped her head around, then leapt from the couch to face him. He said something and she picked up an object – an ashtray. I watched, like somebody tuned into his own personal soap opera, as she flung the heavy ashtray at him and he ducked. When his head came up, his face went through the motions of shock, bewilderment, hurt, then anger, his features contorting until they showed fury.

My heart thumped faster as I stared through the binoculars, pressing them so hard against my eyes they would leave a mark there for hours. For the second time, I thought, *He's going to kill her*.

And what would I do if he tried?

Would I let him – and make sure that the sentence he eventually got was for life? I didn't know that much about the law in 2007, but even then I suspected that the punishment for a hit-and-run, especially after his expensive lawyers were done, would not be enough for the crime he'd committed.

The wife got angrier. McNamara sneered at her and snapped something back.

She threw her arms in the air then started to leg it to the door on her side of the room.

Her husband was too quick for her. He made it across the floor space between them in seconds and grabbed her, roared something and flung her to the couch.

I nearly covered my eyes. I didn't know if I had it in me to watch any more. To look on as he attacked his wife, no matter how much I wanted him punished for what he'd done to my sister.

I didn't have it in me.

Did I?

Julie

'Are you kidding me?'

Harry had lost it with me plenty of times over the years. But I hadn't seen him like this before. The veins throbbed in his temples and his lips curled back in rage.

I faced him, my whole body shaking. I was afraid, I realized.

Who was this stranger? What sort of man would let his wife believe that she'd caused somebody's death? What did that take in a person, to lie like that?

'I remember,' I said, holding my ground. 'I was in the passenger seat. I saw her, Harry. I saw the car hit her on my side and then . . . then she landed on the bonnet. I remember the thump. I looked at her face. You were driving, Harry. You were.'

My husband planted his hands on the back of the couch I'd been sitting on and glared at me.

'That's what you remember, is it, Julie?'

His voice was low, threatening.

'It's what fucking happened!' I said, appalled. 'How could you lie to me about that? How could you tell me I was driving?'

'No,' he said.

'No, what?'

'I never said you were driving.'

'B-but . . .' I shook my head. 'Are you admitting you were driving?'

'Of course I was driving, you stupid woman. Do you honestly think I'd have let you behind the wheel of that car, the state you were in? You could barely stand. Everything that happened that night was your fault. We should have still been at the party. We only had to leave because you mortified us. I'm not letting you make me take all the blame.'

I was still shaking my head, listening and in denial at the same time.

'You – you made me drink that night. You goaded me into it, flirting with women in front of me. I remember telling you I wanted the keys, that I didn't want you to drive me home. In the hotel lobby. I remember that. Then everything was a blank. But that morning, when I found you cleaning the car, you said I'd caused an accident . . .'

I stopped. I was confused. Panicking. I didn't understand what was happening. No, he hadn't said I was driving. But he'd told me I'd caused the crash, and I'd interpreted it to mean I'd been driving.

One clear thought surfaced through the chaos in my head.

'It wasn't my fault!' I screamed. 'Just because I was drunk. It wasn't my fault you hit her, you bastard. You let me think . . . You're fucking evil, do you know that, Harry? All this time, all the things you've done. You've cheated on me and betrayed me. Oh, for the love of God, I know you have – don't bother shaking your fucking head. You've lied to me and hurt me and you . . . you drove me to fucking drink! You made me what I am. I should have known this was coming. The women who said you *raped* them. The way you let Richard get away with what he did. But to do this to me? You . . . urghh!'

I couldn't even summon the words for how much I despised my husband in that moment, I was so full of rage.

'A girl died,' I choked. 'Charlene Andrews. You killed a girl, and I'm not letting you get away with it. She was only a kid. No, Harry. This ends now.'

'So it was okay for you to get away with it when you thought you'd killed her, huh? My wife, the centre of the moral universe.'

'Stop it! You're insane. There's something wrong with you.'

Harry sneered, his face unrecognizable.

'Something's wrong with me? Yes, because I'm the only one with the problems around here, aren't I? I'm the only one with weaknesses and flaws. Well, there's the fucking door, darling. Feel free to use it. Leave me to my evil deeds while you float off on your cloud of innocence and purity. Yes, all right! Yes, I slept with other women! Any man married to you would have done the same. Do you know how many times I've cleaned you up after you've got plastered? How many times I've carried you upstairs and come back down to mop your vomit off the floor? You're an alcoholic, Julie. You have been for years. So, go on. Leave.'

I clutched my stomach. To hear those words, his confession to being unfaithful, finally.

It felt like a relief and a punch at the same time.

I swallowed the pain and steeled myself.

'Are you joking? You admit you've cheated on me, and *you're* trying to throw *me* out? I'm going to ruin you, Harry. I'm going to take everything you have, all that stuff that means so much to you and nothing to me. None of it ever meant anything. Do you understand that? I loved you and you've destroyed it, so now I'm going to destroy you.'

'Bring it on. And yes, I'd throw you out rather than listen to another self-righteous word out of your stupid mouth.'

'A girl is dead,' I repeated, shaking my head. 'You killed her! Does that mean nothing to you? I can't do this. I n-need a drink.' I spluttered out the words and turned to the door beside me.

I'd barely moved when I felt his arms grab me.

He flung me on to the couch.

And I didn't have time to react when he pinned me down so forcibly that I couldn't move.

'Don't you dare. Don't you fucking dare,' he said, his eyes bulging, his face set in fury. 'If you touch another drop, I swear – I'll kill you, Julie.'

'Let me up!' My spittle hit his face. 'It's none of your business. After this? You're a murderer. You're a cheat. You're a disgusting human being. I'll drink this house dry if I want and you'll do nothing. We are over. Done. I want a divorce. And I'm going to ring the police and tell them what you've done: driving into that girl, and every last seedy and corrupt little thing. I'm not taking this any more. Let me up.'

I strained against him, clawing like a cat. I wanted to hurt him any way I could.

'Shut up! Shut up! Shut up!' he roared, and he shook me. The force of him shocked me into silence. In that moment I really felt like he could do it – he could kill me – and the whole of our relationship flashed before my eyes. This man I'd spent my life with. The only man I'd ever loved.

Tears filled my eyes.

Do it, I thought. *End it. Do what I haven't been able to do.*

'Don't you remember, Julie?' he choked. 'Don't you remember what happened that night?'

I stared at him, bewildered.

Then he leaned down and whispered the words into my ear.

At first they meant nothing.

Then it came back to me.

I closed my eyes, my brain reconfiguring, all of the pieces slotting into place.

My arms fell slack and he collapsed back on the floor, his hands covering his eyes as he sobbed.

Oh, God.

I remembered.

I remembered everything then.

JP

I watched the scene unfolding in the sitting room like it was another car crash.

I didn't want Harry McNamara to murder his wife, but I wasn't able to move a muscle to help her. He was leaning over her on the couch, his arms straining as he held her down, but I couldn't see what he was doing. Did he have his hands over her mouth? Around her neck? Was he smothering her with a pillow?

Within minutes, he fell back on the floor. She lay there, unmoving.

Every part of me started to shake.

I had just witnessed somebody being killed and had done absolutely nothing to stop it.

What did that make me?

I didn't know what to do. Should I ring the police?

While I stood there, frozen to the spot, unable to process what had happened, the wife got up. Using the back of the sofa, she pulled herself into position and sat upright, swaying for a minute.

I couldn't make sense of what I was looking at. Harry was on the floor, his shoulders heaving like he was crying. Had he tried to kill her but not been able to do it? Was she still at risk? I would act this time, I swore to myself. If he tried again, I'd smash the window in if I had to.

But . . . she didn't look frightened. Not of him, at least. She looked like she'd just seen a ghost.

She dropped off the couch on to her knees and crawled beside her husband, then wrapped her arms around him.

She was comforting him. And then he placed his arms around her.

The two of them sat like that on the floor, rocking together.

I watched, completely at sea, not knowing what had happened or why and unsure what to do next. I started to weep.

It was messed up.

I'd come here to get the truth for my sister. What had I found instead? That there was something rotten inside of me. I couldn't think straight and I couldn't stop the tears. I lowered the binoculars and turned on my heel.

Part Four

Part Four

Julie

That August night in 2007 was the first and last time Harry and I properly discussed what had happened to Charlene Andrews.

Her death and our guilt in not disclosing the truth weighed heavy on our respective consciences. But when something that awful happens, you only have two options. Deal with it properly, or try to pretend it never happened.

Given how flawed we both were, we were never going to choose the tougher route.

After the *Crimecall* show, though, we talked.

We talked about her, and the days and months that had preceded the accident. We began to talk about Harry's confession that he had cheated, but I had to stop him.

'I can't, not tonight,' I cried. 'We will discuss it and we'll get help, but I don't have the strength to deal with that now, as well. I knew all along, Harry. It's not news. But right now, that girl's death is enough for us to have to cope with.'

He nodded, but I could see he was burning to tell me something else. It was like a dam had opened and Harry wanted to spill everything.

'What?' I sighed. 'What is it?'

And then he told me.

The bank, he said, was going to implode. It wasn't just his imagination. He'd seen the figures. And it wasn't just HM Capital. The whole system was collapsing. It would be a financial crash of such magnitude, the Irish economy would fall apart. He could end up in prison, though he'd done his utmost to ensure that Richard Hendricks would carry the can for what was about to happen.

'Richard?' I said. 'Oh my God. You were telling the truth?'

'Of course. You didn't understand and I'm sorry I couldn't make you. How could you think I wouldn't make him pay for what he did to you? I just chose to get him in the long grass.'

'How could I understand it, Harry! You didn't tell me what you suspected was coming at the bank. We had a deal, remember? All last year, when you knew the shit was going to hit the fan – you should have been confiding in me all along. Jesus, don't you realize how differently things might have turned out if we'd planned this together? And you know it was still wrong, what you did. Yes, maybe Richard will suffer, but he should have suffered immediately. He's been going around thinking he's got away with it. It makes me feel sick. It should have been my choice, from the start, how he was punished. You should have discussed it with me.'

'I didn't want to utter that bastard's name to you. When you asked me had I fired him, I was genuinely shocked. I had to be cleverer than that. I'm sorry if I let you down, but that . . . that scum was always going to pay for what he did to you. I really did try to do the right thing.'

Oh, the irony! You know, I've watched those soap operas where you're just longing for the two people on the screen to talk to each other, to say what they really mean. Those scenes when you get frustrated and shout at the telly, 'Just bloody listen!' And there was Harry and me, soap stars in our own bloody lives. I'd refused to hear what he'd had to say and he hadn't been able to get through to me.

Look at what we'd done.

I did protest, weakly, that we should go to the police about what had happened with Charlene. And he agreed, equally weakly.

We were both cowards. What good would it do, we asked ourselves. Nothing was going to bring the poor girl back. Harry was already facing into the eye of a storm. He had the smallest chance of escaping jail following the bank collapse. He would have absolutely no chance if he was up on a hit-and-run charge.

We were protecting each other. Mutually assured survival.

So we held tight, and time began to pass. It was like the universe had staged an intervention and we weren't going to wreck the chance we'd been given.

Slowly, gradually, we rebuilt our life together, knowing it would never be the same but that we had to try.

We started to deal with Harry's cheating. I couldn't bear to hear the details. I didn't want to know who, I didn't want to know when. I just needed to know why and that I'd been right and I hadn't been paranoid or mad. It caused a terrible rift in our marriage, one we would never recover from. If I'd known then about the rape, I wouldn't have stayed. But his affairs seemed so petty in comparison to what we'd been through the night of the accident.

'I couldn't help it,' he said in one of our counselling sessions.

349

'I know that sounds like an excuse, but it's the truth. I would say to myself, *I can't do this to Julie. I don't need to sleep with anybody else. I love that woman more than life. What's wrong with me?* And then I'd swear I'd never do it again. But every time, it was like, once more can't hurt anybody. Julie doesn't know. I'll just be with this woman and I won't do it again. I'd come home and stand in the shower with the temperature nearly burning my skin off, I'd be that ashamed. There was nothing you could have done. You are the most beautiful woman in the world, the sexiest. I used to try to blame you, in my head. You'd drink and I'd stay out all night. But the truth is, I cheated on you before you started drinking properly. I'm a weak man, Julie. It wasn't your fault at all.'

'How can I not feel that was my fault?' I said in hushed tones, conscious of the counsellor's presence, the only thing stopping me from giving in to my instinct to murder my husband. What he told me hurt so much it broke my heart. And yet I had to cope with it. It was cope or leave. And I couldn't do that.

'It's common,' the counsellor said, an older man who looked like he'd heard the secrets of the world. 'Especially with successful men. Harry felt abandoned by his parents and sought out constant company and validation. Affairs gave that to him, but it was more than that. You are a driven man, Harry. Part of what drives you is your addiction to risk in the extreme, which most people are averse to. Your work involves risk. Your affairs involved risk. Even staying with Julie, when she had problems of her own, entailed risk. It can be a good thing, for a man like you, to have that inclination, but only when it's managed, which clearly it hasn't been. You're addicted to risk.'

That was my husband in a nutshell.

His affairs had damaged our relationship so much I couldn't even consider IVF. I was trying to come to terms with us staying together. I wasn't bringing a baby into that mess.

I joined AA, burning up with shame. I was a failure, I told myself. I'd had everything, compared to most people, and I'd still felt the need to drink. And believing I was a failure made me want to drink. Throw in the knowledge that my husband had slept around behind my back and, Jesus, that made me want to drink everything.

It was only sheer persistence and willpower that got me through.

That, and constantly reminding myself what could happen if I let myself slip – what had happened already.

Throughout all of this, we had to deal with what was taking place at the bank, and, ironically, that really brought us together. I hated what they were doing to Harry, trying to make him into a scapegoat. He had made mistakes and sometimes what he'd done wasn't strictly legal, but he had been a brilliant businessman. He'd driven development in Ireland like nobody else. Yes, it should have all come to a halt earlier than it did, but that wasn't Harry's fault. Everybody else had jumped on board at that stage and they were all leading the same charge. It was like everything good he'd ever done was to be forgotten and instead he was to be painted as the devil incarnate.

I was fully on his side, on that front. It had always been the way. I could quarrel with my husband and he with me, but once an outsider picked a fight we joined forces. And we'd a lot to contend with during the financial crash.

Nothing made us closer, though, than the shared knowledge of what had happened to Charlene Andrews.

It was like we'd had a near-death experience ourselves. Having survived it, we clung together like we were the only two people in the world, me supporting him, him supporting me. Everything that had gone before was like a horrible dream.

Perhaps that dream-like quality that I attached to the Andrews girl's death made it easier to live with, like it hadn't quite happened. For five years, we were in denial.

It had happened though.

I thought nobody knew our secret. But somebody must have.

JP Carney had to have known.

I don't know his link to Charlene Andrews and, to be honest, I could just let it go. But Alice was right. Once I buried Harry, my mind had gone right back to wondering why Carney had come to our home and what had led him to turn himself in.

I don't want people to know about our role in the Andrews girl's death. Harry's dead, but I'd be left living with the consequences. The shame. Having realized Nina Carter was telling the truth, I refuse to bear any more for Harry's sins, no matter how much he did for me.

But I can't be sure people won't find out about Charlene unless I figure out what Carney knows and what he might reveal.

There's only one way I can do that.

I have to talk to him.

JP

I suppose, looking back, I suffered with depression in the wake of Charlie's death. I didn't put a name on it. I didn't go to the doctor – not at first, anyway.

That was for weak people. I wasn't weak. I'd been strong my whole life.

But there was something that worried me. The way I'd reacted when I thought McNamara was about to kill his wife – that *scared* me. It was a part of my personality I hadn't seen before and hadn't realized existed.

I started to read up a bit, to try to figure out why I was the way I was. I didn't think I was a psychopath or anything. But I did begin to accept that maybe I'd been under too much pressure. Grief is overwhelming at the best of times, but Charlie's death coming on top of a life of various traumas did things to my head.

That night outside the McNamara home, I had a breakdown of sorts.

Afterwards, I tried to make sense of how I'd been behaving – the things I'd done and how far I'd been willing to go. And also of what

I'd seen of the McNamaras. What had gone on between the pair of them in that sitting room? What had been said?

The thing is, I just didn't know what to do. The mourning I had postponed so I could get to the bottom of what had happened hit me like a tsunami. I was overcome, and the only firm ground I could grasp was the desperate need to see Harry McNamara pay for what he'd done.

Julie McNamara knew the truth. I was sure of it. There was no other reason for her to have watched that show, got so upset and have had the big blow-out with her husband.

Yet even when Harry had grabbed her and it seemed like he was hurting her, she'd done nothing.

Did I have it wrong? Was she afraid of him?

No. That wasn't it. I'd seen the way she held him that night. She had chosen to support him. All this time, I thought she might be a potential ally, but for all I knew she would give her husband an alibi. And with his car fixed, what evidence would I have that it had been Harry who'd killed my sister? Tony would never testify to repairing the Mercedes – it would put him up shit creek.

I had been expecting that Harry would cave when I confronted him with the truth but really, would that have happened?

Then events overtook everything.

I had gone to their home in August 2007. By the end of the following month, Harry McNamara's life was in freefall. His bank was perhaps the biggest player in the financial crash that hit that year. HM Capital was billions in debt. The whole country was going to shit. As trainwrecks go, Harry's was impressive.

I watched from the sidelines as his business collapsed, as he was declared bankrupt and the coppers opened a file on him.

I lived through the months that followed in a sort of daze. McNamara was in the papers almost every day. I was in limbo. What could I do when the man was in the public eye and already under the scrutiny of the Guards? It felt like God had stepped in to decide this man's fate and I could do nothing other than watch.

So that's what I did.

It didn't give me the same satisfaction. Not like it would have if I had exacted my own justice on the man for Charlie's death. But I was still in shock after that night in Dalkey. I was coming to terms with the fact that should opportunity provide itself, I could be capable of something evil too.

I slipped further into the darkness.

By 2010, I looked for a bit of help. By that, I mean I went to the doctor and told him I hadn't slept in months and asked him to give me some pills. He talked to me for over an hour, made me come back for a second session and diagnosed severe depression. Instead of sleeping pills, I got antidepressants.

I considered taking them all. That was how low I'd gone at that stage. I counted them all out on the table one night and poured myself a glass of whiskey.

It was the table where I'd shared breakfast with my sister the morning before she died. And just thinking that – how much she'd have given to live – made me see sense. I poured the whiskey down the sink and put the tablets away.

I would see McNamara's head served up on a plate, even if it was taking aeons. Every time a trial date was set, it was postponed. Teams of lawyers were pictured on the news looking very important, dashing from Chambers out to their brand-new BMWs.

Then, in 2012, Harry had his day in court.

His wife held his hand as they arrived for the opening arguments. The papers wrote about how strong the couple looked, how supportive she was, how she'd chosen to wear a high-street skirt suit rather than her usual designer labels to send out the message that McNamara had not benefitted personally from his bank's dodgy dealings. This, despite the fact they lived in a house worth millions.

I followed court proceedings every day, even when most of it went over my head. A few journalists managed to do a decent job of breaking down the exchanges and the evidence for normal joes like me. Some of the reporters obviously hated McNamara and wrote about how he had managed to pull a fast one by stepping back from the bank's top job in 2006 and handing it to some chump called Richard Hendricks. Hendricks had already been prosecuted for multiple counts of market and accountancy fraud. He was the first banker in the state to be sent down for actual jail time. I'm sure he was gunning for McNamara.

As the months wore on, I began to get a sinking feeling.

McNamara wouldn't be found guilty.

His defence team was running rings around the state. Magazines were starting to do fluff pieces about McNamara and his wife, painting the couple as the injured party. Had McNamara stayed at the head of the bank, maybe nothing bad would have happened. The man was a business genius, a lovely guy. He had flaws but he knew how to run a bank. Hendricks hadn't the same experience, and he and the senior executives got carried away. Hendricks had even driven his own former business, some airline, into the ground.

The tide of public opinion was turning in McNamara's favour.

It was a double blow and one that tipped me over the edge.

I had to change my plans.

He had to suffer, whatever the outcome of the fraud trial.

In fact, it would be even better if it was when he thought he'd got away with everything that I made him pay.

Alice

'Do you think it's a good idea?'

'What?'

'I just told you,' Alice tutted, exasperated. 'Letting them talk to each other. Carney and Julie McNamara.'

Gallagher shrugged. Doherty had just wiped him and half the station out at cards again and he had no coins left for the chocolate machine on the landing. He thumped it, in the hope a bar might just fall out, but nothing happened.

'Have you got two quid on you?' he asked.

'Of course. I'm always flush. It's the incredibly generous wages.'

Gallagher inserted the coin and selected a KitKat. While his blushing bride-to-be seemed intent on starving herself into a size-too-small wedding dress, he was going to the other extreme. It was probably being around Moody all the time. She never stopped stuffing herself. Obesity was contagious. He'd read that somewhere.

'Here,' he said, breaking the KitKat in half and giving her two fingers. 'So. Your question. It's not a *bad* idea. Victim/perp reconciliation and all that palaver. Where's the harm in it?'

Alice sighed, taking the chocolate.

'I suppose what's pissing me off is that I can't listen in on the exchange. They'll be on their own.'

'Is that safe?'

'Hospital security will be there, obviously. And he won't be allowed any golf clubs.'

'Ha! You reckon he's going to confess or something when he sees her? Tell her that he had a motive?'

Alice shrugged.

'To be honest, I'm curious as to why Julie wants to go see him. I think that's what she believes – that he'll tell her why he did it. She doesn't realize that's absolutely no use to us, if he tells her but won't repeat it for the record. I have a feeling she could be opening a Pandora's box, going in there. She might learn something that, ultimately, comes to nothing but tortures her. She's raw. It's only six weeks since it happened and hardly any time since her husband died. She doesn't know what she's doing.'

'Yeah, but you can't do anything about it.'

'Hmm. Thanks for the chocolate. How's your wedding diet going, Sarge? Did you buy a suit that was too big or something?'

'Fuck off. Haven't you work to be getting on with?'

'Just trying to be helpful. Yeah, they found a poor soul dead in a bedsit in Dún Laoghaire. Working girl, overdose. Arsehole pimp probably gave her dodgy gear. Toxicology want to have a chat.'

'Well, hop to it, then. I'm sure Julie McNamara will ring you if Carney decides to spill his guts. At least then you'll have the satisfaction of knowing.'

Alice raised an eyebrow.

359

'There is that, yeah. Oh, before I do bury the file on this though, there's one other thing I want to follow up on.'

Gallagher got the distinct impression she'd thrown that in to sound like it was an aside, when really it was the purpose of their whole conversation.

'What's that, then?'

'I stopped waiting for our colleagues in the Met to send us something and did a search on Carney's history in England. You were right. I shouldn't have left it to Doherty. He is a useless shit. Anyway, I looked myself into Carney's early days, when his folks were together. There's something he didn't tell us.'

'Brilliant. So you're telling me you cocked up, and to fix it you conducted an unauthorized investigation in a separate jurisdiction on a closed file. I'm sure that won't come back to haunt us at all. What did you find out?'

'Carney wasn't always our boy's name. Prior to 2006 he was John Paul Andrews – he used the father's surname. I spoke to an old neighbour of theirs when they lived in London – Rose something. She kept referring to him as the Andrews boy. So I checked in with the High Courts, and he lodged a deed poll with them a few years back. The neighbour said there was a sister too. Charlie. Said JP doted on her.'

'How the fuck did we miss that? But what's his bloody sister got to do with anything?'

'Well, where is she? Why hasn't she come to see him?'

'Maybe she doesn't talk to him any more. Or she's dead. Besides, if Julie McNamara knew of a Charlie Carney, she'd have said something.'

'Maybe.' Alice shrugged. 'But doesn't it seem unusual that JP wouldn't have mentioned her at all, especially if he was fond of her? Anyway, I'll look into it. Doherty searched for Carney siblings but it never dawned on him to check for siblings under Andrews, and there's nothing to say Charlie went back to her mother's surname too.' Alice winced at the look on her boss's face. 'I'm sure he'd have got there eventually. There's no need to fire him, or anything. I have his balls in my pocket. He's suffered enough, Sarge.'

'What's your point, Moody? Carney didn't tell us he'd a sister. He didn't tell us anything. We had to find out everything. I'm not sure I see where you're going.'

'I don't know. Maybe nowhere. I checked through the system this morning for a Charlie Andrews but got nothing in the preliminary search on our files. She's no criminal record, anyway.'

'Hm.' Gallagher scratched his beard. 'The name does seem familiar. I don't know why. Charlie is unusual for a girl. Try Charlotte, or Charlene maybe. Charlie's probably not her birth name. What are you telling me for, anyway? Isn't your MO to just do whatever the hell you want?'

'I thought you were gung-ho to be involved in this investigation. Are we not the new Starsky and Hutch?'

'I wouldn't go using that line, Alice. Our lot will very quickly turn that into Starsky and Butch.'

'Aren't you very funny. I just need you to give me a little breathing space and not mention any higher up that I'm still pursuing the McNamara stuff. Maybe if I put the word out that JP Carney is John Paul Andrews, somebody will come forward. You know, Harry could have had his wicked way with JP's sister and dumped her with a sprog – something like that. He did have a way with the ladies, by all accounts. Maybe that's what drove JP to batter him.'

361

'That would be one possessive big brother. And the girl in Dún Laoghaire?'

'I'll throw my eye over the case and put somebody on it.'

'Jaysus, Alice. You're relentless.'

'Thanks, Sarge. Stay off those bars now, won't you? I won't always be here to lighten your calorie load, ya big fat bastard.'

Gallagher stared down at his midsection, which was straining unhealthily against the seams of his trousers, as Alice plodded off. All those unkind thoughts he'd had about Moody's weight. Karma was giving him a big kick in the arse.

He dropped the remains of the bar into the bin and trudged back to his office.

JP

Julie McNamara is coming in to see me.

I've been waiting for this. God, I've been waiting for this.

What does she want? Is she looking for some sort of apology? Or has she figured it out?

Is the truth about to come out?

It's only been six weeks. If any more time passes, that detective is going to figure everything out. Somebody will come forward and talk about Charlie. There are still some people who remember me from back then. Somebody will make the connection.

I don't want it to happen like that. I have other plans.

I agree to the visit, after pretending to think about it for a day or two, feigning nerves. I say I should meet her, because it's the right thing to do. But I have conditions. I say I'll meet with her alone. No cops. No solicitors. No doctors. This is a reconciliation meeting – it has nothing to do with the law. The hospital attendants will be there, but I don't care about them. They're like stone columns; their only job is to keep the ward standing. They won't repeat anything. They hear all sorts, every day.

They say it's not going to go down like that but then she says that's what she wants too. Just the two of us.

It's on.

On the morning she's due, I lie in bed a bit longer. They don't force me to get up, to join the queue of oddballs and crazies for a breakfast of pills and cold toast and milky tea. They imagine I'm stressed out because I'll be facing my victim's wife. All of my behaviour so far says that I'm only dying with guilt and remorse. Today could set me off. Plans are afoot to place me on suicide watch when she's gone.

I stay in bed because I want the quiet and solitude. I want to think. I want to remember.

Not what I did to Harry McNamara. Well, not directly. I want to think about the day I knew I had it in me to kill him. The day I realized I was capable of murder.

It was 2011 and I'd just finished up work. I'd gone back into office supplies. Not the original company. That one had closed. But my old gaffer had set up a smaller outfit and gave me a job when I came knocking. It wasn't as well paid and there was no chance of promotion. The whole country was in the pits because of Harry and his mates. It wasn't even looking too good for the boss's new venture, and he would eventually lose that too. But at the time it paid the rent and kept me honest. It was important that – seeming honest. Just in case I had to do something at a later date. Even then, I was plotting.

On that day, I decided to walk home from town, taking the old route through Drumcondra that I used to stroll with Charlie when I moved into my first flat. It was well out of my way, but I felt restless. I'd cleared out her bedroom the previous week, after four long years of watching dust accumulate on her belongings, her treasures. A layer of grey that had settled and grown and reminded me every day that there was no more Charlie, only things. I was thinking of this when I saw him.

Seamie, our dad.

He was sitting on a bench by the canal, sipping from a bottle in a brown paper bag, looking out at the swans. The same wide shoulders, shaggy black hair, now a drink-mottled face. Older, but he'd never looked particularly young.

I don't know what made me decide to approach him. It might have been because I was so alone in the world and he, for all that I'd given up on him years ago, was the closest living connection I had to a time when I had a family. I felt drawn to him.

Seamie looked up when I appeared in front of him and recognized me straight away.

'Well, what do you want, John Paul?' he said. No 'Hello, how are you?' Just 'What do you want?' As though time hadn't passed.

It was like an electric shock, hearing my name from his lips after so many years.

'Come for a drink with me,' I said.

He eyed me suspiciously but stood, a little unsteady already, and walked with me to a nearby pub.

I didn't talk much. I felt like I was in a dream. Like time had gone into reverse.

He filled the silence with tales of how hard his life had been. He didn't ask how I was. How Charlie was. She'd lived with me for years without so much as a phone call, a birthday card – nothing from that man. It was one thing for us to forget him but I still couldn't get my head around him giving up on his own children, especially considering how young we'd been – how young she'd been – when we moved out.

'You look like you've done all right for yourself,' he said, giving me the once-over. I didn't look anything special. I was wearing one of the two cheap suits that I owned and had worn that day to accompany the boss to a sales meeting.

But I was clean and sober – positively civilized compared to Seamie those days.

'You should have been helping your old dad out all this time,' he said, that bitter accusatory note in his voice that all drunks seem to master.

'That right?' I said.

'Yeah. You and that sister of yours. Lazy wagon. What kind of a daughter abandons her own father? Where is she, anyway? Run off and marry some fecker, did she? Just like her mother.'

He threw more drink into him, grimacing when he realized he'd reached the bottom of the glass.

'Charlie is dead,' I said, staring at the bar counter.

His eyes widened and his mouth fell open.

'Fuck. When?'

'Four years ago.'

'What . . . Why wasn't I told?'

I stared at him.

'Seriously? You ignored us for years and you think I should have contacted you? Charlie came to live with me when she was still just a child. You were already getting plastered every day by that stage. You were never a proper dad to her. You'd no right to be there.'

He closed his mouth.

His eyes filled with tears. I almost felt sorry for him. Almost.

'I deserved to be told,' he spat. 'I did my best for you. Both of you.'

'No,' I said. 'You didn't.'

We left the pub late, walking down the canal, him staggering but still standing. He had some capacity for the drink, I'll give him that. Any other man would have been on his ear by that stage.

I walked ahead, just like I used to when we were kids and he got drunk. It used to embarrass me, people thinking I was with that man who was roaring at total strangers.

Charlie had always stayed with him, trying to hold his hand, even when he could barely walk straight. Despite everything, she showed loyalty. She so badly wanted Dad to love her, a man who'd more or less stopped giving a toss when she was still a tot.

'What happened to her?' Seamie called out. We'd spent another hour in that pub and he hadn't thought to ask that until now.

I stopped and turned to face him.

'She was killed in a hit-and-run. A man drove into her. A rich bastard. The cops don't know who he is, but I do. He got away with it. He drove into her and left her body broken on the road like she was dirt, and he got away with it. It was on the news. On *Crimecall* – everything. If you'd lifted your nose out of the glass for five fucking minutes, you might have seen it.'

Why did I bother telling him? I don't know. I suppose I wanted to provoke a reaction, something deeper than the *poor me* crap he lived for, after years of poisoning his own body.

He had a look in his eye – that same cruel expression he'd had the night he told me what Betty had done to me when I was a baby.

Seamie's defence was always to go on the offence.

'Well, you didn't do such a good job of minding her, did you,

John Paul? You throw that in my face, but maybe she'd have been better off with me. And what have you done to make sure this man doesn't get away with it? What kind of a brother are you? This scumbag murders your sister – my girl. You know who he is and you do nothing? Chickenshit. I bet Charlene would have thought that and all. My brother, the coward. You should have killed him.'

'And you should have been there for her,' I snarled. 'For both of us. You're a joke, Seamie. Shit, I don't even know what I'm doing here. Wasting my time on a useless pisshead drunk like you.'

'I'm your father.'

'You're not my father. You haven't been for years. And you were never a father to Charlie. I was the closest thing she had to a dad.'

I turned and walked away from him. I could feel something building inside me, a rage so huge there'd be no coming back from it. My head was going to explode with it.

It angered him, me ignoring him. It was like he wanted to provoke a fight.

'How dare you? I lost everything because of her. Betty was doing all right before that baby came.'

I stopped, turned around slowly.

'What did you say?'

'I said it would have been better if Charlene hadn't been born.'

It took three steps. I grabbed him and dragged him to the water, the two of us stumbling in with a splash.

He didn't put up as much of a fight as I'd expected. All that strength he'd once had was gone – his body was just skin and bones. He resisted a little, but then it was like he just gave in.

Later, the post mortem would reveal he had advanced cirrhosis of the liver. He wasn't long for the world.

When I learned that, I realized he'd wanted to end it all.

He was at the end of his life with nothing to show for it and only a slow, painful death ahead of him.

Maybe he'd deliberately provoked me so I'd put him out of his misery. Whatever the reason, that was the night I found out what I was capable of. Holding a man underwater until he can't breathe is as violent as you get.

And if you can murder your own father, you really can do anything, can't you?

Julie

I had no idea what the Central Mental Hospital would look like until I was in it. If you'd asked me, I'd have come up with a description of some outdated Victorian building with iron grilles on the windows. I'd have pictured long grey corridors, manly-looking nurses in starched uniforms and patients in straitjackets. Pretty much whatever I'd read about psychiatric institutions in the classics or seen in movies.

Not this place. I'd never have imagined this place, with its pastel colours and modern, open rooms, the glass instead of bars, the friendly staff and the illusion that you can just walk in and out whenever the mood takes you.

It will be Christmas in a month and the place is already decorated with artificial trees and tinsel. Papier-mâché stars hang from the ceiling. It startles me. I haven't thought about a single normal thing since the attack. I haven't shopped. I haven't watched television. I certainly haven't thought about getting a tree or buying a gift.

Maybe after today I should try to do something small. A first step. Go and buy a coffee and a magazine, that sort of thing. Get something for Mam and Dad and Helen to say thank you.

The doctor in charge of Carney's care speaks to me first. He insists on getting me a cup of weak tea. Then he explains that his patient has been making good progress in coming to terms with what happened in my home that night but still doesn't know why it happened. Carney is racked with guilt, apparently, and that's why he's agreed to meet me. He's grateful for the opportunity, in fact, to be able to apologize in person.

I nod along at all the relevant spots, appearing outwardly calm, if a little distressed.

Inwardly, I'm trying to keep a lid on the turmoil I feel.

I have no doubt that JP Carney knows exactly why he did what he did that night. To still be putting me through this is just cruel and unusual.

I almost didn't come this morning, thinking I couldn't bear to meet him. The last time that man saw me I was sitting on my chair, gawping redundantly while he battered my husband to death.

Sometimes I don't know what I'm angrier at – his lies and how people are lapping them up, or how I reacted to his onslaught.

'We've set up one of the counsellors' rooms for you,' the doctor says. 'An orderly will sit in the corner, but he's only there for your safety. He won't be listening in on your conversation. He'll have earphones in. This meeting is for you and Mr Carney. As you both agreed you wanted it like this, we will respect your privacy. We take reconciliation very seriously.'

He hesitates.

'I know you have suffered a grievous loss at the hands of my patient, Mrs McNamara. I hope you attain some small degree of comfort from meeting JP and seeing how sorry he is. We have found that this type of one-to-one is extremely beneficial for victims and their relatives, as well as for the perpetrators. Normally, it's after more time has passed. It's a testament to your strength of character that you wish to have this conversation now. And if you want to talk to me afterwards, I would be more than happy to oblige. But – and I imagine somebody has explained this to you already – please know that there is no point in looking for answers or reasoning. The type of psychosis that came upon JP on the night in question is one of the many inexplicable workings of the human brain. There is no logic to it. It's one of those things that we will never understand. He is being punished, even though he is in here and not in jail. Both through his incarceration with us but also because he has to live with knowing what he did, even if his crime was out of character.'

'I know,' I say, biting my tongue.

He brings me to the room and makes sure I'm sitting comfortably while he goes off to fetch Carney. It's a basic space. Two armchairs are inclined towards each other, a table bearing a bouquet of flowers and a box of tissues between them. There's a lamp in the corner throwing out soft lighting. It's warm and comfortable, a safe place to relax and open up.

There's a chair by the door, and an orderly has already taken up residence. He smiles at me politely then puts his hands on his knees and stares into the distance. I turn from him and observe the painting on the wall. It's impressionist in style – twinkling stars in a clear sky, a bench in a park filled with a pair of lovers holding hands.

The door opens and then he's there, in the chair facing me.

Carney.

He seems so young, his dark eyes wide and full of fear. I see them fleetingly when he sits down, then he casts them back to the ground, unable to meet my own.

He's grown a beard since I saw him first, a tight-cut, dark mass of hair that makes him look even more handsome, accentuating rather than hiding his strong jawline.

'JP, this is Julie. Julie, JP.'

The doctor introduces us like it's the first time we've met.

'I'll leave you to it, so,' he says, hesitantly. I can tell, for all his good intentions, professional curiosity is killing him. Maybe he has his own doubts about JP. He leaves, anyway. The orderly replaces his earphones. It's almost like being alone.

We sit there in silence for a few minutes. I thought I would know what to say but, now he's actually sitting there, I'm lost for words. Looking at him forces me to relive that night, and even though I know I'm safe, I'm hoping I don't wet myself again.

He speaks first.

'I'm so sorry about your husband,' he says, still staring at the ground.

It's the first time I've heard his voice.

He's soft-spoken. Baritone, and with a twang of northside Dublin, but not aggressive.

You'd never guess what he's capable of.

I flinch. I can't respond immediately.

Is he testing me? I wonder.

Wanting to know what I know, questioning why I'm here?

Well, I won't play games.

I lean close, but not close enough to alarm the attendant at the door.

'No,' I say. 'No, you're not. Why did you do it?'

He lifts his face now and studies me. His expression hasn't changed. It's still the sad haunted-soul look. It's only in his eyes that I can see the truth.

His pupils are darker. Black. Like there's evil behind them that only seeps in when he wants you to see it.

'I don't know, Julie. May I call you that? The doctors say—'

'Don't call me anything,' I interrupt. 'I don't want to hear my name on your lips. And I don't want to hear what the doctors say.'

His expression changes slightly now, a hint of . . . what is that? Is he amused? Is it because I'm not afraid of him?

'Whatever you want,' he says. 'You're the victim.'

He pauses. He's made a decision about how he's going to act.

'I was happy to meet you so I can tell you how sorry I am. I'll always have what happened on my conscience. Even when they let me out, which the doctor says could be as soon as in a few years, if I go through the treatment process okay. Imagine that. To do something so awful and be allowed back out on the streets, still a relatively young man. It's shocking, isn't it? And yet your husband is gone and you have to live with what you saw for the rest of your life – you have to live with the knowledge that you sat there and watched as I beat your husband to death and did absolutely nothing. It must be terrible. I can't imagine what it must feel like to witness such a thing. I'm so sorry.'

It's like being punched in the gut. It's an effort to keep breathing.

I close my eyes and see white dots dancing. And in the dots there's Carney, smashing Harry's body with the golf club over and over.

I take hold of the sides of the chair to steady myself and open my eyes.

He's smiling.

The bastard is smiling.

'Do you think,' he says, 'that a tiny part of you wanted him to suffer? Is that why you didn't leap to his defence, Julie? Had he hurt you so bad that you were happy for him to die? Had he done something so bad that you thought, *He deserves this*?'

I can feel a panic attack building. This is an admission that he knows what Harry did, but I can't respond to it because he's tapped into something so private, so utterly terrifying, that I want to cry. I start to shake my head, and then I am shaking it properly, and then the words come. Weak at first but then stronger. I can't live with the idea that I wanted Harry to suffer. I won't live with it. For all the things he did to me in the past, we had some good years at the end. I didn't know the real truth about Nina Carter on the night of the attack. I hadn't yet heard what she had to say. But even knowing it, I wouldn't have wished Harry dead. Divorced, yes. But not beaten to death. My deepest fears about my own motivation that night are just that – fear. Irrational, and not real. Not the truth.

'No,' I croak. 'I – I was . . . I was frightened. I was scared. But I didn't want to see my husband hurt. Not then. How dare you say that? You knew nothing about us.'

He shrugs.

'Fair enough. Whatever you need to tell yourself.'

He's so smug, so glib.

'Why don't we talk about Charlene Andrews?' I say, my voice even.

His face flushes but then settles, that slightly amused and innocent look descending once more.

'Who?' he says.

I exhale. I know I'm not wrong. Not now.

'Who was she to you? Your girlfriend? A relative?'

He says nothing, just stares at me.

'I must be wrong,' I say, taking charge of the game now. 'Maybe she didn't matter to you at all. Maybe she didn't matter to anybody. Nobody seemed too worried about her death. I thought you might have been a boyfriend, but the reports about her never mentioned one. Unless you were, and her family didn't consider you important enough.'

His eyes flash to the orderly and back again. We're speaking in hushed tones and he's got the earphones in, listening to a football match so loudly we can hear the crowd cheering. JP is having his own private battle. To keep up the game a little longer, dangling me like I'm a mouse, pretending he's ignorant and blame free; or to let me know that he has his claws well and truly dug in.

He can't wait. Or maybe this is what he's been waiting for all along.

'She was somebody,' he says. 'She was my sister. Charlie. I was hoping you'd bring her up. Now we can have a proper conversation.'

I close my eyes. Her brother. I'd read afterwards she had a brother. How did I not make the link? But he looks nothing like her – so dark to her fairness. And the name is different.

'Is that what you said?' I ask. 'When you whispered to Harry at the end, did you say her name?'

'Yes. I said, "This is for Charlie." I hope he heard me, but who knows at that stage? I guess the last thing he was conscious of was you sitting on the couch watching him get battered.'

We stare at each other, eyes unblinking.

I drop my gaze first. He's hurt me. And in his face I can see a reflection of my own grief – something stronger, in fact. And it isn't pleasant.

'I see.'

'Yeah,' he says. 'You see.'

We're quiet again.

'Why?' I say. 'Five years. It's so long ago. Why?'

I mean, why now? Why did he wait? But he answers me as though I've asked why he couldn't just let it go.

'She was twenty-two. She'd have only been twenty-seven if she were alive today. It's not something time heals. Five, ten, fifteen years, I'll still feel the same. About her and the bastard who murdered her.'

I wince.

'Why did you have to kill him?' I ask, my voice barely louder than a whisper. 'Why not report him? And why not me? Why did you do it in front of me but not kill me? You must have known I was in the car as well.'

JP lifts his hand and scratches at the beard on his chin, examining me as though I'm a student who's asked a particularly fascinating question.

'I knew you were in the car,' he said. 'And then I realized that you knew what he'd done. I don't know why he drove into Charlie. Maybe it was an accident. Maybe he was too frightened to come forward. He probably made his decisions out of fear. But you – you chose to stand by him, to support him. To help him cover it up. That's why you had to be there when I went after him. And now you have to live with that. By the look of you, it was the worst thing I could have thought up for you.'

He flicks his eyes over my diminished frame, my sunken face.

'There was no point going to the cops,' he continues. 'Look at what your husband got away with after bringing the country to its knees. What proof had I that he killed my sister? He sorted the car. You could have given him an alibi. He'd have got away with it, just like he got away with everything he did in his bank.'

I shake my head. It's what I suspected, this exchange. But I'm still horrified. Appalled. All that time he waited and waited, and then, just when we imagined our lives were back on track, he struck.

A reckoning.

'Harry never got over your . . . your sister,' I say. 'He went to her funeral. It was risky, but he went anyway. He had to. He lived with her death every day. We both did. But there was nothing we could do. She was gone.'

'Responsibility,' he says, eyes boring into mine. 'He never took responsibility for what he'd done. Neither of you did. It might have been an accident, but he killed her and he should have come forward and admitted it. You should have made him.'

I feel my shoulders slump.

'Ah,' I say, as it hits me. 'So that's what this is about? This little act. The insanity plea. You're not taking responsibility for what you did. But why hand yourself in at all? Why not run?'

'Because you saw me. I wanted you to see me. If I'd run, you'd have described me and they'd have found me. If I'd denied it, it would have been the denial of a guilty man. It would have showed a level of planning that my temporary insanity wouldn't allow, I'm afraid. This way, I'm guilty but I won't be held responsible. Just like Harry.'

I nearly choke at the devious ingenuity of his plan.

I have so many questions. So many things I want to know. How did he find out it was Harry? How did he find us? Had he been watching us all those years?

All of it so trivial and irrelevant in this moment.

What I really want to know right now is, why is he telling me the truth? What is his game now?

'How do you know,' I ask, 'that I won't just go to the Guards and tell them everything you've just said? I know you can deny it all, but now I know there's a link, they can make the connection with evidence. You can't have been that clever. You had to ask questions, you needed to find out information about our lives to bring you to us. And they're bound to make the link to Charlie. Eventually.'

He shakes his head slowly, smiling at me.

'Julie, Julie, Julie. How do you know that isn't exactly what I want to happen? What I want you to do? What if I told you right now that you have a choice to make? You can choose to go to the Guards, but you probably won't. You could have gone already. You're stuck, and you know it. It can't have taken you this long to figure out the attack was linked to Charlie. But if you tell the Guards what I've told you, then you'll have to confess to keeping Harry's secret for the last five years. He murdered somebody, and you told nobody. The truth about your precious husband will be out. And you'll suffer. Charlie will finally get justice.'

'What if I say I wasn't in the car and didn't know any of this? What if I claim you're a fantasist and you've told me all this but it has nothing to do with Harry?'

'If I'm a fantastist, that doesn't change a thing. They'll leave me here. I'm mad, aren't I? But let's say I tell the cops and you claim it's all lies. Maybe they take me seriously and they reopen my sister's case. But this time they're looking at where you and Harry were the night she died. And then you claim you weren't in the car. But they find out you were pissed and he dragged you out of a party. It will be hard for you to play the innocent. It will be easy for the Guards to establish that the pair of you didn't stay in that hotel that night, and then it's obvious he drove you home.

'But I don't want to do that, Julie. I want to see what you'll do. It's much better if it comes from you. If you want to see me punished, you will have to admit that Harry killed my sister and that you knew. Will you do it? Will you tell the truth? Or wait for DS Moody to bring it to you? I've great faith in her, but she might still fuck it up. She mightn't find out about Charlie. And I'll stay here and get out in a few years. And there's something you should know. I don't give a shit about what happens to me. This was only ever for her.'

Tears well in my eyes at how clever he's been. He's right, of course. I can't relay this conversation to DS Moody unless I want to implicate myself. This is what he wanted all along. To have this conversation with me. To bring me to this point. And chances are, even if I try to get away with it, she'll figure it out anyway.

Oh, that night. That awful night.

All along, I've had a terrible feeling that Carney was connected to that.

He's looking at me with a self-satisfied, smug expression on his face, like he's won all over again.

He says he wants me to do the right thing, but he must know I won't. Otherwise I'd have done it already.

He's smart.

But not as smart as he thinks he is.

I lean closer.

'So you created a little trap,' I say. 'The person who killed your sister had to die, and the person who helped cover it up would be forced to live with another cover-up, unless the truth came out. In the absence of us telling the real story, you deemed that a just sentence?'

His brow furrows and he swallows.

The tears are gone and I sound confident. He's wondering what's come over me.

'The thing is, JP,' I say, 'I think you fucked up. It should have been the other way round. Or you should have killed us both.'

'What?' he says, genuine confusion on his face now, mixed with panic; none of the cunning. The man is a mess. He is unstable, no matter how in control he thinks he is.

'I told my husband to do it. I told him to kill your sister. It was to prove his love for me. I'm the reason she is dead, JP. You see, Harry always said he'd do anything for me.'

'I don't . . . I don't understand. What are you saying?'

'I'm saying that Harry may have been driving that night, but I caused the crash. I killed your sister.'

Julie

That night, 2007

Here's what I remember.

I remember Harry laughing at me when I asked for the keys in the hotel lobby. He grabbed my arm then, and dragged me out to the car. I screamed abuse at him, vile, nasty words, while he held his tongue and manhandled me into the passenger seat.

I bit his hand and he yelled that I was a fucking bitch.

The two of us, utter disgraces.

He buckled me into the car even as I tried to fight him off, then slammed the door with such force that it nearly came off the hinges.

When he got in on his side he was silent again, hands gripping the wheel, jaw clenched in the face of my continued verbal onslaught.

He drove fast.

I hated that he was being silent and ignoring me. It gave him the upper hand. He was making it clear that I was the crackpot, unable to control my rage, humiliating myself.

I stopped yelling and started to cry. The thoughts that had gone around in my head so often over the last few months resurfaced.

When we got home, I was going to do it. When Harry fell asleep, I was going to lock myself in one of the rooms and take a load of pills. End it all.

I don't think I meant to say it out loud, but maybe I did. Perhaps I wasn't as determined as I thought – maybe I was frightened that I would actually commit suicide and self-preservation kicked in.

'I'll kill myself,' I whispered.

'What did you say?' he said.

'Nothing.'

'Julie, what the hell did you say?'

'I said I want to die! I want it to end, Harry. It's the only way I'll be rid of you. I hate you. I hate you almost as much as I hate myself. I can't live this life any more. This twisted fucking loyalty we have, this co-dependency. I can't do it.'

'Julie.' His face was ashen. He brought the car to a halt.

'You know what I wish? I wish Richard Hendricks had killed me. Then it would have been all over. I'd never have known that he meant more to you than I did. That your bank meant more. I wouldn't have . . . I wouldn't have killed the baby. I killed my baby, but it should have been me. Not that little innocent. You were wrong. When it bled out of me, I knew I wanted it. I didn't just want to be pregnant. I really wanted that child, and I didn't understand until it was gone.'

I was crying hard and he with me.

He tried to console me, struggled to put his arms around me.

'I despise Richard Hendricks,' he said. 'I only left him at the bank so I could make him suffer. I keep telling you.'

'And how dare you?' I sobbed. 'How dare you use what happened to me like that? You don't care for me. You're a liar. Don't touch me. Just get me home. Now!'

He gave up and started the car again.

'I've always loved you, Julie,' he choked, as he began to drive, tears streaming silently down his cheeks. 'Don't you know that? I can't live without you. I couldn't live with myself if you . . . if you hurt yourself because of me.'

I snorted, so drink-sodden that I couldn't even hear the real emotion in his voice, just the same hollow words he'd repeated over the years.

'You don't know how to love!' I spat. 'You've lied to me for years, Harry. Made me feel like I'm paranoid and crazy when I've known – I've just known – that you've been screwing other women. If some woman knocked on our door tonight and dropped her knickers, you'd be in there in front of me, still denying it. Look at how you were with that girl on the dance floor. You have no control over yourself. I've been so loyal to you. So faithful. "*I can't live without you.*" You make me sick.'

'I married *you*, Julie,' he said, his voice thick. 'You're my family. My only family. I'm sorry I've hurt you. I'm sorry you feel this way. But you've hurt me too. I want us back. I wish we could go back to the way we were.'

I saw her before he did.

A girl. Long blonde wavy hair. Petite. Ahead of us on the long, empty stretch of road.

'Is that the girl you were dancing with?' I cried. 'I can't believe this. Go on, then. Stop and ask her. You can pick up where you left off. Ask her to come home with us, Harry. I can watch. I've

384

no dignity left. Let's stop pretending. You can have her in our bed. Go on.'

'Stop it, Julie!' he cried. 'Stop it.'

'You wanted her, didn't you? Well, go on! I'm giving you permission.'

'She's nothing, Julie. Nobody. I would climb over her to get to you.'

'Prove it.'

The words hung suspended in the air.

'Prove you'd do anything for me, Harry. Prove how much you love me. Show me those women mean nothing to you. Show me she means nothing and I'll stop drinking. I'll love you again.'

'Jesus, Julie.'

He put his foot on the accelerator so we would speed past the girl and she'd be behind us.

And then it happened.

She was metres from us.

I leaned over and grabbed the wheel. He shoved me back into my seat, furious.

'I said, fucking stop!' he roared, and tried to right the car.

It was too late.

That's what I told myself, afterwards.

Our car was on top of the girl before he had time to straighten it on the road.

I don't like to think of the look in his eyes in those last few seconds. When she turned and he saw her full on – a young girl, not the girl he'd danced with but a total stranger, yet one who looked like me. And his hands, just for a second, loosened their grip on the wheel so the car didn't veer away but instead hit her full on.

No. It wasn't intentional. Was it?

Just because she looked like his wife and he was so angry.

Just because I'd told him to prove his love for me.

I had grabbed the wheel. It was deliberate but it was also just stupidity. Drunken, maniacal stupidity. An unforgiveable moment of madness.

But . . . the night of the *Crimecall* episode, when Harry was huddled on our floor, tormented, in agony, and we looked at each other.

I knew really.

He'd let the car hit her.

He'd done it because I wanted him to kill her, to prove all the other women meant nothing to him.

He'd done it because he hated me in that moment and wanted to kill somebody.

He'd done it because of me.

Epilogue

Late one night a man came into my home, murdered my husband and made me watch.

He did it to teach us both a lesson.

It was a lesson we probably deserved.

Only JP Carney and I know the truth.

And that's where I could choose to leave it. We could both try to get away with what we've done, as far as the law is concerned.

Two strangers, inextricably linked by brutality, lies and revenge.

Or I could tell the world what we did to his sister and what he did to my husband.

Does Carney really, truly want that? Or is he testing me?

Harry is gone. He was the love of my life, even if at times we ripped the very hearts out of each other. If he had lived, what would have happened? I don't know. We wouldn't have stayed together. But perhaps we'd have stayed in each other's orbits. When you live a life together, can you ever really live apart?

And JP is wrong. Harry did one good thing. He took responsibility for Charlene's death. He took it as far as I was concerned. He discharged me of my involvement.

'I ruined your life,' he said, that night after the *Crimecall* episode, when the full truth came spilling out. 'It's all my fault. How you acted that night, and that girl dying. I could have turned the wheel. I should have turned the wheel. I know you didn't really want to hit her.'

'I did, Harry. I did in that moment,' I said. 'I thought she was the girl from the dance floor. She was yet another woman you were looking at instead of me. Somebody else you might cheat with. The final straw. I wanted her to die, and I didn't even know her. I was insane.'

'It's still my fault, Julie. Not yours. It will never be yours.'

Every day for the five years that followed, he tried to make it up to me for the bad times. It was as though if we could make our marriage work, that poor girl's death wouldn't have been for nothing.

Twisted, I know.

But the thing is, sometimes we were happy, despite the fraud charges and the court hearings and the publicity. We were happy the night JP Carney walked into our sitting room and attacked us. And that was wrong. We shouldn't have been able to live with what had happened. None of it.

It was toxic, but it's over now.

I know Carney will be stewing after what I said. If he believed me. He might be telling himself that I made it up, a nasty attempt at revenge on my part.

I don't think so though. I think he could see in my eyes that I was telling the truth.

I could leave him suffering with that, the torture of thinking he had got it so wrong. I have the house. I have plenty of money. I'm still a relatively young woman. I could start again. Live a healthier, better life. If I got away with his sister's death then, I could get away with it now.

But I know it won't be like that. A life built on a glossy surface that's rotten underneath? That could never last. All of my past experiences tell me that.

In the first instance, in a few years Carney will get out, and he will come after me. I know it for certain.

More importantly, there's a young woman's death to atone for.

Charlene Andrews did nothing to Harry and me. We killed her, and she never got the justice she deserved. Not even from her brother, who, instead of reporting the truth, took the law into his own hands.

Nina Carter never got justice.

Even the people who suffered because of Harry's bank – they were left with the consequences.

Eventually, I make the decision. I will take responsibility for what Harry and I did to Charlene Andrews.

It will all come out. Everything. I'll suffer. My family will be ashamed of me. My parents, Helen – I've let them down so badly. I can only hope they love me enough to stand by me.

Right up until she answers the phone, I consider changing my mind.

But no. It has to stop.

'DS Moody,' she barks.

'DS . . . Alice,' I say, forcing myself to speak. 'It's Julie McNamara. I need to talk to you. It's about what JP Carney said to me when I met with him. It's about his sister.'

And then the words come.

It strikes me, at one point during my monologue and her single-syllable responses, that she already knows. That she's been waiting for me to call. She's a smart woman; I wouldn't be surprised if she got there before me.

It doesn't matter. It has to be me who tells her. She won't have to prove her case.

I'll give it to her.

I'll confess.

Acknowledgements

Things I've learned as a writer: I do okay when I write on my own, I do a whole lot better when I write with a team.

A few people in particular made me work extra hard on this book.

Martin Spain, you were irritatingly right on all the early plot holes, as always. Still love you, my favourite person in the world.

Nicola Barr, thank you for pushing me and yes, you knew what you were doing. Look at this beauty. I solemnly take back all those times I saw your name in my email box and thought, for the love of God, please, no more edits!

Stef Bierwerth, who took what I reckoned was already a fairly finished draft and pointed out all the work still to be done – brilliantly, so you're forgiven too. Where would I be without you Stef? Editor and friend. Few are so lucky.

Rachel Neely and Sarah Day who between them sub-edited and proofed *The Confession* to within an inch of its life. Rachel, especially, for your inspired title. Actually, I'm pretty sure that makes you the book's godmother!

All my early readers, the whole incredible team at Quercus and particularly the design team for this mind-blowing cover: I'm proud to work with every single one of you.

Last but not least. All my friends and family, especially my four biggest cheerleaders, my lovely children Izzy, Liam, Sophia and Dom the baby despot – thank you for endless love and support. I can only reach for the stars because I have all of you lifting me up.

Read on for an exclusive extract of
the second psychological thriller from Jo Spain:

Dirty Little Secrets

Coming early 2019.

PROLOGUE

Death stalked the Vale.
In every corner, every whisper.
They just didn't know it yet.

The bluebottle had no idea it was about to die.

It zipped upwards in the blue sky, warm sun shimmering on its wings, bright metallic stomach bloated with human skin cells and blood.

The bluebottle didn't see the blackbird swoop, beak open in anticipation. It didn't hear the satisfying crunch that brought an untimely end to its short, blissful life.

The blackbird continued its descent. There, just beyond the sycamore, streaming from the chimney of the cottage, were more mid-flight snacks. Hundreds of them – fat, juicy, winged insects.

The bird didn't see the boy, with his Extreme Blastzooka Nerf gun and the bullets he'd modified to cause maximum damage from what was supposed to be a minimum-impact toy.

When the missile hit, slate-coloured feathers exploded in all directions. Death and gravity cast the bird onto the top branches of the tree, from where it *thump, thump, thumped* the whole thirty metres down to a soft patch of grass below.

The boy, breathlessly running towards his felled prey, didn't see his mother throw open the kitchen door and bear down on him – the bird's squawk and the boy's squeak had jolted her from all thoughts of her absent lover.

Instantly, she saw what her son had done.

But before she could grab him, the boy pointed up and said, with more awe than even the dead bird had incited: *'Fuuuuck!'* And despite the itch to now punish him twice as hard, the mother's eyes were drawn to the cloud on the periphery of her vision, a black, menacing, humming mass of bluebottles rising out of next door's chimney.

The mother clamped her hand over her mouth. That swarm could only mean one thing, and it wasn't anything good.

Whatever had happened next door, the mother certainly hadn't seen *that* coming.

Once upon a time, they'd all tried to be more neighbourly. As recently as a couple of years ago, that effort had taken the form of a street party.

Nobody could remember who had suggested it. Alison, a newbie at the time, reckoned the street party was Olive's doing. Chrissy thought it was Ron's. Ed presumed it was David's. Nobody supposed George had come up with it. Not because he wasn't a nice guy, but he was painfully shy and you just couldn't imagine him saying, *Hey, let's have a bit of a party, mark the start of the summer hols!*

George, though, had put in the most effort. His house, number one, was the largest on the Vale and, therefore, he clearly had the most money (well, his family did – they all knew his father owned the property). That day, George, very generously, brought out four bottles of champagne, a crate of real ale and giant-sized tubs of American toffee candy and wine gums. They were added to the haphazard mix of sweets and savouries already laid out on the trestle table. The sugary wine gums sat between the large bowls of Jollof rice and fried plantains that David had provided.

The adults had floated around each other nervously, despite the fact that most of them were professionals, used to networking and performing. Matt was an accountant. Lily a school teacher. David worked in investments. George was a layout graphic designer. Alison owned a boutique. Ed was a retired something or other – whatever he'd done, it had left him very wealthy. They all had money, in fact. Or at least appeared to. They were social equals and the majority of them had lived in proximity for years.

And yet there was a shyness amongst the grown-ups of Withered Vale. In a domestic setting, out of the suits and offices, metres from their own private abodes, each of them felt an odd sense of discomfort, like they should be more relaxed than they were. Like they should know each other more than they did.

The children, forced into being the centre of attention and with far too much responsibility on their tiny number, had awkwardly played football in an attempt to entertain. The twins were useless. Wolf kicked the ball with such intensity it was like it was diseased and he needed to clear it as quickly as possible. Lily May, his sister, defended herself, not the goal, twisting her body in knots any time the ball was aimed in her direction, at all times nervously sucking the ends of her braids. Cam, a couple of years older and many degrees rougher, was brutally violent, with John McEnroe's

indignant temper whenever he was called to order. And Holly –
well, she stood slightly aside, old enough to babysit, too young to
be in the adults' company, painfully self-conscious and bored and
mortified.

Somehow, despite the alcohol, the generous food portions, the
sun's gentle warmth and Ron's best attempts to get an adult football
game going, the party just didn't come off.

If you'd asked any of them why, they'd have all shrugged, unable
to put a finger on it.

But if you'd made them think hard . . .

Olive Collins had moved from group to group, chatting to the
women, harmlessly flirting with the men, trying to amuse the children, generally being a pleasant, sociable *host*.

Of all the seven homes in the privileged gated estate of Withered
Vale, Olive's was the smallest and the one that stood out as the most
different. Of all the residents, she was the one who probably
belonged the least. Not that anybody would think that. Or say it,
when they did.

The horseshoe-shaped street was a common area. And with the
exception of Alison, nobody believed the party had been suggested
by Olive.

Olive preferred one-to-ones.

But she'd taken over. Olive, Withered Vale's longest resident,
had an awful tendency to act like she owned the place.

Slowly, they peeled off. Chrissy, a reluctant attendee in the first
place, steered Cam firmly by the shoulder towards home; Matt
sloping loyally behind his wife and son. Alison linked arms with
her daughter, Holly, smiling and thanking everybody as they left.
Ron, the singleton, made away with two bottles of ale and a cheeky

wink. Ed half-offered to keep the party going in his house until his wife, Amelia, reminded him loudly that they'd an early flight the next day. David, eager to return to his own kingdom, brought the twins Wolf and Lily May home, all walking in a row like ducks.

Lily told David she'd follow on shortly and offered to help George carry the remains of the crate back to his house. Of all the residents, these two had managed to strike up an unlikely but genuine friendship – just chit-chat on the footpath, little more, but some neighbourly engagement in an otherwise very private estate.

Only Olive was left, folding up the chequered tablecloths she'd supplied.

'Olive looks a bit sad,' George remarked, when they were out of earshot.

'Does she?' Lily said, casting a discreet backwards glance at their neighbour, the ponytail of dreads she was wearing in her hair that day swinging on her bare shoulders as she turned.

Olive was pulling together the corners of the cloth, mouth turned down, fringe falling into her eyes, her cardigan buttoned up to the neck. A lonely figure.

'Well, you're an eligible bachelor, George,' Lily said.

'And you're the neighbourhood saint,' George retorted.

'I have to put the twins to bed.'

'I have to put myself to bed. Alone.'

They both smiled tightly. Neither could bring themselves to invite Olive over for a nightcap.

Their neighbour was always perfectly amiable but both Lily and George knew the wisdom of the saying 'if somebody is gossiping to you, they're gossiping about you'.

'Maybe Alison . . .' Lily said, catching sight of Holly's mother making her way back down her drive towards Olive. Alison hadn't yet got the measure of everybody but everybody reckoned they had the measure of her. She was a soft soul. Kind.

'Ah,' George said. They were off the hook. Alison chatted away to Olive and the other woman nodded happily. Then the two women made their way into Olive's cottage.

Thank goodness for lovely Alison.

Poor Olive. She was so very hard to relax around. Even then.

Even before she properly began to wreak havoc on the lives of her neighbours.

NEWS TODAY
ONLINE EDITION

1 June 2017

The body of a woman found in her home yesterday may have been in situ for almost three months, according to a police spokesperson.

The gruesome discovery was made after a resident in the wealthy gated community where the woman lived contacted the emergency services citing concerns about her neighbour's property.

Local officers had to force entry into the woman's home to ascertain her whereabouts and safety. After finding her body, a police forensics unit was summoned to the scene.

The woman's identity has yet to be disclosed. It has been revealed that the deceased was in her mid-fifties and lived alone. Cause of death also remains a mystery and will be determined by a postmortem, due to be conducted later today.

The woman's home is situated in a quiet residential area just outside the village of Marwood in Wicklow. This morning, locals reacted with horror to the news that her death had gone unnoticed for so long.

At time of printing, nobody from Withered Vale itself has been willing to talk to the media.

OLIVE

No.4

At first, there was just me. Before my house had a number. Before the others arrived.

I hadn't intended to live on the outskirts of the village on my own. I'd ended up there by chance. I couldn't afford any of the houses on sale on the main street. Or the side streets. Or the streets off the side streets. My income from the health board, where I worked as a language therapist for children, was good. Just not good enough.

Priced out of buying a house where I'd grown up, one day in 1988 I drove over the bridge and out past the pretty woods that dotted most of my home county.

Just beside the woods and before the fields that made up John Berry's land, I saw the cottage. Its owner had died months earlier and we all knew his son, by then an illegal immigrant in the States, had no plans to return. A home wasn't much use when you couldn't get a job for love nor money and anyway, nobody left America once they'd got in.

It was just a matter of the estate agent phoning and telling him somebody was willing to take it off his hands. I got it for a song and a promise to ship some personal belongings over.

'Withered Vale?' my mother said, eyes wide and appalled. 'Why would you pick there, are you mad?'

'It's picked me,' I laughed. 'It's the only place I can afford.'

My parents only knew the Vale because of its history. At the start of the twentieth century, an over-enthusiastic and most certainly drunk farmer had decided to tackle pests on his land by going hell for leather with arsenic spray. He poisoned all his crops in the process – they withered and died in the fields.

'But it's miles away,' my mother protested. 'How will I get by without you?'

'The cottage is minutes away in the car,' I said. 'I'm twenty-six. I can't stay living at home forever!'

In truth, it wouldn't have mattered if I'd gone to live on the moon. I still had to call around to my parents' every evening on the way home from work, at least until they both died, a year apart, a decade later.

After the initial period of grieving, I realised I was glad to be able to go directly home each night. The remoteness and the single life didn't bother me at first. I was exhausted from all the running about, before and during my parents' illnesses. I could imagine nothing nicer than arriving home from work to a lovely, clean house, with a takeaway, a video, a bottle of wine; nowhere to go, no duties to fulfil. I happily went on like that for, oh, I don't know, at least a year.

It's true what they say. What's seldom is wonderful and my routine soon became, well, routine.

And as time wore on, I became lonely.

I'd no siblings and no close friends and I hadn't planned on being a spinster. There was no revelatory moment, no decision, when I thought, I'm so thrilled with this life, I think I'll just stay on my own.

If anything, I'd been convinced I'd follow the traditional route.

I wasn't a dainty and pretty woman exactly, but I certainly wasn't ugly and boyfriends were never a problem. For whatever reason, though, I never met anybody I was willing to settle with, or for. I was destined to be *just the one*.

But I did enjoy company.

So, in 2001, when John Berry sprung it on me that the land under my cottage actually belonged to him and he'd sold it to a property developer to build on, the only concern I had was whether my home would remain standing.

'Of course!' he assured me. 'You don't have the freehold, but you've bought the place and it's yours. This fellow would have to buy you out but he has no plans to. He's going to build around you. He's not going mad, either. Just a few houses to see how it goes. It's going to be an exclusive development – large, fancy homes for rich, important types. The ones who like their privacy. Withered Vale, right next door to Marwood, a whole village on your doorstep. Everybody will want to buy a place.'

'Is he really keeping the name?' I asked, amazed. Pockets of these developments had begun to spring up all over the country at the turn of the century, copycat American-style estates for the privileged few. But they all had names straight from the LA handbook: *The Hills; The Heights; Lakeside.*

'Oh, he's keeping it,' Berry said. 'He loves it. Thinks it will make the place unique. He reckons he's going to blow the property values around here out of the water.'

One by one, I watched the houses go up around me in a semi-circle. While they were big, each one was different, and all had a quality of design. And the fact each house was unique meant my cottage, despite its far smaller size, didn't stand out quite as much. In fact, when he brought the landscapers in, the developer added the same hedge border as mine around all the properties. It gave the Vale a feeling of continuity, he said.

Sadly, it was just a tad too tasteful for him. He lost the run of himself and turned us into a 'gated' community. He hung a big wrought iron sign over the railings in case anybody struggled to find Withered Vale, the only outpost for miles between Marwood and the next village on the other side of the woods.

I'd gone from being a one-off cottage on the edge of civilisation to part of an elite club.

As the families moved in, one by one, I greeted them generously and genuinely. The homes were numbered one to seven and my cottage, after some initial wrangling with the developer about where I would sit on his patch, was number four.

Right in the middle of everything.

Some of them came and stayed, some of them moved in and moved out and we got new neighbours. They were all blow-ins to me.

I tried to be friendly with everybody. I hope people remember that. That I tried very hard.

The police men and women beavering around my body right now don't know anything of my story yet. They don't know anything at all, really. They've spent the last twenty-four hours trying to rid the house of flies and maggots and the pests they know are here but can't see – the mice and rats. The gnawing at my fingers and toes speak to their existence. It's amazing there's anything left of me.

It's the heat, you see. After an unusually cold spring and early summer, I was doing okay, sitting there on the chair, silently decomposing. The same chair Ron from number seven bent me over for three and a half minutes of mind-blowing passion the night before I died, leaving with my knickers scrunched up in his pocket.

I hope, for his sake, he's got rid of them.

Then late May came and the weather turned on its head, sending temperatures soaring and bringing all sorts of nastiness into my living room.

It's amazing how long they left me, my *neighbours*. Not one, not a single one, came to check on me. Not even Ron. And Chrissy only rang the police when my cottage looked like a public health hazard.

Was I really that hated?

Those poor detectives. I almost feel sorry for them. It's going to take them forever trying to figure out who killed me.

FRANK

Frank Brazil had never claimed to have a strong stomach. And he wasn't going to start pretending now, in the presence of this body – this carcass. Every time his eyes happened on the blackened, liquefied lumpen form, bile threatened to explode from his oesophagus.

Even his partner Emma looked slightly less orange than normal, her naturally fair skin a few notches paler under the caked foundation cream.

'It's utterly disgusting,' she said, decisively. She hadn't stopped talking since they'd arrived. Frank prided himself on being a modern man – he held to the philosophy that there was no difference between men and women, that the fairer sex were equal – in fact, *superior* – to men in almost every way. First his mother, then his lovely Mona, had kept him right in that regard.

But, Christ . . . Emma. He could not get his head around the girl. So young, with so many opinions and all of them so fixed!

'The poor woman. What has happened to *community*? How could her neighbours not notice she wasn't around? You'd think one of them would have knocked and raised the alarm. You should see what they're saying on social media about the people who live here. And where are her family?'

Frank shrugged. It wasn't that he didn't agree. Frank's home was in an old council housing estate that had been gentrified and while many of his neighbours these days were students or young professionals, there was still a community feel to the place. Only last week they'd had a football tournament of sorts on the green that the houses surrounded. Dads, city-boys, students and children alike all joined in.

If one of his neighbours died, he'd notice they'd gone missing in action and there were far more than seven houses in his estate.

'It's just plain wrong, elderly people being left alone like this,' Emma continued. 'I hope the government runs those ads again, the ones about checking on vulnerable pensioners. They'll have to, in the wake of this.'

'Elderly? Emma, she was fifty-five! That's two years older than me.'

'Well, I'm not being funny, Frank, but you *are* retiring in three months,' Emma said, and Frank clamped his hand to his forehead. How could you ever explain to a twenty-eight-year-old that fifty-three was not old? That he was retiring because he was tired and sad and no longer cared? He'd been working in this job longer than she'd been alive and he'd seen too much. He'd lost empathy. When that went, you had to go too. Every sensible copper knew that.

He turned away from Emma and peered through the window. Somebody had raised the blinds to let light into the room. The entrance gates had made it easy to isolate the crime scene – there was no press throng, it was just the police and emergency vehicles inside the perimeter. And the neighbours, who were still holed up in their houses, having woken up to a shitstorm of epic proportions.

Forensics had taken initial DNA from the scene. There was plenty. Too much, in fact. If it wasn't accidental death or suicide, if it turned out Olive Collins had been murdered, they had tonnes to work through. They'd even, according to the speculation of the forensics team, potentially picked up traces of semen from the floor beside the body.

'She must have had a chap,' he said aloud, to himself and to nobody.

'Do you think so?' Emma said. She pulled on her gloves and picked up a framed photograph from the dresser. Crime Scene was finished in the sitting room – every surface dusted and swabbed, every inch photographed – but the detectives still wore baggies over their shoes and blue rubber gloves on their hands. The picture showed a younger Olive in a large-collared blouse with a striped jumper last seen circa 1985, sporting a bowl haircut. 'She wasn't particularly attractive. And she was . . .' Emma trailed off like she'd thought better of her next sentence.

He shrugged.

'If she was willing . . . That's usually enough for most men. Anyway, I wouldn't go judging her looks on a thirty-year-old photograph; the entire population looked ridiculous in the eighties. Or on what's in the chair, there. Let's find a more recent picture of her.'

The deputy state pathologist appeared in the doorway.

'I'm ready to move the body.'

Hovering behind him was the head of forensics, the likeable, down-to-earth Amira Lund. Frank had a lot of time for Amira, and he liked to tell himself it wasn't just because she was a very attractive woman – big almond eyes, dark skin, long luscious black hair (that he rarely saw, to be fair, given all their interactions took place with her ensconced in a white suit).

'Frank, got a minute?' she asked.

'They're about to move the body,' Emma said.

'Abso-fucking-lutely I have a minute,' Frank said. There wasn't a chance he was hanging around to see Olive Collins' corpse being shifted from the chair into a body bag. Christ knew what was under that saggy mess. His skin crawled just thinking about it.

'You're in charge,' he told Emma, who struggled to hide her delight before she realised what she was about to witness. The smile died on her face.

Frank followed Amira out, ducking his head under the door frame and emerging into the small hallway that ran between the sitting room and the kitchen. He knew already that it led off towards the two bedrooms and bathroom. The cottage didn't have an upstairs but it had a large enough ground-floor footprint.

'Through here,' she said, bringing him into the kitchen. Frank stood aside to let one of her team come out first, his large hands filled with evidence bags.

'Has God said anything yet?' Amira nodded back in the direction of the sitting room.

'He deigned to tell me when I arrived that it's difficult to pick up anything from a body in that state – truly, a revelation of biblical proportions – but there are no bullet or knife wounds, no old blood stains. Nothing you don't know yourself. However she died, it was gentle enough. Maybe she'd a heart attack. Or she took a bottle of pills and just sat down to watch telly, drifted off. The lads who found her said the television was on stand-by, like it had switched itself off after a time but was ready to go with a flick of the remote.'

Amira shook her head.

'I don't think that's what happened.'

Frank sighed. Sudden death was always treated as suspicious. They had to examine all the angles, tick all the boxes. But in the end, all it really created for the police was paperwork. Lots and lots of it.

He'd been happy to come out here this morning because admin was all he was good for. Emma wanted complex, high-profile cases. Day-long interrogations. Sensational trials. She was young, she had the energy for it. Anybody who looked like they got up at the crack of dawn every day just to apply make-up had the energy for anything.

All Frank wanted was an eight-hour shift where nothing of note happened, after which he'd head home to a frozen pizza, David Attenborough on the TV and a good night's sleep free from nightmares.

'What is it?' he asked, tentatively.

'The boiler was pumping carbon monoxide into the house.'

Frank cocked his head, raised a hand, pulled at the tuft of reddish-brown hairs over his upper lip.

'Accidental death from ingestion of poisonous gas. Very sad. They should make those CM alarms obligatory.'

Amira shook her head again.

'Nope. Not accidental. Come over here.'

Frank followed her to the kitchen door, every step heavy and resigned. He watched as Amira stood on a chair and traced blue-gloved fingers around the vent over the door.

'What's that?' she said.

He took his place on the chair.

'Tape,' he answered, and his stomach felt funny.

'Tape,' she repeated. 'Every vent. The doors and windows are well insulated, nothing needed there.'

'What about the front door? Didn't the neighbour say something about the letter box being taped off?'

'It was just the letter box and it was masking tape, not clear tape. And there are fingerprints on it. A couple of sets. One is probably the neighbour who found her. The other, if I were to hazard a guess, is probably the victim's. She had a postbox attached to the front wall, maybe she didn't need or want people sticking post in the door.'

Frank, drowning, clutched for the life buoy.

'So, either Olive Collins had an aversion to fresh air or her death was planned. She wanted the method she chose to be effective. She knew the boiler was leaking or she blocked the pipe. Is it an old one?'

'No. It's brand new. It's in that cupboard on the wall behind you. It's not long since it was serviced, according to the sticker on its front. But the caps were unscrewed and the flue stuffed with card-board. Manually.'

'Well. Suicide it is, so. She taped up all the air vents. I'm surprised she didn't block the chimney. That's what drew the neighbour's attention – the bluebottles.'

'There was nothing in the chimney,' Amira clarified. 'But that wouldn't have mattered. The chimney flue is narrow and not suffi-cient to empty a home of carbon monoxide. She had a painting propped in front of it as well. There was some ash in the fireplace from paper she must have burned, but no open fires for her.'

'Sorry, Amira, what's the point? Something is giving you itchy knickers.'

'I'll tell you what's upsetting me, Frank. This house is crawling with DNA. For a woman who was left dead in her sitting room for nigh on three months, it looks like she had an awful lot of visitors in the run-up. The only place we haven't picked up fingerprints is on the tape over those vents. Nor from the pipes attached to the boiler. They were cleaned.'

'Shit.'

'Yeah.'

'But – come on, it's still more likely she'd have done it herself. How could somebody have taped up all the vents without her noticing?'

'It's not like it would take that long, Frank. And, as you can see, it's clear tape. I didn't notice it until we checked the boiler and I started to look closely.'

'I don't know, Amira. As a manner in which to murder somebody, it's fairly diabolical. I'd go so far as to say it's a little over-imaginative for this day and age.'

Amira shrugged.

'Some people aren't into knives and guns, Frank, and not everybody has the strength or capacity for strangulation, despite what the movies tell us.' She hesitated. 'There's more.'

'You're upsetting me now,' Frank sighed.

'Wait for it. Her phone was beside her when we arrived. We dialled the last number. She rang us.'

The colour drained from Frank's face.

'No.'

'Yep. I've done your homework for you. She dialled the emergency services. 3rd March, 7 p.m. You might want to sit down for the next bit.'

'I think I might.' Frank pulled out a faux-leather brown chair from the kitchen table and plonked his arse on it.

'It was recorded as a distress call. Two uniforms were sent out. They got in the main gate, knocked on the door.'

'They knocked on the door?' Frank felt like Alice, plummeting down the rabbit hole.

'Blinds were drawn. Nobody answered. No obvious sign of distress. They were going to go around the back but the man next door pulled up and the three had a little tête-à-tête. The neighbour said he hadn't seen or heard anything unusual and that if the blinds were down she was most likely away. So they put it down to a hoax call and left. And the blinds stayed down for another three months, until we arrived. Here's another little tidbit for you – the Champions League was on the night she phoned. Kick off was 7.45 p.m. Do you think the lads might have had an interest in the match?'

Frank laughed. It was nervous and it was involuntary.

'I've never been so glad to be retiring,' he said. 'Country cops cock up again. There's your headline. What did she say in the call?'

'In a very agitated tone, she said, and I'm quoting, *I think something is very wrong.* Then she hung up. Abrupt.'

'Clearly just a hoax, then. Idiots.'

'Yeah,' Amira said. She pulled out the chair beside him and sank into it. 'You're screwed, aren't you? Sorry, if I'd known earlier, I'd have rung and told you to call in sick. Fancy a drink later? I'll buy.'

Frank shook his head. Like that would make up for it. Three months. That was all he had left. And now Emma would be foaming at the mouth. There'd be an incident team. Press conferences. Weeks of interviews. Unpaid overtime.

Unless . . .

His only hope was that the bosses wouldn't want him to immediately classify it as murder. Resources were tight, statistics were everything, and a lack of fingerprints wasn't an absolute indicator of criminal intent. Frank and Emma could spend a couple of days looking into the dead woman's life, interviewing the neighbours, that sort of thing, while they waited for the post-mortem and forensic results. Try to determine if there were any actual motives for somebody to want to kill the woman.

With any luck, she'd be whiter than white and the coroner would record it as death by suicide.

Frank almost laughed at his own desperation.

GEORGE

No.1

Wolf Solanke was in George Richmond's back garden again. George could see his little head of tight Afro curls bobbing up and down as he laboured at the patch of earth he'd chosen to transform that morning.

Lily had bought the twins gardening sets for Christmas last year. But George knew Wolf's father David had OCD when it came to *his* lawn. Everything in the Solankes' backyard might look as if it was thrown together devil-may-care, but it was a cultivated chaos. There was no way David would let his kids muck around out there with mini trowels and spades.

So Wolf liked to play in George's extremely expensive land-scaped flower beds and George didn't mind a jot. The gardeners came, they did their thing, he was grateful and oblivious at the same time.

It was nice to have a little company, even if it was an eight-year-old kid.

He sauntered across the lawn to Wolf, who was so focused on

whatever he was up to with his small rake that he didn't notice George's approach.

'It's hot today, isn't it?' George said.

Wolf jumped.

He looked up at George with big brown eyes, then looked away again, scratching at his dark cheek with mucky nails.

'It's very warm,' Wolf said. 'The weather woman said twenty-eight degrees by noon.'

'Wow. A heatwave.'

'That is not a heatwave,' Wolf replied.

'Well, technically, no . . .' George trailed off. He'd learned early there was no point having arguments with Wolf about specifics.

'Fancy a drink, kiddo?'

'No, thank you. Mr Richmond, you really need to put something down for these begonias. The slugs are eating them.'

George, while impressed by Wolf's knowledge of his shrubbery, merely shrugged.

'Circle of life, pal. Slugs have as much right to eat as you and I.'

Wolf looked aghast.

'But you'll have no flowers.'

'I'll tell my gardener to grow some that aren't so slug-friendly. 'Course, then I might get other bugs. On the scale of things, I don't mind slugs. I've heard whitefly are like locusts. Eat everything they see. Bloody insects, eh?'

George was shocked to see tears well up in Wolf's eyes.

He dropped to his hunkers so he was level with the kid.

'Hey, pal, what's the problem?'

Wolf didn't answer. Instead, he rubbed angrily at his eyes,

gathered up his equipment and started off down the garden, disappearing into the gap in the hedge he used to transport himself home.

George stood there, metaphorically scratching his head.

Alone again, he turned and made his way back into his house and climbed the stairs. His destination was the landing window, the one that gave him the best view.

The Vale was normally so tranquil. Nothing ever happened in it. Nothing anybody talked about, anyhow.

But right now, it felt like bedlam. There wasn't a single person George knew out on the road. Just lots and lots of police.

He rested his head on the cool glass, the rich net curtain leaving triangular indents on his forehead, and closed his eyes. The familiar anxiety began to bubble, a feeling that he could only respond to in one way.

A door banged outside and George's eyes shot open, just in time to see a flurry of activity at number four. They were bringing out her body.

He shook his head. It was her. Really her. He was watching his dead neighbour being wheeled out of her home on a stretcher and what did he feel?

Nothing.

But then, George was never very good at proper emotions.

That's what his father had told him when George had lost his job – when he'd been fired from the newspaper. It had taken all of the great Stu Richmond's power to keep what had happened quiet. And George hadn't even seemed upset. Or grateful. So Stu said.

He'd been almost right. George's main emotion had been relief.

Not because he'd been *saved,* but because he no longer had to keep up the lie.

Any one of his journalist 'friends' would have happily run with the story, that's what George's dad had said. He was probably right.

Luckily, management were terrified of falling out with Stu Richmond. George's father was the country's leading music mogul, the Irish Simon Cowell, and a big deal in the States. If his artists boycotted the paper's entertainment section, well . . . It was decided that George losing his job was punishment enough.

His father had done him that one favour and then more or less washed his hands of him. Bar the house and the monthly cheques.

'Don't ever embarrass me again,' he'd said.

George had tried. He'd gone to counselling when he'd been fired, attempted to get to the bottom of what it was that made him such a screw-up. He went weeks without leaving the house, not reaching for distraction with his computer or TV, meditating even, in an effort to fix himself.

At one point in his sad little existence, he'd considered putting a dating app on his phone and trying to find a girlfriend. He wasn't a bad-looking man and he was still youngish, only thirty-five. The counsellor said he had to stop shying away from intimacy. There was still time to come back from the brink.

But no matter what he did, it crept in again.

People had no idea.

George reckoned what was wrong with him was worse than being addicted to crack cocaine.

Just looking at all the activity outside was too much for him.

Olive bloody Collins.

George felt the familiar urge come over him. The stress, the desperation. He could think of nothing else but doing what he had to do. Right there, right then.

He reached for the wipes on the windowsill.

Good riddance to bad rubbish, he thought, as he scrubbed the wood clean.

OLIVE

No.4

When Stu Richmond moved into number one, it was very exciting. In a country of B-list celebs, he was a shining star because he'd made it *in the States*. The man who'd launched many a career and garnered millions in the process. He was more famous than half the bands he'd founded, probably aided by the fact they had a habit of crashing and burning when the egos properly landed.

I insisted on calling him Mr Richmond. I did it partially because I was old-fashioned, but, if I'm honest, mainly to annoy him. He was one of those people that just provoke the rebel in you. 'Stu' fit the image he was trying to project and that image was of a man that wasn't out of place with a girlfriend who was younger than his adult son; a man who had a red Porsche in the driveway; a man who routinely flew 'Stateside'; and, God bless him, a man who had a personal trainer and hair plugs.

First the girlfriend departed. Then Mr Richmond headed back to his US home. The charming countryside and fabulous Withered Vale lost its allure over the course of one damp winter.

It was George's turn to live in the mini-mansion.

George was far quieter than his father. A real lone wolf – isolated even, you might say. We were such a small community, it was a terrible waste.

At first I thought he might be gay and a little shy because of it. It was clichéd, I know, but he was young, handsome, kept the exterior of his home immaculate, and I never saw a girl call to his house, never saw a woman on his arm.

That summer, I stuck a Pride sticker in the sitting room window to show some solidarity. Maybe that was all he needed. Some outreach.

I watched to see if he'd do the same. He didn't.

It turned out George wasn't gay.

George was something else altogether.

Jo Spain has worked as a party advisor on the economy in the Irish parliament. Her first novel, *With Our Blessing*, was one of seven books shortlisted in the Richard and Judy Search for a Bestseller competition and went on to be a top-ten bestseller in Ireland. *The Confession* is her first psychological thriller and first number one bestseller. Jo lives in Dublin with her husband and their four young children.